Ali Lowe

The Trivia Night

First published in Great Britain in 2022 by Hodder & Stoughton
An Hachette UK company

This paperback edition published in 2022

1

A CIP catalogue record for this title is available from the British Library

Paperback ISBN 978 1 529 34883 5
eBook ISBN 978 1 529 34884 2

Typeset in Plantin by Manipal Technologies

Printed and bound in Great Britain by Clays Ltd, Elcograf S.p.A.

Hodder & Stoughton policy is to use papers that are natural, renewable and recyclable products and made from wood grown in sustainable forests. The logging and manufacturing processes are expected to conform to the environmental regulations of the country of origin.

Hodder & Stoughton Ltd
Carmelite House
50 Victoria Embankment
London EC4Y 0DZ

www.hodder.co.uk

For Rob, my everything

CONTENTS

Darley Heights Public School's Trivia Night

TABLE PLAN

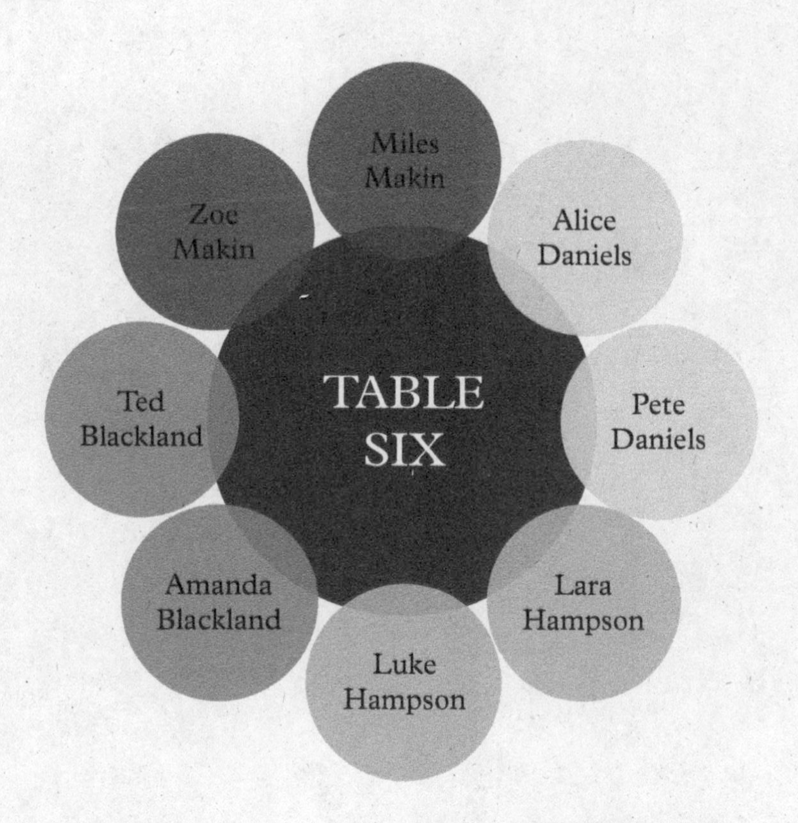

Prologue

My dear husband,

I am at the place we used to come to, when we loved one another. Pen and paper on my knees, writing to you like I used to do, back in the day. Out front, waves thump the shore, turfing out early-morning surfers in their deadly roll, like debris being shaken from a rug. Heads bob up, followed by black rubber-clad bodies, invigorated by the cold and the ferocity of the swell. The dawn glitters off the ocean; how quintessentially Australian!

Behind me, the residents of Darley sleep as though drugged. Soon enough, the people we used to mingle with over cocktails and finger food, the creme of Sydney's beach-lined peninsula, will stir in their linen-covered king beds, inside Balinese-styled homes, hands feeling out for switches to flood the world with artificial light until the sun makes its show. But here on the beach the light is real. A deep, rusty glow that blurs to peach slower than the eye can see (but blink and you'll miss it), bringing with it a hug of warm air, a taste of the heat we've been promised. Summer is here again! The earth has done another circuit around the sun. It's hard to believe it's been a year since it happened, isn't it, my dear?

I can't help but think back on it all as I sit watching the waves. Isn't the feeling of cold sand sliding through your toes positively delicious? Each grain the perfect weight and consistency to make it flow like silk – until it is ruined by the weight of water. But everything beautiful is ultimately sullied, isn't it? Like love. Like marriage. Oh, I can still picture it now. Eight adults – eight responsible parents – drunk on vanity and booze, eyes greedy, limbs poised, mouths frothing with innuendo. Eight lives merging for better or worse, like globules of hot wax fusing, irresistibly, inside a lava lamp.

There was something so utterly delicious about the predicament they were all in and I honestly believe it would have been remiss of me not to act, especially given what I'd been through. After all, I didn't make them do what they did. I didn't force them into anything. They did all of that themselves – I just helped a little afterwards. I just made the situation work for me. And didn't it work, my darling? It worked a dream!

But I do sometimes wonder how things would have gone if Amanda Blackland had never joined Darley Heights Public School. If the trivia night had been cancelled for some unforeseen reason. If they hadn't all been so selfish. Perhaps there would have been no funeral. No children standing at the foot of a polished mahogany coffin, tears spilling from woeful eyes and collecting sorrowfully at their tiny feet.

I guess we will never know, will we, my dear?

Yours fondly,
Me xoxo

Part One: Trivia Night
One Year Earlier

Chapter One
Amanda

Ted stood on the pavement and loosened the collar of his white work shirt. It was the hottest January for something like twenty years, and I was still in the passenger seat of the car applying mascara. He had turned off the engine, and the air-con along with it, presumably in a bid to force me out through heat exhaustion. Outside, swarms of dishevelled primary-age children trudged up to the school gates, devoid of energy, like last-place marathon runners.

My husband knocked on the window and tapped his watch with an indulgent smile. I held my index finger up, the universal 'one more minute' sign, and turned back to the overhead mirror. Not striking, but passable. I flipped up the mirror, and stepped out of the car.

'Beautiful, my darling!' Ted smiled. Beads of sweat had collected in rows on his forehead – not in a gross way, but in a sort of orderly, masculine fashion. He held out his hand. 'Ready?'

I nodded and clipped shut my tan clutch. Perhaps it was a little too much preening for the year 1 assembly, but I could hardly go make-up free for my first Darley Heights Public School event. All the other mums had known each other for the entirety of kindergarten year already, enjoying playdates and school socials and whatnot, while I'd wast-ed four terms greasing up to the humourless flock at St Cecilia's, the private primary school down the road (and paying top dollar to do it). There was something so terrifying not only about stepping from a small private school community into a larger state one, but also in joining a flock that was already well formed. It felt like arriving late to a party where you don't know anyone except the host – although in this instance, without the benefit of a sneaky glass of Prosecco beforehand. But if I was a fifteen out of ten for nerves, my daughter was only a one. Evie may only be seven, but she wasn't remotely fazed about starting at a brand new school. She had already taken herself off on an exploratory mission. *Be more like Evie*, I told myself.

Although she had disappeared entirely.

'Where's she gone?' I shrugged.

Ted nodded to the other side of the car park, where the small body of our second-born hung by her hands from the branches of a tree like a monkey, in a green-and-white tartan summer dress.

Evie's long brown hair swung about her shoulders wildly, despite me having detangled it ten minutes previously with a brush and brute force, and her brand new, seaweed-green school hat lay in the arid dirt below. She was such an active child and so unlike the rest of the family. Sam wouldn't be caught dead up a tree – mind you, he was at high school now, so that wasn't exactly a surprise. For him it was all about hoodies, YouTube gaming channels, and skateboarding to KFC with his mates. This morning he had sloped out of the house en route to the school bus with his rucksack hanging so low off his shoulder that his lunchbox had fallen out.

A young female teacher with sweat patches under the arms of her silk blouse, and legs that were losing the battle to walk quickly within the confines of a too-tight navy pencil skirt, passed the tree and smiled up at Evie.

'Sorry.' I shrugged. *Sorry my daughter is swinging from a tree.* The woman smiled and shook her head. *No worries. I've seen worse.*

How different Darley was to St Cecilia's! At Saint Cee's, Evie would have been lynched by the school principal for scarpering up a tree trunk like that, in regulation uniform no less. But then, Margot Walsh had been notoriously strict. It hadn't been hard to affront her overzealous sense of propriety. It seemed like Darley Heights Public School wasn't too hot on formality.

'Careful you don't rip your new school dress, Evie,' I called as I watched the cotton of the green tartan scratch roughly against a branch. She ignored me and clambered higher.

'Evie! Be careful!' shouted Ted, letting go of my hand and moving underneath the branch that held our daughter, to act as a human crash-mat.

'Honey, she's fine,' I told him. I prided myself on being relaxed about these things – too relaxed, my husband said.

Behind Evie, at the base of the hill, the town of Darley stretched out like a grid, one side lined entirely with blue ocean. Houses, mostly with white or dove-grey facades, sat in neat rows in the middle of the bustle, flanked by the green of the golf course and the tree-lined cricket oval on one side, and the tidy, manicured lawns of St Cecilia's on the other. Half a kilometre away to the left was the sprawling compound of Darley Mall – its red illuminated sign likely visible from space – where teenage girls hung in packs in sweet-smelling, over-lit make-up stores;

high-school kids held hands and probably more in the back row of the cinema during the day; and young mothers with small babies and dark circles loaded up on coffee.

From up here, it all looked like perfect coastal bliss. Lush green grass, azure blue water, white picket houses – the kind a child might draw, with triangular roofs, trees in the front garden and pristine, landscaped paths leading up to symmetrical fences. Curtains neatly bunched like the letter 'R' in each of the four front windows. I could pick our house out from its position on Mentira Drive, along the edge of the golf course, its aluminium roof sloping down towards the garden, and the oblong, turquoise pool littered with gaudy inflatables. I'd always thought our home, with its slightly darker coat of paint, more charcoal than pigeon-grey, stood out a little more than the others on the street, but from this vantage point, it looked just the same as the others. Nothing notable, nothing special.

Evie's dress caught the branch again and the hem strained against her knees.

'Your *dress*, Evie!' I called again, feeling a familiar flare of anxiety. I didn't want anyone to be looking at us here, to be singled out again for any reason.

'Kay!' she yelled back.

'C'mon kiddo, down please.' Ted held out his arms. Evie let her body drop, landing with a puff in the dirt beside him, transforming her socks from pristine white to mud grey. Her smart new shoes looked like they'd already done a couple of terms of hard graft in the playground.

'Fabulous,' I said. 'There go the Mary Janes.'

'Mary Jane who?' Ted said, confused.

'They're a type of shoe, darling.'

'Well, I wouldn't worry too much. Look at them all.' He nodded at the large group of kids ahead who were pushing through the school gates ahead like parents at the Aldi ski sale. 'Not exactly military about the uniform upkeep here, are they?'

He was right. The students at Darley Heights really were a motley crew – shirts in varying shades of white emblazoned with ink stains in red, white and blue; hats faded from dark green to an insipid olive colour thanks to the sun or the washing machine, or perhaps a combination of both; and trainers in rainbow hues that loudly flouted the 'black shoes only' memo we'd received in Evie's new starter pack a month before.

Ted put his hand on my lower back, as if to guide me up the pathway towards the school. In the old days this smooth manoeuvre was an indicator of chivalry to lead me through doors and the like, but over the years it has developed into a ploy to get me to hurry along. I could tell by the fact the gentle nature of the push had just about doubled in pressure since 2010.

'True,' I said. 'The cars, though . . . look at them, they're pristine!' I flicked an eyebrow to the kiss-and-drop zone on our right, where a row of shiny black SUVs with tinted windows and personalised number plates spat children out on to the pavement. The car game was strong – definitely more so than at St Cecilia's – and that was a private school. Evidently, the thousands of dollars all of these parents were saving on school fees were being heavily invested at Bruce Barclay Motors in the next-door suburb of Coral Plateau.

The school itself was small and neat, if not a little dated. The main building was clad with canary yellow weather-board, and was surrounded by the lower-school classrooms – portable buildings called demountables, that were raised up from the ground on stilts like large granny flats. Inside the circle was the concrete quad, where we'd been told students lined up in rows after the nine o'clock bell before class, and beyond that, across from the netball courts, canteen and uniform shop, were the upper-school rooms for years 3 to 6, which ran in a spacious semicircle around the sporting oval.

Ted and I had looked around the school eighteen months previously, prior to choosing St Cecilia's, and on that wet, winter day, with the children in their classes and the quad quiet and neglected, it had seemed so outdated, so dull. But today it was different. The grass was green, flowers bloomed along the pathway that led from the gate to the main buildings, and laughter bounced off the walls as freely as the numerous handballs that were being lobbed across the quad. Kids raced across the oval, teasing one another with boisterous pushes towards the large sprinkler that rained down on the grass, relieving it from the ravages of the summer sun. The entire school hummed with something that was so much more vital than the stiff aura of St Cecilia's, with its circular water fountain, clipped hedges and eerie, silent halls. The children here seemed so much more content, *happier*, so much more like kids – even if they were scruffy as all hell.

I scanned the number plates as we walked along. AMY 06Y was nudged in ahead of MOM 079 and MICH 4EL.

'HAM-5ON,' I said, reading aloud the number plate of the car we were about to pass.

'Maybe they're butchers,' Ted quipped.

As we levelled with the car, a blonde head shot out of the passenger seat window like a sideways jack-in-the-box, scaring the absolute bejesus out of me. The hair was caramel in colour and messy. It smelled of coconut.

'Sienna, put your hat on *now*,' the woman yelled up the hill towards the school gates. She was blonde and tanned, with tiny features. Unquestionably stunning, even with her face contorted in a shout. When she didn't get a response, she cupped her hand around her mouth, creating a sort of fleshy megaphone, and as she did so, the giant solitaire on her wedding finger sparkled in the morning sun.

'Sienna! Hat! Now!' she called, shriller this time. The piercing screech was all wrong coming from such a tiny head, and I must have jumped back a little, because she began to laugh and reached her hand out of her window in an attempt to touch me. Which was a little odd because I was about a metre away.

'Oh my *gosh*,' she cooed, tugging on the little discs of her gold necklace. A henna tattoo snaked up the inside of her wrist. 'I'm *so* sorry! I'm such a terrible nag. "Put your hat on!"' She put hands around her mouth again and mimicked her own screeching. 'I didn't mean to startle you. It's just I can never get Sienna to wear her hat and it's ridiculously hot today – or at least it's going to be. The forecast says thirty-four degrees, can you believe it? Not a day to go hatless, is it? Mind you, I don't blame her. It's not the most fashionable head-wear.' She grimaced. A few metres ahead, a pale child who looked about the same age as Evie, with white blonde hair falling down her back, reached in her rucksack and pulled out a faded bucket hat, which she plonked moodily on her head before turning to the car and glaring as if to say, 'Happy now?'

The woman seemed totally unfazed by her daughter's rudeness. If it had been me, I might have stuck my hand on my hip and done the old what-did-you-just-say-to-me? routine, but HAM-50N just sat there, her turquoise eyes sparkling with pride and freckles dancing all over her annoyingly pretty face as she smiled. Not a jot of make-up to be seen, which, I'm not going to lie, was a little irksome since I'd just spent the last half an hour preening.

'Oh, please don't worry.' I smiled and took a step forward, giving Evie's hand a gentle tug.

But she hadn't finished with us yet. 'Are you 1S parents too?' she asked, sticking her head further out of the window. 'Miss Sawyer's class?' Her feet were still in the driver's seat footwell, but her body stretched across the passenger seat. It didn't look comfortable in the slightest. The car behind, obviously keen to pull in and drop off its own unkempt offspring, let out an aggressive beep. I looked back at the driver and winced apologetically.

'We are. I'm Amanda and this is Ted,' I said, gesturing towards Ted, 'Amanda and Ted Blackland, that is. And this is Evie.'

'It's so lovely to meet you.' She smiled and turned her head towards Evie, dropping her voice into child speak. 'Hi Evie. I'm Lara, Sienna's mum. How are you?'

'Good thanks,' Evie mumbled, and kicked the pavement, adding a scuff to her already filthy shoes. I made a mental note to buy them from Kmart next time instead of the extortionate kids' shoe shop at Darley Mall.

Lara gripped the window frame enthusiastically. Her hair was loose around her shoulders, all salty and sun-kissed, exactly like her daughter's. She looked like she belonged in an orange combi van in a hippy commune in Byron Bay, not in well-to-do Darley, driving a bullet-proof 4×4 with personalised plates. It was a weird juxtaposition, like turning up to work at a soup kitchen wearing diamonds. I wondered if she was one of those insufferable trustafarians – the trust-fund recipients that dress like grungy hippies but rely on Daddy's dollar to pay their way. She was way too unhassled to work for a living and certainly didn't seem in a rush to get anywhere.

I realised I was smiling excessively as I silently analysed her, because my cheeks started to hurt. 'Well, it's lovely to meet you,' I said, scolding myself for being so judgemental.

Lara smiled and nodded.

'Okay, well good to meet you, Lana,' Ted said. He cast a not-so-subtle look at his watch and placed his hand on my lower back again. 'Right darling, shall we?'

'Luke's meeting me in the hall,' Lara garbled. 'My husband. He's following on in his car because he's been at work since a sparrow's fart. I'm sure you'll meet him in the hall. Anyway, I'll see you up there. Bye!' Then she smiled, flicked on her right indicator and pulled out aggressively, narrowly missing a black people carrier passing on her right.

'I just love small talk.' Ted grimaced, dodging to avoid two gangly boys barging past him, their schoolbags flapping about haphazardly on their shoulders. 'Bloody hell, it's like the charging of the fucking bulls.'

'Yay!' Evie punched the air. 'That's two dollars for the swear jar, Dad. If you keep on using bad words, I'll be able to buy another Beanie Boo this weekend!'

I'd just opened my mouth to admonish Ted for swearing (it really was something that irked me to high heaven), when a woman with flaming red hair and carrying a Louis Vuitton shoulder bag barged into my left hip.

'Fuck,' I said.

'Ugh! Sorry,' she sighed in a manner that suggested she wasn't sorry in the slightest. 'Otto! Charlie! Come here *now*!' she called behind her.

'Wow,' I said, rubbing my hip.

And that's when the smell hit me. Dior Poison. Sweet and plummy, but also kind of deadly and calculating with all those musky, sandalwood base notes. I stopped dead on the pavement and took in a sharp breath because I was suddenly back there at St Cecilia's. Back in the playground where glances crossed like swords and tuts clicked like thunder; back in that pristine colonial-style house with the stark white deck and the colourful, single-knotted Moroccan rug, where everything had gone, quite alarmingly, pear-shaped. Where the thing had been done that could never be undone, which had changed the very course of my life, *all* of our lives, and led us here to Darley Heights Public School for a fresh start. My head swung around instinctively – left to right, behind, in front – but the only familiar face was Alice's, up ahead. The coast was clear, and I allowed my lungs a relieved exhale.

'Darling?' Ted turned back and reached out his hand. 'All okay?'

I nodded and took his hand, allowing him to gently guide my momentarily paralysed body up the hill.

Inside the hall, the giant ceiling fans only seemed to recirculate the sticky late-January air. The main wall to the left of me, painted eggshell blue, was like a giant pin board. One side was decorated with forty or so paintings of native animals – kangaroos nestled side by side with koalas, echidnas and possums. One picture was of a father clutching a beer in one hand and a TV remote in the other, with the words, 'The Native Dad' at the top (give that child an A+ for thinking outside the box). Some of the paintings were jaw-droppingly artistic, others not remotely so, but what these ones lacked in precision, they made up for in charm. Opposite the large patchwork of art, on the right-hand side of the wall, the blue, red and white Australian national flag, dotted with stars, was pinned up on equal footing beside the red, yellow and black Aboriginal ensign, its three vibrant colours representing the people, the sun and the red ochre colour of the native earth. Both flags looked a little like they could do with a wash and an iron, which was sort of symptomatic of the entire place and its students – charming, but a little unkempt.

We made our way towards the rows of faded orange chairs.

'So, let me get this straight,' Ted whispered. 'Not only are we here this morning, but we're also back on Saturday for some fundraising event?'

'Trivia night, you mean.'

'That's the one. And what does trivia night entail, exactly?'

'Fancy dress and quizzes. They do it in most schools, darling. It's the main annual fundraiser for the school year, but it's basically a giant piss-up.'

Ted nodded. 'I don't remember St Cecilia's doing it.'

'No. St Cee's doesn't, none of the private schools do. They get enough cash from fees, I suppose.'

'Bit full-on at the start of the year, isn't it?'

'Well I guess most people are ready to let loose at the end of Dry January and that means they're happy to dress up and get drunk, which ultimately means they donate more in the raffle and auction. Well, that's what Alice told me, anyway.'

Alice knew everything about everything as the parent-teacher committee's events chair, including how to wangle a last-minute spot for the daughter of her oldest friend. She'd certainly pulled some strings for us – it wasn't an exaggeration to say we wouldn't have been in this hall without her.

'What do we have to dress up as? Presumably it's acceptable to go as yourself?'

Ted didn't do fancy dress.

'As a handsome school dad? Unfortunately not. This year's theme is "back to school". It's a big deal, honey. Everyone puts loads of thought into their outfits and there are prizes for best-dressed. Didn't you see the posters up outside?'

'No, I didn't,' he sighed. 'I'd do anything for you, my darling, but this sounds truly awful.'

'Oh come on, Scrooge.' I squeezed his knee. 'You're doing it for Evie, really. Besides, we can't miss the first event of the school year, can we? It'll be the perfect opportunity for us to get to know people, to make friends. It'll be fine. You'll just have to get into the spirit of it. Pop on a white shirt and grey pants like a schoolboy and it'll hardly be a costume at all. I'm sure it'll be hilarious.'

But even as I said it, I knew I wasn't convinced. I mean, it sounded fun for sure, but for some reason it felt a little like a debutante ball, with me as the new girl. My stomach danced – and not in a good way – at the idea of hundreds of cliquey mums huddled in groups, scrutinising the rookie year 1 mum like lions appraising a defenceless gazelle. The dress-up element just made it worse. It's one thing trying to impress your peers in your own clothes, but quite another in costume. It would, quite literally, be like going back to school – and I wasn't under any illusion that the first time hadn't been hellish enough. The only saving grace was the fact that, this time, everyone would have alcohol to numb the awkwardness.

'I'll take your word for it,' said Ted.

We made our way to the nearest available seats, in the middle of the audience, about eight rows back. Just as I was about to sit down, Evie yanked my hand and pulled me upright again. 'Mum,' she said. 'You have to walk me to the front to my class. Look, they're all sitting in a line up there. I don't want to go by myself.'

I looked to the front and saw a row of nervous looking children – Sienna, with her hat sitting haphazardly on her head, a nose full of freckles and delicate, pretty features, like her mother; along with Lottie and Freya, Alice's twins, who were non-identical but disarmingly similar, more so as they got older. Their dresses were pristine, wrinkle free and a good deal brighter than most in the line-up, and they both had their hair pulled back tightly into French plaits. I hoped to God Evie wouldn't sit down next to them in her dusty tunic and muddy socks.

'Okay, okay,' I told Evie, reversing myself back past six pairs of slender legs, and apologising profusely, like you do in the cinema when you need to get out to go to the loo in the middle of the movie. She pulled me along the aisle and I suddenly felt alarmingly self-conscious, as if I were the one on show, being judged as I walked along and not her. Something about it smacked of the new girl doing a weird lap of honour while the regular spectators awarded silent marks out of ten. And even though I *should* have felt confident as a perfectly presentable 42-year-old woman dropping her child off at school, and even though I knew deep down I had as much right to be there as any one of these mothers, I did feel different. After all, I hadn't originally chosen to send my child to Darley Heights, I had ended up here because of the awful thing that had happened. I wondered if some of them knew about it, if they had heard the gossip being bandied around town. Darley was a small place and people did socialise outside of their own school communities, namely on the sidelines at Saturday sport. And even if they didn't know, maybe they'd assume I was a snob for opting to go private for a year when Darley Heights Public was perfectly good, thank you very much – or that I'd only picked their quaint little school because I'd seen the latest round of national primary school ratings.

These niggling considerations aside, there was also the fact that all of the mothers at Darley were so collectively gorgeous. They were all symmetrical, with smooth skin and blow-dried hair pulled up into silky, high ponies. All of them – and not just the few I'd seen in the kiss-and-drop area hanging out of their SUVs – but *every single one*, was wearing activewear, tight-fitting pants in bright colours and floral patterns, flattering their gym-honed physiques. It was like I'd rocked up to a yoga retreat. I almost expected some half-dressed, bangle-wearing guru to pop up on the stage and ask me to get into a downward dog. They all looked so healthy. And that's when I thought, as I looked down at myself and cursed my choice of Zara sundress and Saltwater sandals, *I do hope these people like a drink, otherwise I'm in for an incredibly dull five years.*

What was also strange was the overall appearance of the dads. There were only about a dozen or so in a hall full of women, but the ones that had made the effort to show up were all besuited, smart and well-groomed. *Businessmen and their stay-at-home wives.* I blinked my preconceptions away. *Perhaps they've taken the day off for the assembly, Amanda*, I told myself. *Perhaps all the women are off on a sponsored walkathon afterwards.* After all, community spirit was thriving at Darley Heights Public, according to Alice.

I bent down to kiss Evie, depositing her at the front of the hall, and began the somewhat intimidating walk back to my seat. The women were huddled in impenetrable groups, chatting quickly, conspiratorially, as if they needed to cram a week's worth of gossip into an hour. Ponytails swished back and forth dramatically as they swapped chatter like soccer trading cards.

'Did you hear about Patrick and Jodie Knight?' a peroxide blonde with a shiny, taut forehead said to her immediate neighbour as I approached. I turned my ear in to listen. 'Poor woman! All the while he was screwing that girl behind the coffee machine at Della's Cafe. She had no idea!' She shook her head slowly, her lips pursed white.

'Bet he's got plenty of points on his loyalty card, dirty pig,' her friend replied.

It was juicy stuff and, as drawn in as I was by the subject matter, I also felt a creeping sense of foreboding that I had inadvertently moved from one gossip-sodden school to another. I recalled Alice's reassuring voice when she had told me it was all sorted, when Evie's spot was confirmed. 'Darley Heights really isn't like your last school,' she'd said. 'Everyone is *so* genuine.'

She was proved immediately wrong about the last bit.

'I just love your pants, Tansie,' said a statuesque brunette, completely disingenuously, to the redhead who'd bulldozed me out of the way. I knew it was false praise because the pants were literally plain black. 'They're so slimming, are you off to the gym?'

'Nah, not today, I'm off for a mani-pedi,' Tansie replied. *Her* forehead didn't move either, although her nose wrinkled up like a pig's snout when she spoke. She looked oddly familiar, and I wondered if I'd photographed her house before she'd sold it. I often saw clients of Fair & Brewer – the real estate agency I worked for as a snapper – when I was out and about. They never recognised me, but I knew who they were because I'd often spent ages moving their family snaps out of the way for their sale photos.

I must have been looking at Tansie with a gormless expression on my face, because her eyes flickered up at me abruptly with a glare that said, 'what are you staring at?' I shot my gaze down to the floor and scuttled back to my chair, performing an awkward sort of upright limbo past several yoga-wear-clad knees and neoprene holdalls in the same shade of grey to get back to Ted.

'Clones,' I whispered into Ted's ear, pleased to be in the safe haven of my husband's gentle, albeit sarcastic, aura. He looked up from the paper programme that had been left on alternate seats, emblazoned with the school logo and the words, 'Year 1 Welcome Assembly. Monday 25 January.'

'Drones?' he asked loudly.

'Shhhhhhh!'

'Drones in a school?'

'Ted, shhhh!' I sank into my seat.

Fortunately at that moment Alice bounded up the aisle, smiling and waving at the mums. She'd pulled her brown hair on to the top of her head in a high ponytail, and was wearing tight, three-quarter-length leopard print leggings and a matching crop top. She looked like she was fresh from the Lorna Jane summer sale. Credit to her, her stomach looked amazing. Probably because she only drank the occasional gin and slimline, and did about 20,000 ab crunches a day. She got up at five thirty every single morning for a routine of weights and press-ups on her deck, rain or shine. Rather her than me.

'My favourite couple!' she sang, bending down for an awkward, three-person hug before pulling away. Ted looked her up and down with a smile. 'Hey Alice,' he said. 'Taronga Zoo called. They want their big cat back!'

'Very funny.' She rolled her eyes. 'How are you guys? I still can't quite get over how amazing it is that you're here, at Darley Heights. Honestly, it's just *the best*.'

'Well, it's all thanks to you.' I smiled, gazing up adoringly at Alice. And I did adore her; she'd been my bestie since I was the same age as Evie. She grinned back at me and shrugged to illustrate it was nothing, although that wasn't remotely true because she had gone out of her way for us. I knew it and she knew it, and even Evie knew it.

When things had gone loco at St Cecilia's back in November, I'd called Alice immediately and told her the whole story: what had happened and why we'd had to leave the school right then and there. And Alice had gone straight into the principal's office up at Darley Heights Public and begged Brigitte Denner to find an extra spot for Evie for the new year. Thankfully, Alice had sway thanks to the parent-teacher committee, and even though it was very late in the term to be accepting new students for the year ahead, and even though all the class lists for term 1 had already been printed, Mrs Denner had picked up her big rubber headmistress stamp (or probably just a biro) and marked our transfer approved. She did it, she said, because Alice had made such a tireless contribution to the school, and so any friend of Alice's was a friend of the school. Our luck was in.

And so here we were, in a school hall that was a fraction of the size of St Cecilia's, all squashed together on rows of plastic orange chairs. The centrepiece was the elevated stage, which was fronted with a large, maroon velvet curtain, like an old theatre curtain, weighty and ancient, and presumably cranked open at rare intervals with a large lever. Two sides of the school emblem, depicting two hands clasped together, met in the middle like a broken necklace.

A man in tracksuit pants and a T-shirt, with a whistle round his neck, climbed up the seven or so steps to the stage carrying a lectern, which he positioned in front of the school emblem, bypassing the glass trophy cabinet, crammed with little golden statuettes and photos, celebrating the winners of various sporting and public speaking contests.

The morning sun streamed in through the gaps of the aluminium blinds, and the heat inside the hall was stifling. 'At least after trivia night there'll be some air conditioning in here,' said Alice, reading my thoughts. 'I'll bet it is way more dated than the school hall at St Cecilia's, isn't it? In fact, that whole school is probably a lot swankier than this one.'

'On the contrary,' I said. 'It's so cosy and inviting here. Not to mention titillating! I mean, in the space of fifty yards I heard *all* about Patrick and Jodie Knight . . .'

Alice laughed, and then stopped herself and looked around, presumably to make sure she hadn't been seen making a light-hearted response to the poor woman's misfortune. 'It's a terrible business,' she said loudly. 'Everyone's so sad for her.'

'They don't look particularly sad,' I said.

'Says the woman who never cries.'

It was a fair point. I wasn't a crier. In fact, I hadn't cried for years – not when Ted proposed, not when my babies were born, not when my mother died. Not a single drop. It was like I didn't have tear ducts or something. I mean I felt the emotion, but it was like I couldn't flush it out, couldn't finish the cycle. Sam thought it was fascinating. 'You're evolutionarily advanced, Mum,' he said. 'Like people who don't have wisdom teeth.'

Alice caught my pensive look. 'Honestly, Mand. They're a great bunch.'

'I'm not worried,' I lied. 'But one thing I am surprised about is the uniform. Clearly, I didn't get the memo . . .'

Alice looked concerned. 'Oh no. What's Evie missing? I can run to the uniform shop for you if you like?'

'No, not Evie, *me*, you dimwit! I didn't get the activewear memo.'

'Oh, you're too funny, Mand.'

'There is literally no one here who isn't in yoga pants. Do they sell a range at the uniform shop, too? All in extra petite?'

Ted grinned and put his arm round Alice's shoulders, pulling her in affectionately. I loved how he did that, treated her like a sister. Although it was to be expected really, since she'd been part of his life for the last fifteen years.

Ted loosened his tie. 'Wow, Al. There must be some sweaty crotches in here.'

'Don't be so crude Teddy.' Alice was the only other human being in the universe allowed to call him Teddy. That's the kind of privilege you get when you're forty and have known your best friend for most of your life. 'That's so inappropriate in the school hall!'

I couldn't tell if she was joking, or if she'd suddenly had her body infiltrated by the PC police. Either way, I was starting to get the distinct impression Alice *really* cared what people thought of her at Darley Heights.

Ted grinned and stood up. 'Have I got time to go to the bathroom?'

'Didn't you hear me tell the kids to go before we left the house?'

'I've drunk a venti latte since then,' he said, and strolled off towards the toilet block at the back of the hall.

Alice slipped into Ted's seat and tightened her ponytail, business-like. 'Right,' she said. 'Trivia night is on Saturday, as you know, and I'm sorting tables. Late, I know, but it's all part of Mrs Denner's whole blend-the-tables thing.'

'Her what?'

'She wants to mix it up so that people who don't know each other sit together.'

'Well, that'll be easy for me.'

'Yeah for you it's fine, but a lot of the other parents are a bit annoyed because they want to hang out with their usual cliques.' She caught herself. 'I don't mean *clique* cliques. They just want to be with their mates. I don't really care to be honest, as long as we sell all the tickets.'

She got out her iPad and scrolled to the notes section. 'Okay, so you're on my table, which sort of flouts the rules, but I'm exempt because I'm organising it. Anyway, so there's you guys, myself and Pete, and Zoe and Miles Makin. Zoe is a mum from Miss Sawyer's class too. She's the *curvy* one . . .' She whispered the word as if she were swearing. 'Her husband is the tall bloke who looks like Stephen Merchant, works at Pasadena, as in the restaurant. Their kid is Freddie. He wasn't in the twins' class last year, so I barely know Zoe, but she looks like she's good fun.'

She nodded vaguely at the other side of the room, towards the front. 'They're over there – see? The tall ginger guy and the brunette?'

I turned to see the back of an auburn head, next to a tumbling glossy brown ponytail. I couldn't see the couple's faces, but I imagined they both looked like thunder, since they were sitting about as far apart on their seats as they could.

'Anyone else?' I asked.

'Yes, the Hampsons: Lara and Luke. They're new, like you. They moved from the city last year because Luke set up his practice here, and they don't know anyone. Lara specifically asked that they join my table . . .'

'I just met her outside,' I said, happy to be making connections, however diluted. 'The hippy, right?'

'Yep, that's her. I don't know her too well either, but she seems nice enough. She's a radiologist up at Darley Imaging, you know, where they do the baby scans.'

I suddenly felt bad for assuming Lara was a 'kept' woman.

'Right. She's very pretty, isn't she?'

Alice looked like she hadn't considered it. 'Yeah, I suppose,' she said. Then she leaned in. 'Okay, you'll love this. I'm not gossiping, but . . . I've heard from a *really good* source that Lara and Luke are . . .' She looked from left to right and then straight at me. '*Swingers*.'

'No way!' I leaned in. I should have known better than to lap up Alice's amuse-bouche of gossip, especially since I'd been the focus of the rumours at St Cecilia's, but really, this was tantalising stuff. 'You're kidding, right?'

'Dead serious. Well, you never know, I suppose it could be bullshit. But Tori, who's new on the committee and who is really very credible when it comes to *information*, knows someone who used to have a kid in kindergarten last year with their daughter, Sienna . . .'

'Wow . . .'

'Speak of the devil.' Alice nodded to the front of the room as Lara floated past the stage.

'She doesn't exactly look like a swinger.'

'Who does?'

'She looks like she'd rather meditate in bed than do anything else.'

'It's always the ones you least expect.'

Lara offered us a shy wave as she slid into the row in front of us and towards two empty chairs with the words 'saved' on them in a child's writing. As she inched forward, her floaty green floral kimono, bright and beautiful and fluid amid a sea of black, tight-fitting Lycra, caught on the static from one of the ugly orange chairs and she turned, her overrun hair covering her face, and muttered, 'Sorry, so sorry' as she yanked the fabric towards her. For someone so incredibly beautiful, so *ethereal*, she was a tad on the jittery side, as if she wasn't quite comfortable in her own skin. She made an 'eek' face at Alice and I, and took her seat, clearly relieved to have earthed herself.

'It's okay, you're not late,' Alice whispered, but Lara had already fixed her eyes on the front entrance, looking at the man who had emerged through the doors like a Ralph Lauren model stepping onto the catwalk at New York Fashion Week. A man who was clearly in no rush.

And that was the first time I saw Luke Hampson. He was tall, broad and very tanned, in the manner of a gap year student who'd just got back from six months dossing around in Bali. He had an air of arrogance about him, and evidently the rock-star effect, too, since row upon row of ponytails whipped round to check him out as he strode across the room.

'That's Luke,' Alice whispered in my ear. She threw her head dramatically towards the door. '*Doctor* Luke Hampson. Totally up himself, but very popular with the mums. He's been married before, you know, and has two older kids who live with his ex. I heard he couldn't keep it in his pants, so she left him. Doesn't surprise me. Not that I'm *gossiping* or anything . . .'

'Wow,' I said. For someone who didn't gossip, Alice was incredibly informative. 'What kind of a doctor is he?'

'Botox, fillers and minor surgical stuff. He's already got a very loyal following among the school mums, and he's only been open for business a few weeks. Must have a very good bedside manner . . .'

I was about to tell her I could sort of see why, when Ted appeared again. He nodded towards Luke. 'So, just a little prick then?' he grinned.

'Teddy!' Alice wagged her finger at Ted with a smirk. 'Anyway, I'd better go and sit down. I'll catch you both after the assembly, okay?'

She ran off down the aisle. Ahead of us, the wrinkle doctor was doing his own version of the sidewards limbo.

'My apologies,' he said as he stepped over Tansie's feet.

'No worries, Dr Hampson,' Tansie said breathlessly.

'Call me Luke,' he replied.

I watched the redness creep up Tansie's neck and spread across her ears, and I heard myself emit a sort of contemptuous, Peppa Pig-style snort. Thankfully, Tansie was too busy staring ahead (presumably repeating the mantra, 'Don't go red. Don't go red. Don't go red' to herself) so she didn't notice. But he did. He turned all the way around, a proper 180-degree owl head, to look at me, the source of the derisive sound. His dark eyes shone like a wet stone. The look was so intense it was almost invasive, and I felt the beginnings of the same flush on the skin of my own neck. Thankfully I was able to stop it and regain myself before I had a full-on scratching fit, and that was when he looked away from me and very pointedly up at the clock above my head (even though he was wearing a watch, and a very expensive one at that). Then he returned his gaze to the front of the hall.

Well, I'd be lying if I said I wasn't irritated by his dismissal. Not because I found him *attractive* – no, he was far too arrogant for my taste – but because, without wanting to sound up myself, I'm usually the one to look away. I am not at all bad looking for my age, slim with shoulder-length caramel hair and great skin thanks to my own little anti-wrinkle injection every now and then (I get cash out with the shopping, so Ted doesn't know it comes from the joint account). In fact, I know I look okay, because Fair & Brewer chose me to model for our recent 'You're At Home with Fair & Brewer' campaign, and everyone knows a real estate agents would want someone fairly attractive on the side of a bus to tout for business. So, yes, I was used to getting a second glance and I didn't like the fact this man hadn't offered credit where it was due. What can I say? I'm only human. I was also annoyed because he was so tall and had completely blocked mine and Ted's view of Evie, which was the whole reason, aside from the checking-out-other-parents circus, we were there.

'Just great,' Ted muttered, interrupting my thought process. He gestured to Luke's back. 'Now I can't see a bloody thing.'

I nodded in support and offered a conciliatory pat on the knee, adjusting my body so I could actually see my child, who was seated beyond Luke's right earlobe. This meant I was forced to assess my fellow newcomer by default. His skin was tanned, and his hair clipped with the same precision as a hedge in the Botanical Gardens. It was neat and expertly set, not free-range like Ted's unruly mop, and was golden, the colour of a perfectly fried potato chip. He was clean shaven, a five o'clock shadow creeping across his jaw, and on his cheek was a deep-set dimple that seemed to wink when he smiled. He was perfect. If you like that kind of thing. Personally, I'm not a fan of men who reek of too much time in front of the mirror.

As a couple, the Hampsons seemed to be the most horrendous mismatch. Luke was sterile and perfect, and looked as though he might have a touch of OCD – you know, aftershave bottles lined up perfectly on the dresser – while Lara was verging on unkempt, with her henna tattoos and her bangles and her wacky sartorial palette. She looked like the kind of woman who used deodorant made from coconut oil on her hairy underarms and had a downstairs like the Belanglo State Forest. Her hair, with its cascading golden waves, was too haphazard. It needed a good brush. Or did it? It somehow worked for her. Under the vibrant kimono, which broke up the muted tones of the dull school hall, she was wearing a designer dress from an outlandishly expensive Bohemian store in Byron Bay that I'd seen advertised online. Yes, she was unkempt, but expensively so. And the interesting thing was, she was nothing like the other women in the hall. Nothing at all. I watched her as she gazed adoringly at her husband, and I actually felt very sorry for her. As gorgeous as she was, it couldn't be easy to hold on to a man like that – a man who caused ponytail whiplash whenever he entered a room, and who, if Alice's assessment alone were to be believed, had every single mother at Darley wishing he'd flip them over his surgical bed and give them a jab to remember.

Mrs Denner climbed the steps to the stage, her heels thumping dramatically on the hollow wood, and tapped the microphone on the lectern, which was now dressed with a frilly sort of tablecloth with tassels on the end. The microphone let out a high-pitched squeak, causing a room full of swallowed giggles.

'I do apologise,' she said, her voice weary. 'Good morning parents. Thank you so much for joining us for this important assembly, the first one of term one.' Her public speaking voice was lovely and poetic, unlike the shrill bark I had heard her use at one of the older kids who'd pushed his mate under the sprinkler on the oval just before the bell went.

'I'm very grateful for such a good turnout today,' she continued. 'Especially given most of you will be back in this very hall on Saturday evening for trivia night. We truly appreciate your commitment to our little school. On that note, I'd like to remind you that we still have a couple of tables to fill ahead of Saturday. As I stressed at the end of last term, we are all in new year-groups now, and I'd like to encourage you all to sit with parents from your year that you may not have socialised with before. All of our new families will have received an email over the Christmas break with details about how to buy trivia night tickets, but if you are new to Darley Heights, and have yet to purchase your tickets, or if you have any questions about how to do so, please do not hesitate to reach out to Alice Daniels, who is running the event.' She scanned the room.

'Stand up, Alice,' she said.

Alice jumped up and pointed at the top of her own head with her index finger.

'Lastly,' Principal Denner continued, 'I would like to encourage you to give generously on the night. We will have a raffle with prizes including wine and spirits, a luxury food hamper and theatre tickets; and a silent auction with a mountain bike and a girls' spa weekend in Melbourne up for grabs – thanks to the generosity of some of our parents. So it really is worth bringing along as much cash as you can afford . . .' She stopped and cocked an ear to the left. 'What's that Mr Mattock?'

The sporty man with the whistle, who I had now realised was the Phys-Ed teacher, shouted something up to her from the front row.

'Ahh yes, thank you Mr Mattock. Nigel Mattock has just confirmed we will have an EFTPOS machine on the night, so if you are not able to bring cash, you will still be able to bid on auction items and buy a strip, or strips *plural*, of raffle tickets. We encourage you to spend big! However, we will not allow IOUs on the night.' Principal Denner paused. 'I repeat, NO IOUs.'

'I think we got that,' Ted whispered. 'No IOUs.'

'Shhhh!' I said, holding back a giggle.

'As most of you know, all monies raised on the night will go towards air conditioning for this very hall, which, you will all agree, is well overdue,' Mrs Denner continued. 'We have already had a very generous cash donation from Dr Luke Hampson . . . .' Did she just *swoon*? 'So, um, thank you Dr Hampson!' The room erupted like the pit at a Justin Bieber concert. Luke nodded and waved his hand up and down in a manner that said, 'Thank you, ladies, you may cease clapping (but please do not, because I am basking in it).'

I was so close to him I could smell the arrogance wafting from his pores.

'And there is one thing I feel I should mention.' Mrs Denner's expression was grave. 'I do not like having to discuss this, but last year, it was brought to my attention that a group of parents brought along a type of hand-rolled cigarette that was not made from tobacco . . .'

There were some sniggers from the middle row.

'I should not have to remind you that smoking marijuana on school property is illegal, and will not be tolerated. And while I am convinced none of you here would engage in such . . . *unsavoury* behaviour, I feel it is my duty to remind you that drugs are strictly prohibited on school grounds. Anyway, enough from me–' Mrs Denner gestured towards her feet, where a hundred kids were seated cross-legged, facing their parents and carers. 'Let's hear from some of our wonderful students, who, after the Acknowledgement of Country, would like to begin this special assembly by reading a poem based on our own school motto – "Sharing is Caring" – written by our very own English teacher Mrs Seabold. It is entitled, "I'd Like to Get to Know You Better".'

And as she said those words, Luke turned his head around and looked me straight in the eyes again, for a second longer than the last time, with the faintest trace of amusement on his face. *I'd like to get to know you better.* I can't deny there wasn't the smallest thrill that he had finally noticed there was a bona fide Fair & Brewer model sitting behind him, and this time I was the one who looked away first.

An hour later, we were out of the stifling heat and into the morning sun, which threatened to be just as unbearable. Ted's shirt was wet with sweat patches and Evie looked like she was about to pass out from heat exhaustion, so I made her have a few power gulps from my water bottle on her way to her classroom. She guzzled the lot and ran off before Ted called her back and rubbed sun cream into her face.

'She can do that herself,' I said.

'Yes, but she won't bother. She's seven.'

I shrugged. Sometimes he was just a little too uptight about the kids. I was all for instilling a bit of independence in our offspring.

He took my hand and held it as we walked to the car park, in what I suspected was another 'hurry the wife along' ploy. Chatter rang in my ears as we followed the crowd.

'. . . soooo cute, wasn't it?'

'And when Otto fluffed his lines . . .'

'Oh, *bless* him . . .'

'. . . did you *see* Luke Hampson?'

'Shhhh, Tansie, you're *terrible*!'

'. . . have you got your trivia costume?'

'It's *definitely* school uniform.'

'Ask Alice Daniels on the committee.'

'Yep, BYO.'

'. . . Prosecco, probably.'

'*Another* new girl?'

'Swingers? Says who?'

'She's got a girl in 1S. That's Emma Sawyer's class.'

'. . . moved from Saint Cecilia's.'

Saint Cecilia's. The sound of the words seemed to conjure up that smell again, the smell of Poison, of foreboding.

But no sooner than it had arrived, the sickly aroma was gone again, carried away on the hot summer breeze. Stolen away to tease someone else, to pop the membranes of *their* memory like a balloon.

A few steps ahead, Lara kept pace with Luke's wide stride. She looked like a miniature Schnauzer trotting alongside a Great Dane.

'That bloke,' Ted whispered, nodding at Luke's back, which was broad at the shoulders and then sloped in, like an inverted triangle, 'walks like he's got a hot potato up his arse.'

'Arrogant,' I found myself saying. 'They're such a mismatch.'

'He was checking you out in the hall.'

'No he wasn't!' I tucked a strand of hair behind my ear. 'Really?'

Ted tightened his grip on my hand. 'He was,' he said, bending down to kiss my temple. 'And who can blame him? You were the hottest woman in there.'

I did an over-exaggerated bat of my eyelids and squeezed his hand back.

In the car park, Lara chatted to Alice, who was twisting her wedding ring nervously on her finger. She did a double-take when she saw us.

'Amanda! Ted!' Alice called, beckoning us over.

Lara looked at me. 'Hi again,' she said. 'I was just asking about the trivia night, seeing as how we're all virtual strangers sort of thrown together. But then Alice told me you guys go *way* back.'

'We do,' I said, keen to let Lara know how far. I guess it made me feel a little more secure, showing another parent that I had connections with somebody who was *somebody* at Darley Heights. 'Yes, we go back a very long way. We're cheaters!'

'I'm sorry?' Lara smiled.

Oh God, did she think I was making some swinging joke? Or worse still, suggesting we were up for that kind of caper?

'Um, I don't mean *cheating* cheating,' I heard myself emit a high-pitched laugh. 'Not, I mean, in the *marriage* sense. I mean we're openly flouting Mrs Denner's rule at trivia night about making new friends.'

'Oh, I *see*,' Lara said. 'Well, I'm all for a bit of cheating! I won't tell anyone if you don't.'

Alice threw me the side-eye. Lara seemed to have warmed up a touch from her previous awkwardness. She looked over her shoulder. 'You must meet my husband, Luke!' She stood up on her tippy toes and cupped her hand around her mouth, like she'd done with her daughter an hour and a half before. 'Luke, honey?'

Luke was on the other side of the car park, unlocking his black BMW with a beep-beep. He turned around when he heard his name and pressed the fob again, dramatically.

'Locking it? Is there a crime problem at Darley Heights Public I should be aware of?' Ted muttered.

Luke strode over nonchalantly, in no hurry. I flicked my hair off my neck, where the heat had made it stick.

'Luke, this is Amanda,' Lara said, gesturing towards me.

The wet stone eyes met mine and he stepped forward with a waft of eau de toilette and grabbed my wrist. I barely had time to look down, let alone protest, before he yanked me in for a peck on the cheek. He smelled of expensive soap.

'Hello Amanda,' he said.

'Hi . . . hi,' I stuttered, stunned by the intimacy of his gesture. Then, quick as a tack, he let go of my wrist and turned to Ted.

'Nice to meet you, mate,' he said, holding out his hand.

Ted held out his own hand in response and the two men shook. I noticed Ted had pulled his body upright so that he had a height advantage on Luke, which was really unlike him. I mean, I knew he already thought Luke was a bit of a dickhead, but the uninvited kiss thing must have really peeved him. He was all straight, his chin unnaturally high like a bloke in an old sepia photograph, and, as he held up his head, I noticed Luke was doing the same, so the two of them looked like they were about to square off.

Ted stepped back after a moment or two. 'You too, *mate*,' he said in a manner that suggested Luke was very definitely not his mate.

'Well,' said Lara in a chirpy voice, oblivious to the tension. 'We'd better be off. Luke's got a busy line-up this morning. Nose job today, isn't it honey?'

'That's correct!' Luke said. He looked pleased with himself.

'Really, mate?' said Ted. 'Are you sure you need one? Your nose isn't *that* bad.'

Luke nodded and smiled. 'Good one, *mate*.'

Lara let out a burst of laughter. 'No, no . . . Luke's *doing* the surgery, Ted,' she said, with a flap of her hand. 'He's a plastic surgeon! That's too funny!'

Alice bit her lip to stop herself from laughing.

'Anyway,' Lara said. 'I just wanted to introduce you all to Luke since Alice has very kindly invited us onto your trivia table.'

'It will be such fun,' said Alice. She smiled warmly at Lara.

'Can't wait,' muttered Ted.

'So, see you on Saturday, guys!' Lara sang.

Luke gave a nod and turned away. 'Ciao.' He waved over his shoulder as he sauntered off. I watched his buttocks rise and fall as he walked. Even his arse was arrogant.

'*Ciao*?' Ted scoffed, as he climbed into the driver's seat, brushing off crumbs left by Sam's chocolate croissant en route to the bus stop. 'Ciao? Who's said "ciao" since 1985? Handshake like a wet fish.'

'I know,' I agreed as I watched Luke climb into his car. 'What an idiot.'

Just as Ted clicked into reverse, Alice banged on the window.

'Christ, what does she want now?'

'I don't know,' I said, and let the window down.

'I can lip read,' Alice laughed. 'Just checking you're okay with the trivia table. It just dawned on me you might not want to be with the Makins or the Hampsons. Is there anyone else you wanted to sit with? Not that you actually know anyone else to pick from.'

'No!' I said, rather too hastily, as I watched Luke's car pull away. I didn't want to upset Alice's meticulous planning by demanding she swap someone out. And also, it wouldn't exactly be the best way to win friends and influence people, to reject a couple from the table because the bloke fancied himself, or because they might end up trying to shag us.

'Definitely not,' I reiterated. 'Thanks for sorting it all for us. We're happy, aren't we, Ted?'

'Yeah, sure,' he said, taking his foot off the brake and reversing ever so slowly in a bid to get Alice's hands off the window frame.

'Great! Okay then, just wait while I . . .' She pulled out her iPad from where it was tucked under her armpit and began tapping on the screen with her forefinger while walking backwards along the trajectory of the moving car. 'I just want to sort the table while . . . I . . . have . . . you . . . here . . .'

Ted let out a sigh, put his foot on the brake and ran his hand through his hair.

'Okay, we're all done,' she said, with a winning smile. 'I've confirmed everything online. We are officially table six! Remember the theme is "Back to School", so you'll need to think outside the box because there will be a heap of people just in regular school uniform which is completely dull. Try and make it as exciting as you can. Honestly, guys, trivia night is quite literally the best night of the school year. I promise you: it's going to be a night to remember!'

Chapter Two
Alice

Transcript: The voice of Alice Daniels in the office of Dr Martha Davis.

You want me to start from the beginning? You mean right from trivia night, or earlier? Okay, well I'll start from that afternoon, because I remember it all pretty clearly. The sequence of events is almost like a wall of photographs lined up in my brain, all of it colourful, clear as day. I can remember the conversations, the music, the arguing, and of course when Lara arrived and caused a massive furore. It's like any moment in your life that's significant, good or bad: getting married, seeing a dead body, giving birth. Somehow your brain captures these moments on photographic paper and flashes them in front of you when you least expect it. Isn't it strange how it does that? Amanda calls those life glimpses 'Polaroid moments', the ones that stay. Sometimes I can't remember what I ate for breakfast – in fact, I literally cannot recall what I had this morning (muesli or yoghurt, I suspect, since I'm a creature of habit), but I still have a vivid memory of the time Sally Eden told me I was a fat cow in the chemistry lab when I was fourteen and Amanda stood up and said, 'Shut up Sally Eden, you dickhead!' Believe me, we could do an entire session on that memory alone. Oh, that really was a moment I liked to replay later in life whenever I couldn't get into a size ten pair of jeans. Luckily, I won the battle of the bulge, but only because I work out so much and I'm so fastidious about my diet. Wasn't it Kate Moss who said, 'Nothing tastes as good as skinny feels'? I couldn't agree with her more. So yes, I remember a lot of trivia night, just because of how significant it was in terms of what happened to all of us afterwards.

Was I drunk? I mean, I'd had a little to drink, but nothing excessive. I was organising the whole event, you see, so it wouldn't have been a good look to get paralytic. I'm quite controlled like that. I don't like that feeling of waking up the next day and thinking I've done something inappropriate, the sinking feeling that makes you put your hand to your temple when you know you did something embarrassing, but you can't quite recall what. It's just not in my remit to embarrass myself, to open myself up like that. I worry what I might tell people when I'm in that state, what secrets I might unwittingly divulge. Not to mention the hangovers! I can't deal with feeling fuzzy these days, not with the twins to coordinate (7-year-old girls can be quite a challenge at the best of times, let alone when your head feels like it's trapped in a vice). So no, to answer your question, I wasn't particularly drunk on the night. Tipsy, most definitely, but drunk? No. Anyway, sorry – that's probably more information than you need, isn't it? I'm digressing, my apologies. Let me start from the beginning. Bear with me, won't you?

It was boiling that day, Saturday 30 January. I mean, January is always hot, as you know, but the heat is meant to taper off towards the end of the month as we nosedive to autumn, and there was just no respite from it this year. You must remember it? Darley was bursting at the seams with tourists and teenagers in those God-awful Brazilian bikini bottoms that go right up their backsides. The ones that Amanda says she wishes she could wear, and I think look common as muck. Not that it needs to be hot for teenagers to strip off, but as I've established, it was. Crazily so. The heat in which even mad dogs seek shade.

Pete and I had spent the morning in the garden, watering and mowing, and doing general maintenance. Most people in Darley employ someone to do that kind of thing, as you know, but we like to do it ourselves. It's the same deal with having a cleaner. Everyone I know pays for a weekly clean, but I just can't abide it. No one ever does the job to the standard I like, and Pete agrees. 'If you want a job done properly . . .' he says. I do the cleaning, but the garden we tend to do together, as a family. He mows and the girls and I weed and water. Our front garden is honestly my pride and joy, I could stay out there for hours. It's so spacious and whimsical. That's the style we went for. You know, lots of intertwining branches and wild flowers, and a little stone path leading from the veranda to the front gate.

The inside of the house is a little dated, since it's Pete's parents' old place – you know, 1980s-style kitchen, a corner bathtub, vinyl tiles, carpets throughout, that sort of style, totally needs refreshing. They never really did anything to it, especially as they got older. But from the front, it looks incredible. The first stage of our renovation was an exterior repaint, and so we went from a canary yellow slatted frontage to crisp white, and with a garden that's as lush and watered as ours, it honestly looks like something out of a movie. We're starting the inside of the house in a couple of months, and it will be wonderful to be able to host cocktail parties and the like – at the moment, I just don't have the inclination to show it off. Pete says, 'Never judge a book by its cover.' Our 'book' may have a wonderful cover, but inside the story is less than intriguing. But we'll get there, of course.

So anyway, after a morning sweating it out in the garden, I did an hour of mathematics with the girls. We do at least three hours of maths and English with them every weekend, because in my opinion the school curriculum doesn't push them enough and I want them to end up in the Darley Heights Opportunity Class in year 5. Lottie is a whizz with sums, and Freya's the literate one, so I think they both have an excellent chance. The OC is for bright kids, as you may already know, and it is way better and more intensive a programme than any *private* school could offer. That's why we never considered St Cecilia's ourselves, like Amanda and Ted. The kids at St Cecilia's may get to go skiing and on field trips to China, but who cares about that if they don't get good jobs as adults? There's only so far networking can take you! And I mean, what use is the ability to ski if you don't end up earning enough money to take your own family to Whistler one day?

Anyway, I had a quick shower and cycled up to the school, where I spent the entire afternoon painting signs, decorating tables and laying out raffle prizes inside the hall. It was like an inferno inside the building and I was throwing back the water like I'd been hiking through the Sahara. But since trivia night was my first fundraiser as events chair on the parent-teacher committee and was a massive deal to me, I sort of forged on, despite the sweat. I mean, what else can you do? It was my job.

Thankfully, I was used to that sort of thing. Let me give you a bit of background. Before I had the girls seven years ago, I worked as an events planner in the city, and I would have to set things up rain or shine: weddings, baby showers, engagement parties. It was nice to revisit that environment, to be in charge of an event again (albeit on a much smaller scale) and also, I suppose, to enjoy the kudos that came with it. It had been a while since I'd had the freedom to plan an occasion on a big scale. Pete and I decided I would give up work when the twins arrived. He's very traditional, my husband, and so am I, I suppose. It's the legacy left to me by my own mother, who was the archetypal 1980s housewife with the apron and the curlers setting her hair every night. Our family home was pristine growing up and there was always a square meal of meat and two veg on the table. My father worked, and my mother cooked and cleaned. That was just the way it was, and she did it perfectly, never once complained. It was what had been drummed into me all along, this need to be a pillion of domestic perfection once you were a mother. And Pete is cut from the same cloth.

And for me, giving up work was the right thing to do, at first. Freya and Lottie kept me so busy as babies and I loved being a stay-at-home mum. We didn't really have to worry about money since Pete's parents had sold us the house for way less than it is worth so they could move into this quaint little retirement community half an hour's drive north, so the mortgage was very small. I knew how lucky we were to have the house, because despite the dated interior, it is one of the larger homes in Darley with five bedrooms and a converted attic space, which Pete uses as a study. I loved the place from the start, and in the first weeks of parenthood, I just adored sitting out on the front porch and rocking the girls to sleep and looking out into the garden. It was where I sat and thought about stuff, you know? Where I contemplated life.

But after a few months, I started to want more. I loved my girls more than anything, of course, and I still do, but there was something missing, and, like a lot of women, I gradually began to feel like a decaying piece of fruit left in the basket, never to see sunlight again. I didn't want to swallow it down and just accept my lot gratefully like my mother had done in 1985. My job had always been a huge part of who I am, *is* a huge part of who I am, and I suppose in those first few months of motherhood, after the initial euphoria, the whole 'oh my God, look what I've created' feeling had worn off, I struggled to figure out the woman who was left. I felt as though my extensive skillset had been made redundant, which, I suppose, it had. Instead of organising social events for a hundred people, I had been demoted to personal assistant to two six-month-old children: Monkey Music on Mondays, Baby Gym on Tuesdays, singalong with Jill at Darley Library on Thursdays, Baby Cinema on Fridays. And the incessant hum of *The Wiggles* singing about fruit salad and hot potatoes and cold spaghetti with inane smiles on their faces, playing in the background until my brain felt like cold spaghetti too.

Life became richer in many ways. I mean, nothing compares to those first smiles and giggles. But I stopped bothering with make-up (what's the point when you're only going to Monkey Music?); I gave most of my work clothes to Amanda to wear at Fair & Brewer (she'd gone back to work part-time when Evie was six months old) and devoted an entire section of my wardrobe to leggings; I felt the deafening silence where there was once praise, because there was no round of applause to be had for this kind of multitasking, for the incredible ability to breast feed two babies in tandem – no one to shake my hand and thank me for my skills like they did in the events world, to tell me, 'Well done, Alice, you pulled that off sensationally.' Pete was always there to offer a perfunctory 'you're doing a great job', of course, but it always came with a patronising pat on the shoulder, not from awestruck eyes that sparkled with enthusiasm, like it did from my satisfied clients. I missed that thrill after having the twins.

In some ways, I was lonely. I had Pete to chat with about the ins and outs of daily life, of course, but I needed more than that. I'd gone from working with big groups of people, from air kisses and phone calls with celebrity chefs, to flopping my breasts out in Darley Library's drab meeting room, with its olive green chairs in a semicircle, in front of a small collective of overweight women with dead eyes and bellies that hung over the tops of their porridge-encrusted tracksuit pants. With whom the only thing I had in common was the fact small humans had exited all of our vaginas and now we weren't sleeping because of it. I didn't want to talk about my postpartum bleeding with a bunch of strangers, or the degree of my perineal tearing, or when I was going to 'get back on the horse' with my husband (especially since I wasn't planning to let Pete near me for a good few months). They didn't care any more about my cracked nipples than I did about theirs! I mean, can you imagine?

Thank Christ for Amanda in those days, is all I can say. At least we had one another. She was in the thick of it with Evie, who was three months old when the twins arrived, but she had already done it with Sam a few years before and so she knew the drill. She's always been pretty relaxed with her kids – sometimes a little too much so in my opinion – so she skipped the mothers' group meetings ('I know how to massage my own lumpy tits,' she said) but encouraged me to go, promised me it would get easier, told me to enjoy it. Told me to chill out with the black-and-white books for baby's cognitive development and the abacuses and the swimming lessons. 'They're tiny babies,' she told me. 'They've got plenty of time to be geniuses.' She warned that before I knew it, I'd be back at work again and the girls would be at primary school and I would miss the hectic 'baby' days. She looked out for me, looked after me. Did things like baking 'feeding-friendly' savoury muffins filled with fenugreek and oatmeal to help boost my milk supply, and dropped round batches of frozen shepherd's pie so that Pete and I were well fed. Sometimes she'd just sense I needed a caffeine hit and would turn up with coffee. All I needed to do was phone her with a wobble in my voice and she would whizz round. Quite often, she'd leave Evie with Ted and sit with the girls so I could go for a walk. And I relished that freedom, I really did. Although invariably I'd be home at the twenty-minute mark because I didn't like to leave them too long. It was strange really – I was desperate for 'me' time, but I didn't want to be away from my babies, either. I also didn't want anyone to see me out and about without the girls and judge me for taking time off. I mean, people can be pretty judgemental, can't they?

Amanda had it all under control at that point in her life. She was at her best with a newborn. Sam was already in year 1 at Darley Heights when Evie arrived, and it was almost as though she forgot about some of her own issues when she was flooded with new baby pheromones. She is a very practical friend, Amanda. She doesn't always get it right in her own life, not by a long shot, but when the chips are down, she rises to the challenge. She's there for you, you know? She's always been like that, even at primary school. I'd sort of bumble along looking after her, day in, day out, because she had such a shitty home life and mine was pretty near perfect (you know, parents still together, lovely big house with a back door pool, piano lessons on Tuesdays – the complete opposite to hers) but if something bad happened to me, she would jump on it like a cat on a mouse. So, while I might be sharing my lunch with her because her mum had forgotten to pack it, she'd be squaring up to the likes of Sally Eden or Jonty Duncan because he'd yelled something crude about my boobs not coming in. It's been like that as adults, too. We've weathered it all: the break-up that rips your heart in two, commitment, marriage, babies. We look after one another, and, even though Pete thinks that I do more of the looking after in our friendship these days, he doesn't realise what Amanda and I have been through together. Life goes in cycles, right? And one day, the balance will shift again.

Anyway, to cut a long story short, it was Amanda who suggested I start up my own business so I could work on my own terms and within childcare hours. She championed it, in fact, and so when the twins started at their Montessori day care, I started Abloom Events, offering party planning and the like – fortieth celebrations, christenings and so on. It was immediately successful, partly to do with the fact that Darley is such a wealthy suburb, I suppose, and so people have the cash to be extravagant. But also because there are no other local event hubs. If you want a party planner, you have to call them in from the city, and no one can be bothered with that!

It has been wonderful and I'm truly grateful to have found my niche (Amanda was right!), but I'm also a Type A personality, always have to be adding to the to-do list, and so I joined the parent-teacher committee when the girls started at Darley Heights Public a year ago. Luckily for me, the entertainment chair Sandra Curtess announced she was stepping down from the role, because her son Curtis (Curtis Curtess! I know, right? Of all the names! What was she *thinking*?) was off to high school, and I jumped at the chance to take the role. So, as you might understand, the trivia night was a big deal for me because it was my first chance to showcase to the committee and parents exactly what I was capable of and how well I could organise a fundraising event on a large scale. Because that's what it's all about, raising money, and Darley Heights Public needed a new air conditioning system for that damn stifling hall, even if it was rather ironic that we were fundraising for it at the end of the summer and the date of install was likely to be mid-winter.

Pete helped me decorate that Saturday afternoon along with a couple of kindergarten mums and it was all going swimmingly until *she* turned up. She was the last to arrive. And as soon as she'd introduced herself as Victoria Day and told me she was a new parent who'd transferred two of her three daughters from St Cecilia's Primary, I realised poor Amanda was in for it. Amanda had left the school to escape that very woman – and for good reason – and now here she was in the school hall at Darley, paint brush in hand, tearily telling me all about how her two youngest angels had been forced to leave the highly respected Catholic school very suddenly at the end of the previous year, because their father, Nico, had lost his ludicrously well-paid job in finance. It was a case of either pay the school fees for all three girls or lose the house, and they'd picked the house – as you would, of course. She told me the whole story: all about how she'd had to pretty much get down on her knees and beg Mrs Denner for not just one spot at Darley Heights for the new term, like I had on Amanda's behalf for Evie, but *two* places for her highly gifted girls, and how it couldn't have come at a worse time, since the kids were in mourning because the family dog had been run over not long before, and they were 'devastated, broken'. I actually felt sorry for the woman for a nano-second because her sob story was so . . . raw. But then I reminded myself what this woman had done to Amanda, how atrociously she had bullied her, and how my best friend had held her head up, achingly, while Victoria and her cronies berated her and gossiped about her. I found it incredibly hard after that to be polite to the woman as she stood there painting a canvas signboard, and it was particularly gratifying to correct her grammar and inform her that it was actually 'Get *your* punch here' and not 'Get *you're* punch here', which was what she had painted. I even told her – and this was probably erring on the mean side, but whatever – 'Victoria, grammar is the difference between helping your Uncle Jack off a horse, and helping your uncle jack-off a horse' and she looked at me as if I was mad. But she did it anyway – she painted over the word 'you're' and started again.

Anyway, while we were decorating, Pete took me to one side, behind the musty stage curtain, which desperately needed a steam clean, and told me that I was duty bound to warn Amanda that Victoria Day was now a parent at Darley Heights. I thought it was rather generous of him actually, seeing as he wasn't Amanda's biggest fan at that point in time, but that's Pete through and through. He has a strong moral compass and he likes to do the right thing. He said, 'Alice, you and I both know Amanda will get annihilated and do something stupid if she bumps into Victoria tonight and she hasn't been warned beforehand.' I knew he was right – there was nothing more likely to push Amanda to her limits than finding out her tormentor had evicted her from one school, only to show up at the next.

But here's the thing – I couldn't do it. I just could not bring myself to forewarn her, and I think there are a number of reasons why. The first was that I didn't want to push her back into that bottomless, depressive pit she'd only just scratched herself out of now she was away from toxic St Cecilia's. But in more immediate terms, I didn't want to ruin her night. I couldn't do it. I wanted her to embrace the anonymous and enigmatic persona she'd been clutching as she wafted into Darley for just a tiny bit longer. She deserved that much, after everything she'd been through. Also, in practical terms, I had a hall to decorate and I didn't have time to get on the phone to Amanda for an hour while she agonised over the fact her nemesis had not only arrived on her new doorstep, but was now decorating it. It would have totally thrown my timetable out.

So, for that part, I take the blame. I can see how my decision not to pre-warn Amanda ultimately made the sequence of events unfurl. Then again, as Pete pointed out to me later, *I* didn't make Amanda do what she did at St Cecilia's. *I* didn't pour the cocktails down her throat and make her mess everything up. Nor did I make Nico lose his job, or influence the Days' choice of Darley Heights as their next best option to private (although, as the best state school in the area, it was no great surprise). And, of course, I couldn't control what happened at trivia night, or foresee Victoria's involvement in that whole sordid episode.

But I do sometimes wonder if, had I told Amanda that little bit earlier that Victoria was at Darley Heights, rather than just chucking it at her like a wet rag at the very start of proceedings on the trivia night, she might have behaved differently. Or maybe, just maybe, she might have stayed at home. But I suppose you can't go through life thinking 'what if?', can you? What is done is done.

Oh gosh, I'm so sorry, is it that time already? Yes, of course, I understand. I guess the rest will have to wait until our next session.

Chapter Three
Zoe

From: Zoe.m8kin79@realworld.com.au
To: pho_e_b_wallis@zapmail.com
Subject: The truth

Dearest Phoebe,

Where are you right now, sis? Which continent? Dancing? Drinking? Chilling out on a sun lounger with a pina colada? Where will you read this? And do you even have Wi-Fi? I really wish you'd make contact just to let me know you're okay. I understand why you needed to get away after what went down, I really do, but just some kind of contact would put my mind at ease. Please, if you could find the time, I'd be so grateful.

Okay, so I know I've mentioned the trivia night saga before, but I never really told you the full story, so this is it, warts and all. Remember the diaries we both used to keep when we were kids? Pages and pages in the leather-bound books mum got from Fred's the Stationer? Red hardback books with the thin lines! I'd fill mine with all the exciting stuff – which year 10 boy I wanted to kiss (always Paul Wright) and how I hated Dad because he'd grounded me for climbing out of the window to go roller-skating. (I remember him telling me, *When you're a parent, you will understand!* Of course I probably rolled my eyes, but now I totally get it.) You filled your book with all the places you wanted to go and all the stamps you wanted to get in your passport, do you remember? Mine was a stream of colourful consciousness, and yours was just lists and lists in black and white. Morocco, Venice, Kenya, England! Or bridges, *always* bridges: The Golden Gate Bridge, London Bridge, Tower Bridge (you said England had the best ones), Brooklyn Bridge, The Ponte Vecchio . . . You'd hyperventilate with excitement whenever we went over the Sydney Harbour Bridge, and I'd say, *Wow, Phoebs, another bridge, that's so exciting.* I can't remember the others, but there were loads. Memories, Phoebs, memories!

So anyway, in the spirit of sisterhood, and since I can't tell anyone else exactly how it all unfolded, I'm going tell you (and only you) what happened that night, because I know you won't judge. I'm looking upon it as a kind of electronic diary that only we are privy to. Let's just hope I don't get hacked!

Are you ready? Okay, so here goes.

On the Saturday (trivia night *day*) I went to get some crackers and dips etc. to take with us that night because it was a bring-your-own affair, including food. Can you believe that? $30 per ticket and no food? I wasn't in the best of moods because Miles was off playing golf and so I had to prep with Freddie in tow. Not that I don't love him being with me, you know that, but I had so much to do: go to the hire shop to get my costume, pick up booze from the off-licence, get cash for the babysitter. You know, all the stuff you have to do before you go out? I whizzed round the supermarket like I was on speed, flinging stuff into the trolley, trying not to hit Freddie, who was in the back on the iPad, and trying to calm my nerves about leaving him with the babysitter, because you know how anxious I get when I'm not physically with him. And the whole time I was snapping at him 'cos he was saying, *Let's get some stuff from the baby aisle just in case we get another baby!* Of course he didn't know I was already on edge since I was ovulating for like the twentieth time since we started trying two whole years ago and it still wasn't bloody happening, and that frankly, I couldn't be arsed with it any more. So I wasn't in the mood to deal with Freddie trying to grab newborn nappies off the shelf, not least because he was hanging over the edge of the trolley and I was terrified he might fall and bang his head or something. I read about a kid doing that in Arizona – he fell out of a trolley in the supermarket right on his head, and boom, dead!

I'd also woken up looking like total shit, with saggy eyelids and high-school skin, and he was like *Mum, can I have a Kinder Egg? Mum!* And I was like, *FOR GOD'S SAKE FREDDIE, SHUT UP*, all snappy, and he went, *Mum look, there's Evie Blackland from my class!* And I looked up, and there was the new kid from Freddie's class that I kept hearing about, with her dad, who was really very attractive. And I was pretty flustered, I'm not going to lie. If I'd been looking good that day, I might have acted a bit cooler. Anyway, the little girl was waving and yelling, *Freddie! Freddie!* so we had to stop and talk, which was awkward because I was in a pair of crappy yoga tights and I hadn't even showered. He was wearing grey tracksuit pants and a white T-shirt, which you know

I'm a sucker for, and he smiled with this giant toothy grin like he was in an ad for toothpaste or something, and said, *Well hi there!*

I was like, *Oh, hi!* And he goes, *I'm Ted and this is Evie!* and I go (and I'm not sure what I was thinking, but I said it anyway), *Oh, really? And here's me thinking you stole her off the street!* And it was pretty awkward until Freddie laughed and said, *Mum, you're so silly!* and Evie joined in and Ted's blue eyes crinkled at the corners like the folds of an accordion.

We made small talk for a minute, mainly about the trivia night, 'cos once we'd worked out who the other one was, we realised we were going to be on the same table, along with the doctor and the hippy, plus Alice (the one who organised it) and her husband, Pete. The chatter went, *Well, it should be a fun night!* and *Yes, I hope so!* and *How's your costume going?* and *Fine!* And after a minute, I said *Okay well, happy shopping!* And he said, *You too!* and went to move his trolley to the left while I moved mine to the right, so there was a totally awkward trolley collision right there on the corner of the toiletry aisle and the canned soups. We pulled the trolleys apart, but then, get this, we both moved to the *other* side, so it was like we were doing some kind of trolley dance in aisle eight, and we both laughed in a mortifying way. Then Ted said to Freddie, all serious: *Tell your mum to look where she's going.* I was a bit affronted, until he smiled and said, *Zoe, that was a joke!* and I let out a hysterical laugh, like I'd been sucking on gas and air or something. Then we both went at the same time, *Okay, then!* And Freddie and Evie both yelled, *Jinx!* and then,

Double jinx! when they realised they'd also said it in unison, and I just wanted to get the hell out of there. *Well it was great to see you Ted,* I said, and yanked us out from the two-trolley pile-up. As soon as we were properly around the corner, I put my hand up to my pink face and I said to Freddie, *Oh my God, I carried a watermelon!* And he looked at me blankly, and said, *You carried a what, Mum?*

I was still burning with embarrassment when I got home to our knackered little apartment to find Miles cleaning his golfing shoes in the kitchen sink – which he won't be allowed to do if we can ever afford to renovate – and to cut a long story short, we ended up having another stupid fight about the whole baby thing, because I suggested we fit in some nookie before the trivia night, in case we were too drunk when we got home (even though, as I said, I really did not have the inclination in any way, shape or form). He looked at me like I was an idiot and said, *Well what are we meant to do with Freddie, exactly? Is he going to watch? We're in a two-bedroom apartment, Zoe* (the inference being that if we hadn't spent so much cash on IVF, we might have finally upgraded), and I lost it at him, because he seemed to be implying I was a bad mother when all I was suggesting was we put on a Pixar movie for Freddie and quickly get to business. Nothing flashy or romantic, just a functional quickie in order to procreate. But being told it was a stupid idea really got my goat and we ended up screaming at each other, which I was fully aware was way more harmful for Freddie than twenty minutes of *Cars 2*. And I told Miles that and he went, *For fuck's sake, Zoe, why does this circus always end up my fault?* And I was so resentful he called it a circus that I threw a bowl of cold pasta at him, sauce and all, (which was annoying because it was the incredible one he brings home from work with the crayfish bisque) and it sort of hung off his hair and dripped into his eyes. It really pissed him off and, after he'd wiped his face with a tea towel, he hissed, *Well, if I didn't want to have sex with you before, I definitely don't now!* Then he stomped off outside, flicked off the top of a bottle of amber ale and let the cap drop somewhere on the grass that he hadn't bothered to mow because he'd been dicking about on the golf course. I watched him in our postage-stamp-sized garden with the faded, dead grass and the crumbling wall and the dried-out hydrangea bush, my heart pounding with anger and disappointment and wondered where it had all gone wrong. I thought back to when I first met him and how much I loved him right from the start. Right from the moment he pulled into a no-stopping zone in his beat-up Honda and stomped over to confront me about stealing the last parking spot in the row outside Pasadena.

I don't know if you remember this story, but I'd pulled into the space when he was indicating, and he wasn't happy! He was late to work you see, and it was before they'd made him head chef, so he was desperate to make an impression. Oh, his face was so adorable. I can still see the look on it when he saw I had a flat tyre and he said, *Oh shit, I really am a miserable fucker! I was about to have a go at you!* And he stuck his head in through the restaurant door to tell them he'd be there soon, he was just helping a 'beautiful stranded lady' change her tyre. I can actually see the muscles of his back as clear as day through the white

T-shirt he was wearing as he bent over and changed the tyre, all manly and chivalrous and efficient, and then how his face melted into that gorgeous smile when I said, *Has anyone ever told you you look a bit like Prince Harry?* And he said, *Once or twice . . . a day.*

And that's the way he was from that point on. The looker-afterer, through everything: through those awful, dark days three years ago (Phoebs, I would never want to go back there, not in a million years). Through Freddie's delivery, where he was the most amazing birthing partner, and those incredible, but tiring, first weeks as parents. Through the anxiety, you know, the fear I've had that something bad might happen to Freddie, because as you and I both know, bad things DO happen to good people. We've been through so much, Miles and I, but despite all of it, we've come unstuck. Somehow this whole trying-for-another-baby thing managed to beat us down when nothing else could.

Anyway, where was I? Right, so Cassie, the 16-year-old sitter, arrived at seven o'clock with her mum's home-cooked dinner in a takeaway container and a bag of red grapes, which I told her she needed to keep well away from Freddie because I read about a kid in the UK, London I think, who choked on a seedless Californian green grape in the supermarket checkout queue (can you believe that? A 7-year-old choking on a *grape*? Supermarkets are actually pretty dangerous places for kids when you really think about it). Anyway, Miles and I were both still fuming at that point, and neither of us was remotely up for a night on the sauce, least of all at school with a load of random parents, so I very nearly pulled the pin. Worse still, Cassie seemed really young for her age, and I had a sudden panic like, what if there was a fire in the apartment, or what if Freddie needed CPR, and would she know what to do? But I talked myself down because I'd spent sixty bucks on a cheerleader's outfit, and another sixty on tickets, and I didn't want Miles to whinge that he'd taken the night off work for nothing AND we'd thrown 120 bucks down the shitter. So I reminded Cassie the emergency number was 000 and made her repeat it even though she eyed me like I was deranged, and we rushed out of the door and climbed in our Uber. And Miles said, *Why the hell are we in a cab when it's only a kilometre away?* And so I let out a massive sigh and pointed aggressively at my heels.

(Ahh, the Bridge of Sighs . . . that was another one. Have you been there yet? Is it Venice, or Vienna? I can never remember.) Damn it, Phoebs, I just looked at the clock! I'm wide awake, but I really need to try to get to bed. Freddie's been waking up at five thirty the last few mornings. He's so unsettled at the moment (not surprising really, is it?). I don't really have a solution, just patience I guess, just time. Well, that's what everyone is telling me. Huge life changes like this one are really tough on kids, and I need to make sure he doesn't bottle it all up. Talking is good, isn't it? I've learnt that the hard way. So, let me know, if you can, sissy, that you're okay – it would mean the world to me. Xoxo

Chapter Four
Amanda

Alice was at the school gate, holding a clipboard. I wasn't sure if this was ironic or not, since she ran her entire life on an iPad, and here she was with a bit of plywood with a large plastic clip on it. She looked guilty as hell when she saw me.

I looked at her sideways. 'What's up?'

'I need to chat to you about something,' she said, flapping the clipboard under her armpits. The heat was still unbearable, even early into the evening. 'Not now, but soon, once I've ticked all the names off. I'll come and find you.'

'What? Is it my costume? Did I get the theme wrong?'

I was dressed like Britney Spears in the video for 'Hit Me Baby One More Time', in a pigeon-grey miniskirt, white shirt (unbuttoned) and Sam's grey school cardigan. I'd felt pretty good leaving the house until Sam had said, 'Eww, Mum, aren't you way too old to be wearing that?' and Tara, the 14-year-old babysitter (cheap as chips at twelve dollars an hour) snorted so hard she had to blow her nose.

'Amanda, look around you.' Alice gestured down at her own Hermione Granger outfit. 'Of course you didn't get it wrong. You look great.'

'What, then?'

'Look, I can't chat right now, just . . . I'll find you in a bit. We're on table six, okay?'

'Sure,' I said, giving Ted a 'WTF' look.

He put his hand on the small of my back and leaned in. 'Don't worry, darling,' he whispered as we made our way across the playground towards the hall. 'She's probably going to tell you she's forgotten to put Wham! on the playlist or something.'

I smiled and put it to the back of my mind. Ted was always good at offering reassurance. Behind the biting wit and the endless sarcasm was a loving husband who always put me first. Ted was kind, and funny and generous, and never so much as looked at another woman because he said he'd already found the best one. Alice always said I was 'beyond lucky' to have found a man like Ted and ranted on about how patient and devoted he was – a comment which she quickly followed up with something along the lines of, 'well of course he's lucky too'. I *was* lucky, but in the last few months, something had changed. It was almost as if Ted was becoming a little too serious, the further he trod into his forties (and he was only forty-two). The things he used to laugh at, or find endearing, often elicited a fatherly eye-roll these days. A couple of nights previously, he'd given me a right telling off about Sam walking home from the bus stop on his own.

'It's only one major road to cross,' I'd protested. 'Sam is thirteen and perfectly able to remember the green cross code.'

'Amanda,' Ted had replied. 'You told him you were picking him up! He was worried.'

'Rubbish!' I turned to Sam. 'You weren't worried, were you, sweetheart?'

'Well, you did say you were coming to get me . . .' Sam ventured, opening a packet of Doritos.

Ted did an 'I rest my case' shrug.

'It was just a miscommunication, darling,' I'd said, ready to forget the matter.

But Ted didn't want to drop it. 'You know, Amanda,' he said, 'you don't *have* to have a glass of wine every single night. Maybe then you wouldn't forget stuff!'

'One wine is normal,' I'd snapped back. 'What is *not* normal is to only want to watch Netflix every single night!' (I think there was also an 'I'm sorry, but are you my husband or my father?' thrown in for good measure, too, but the details are hazy). We didn't stay angry for long, we never do, and Ted had apologised in bed for being a grumpy old fart.

A few steps ahead of us, Danny and Sandy from *Grease* walked alongside Cher, the spoiled girl from the movie *Clueless*. Beyond them was a man dressed as Dewey Finn, *School of Rock*'s fraudulent teacher, striding along, guitar in hand. I recognised him as Mr Mattock, the Phys-Ed teacher from the year 1 assembly. I wondered what he'd make of Ted's lame grey pants, sweatband and whistle ensemble.

'Awesome get-up,' Ted said, offering the teacher a nod. Mr Mattock did the half splits and strummed his guitar in response.

Outside the hall, a group of women chatted in a circle, fanning their faces with flat clutch bags and electric fans. I could only see their mostly blonde heads, but ascertained from their pink skirts, cardigans and Alice bands, that they were the bitchy girl gang from the movie *Mean Girls*. Tansie was one of them, I recognised the red hair. And as for Harry Potter – well, I'd never seen so many maroon and yellow scarves, zigzag scars and plastic wands in one space.

Ted leaned in. 'Bloody hell, it's like Hogwarts in here. Sam would *love* it.'

'He's way past the Harry Potter phase,' I said.

'No he's not.'

'You just don't want him to be.' I smiled. 'Let's get a drink.'

'Sure,' said Ted. And he looked like he was going to say something else, which I assumed from my intricate knowledge of him was going to be along the lines of, 'Take it easy on the booze tonight, okay?' but he didn't, which pleased me no end, because it meant that maybe, just maybe, he was going to let loose for once and we might get to have a little fun together.

I scoured the room for the cocktail bar (and I use the word 'bar' loosely, since it was actually a wonky-looking trestle table with a white paper tablecloth on top) and dragged Ted over by the hand. Above the table, manned by the librarian Mrs Macey, was a rather amateurish sign saying, 'Get your booze here!' You could still see where the original sign underneath had said 'you're booze', which wasn't the best look for a primary school that prided itself on exceptional grammar.

'Look,' whispered Ted. 'Someone got the finger paints out.'

'Behave,' I warned him. 'Alice put a lot of effort into this!'

'Really? I'd hate to see it when she doesn't make an effort. Isn't she meant to be an events planner?'

'Exactly – not an artist. You're only as good as your tradesmen.'

'You mean the kindy kids?'

Mrs Macey was wearing a Tiffany-blue tabard. She held out a kitchen ladle and a brown-card cup as we approached. 'Alcoholic punch, kids?' she sang.

Ted laughed. 'That sounds incredibly menacing coming from one of our daughter's new teachers, but yes, please, we'll have some.'

She chuckled and waved a hand at Ted, as if she were batting away a fly. 'Welcome to Darley Heights,' she chirped.

'Thanks,' Ted grinned. He passed me a cup and wandered down the hall to look at the year 1 paintings.

I was just working out how to carry my punch, my bag and my ticket so I could get out of the way of the now-thriving bar, all whilst tying my shoelace, when a voice beside me laughed and said, 'You look like you're struggling. Can I give you a hand?'

He was tall, very tall with olive skin and a warm smile and was dressed as Severus Snape. I glanced at Ted who was halfway down the hall, oblivious to my juggling act.

'Oh yes, that would be great, thank you so much. If I just hand you my purse, I can tie up my shoe!'

'Of course. It's always a marvel how much stuff you ladies have to carry.'

I smiled and handed him my bag. 'You're lucky you have giant pockets in that gown. You could be stashing a whole load of stuff in there for all I know!'

Severus laughed and his brown eyes sparkled.

'You make it sound so exciting. I think I have my wife's lipstick and a fifty-dollar note.'

'Big spender.' I smiled.

He fumbled with the clasp on the bag and then hesitated. 'Should I put the ticket inside for you?' he asked. 'I don't want to take liberties opening this thing up. That wouldn't do.'

'Oh please, go for it,' I said.

'Done,' he said, shutting my now-bulging purse and tucking it under my arm for me. 'Have a great night.'

'You too – and thanks again.'

'You're welcome.' Severus smiled and strode across the room in his gown.

I caught up with Ted, taking a giant swig of my punch on the way. It wasn't half bad for something that had been created in a black plastic rubbish bin.

'Who were you chatting to?' he asked.

'I don't know,' I said. 'Some dad. He helped me with my purse. You know, *chivalry*?'

'Oh God, I'm so sorry darling. Did I wander off and leave you fighting with all of your evening-out paraphernalia?'

'Hmmm.'

He patted my bum and looked over at Severus. 'He looks familiar.'

'Of course he does, he's Severus Snape,' I said.

'No, I mean his face is familiar.'

'I've never seen him before.'

Ted shrugged. 'He must be boiling in that get-up.'

'Doesn't it look great?' I nodded towards the middle of the room where ten large circular tables, each dressed with white paper tablecloths and graffitied with felt-tip pens, skimmed the dancefloor. 'There's table six. Right next to the photo booth!' I flung my bag on to one of the chairs at our table, downed my punch, and grabbed Ted's hand. 'Come on!'

Inside the booth, he pulled me on to his lap and did his serious face. 'Take it easy, tonight, darling,' he said.

There it was, I *knew* it! The early-evening warning. It was always the same.

'I will,' I pouted. 'You say it like I'm an *alcoholic* or something!'

He didn't say anything.

'Ted?' I felt my body go stiff.

He kissed me on the neck. 'Darling, you have to admit you've been getting a little *over-excited* recently,' he said. 'I know tonight is daunting for you, meeting all these new people and wanting to fit in.'

'What are you saying, that I'm going to get wasted because I want people to like me?'

It was exactly what he was saying. He knew me too well. However, his answer was far more diplomatic.

'I'm just looking out for you,' he said. 'I'm saying take it easy, that's all.'

'Sure.' My voice had a note of sulkiness.

'Oi you,' he said, pulling me in tight. 'I love you. Come on, let's take some photos.' Then he tickled me on the side of my ribs and it made me giggle, so I couldn't very well continue with my sulk. I never held grudges for long, I couldn't, not with Ted. He always had the words to make things better, and the inclination to say them. I loved that about him, I always had. So we pouted, pulled faces and kissed between flashes. Immediately the machine began to whir as it processed our silly snaps and spat them out.

'Oh my god, this is great,' Ted laughed, pointing to the one where he'd plonked his face into my boobs.

'You can have it for your wallet,' I said, resting my head against his arm.

We were just about to sit down when Madonna's 'Like a Virgin' began to pump from the speaker at the front of the stage, and the disco ball began to throw flashes of green and red and yellow across the floor and up the walls. I heard a few 'whoops!' as a group of mums who were already a little greased-up raced to the dance floor.

'Come on, Teddy,' I said, beckoning him towards me with my forefinger.

He rolled his eyes, but followed nonetheless, jigging his hips and clicking his fingers, in what was undeniably the very definition of 'dad dancing'. *Sam would die if he saw this*, I thought. Ted threw his arm round my waist and yanked me in close, almost winding me. I laughed. It was a while since we'd been this silly together, and it felt good.

Madonna cooed the chorus.

'Are *you* a vir-er-er-er-gin?' Ted whispered in my ear.

'Yes,' I said girlishly. 'I'm waiting for my wedding night. But if you're very lucky, I might give you a nice, long blow . . .'

'Well helllllooooo!' A sickly smelling head popped between us. 'Sorry to interrupt, but I wanted to say hi!'

She was wearing a cheerleader's outfit which looked like it was about four sizes too small. Flesh was pouring out of her top, like muffins spilling over the edge of an oven tray. Her sleek brown hair was in a high ponytail, and two large pom-poms shimmered in her hands.

'You must be Amanda!' she said.

'Yes, I am,' I replied, the undertone being, 'and who the hell are you?'

She laughed. 'I recognised your handsome husband! I'm Zoe.'

Ted looked as if someone had opened the 2022 Pirelli calendar and shoved it right under his nose. The same Ted who found soccer sexier than the female form – or so I thought. 'Oh hi, um, Zoe,' he said. 'It's good to see you again!'

'Again?' I smiled thinly.

'Yes. Zoe and I ran into one another earlier today in the supermarket.'

'Literally,' she laughed.

'I almost ran her over,' Ted said jovially, like a groom explaining in his wedding speech how he'd met his bride. 'With my trolley!'

'Oh,' I said, pouting. 'You didn't mention . . .'

'I must have forgotten.'

There was an awkward silence.

'Well, it's lovely to meet you,' Zoe said to me. 'You look just . . . stunning. I'm guessing you're Britney Spears, right?'

'That's right.' I felt myself relaxing, but was still on guard. 'This is my son Sam's school cardigan, which feels a little wrong.'

'What a great idea,' she said.

'You look great too,' I told her, because I thought I should. But really, she looked like a bit of a slapper.

'Thanks,' she laughed. 'My husband Miles is in his element, he always wanted to date a cheerleader.' She laughed and tossed her ponytail off her shoulder like she was in a shampoo commercial.

'I bet,' said Ted. I shot him a look and he mouthed 'What?' at me and shrugged.

'What perfume are you wearing?' I asked, trying not to turn my nose up at the overpowering floral whiff. 'It's really familiar.'

'Oh this?' she batted a hand. 'It's Chanel Number Five. The scent Marilyn Monroe said was the only thing she wore to bed . . .' She glanced at Ted.

By this point I was starting to feel uncomfortable. This woman was far too sexually charged for my liking. I wondered if she was on heat or something.

Ted let out a splutter. 'Sorry,' he said, tapping his chest peculiarly. 'Indigestion.'

Just then a tall, red-headed man with a face full of freckles appeared next to Zoe.

'Oh, hello Miles,' Zoe said. Her voice was cold. 'Meet Amanda and Ted, they're on our table. Amanda and Ted, this is my husband, Miles.'

He held out his hand to me and then to Ted, and said, 'Nice to meet you both.' Although the look on his face suggested he'd rather be anywhere but in a hall full of adults in fancy dress. He evidently wasn't into dressing up, because his 'uniform' was black board shorts, a white wife-beater and a tie with flamingos on. Totally lame.

'As you can see, Miles put a lot of thought into his costume,' Zoe said, reading my thoughts. 'He's meant to be a schoolboy.'

'Well, thankfully one of us realised it's a complete waste of money to spend sixty bucks on some cheap polyester,' he said directly to me.

'Um, right,' I said, feeling decidedly awkward. 'So, whereabouts do you guys live in Darley?'

'We're in the Sunshine Apartments block on Avalon Parade,' said Zoe.

I knew the apartments because Fair & Brewer had refused to put one on the market – the value was way under the kind of cash they liked to pull in for a sale. A million dollars was the company's starting point, and the Sunshine Apartments never fetched more than six hundred thousand.

'I know them. What a nice spot,' I said, hoping I didn't sound too fake.

I was about to ask what they both did for work, and then I remembered Alice telling me that Miles was head chef at Pasadena, the seafront fish restaurant with the white tablecloths and the crazy-long waitlist. We'd been a few times.

'How about you guys?'

'Oh, we have a little place on Mentira Drive,' I said, trying to emphasise the 'little', so we didn't come across as the landed gentry. There was some truth in it – our grey-fronted four-bedroom weatherboard with its Moroccan tiled porch wasn't the biggest in the street, far from it. But it was deceptively spacious. We had gutted it when we moved in, turning the separate kitchen and dining areas into one extended living area that opened up into the north-facing garden. Plus we'd splashed out on landscaping and a new pool. It was the perfect place to sit with a glass of rosé in the sun.

'We're by the huge palm on the brow of the hill – the only palm on the street,' I told Zoe.

She nodded. 'I know it, I run past it. It's a beautiful house. All of the houses on Mentira Drive are stunning.' She looked at Miles wistfully and said, 'One day.'

Now if I'd thought Luke and Lara were a random combo, then these two were even more mismatched – she the curvy, dark-haired beauty, and he the gangly hipster type who looked like he might blister if someone so much as said the word 'sun'. *Well, there's a lid for every pot*, I thought.

'Freckles,' Ted announced, trying to break the silence.

'I'm sorry, *mate*?' Miles said, evidently wondering if Ted was taking the piss out of his own lightly speckled skin.

'Why are all the schoolgirls wearing freckles? Why is it even a stereotype? I don't know a single schoolgirl with freckles . . . It's like going to a French-themed party wearing onions and a baguette. If I was a schoolgirl, I'd be seriously offended.'

Miles smiled thinly and took a swig of his beer. 'Original, eh?'

'You work at Pasadena don't you, Miles mate?' asked Ted, in an attempt to draw some conversation out of Miles. 'Great place. The food is out of this world.'

'Cheers,' said Miles. 'Yeah, it's not a bad spot.'

We were all silent for a while when Ted, who isn't a fan of dance floors or small-talk, suggested we head over to the table.

A moment later, Alice arrived, eyeballing me intensely, and I remembered there was something important she had to tell me. She grabbed my arm, and was about to lead me off somewhere, when Ted nodded to the middle of the room, where Mr Mattock, dressed as Dewey Finn, was break-dancing. It was only seven thirty.

'Check out the Phys-Ed teacher,' he said.

'School of *Cock*,' said Miles.

Zoe let out a sigh, one of those big ones you do in yoga that sounds like an airbed being deflated. 'So crass,' she snapped.

'Ohh I love a good wordplay,' giggled Alice.

'Look, there's Pete.' Ted nodded to the centre of the hall.

Alice's husband, dressed as a professor in a long black gown and a square cap with a tassel, waved as he approached the table. Predictably enough, he'd opted for the most boring outfit possible. Party-pooper Pete, always playing Captain Sensible.

I picked up the nearest bottle of Prosecco and peeled off the golden foil on the bottle top. But before I could wriggle out the cork, Alice took the bottle out of my hands and placed it back on the table. 'Before you do that, I need to talk to you,' she said, dragging me to the photo booth, and swapping her party face for her serious one again.

'If you wanted to get some photos, you don't need to be so grumpy about it,' I said, trying to lighten the mood.

She didn't smile. She just came out with it. Ripped the plaster right off.

'Victoria's here,' she said.

'Victoria who? Beckham?'

She sighed. '*Victoria*, Victoria, Amanda.' Now that *was* confusing. I repeated it in my head and still didn't get it.

'Victoria Day.'

'What?'

'Victoria Day is here at Darley Heights, because Nico lost his job and they can't afford the private fees for St Cecilia's anymore, and you're going to have to be really quite mature about this and turn the other cheek because you can't change it. There, I've said it.' She let out a sigh. 'I've said it. Victoria Day is at Darley Heights Public!'

I was still confused. 'What do you mean Victoria Day is at Darley? What you mean, *now*?'

I felt a jolt in my stomach.

'She's over there with her husband, Nico. Her kids go here now, well two of her girls, anyway. She turned up to decorate the hall this afternoon, Mand. I didn't realise who she was until she told me this whole sob story about having to leave St Cecilia's because of the fees, and going on about how her kids were having a shitty time of it because their dog had died.'

She drained her glass and looked at me expectantly.

The dog in question had been a Dachshund, long-bodied and smooth-coated, with a cold wet nose that left a trail of snot on your ankles. His name was Mr Perkins. Victoria used to bring him up to St Cecilia's in the afternoon when she picked up her three girls, more often than not tethering him to the lamp post outside the school gates and letting him yap annoyingly at the kids as they poured out after the bell had sounded. Yip-yip-yip-yip, he'd go, throwing his head up and down like one of those annoying battery-run dogs that barks repeatedly before turning a somersault. Evie called him the 'cute yappy poo', as in, 'Mum, can I go and stroke the cute yappy poo?' To which I'd reply something along the lines of, 'Eww, you want to touch a poo? Well you'd better wash your hands after.' It was our schtick.

On that November day, the day when life as I knew it went decidedly tits-up, Mr Perkins had been at the front door to greet me as I joined Victoria and about fifteen other mums in cocktail dresses and fascinators to watch the Melbourne Cup. Scoring an invite to see the race at Victoria's house was a *big deal*, like getting a golden ticket in a Wonka chocolate bar. It wasn't just a measure of friendliness, but a social score, a top rating on the popularity barometer – because Victoria Day was St Cecilia's Queen Bee. Everyone had heard of her, not just because she owned the biggest house in Darley – a renovated Queenslander with an unusually large front yard which everyone cooed over on dog walks and drive-bys – but because she was heavily involved in the parent-teacher committee and her girls were constantly being awarded public-speaking trophies, or art prizes or athletics ribbons. She was tall, unnaturally so, with a large, prominent nose, a blonde bob and a stare that could turn people to stone, and, if this was not intimidating enough, she was always flanked by a group of year 4 mums who followed her around like rock groupies. You could tell it was Victoria, and not any of the other women, who was the leader of the gang, because she always seemed to walk out front, ahead of the others, like the point of a triangle, and if she did something, such as tighten her ponytail, the others would follow like human dominoes.

Most of the mums invited to Victoria's Melbourne Cup luncheon had children in the school's upper years like Victoria (she admitted herself she hadn't made much of an effort with the mums in her youngest daughter Darcy's kindergarten year), and I was the only kindergarten mum to make the invite list. It only happened because Darcy and Evie had dance class together every Thursday after school, and by term four, Victoria and I had racked up at least six hours of small talk inside Darley Scout hut. It didn't come about naturally, because Victoria didn't have even the remotest whiff of a welcoming air about her – she never made eye contact and sat almost awkwardly upright with her back slightly turned from me. It wasn't a congenial gait. I honestly think she only spoke to me the first time because Evie dragged Darcy over at fruit break and said to me, 'This is my new best friend, Darcy. We're friends, so *you* two have to be friends!' Darcy had insisted we shake hands.

So Victoria could hardly ignore me from that point on, especially since I made a point of chatting to her, even though she was a cold fish. It sort of became a project for me, to warm her up. So I would chat and Victoria would nod her agreement, interjecting with the odd point in her deep, commanding voice. As the weeks progressed, her terrifying façade slipped ever so slightly, so much that sometimes she would even initiate the conversation – usually chatting about other mothers at school. She had everyone pegged into groups, like the 'losers' or the 'boozers' or the 'geeks'. Christ only knows what category she'd filed me into, and I didn't fancy finding out.

Even though we chatted for almost an hour a week, and had even swapped numbers in order to arrange a playdate (which hadn't happened yet), Victoria still didn't give me much attention at school, just a perfunctory nod when we passed one another. However, once or twice I noticed her observing me as I chatted to the other mums outside class.

The shift came in late October, when she turned up to dance class with her sunglasses on and the collar of her pink polo shirt up high. It didn't take me long to work out she had been crying.

'Are you okay?' I asked.

She nodded.

'Can I get you something?'

'No.'

Her chin wobbled, her face flamed.

'Victoria, are you . . . ?'

She held her hand up, shook her head, told me not to proceed.

'Okay, well if there's anything . . .'

'Actually there is,' she said and stood up. 'I need to . . . leave now. Please can you drop Darcy home after class?'

'Of course, Victoria.'

She nodded her thanks.

'No worries.'

'And Amanda?'

'Yes?'

'Do not tell anyone about this.'

'Of course not.'

When I dropped Darcy home in the car, Victoria didn't come out to greet me, just held her hand up at the door and nodded. And while my fingers hovered above my phone later in the night, agonising over whether or not I should follow up with a text, all my instincts told me I should leave well enough alone. So I did.

The following week, back at ballet, when I asked her if everything had been okay, she said, 'Last week? That? Oh darling, that was just PMT.' And she laughed.

I doubted it had been just PMT, but I took her word for it nonetheless, and that was when she asked me. Invited me into the fold.

'Thank you for your concern last week, Amanda,' she said with a straight face, as if she really didn't like me. 'Presumably you have no plans for Tuesday? For Melbourne Cup?'

She clearly didn't think I was the kind of person who would have plans for Melbourne Cup, which was vaguely affronting, but the fact was, I didn't. Alice was organising some corporate do and she was usually my Cup 'person', so I had nothing in the diary at that point (needless to say I would have sorted something, because I haven't done Cup day without a drink since I was twenty).

'Not at the moment, actually . . .' I told her.

'Well then, you *must* come to my luncheon party on Tuesday. Dress to impress. Kick off – or should I say the starter gun – is at one-ish, so get your kids a playdate for after school so you don't need to do pick-up.' She didn't wait for an answer, just grabbed Darcy's hand and turned to leave the Scout hut. 'Come along, Darcy.'

So, you can see how much pressure I was under on the actual day to make a good impression – if I didn't, I'd be filed in one of the baskets Victoria talked about: the try-hards, the geeks, the social lepers. And, like the next socially anxious school mother, I was prone to taking the edge off nerve-wracking situations by downing a medicinal glass or two before they got underway (and I'd like to point out I am not alone in that. I know plenty of people who'll have a dram of whisky or a beta blocker before a stressful work event. *Plenty.*) It just made things a little easier for me, allowed me to think of things to say and to have the confidence to say them. Lubricated my vocal cords, I suppose.

I arrived at Victoria's home at one thirty, half an hour later than had been stipulated, as I'd been taking photos of a sale home in Dale Street first thing and it had pushed the whole morning out. Victoria's house was even more impressive up close, with a spotless veranda that hugged the main building like a planetary ring. Tall, neatly trimmed hedges lined the driveway, bordering neatly mowed grass, and a high gate cut off the front of the house from the backyard. It was about three times the size of my own home (and I'd thought we had quite a sizeable place), and I felt my stomach twist as I tried to swallow down the nagging sense of imposter syndrome.

Victoria opened the door, and the smell of musk, sandalwood and jasmine hit me.

'You smell amazing,' was the first thing I said.

'Dior Poison.' She smiled. She was all red lipstick and feathers hanging from her mauve headpiece. She wore large black sunglasses like Jackie Onassis and it took me a few seconds to notice the yellowing at the side of her eye. She clocked my interest and pushed her sunnies further up her nose.

'Are . . . are you okay? I mean, your eye?'

'Oh this?' she put her fingers on the bruised flesh. 'It's nothing. I just walked into a door. I actually did. It's not some cover-up for domestic violence or anything.' She laughed a little too hard. 'I'm terribly clumsy! Poor Nico! He's worried everyone thinks he's a *wife-beater* or something terrible.'

I smiled, reassured. I didn't have much time to extend my line of questioning, because I was almost bowled over by Mr Perkins, sniffing at my feet like I had a juicy pork chop strapped to each one, and I remember thinking, *Thank God he isn't crotch height, otherwise this would be really embarrassing* (because no one wants people thinking they've got an odour problem).

'Stop that sniffing, Perky Poo,' Victoria told him, but she didn't drag him away or anything, just said it to him, like he was a 5-year-old child who might nod his head in a conciliatory way and retreat back into the house. Instead she stepped over him and leaned forward to kiss me on both cheeks, affording me another waft of Dior Poison, with its 'notes of clove, amber and musk', a smell that was as strong and determined as she was. She stepped back and looked me up and down in my calf-length black dress, and I couldn't really tell what she was thinking – whether she liked my outfit or was about to tell me the crematorium was a kilometre up the road.

'Wow, black for Melbourne Cup,' was what she said. 'The lady is a vamp! Come on in.'

'Well, now you've invited me in, I'm allowed to eat you,' I quipped.

'Sorry, what?' she said, momentarily distracted by the four-legged turd weaving in and out of her ankles.

'Oh, I was just making a silly joke about vampires, because they have to be invited over the threshold of a house, to um, bite people, and you said I was a vamp . . .'

'Oh, too funny,' she said, evidently not remotely amused. I didn't blame her – it wasn't one of my finest. She bent down and scooped up the dog. 'Don't mind Mr Perkins. He's my fourth baby, aren't you, Perky Poo?' She let him lick her mouth with his jabby pink tongue. 'Don't worry, he doesn't bite.'

'Oh, I'm not worried,' I smiled. 'I've eaten steaks bigger than him.'

She looked at me oddly. 'Well,' she said, her arms open in the manner of a game show hostess. 'Come on in!'

And just like that, my fate was sealed.

The house was beautiful inside – all white walls, and colonial touches: rattan fans and baskets, along with large indoor palms with shiny green leaves. There were no kids' toys, no garish plastic landfill scattered across the floor, or drawings of stick men on the kitchen fridge. That made me even more nervous – there is something about kids' clutter that makes a person feel more at ease. On the side table, there were two black and white family photos and a sepia one of Nico and Victoria on their wedding day, presumably during their first dance. You couldn't see his face, just the back of his head and Victoria was laughing over his shoulder. It almost looked like the kind of stock photo you get inside the frame before you've put your own one in. Modelesque, ecstatic, so in love. Even without his face on view, it was clear from the placement of the photo and Victoria's uncharacteristic smile within the frame, that theirs was a happy marriage. Beside it was a snap of Victoria's three girls together on the beach, another of Darcy and Iris in their St Cecilia's uniforms, and a single portrait of Clara in a Milton Abbey Ladies' College uniform with a bow in her hair and gold studs in her ears. She was the spitting image of her mum.

'What a beautiful home,' I marvelled. I'd never asked what Nico did for a living, and Victoria sure as hell didn't work.

'Nico's in finance,' she said, as if reading my mind. 'He's a trader. Stocks and bonds.'

'Oh, right.'

'It's okay, everyone asks the same thing when they see the house. I'm aware that it's rather grand.' She laughed to suggest she was embarrassed by the excess. 'The actual build was modelled on the home my parents built on Lyre Street, just down the road. Only way bigger. I just love the colonial look.'

'I know that street,' I said. 'I've worked at a few sale houses there.'

'Oh!' Victoria smiled.

She led me through the hall towards the group of twittering women in their designer dresses in bold, primary colours. 'Everyone, this is Amanda,' she announced, wafting a hand in my direction. 'She's a mum from Darcy's kindergarten class, so let's make her feel welcome.'

Ten pairs of eyes turned to me. 'Hi, Amanda,' they cooed together. It reminded me of the time I'd gone into Evie's class for literacy sessions and the kids had been instructed to say hello, and they kind of chorused, 'Good-mooooorrrning-Mrrrrsss-Blackland' with no sincerity whatsoever. I smiled and felt my tummy tighten at the intensity of the eyes looking me up and down, assessing my figure, my outfit, my composure. They were all so stylish and so coiffed. Evidently most of them had been for a blow-dry that morning and dry-cleaned their cocktail dresses – I'd thrown my hair up in a messy bun and wiped a suspect white mark off my dress with a kitchen scourer. My bag didn't really match, but I hadn't had time to think about it, what with work. I felt like a fraud, a reality TV star at the Oscars.

I scoured around for some booze and picked up a glass of champagne from the table next to me, without being asked. I drank it down in one, shaking off Mr Perkins, who had clamped his front paws around the strap of my knackered old Jimmy Choos and was humping me like there was no tomorrow.

'Oh Perky, get down,' Victoria sighed. 'Randy little bugger! He obviously likes you! Can I get you a cocktail? A Margarita? Singapore Sling?'

'A Singapore Sling would be amazing, thanks!' I hadn't had one of those for ages, and to be honest, if she'd asked me if I wanted a glass of anti freeze I would have said yes.

'Done.' Victoria whirled around to the breakfast bar, where a woman in black was rolling out pizza dough. 'A rustic margherita,' Victoria barked, scooping up Mr Perkins and chucking him like a football across the room.

'Um, actually, I'll try a Singapore Sling if that's okay?' I repeated.

'Oh, you are so cute.' Victoria put her hand on mine. 'No, no, the *hired help* is making margherita pizzas as well as cocktails. Too funny!'

I wasn't sure how appropriate it was for Victoria to call the woman the hired help to her face, even though admittedly she was helping and had been hired to do so. Or how comfortable I felt with her neglecting to say 'please' or 'thank you' to the tired-looking woman in the black trousers and black cotton blouse, but I wasn't about to mention it. So I smiled apologetically and mouthed a pathetic 'thanks' instead.

I was totally confused by this world I'd stepped into, of unfamiliar women in giant feathery fascinators and catering staff. And the thing was, they were all like Victoria – all of them weighed down by stacks of bling and genuine Chanel handbags. I felt ashamed of my ancient and battered Kate Spade offering (bought in New York circa 1998) and my significantly smaller diamond ring. Ted hadn't been a qualified architect when we got engaged, so my ring wasn't the showiest. But I loved it nonetheless, until that day, when I wished it had been a *teeny* bit bigger. By approximately twenty times.

A woman in a mint-green dress called Nicole sidled up to me. 'So, what does your husband do?' she asked snootily.

'He's an architect,' I said. 'He's designed the Milton Tower in the CBD.'

She looked impressed, so I continued. 'And I'm a photographer. I take photos for Fair & Brewer, the real estate agent . . .'

'Oh, you *work*? How lovely,' she said and wafted off.

The feeling I was out of my depth didn't go away when one of Victoria's chums called Madeleine – who I recognised as a year 3 parent – came around to collect money for the Cup sweepstake. 'Come on girls, green dollar bills only,' she sang. 'It's one hundred dollars if you want to be part of the sweepstake.'

'Oh,' I said, when she got to me. 'I'm so sorry, I didn't realise. I only have a twenty-dollar note.'

Madeleine sighed. 'Does anyone have a hundred dollars they could lend Amanda, please? She doesn't have any money!'

Oh God, I thought, *this is horrendous.*

'I do have money at home, I mean I . . .' I started. 'I just didn't . . .'

'Here you go, darling,' said mint-green Nicole, opening her purse to reveal a stash of green hundred-dollar bills that matched her midi-dress. 'Have a bet on me!' She pressed the note into my hand and gave me a reassuring nod, like my Uncle Mike used to do with a fiver when he'd come over to see my mum. The only difference was that Nicole wasn't encouraging me to go and buy an ice cream.

'I couldn't possibly . . .'

'Oh please,' Nicole sighed. 'I won't hear anything of it. No, no, no!'

'I'll make sure I pay you back,' I said, gratefully.

'Oh,' she said, and looked at me pityingly. 'That is the sweetest thing. No, darling, it's a gift. That's one thing I don't have to worry about . . . money.'

It was a horrible feeling – especially since I'd always considered us to be pretty comfortably off. But these women were in a completely different league, and however many of them I chatted to about school, or living in Darley, or what I was watching on Netflix, I could not get myself over the achingly big financial divide.

So I drank, and drank some more, and filled my stomach with acrid liquor instead of the pizza that had been prepared with the express intent to soak up everyone's booze, only taking the edge off with the occasional salmon blini that made its way round the room thanks to the *hired help* (who at some point in the evening told me her name was Helen). Even when my surroundings began to spin round me like the blurry lights of a fairground ride, I had another, for Dutch courage, kicking off my shoes and dancing barefoot and alone, on Victoria's garden deck. I was aware of a few people looking at me, and Victoria's face wearing the steely glare she'd had the first few times we'd gone to after-school dance class, so I decided to take a breather and accept the salmon blinis being offered to me, one after the other, by Helen. I vaguely recall her saying, 'Line your stomach, love. I'll get you some water.'

It wasn't as if I was *really* drunk, just a little tipsy, so when I started to feel sick, I assumed it was the salmon

(I mean, it's proven to be a major cause of food poisoning. There's a reason pregnant women can't eat it.) Then, when the lurch in my stomach turned into a dry retch, I thought *Uh-oh, I need to get to a bathroom, now!*, but I couldn't remember where it was. I saw a woman's hand – maybe Helen's? – pointing upwards, and so I threw myself towards the staircase, lolloping up it like a bear. But unfortunately, I totally misjudged the placement of the top step, and landed with a heavy jolt on my stomach, my five pink Singapore Slings spewing violently from the V-shaped space between my fingers. Even in the state I was in, the wide reach of the vomit astounded me. It didn't just land in a ragged oval puddle on the woven Moroccan rug, but seemed to spread, like blood spatter, onto the cream carpet beyond, as well as all up the walls, the cornices, the corners of the staircase and the balustrades.

I looked behind me at the group of aghast faces in a cluster on the bottom step. Heard a stifled giggle and then saw Victoria emerge from the middle of the group like Roald Dahl's Grand Witch, her face white and her eyes like fire. She stomped up the stairs, stopping halfway because of the smell, and stared at me with the sleeve of her new Zimmermann maxi dress covering her nose and mouth. I heard someone whisper, 'Oh my God, she is *wasted*,' from the bottom step and I wasn't under any illusion they were talking about our host.

'Victoria, I . . .' I heard myself slur. 'Do you have a cloth I could . . . ?'

She didn't speak, just shot daggers at me from narrowed eyes with pin-prick pupils.

'I'll just get a cloth from the kitchen . . .' I stood up on shaky legs, which wasn't really working for me, so I sort of bear-crawled backwards down the stairs. Someone, a woman called Leonie, had run in to the kitchen, and was now offering me a wet dishcloth.

'Don't anyone give her a cloth!' wailed Victoria.

Leonie jumped and scarpered back into the kitchen.

As I backed past Victoria, I allowed her the first uninterrupted view of the vomit stain.

'My rug!' she screamed. She threw a bony finger towards the door. 'Get out!'

'I'm so sorry,' I said, retreating down the hallway. 'I think maybe the salmon was off . . . ?'

'Off?' she snapped. 'Off? That was fucking champagne-infused gravadlax and it cost forty dollars a packet. It wasn't the fucking salmon!'

'I'm so sorry,' was all I could manage as I bent down low and backed out of the front door.

Now, if the story had ended there, it might have been okay. I might have been able to claw myself out of the quicksand of social annihilation, to heave my body up onto the banks of redemption. But it didn't.

Instead, I stumbled home and hatched a plan to absolve myself. An apology, I reasoned later that evening, as Ted peeled me off the sofa and tucked me into bed, might be well received, and, unlike most decisions made under the influence, I still believed it was the best course of action when I woke up the next day.

So I pulled myself together and I returned to Victoria's after lunch. I took the car because I planned to pop to the supermarket afterwards for some more rehydration tablets, and as I drove up her neat cement driveway with its border of frangipani trees (fruit salad, of course – no one in Darley would ever plant the garish *pink* ones), I felt like I might puke from nerves. I felt awful about my behaviour. Yes, I'd been intimidated the previous afternoon, but it hadn't been an excuse to behave like a teenage girl who'd just downed a bottle of her dad's vodka. I was ready to tell Victoria this, too.

The moment she opened the door, I could tell she wasn't in a forgiving mood. Mr Perkins, on the other hand, appeared delighted by my visit, and sniffed at my feet enthusiastically.

'Well, well, well,' Victoria said, her hands on her hips. 'You've got a nerve, haven't you?'

I had imagined she might have calmed down a little overnight, but it seemed not.

'Victoria,' I said. My mouth was drier than a pig pen. 'I am so sorry. It was terrible, inexcusable. I'm so very sorry about what happened to your . . . carpet.'

'You mean the rug that was hand-woven by native Berbers in the Atlas Mountains?'

'Um, yes,' I mumbled.

'The irreplaceable rug that now has vomit woven into its fibres?'

She glared at me, but I carried on regardless. 'I just don't know what happened,' I told her. 'I don't understand . . .'

She looked at me, her eyes black, and I knew then I was in for it. And rightly so.

She pointed a yellow, rubber-clad finger right in my face. It smelled of disinfectant, which may or may not have been recently applied to her rug. If she'd been wrist-deep in puke when I turned up, it certainly hadn't done anything to ingratiate me towards her.

'What happened?' she yelled. 'I'll tell you what happened. You got shit-faced and ruined my antique rug. There's still a fucking salmon-pink stain in the middle of it that no amount of shampooing can get rid of.'

'Oh Victoria.' I shook my head, mortified. I realised how embarrassing my behaviour was for her and how costly the whole episode had been. Not to mention the fact I had ruined her party. 'Please can I offer to pay . . .'

'And the smell? Don't *even*! I can't get the fucking dog away from it.' Her face was red. 'Perky!' she yelled and clicked her finger. 'Come here, now!'

The dog ignored her and lifted his leg against the side of my tyre.

'My husband is fucking livid. Livid! Do you understand what that *means*?' She was yelling, but her voice cracked a little when she said this, which actually made me feel terrible.

I shook my head again.

'Victoria, I can't apologise enough . . .'

'Apologise? Is an *apology* going to fix anything?' She was wagging her finger now. 'Is an *apology* going to undo what happened? No, I don't think so.'

She was completely riled, and I understood why. I did. I unzipped my purse with shaky fingers, took out four crinkled fifty-dollar notes, and lamely handed them to her.

She laughed meanly. 'Two hundred dollars? *Really*? You think *two hundred dollars* is going to cover the cost of cleaning an *antique* Moroccan rug?'

'Okay, well please just let me know the amount and I'd be happy to . . .'

'You'd be *happy* to? Well isn't that generous?' She laughed like a lunatic. 'Get the fuck off my driveway. *Perky, come here!* Just leave.'

I figured I couldn't do anything more. Couldn't offer anything more than remorse and reimbursement, and so I turned back to my car, resigned to a life of social ostracisation at St Cecilia's now that the Queen Bee had told me in no uncertain terms how unwelcome I was. As I fastened my belt and pulled the gear into reverse, Victoria was still pointing wildly at the end of the driveway and shouting something, but I couldn't work out what. Later I realised it was the word 'stop'.

I put my foot on the gas and released the brake. As soon as I felt the bump I knew I'd hit something. I yanked up the handbrake and opened the door to see Victoria sprinting past me to the back of the car.

She let out a high-pitched scream and fell to her knees, and that's when I saw the blood and felt my own go cold. Mr Perkins was lying, motionless, beside my back wheel, flatter than a kangaroo on the highway.

Back in the hall with Alice, I was suddenly aware of my empty hands. I needed a drink. Anything would do. I picked up a half-drunk glass of punch from a chair beside the photo booth, complete with a fuchsia lipstick print on the rim, and downed it. I didn't know who it belonged to. Alice watched me, but she didn't say anything.

'Where is she, then? I can't see her,' I asked.

'She's over there with the Mean Girls.'

'That figures.'

I turned to look at the group of women in pink at the far end of the hall. I was surprised I hadn't picked her out when I'd seen them from behind earlier, with her sleek, blonde bob and six-foot frame. It was her, alright. Unmistakably Victoria. The reaction was visceral. I felt winded, like I was suffocating under a heady, intoxicating blanket of Poison. Suddenly she was everywhere – my senses were full of her. I flopped down on the chair, defeated.

Victoria was talking animatedly with the other four women. She looked like she'd been at this school for years – so effortless, so easy. Unlike my awkward chatter with Zoe, Victoria looked like she *belonged*. Beside her was a tall man in a long wig – the man from the bar.

'Is . . . that Nico?' I asked Alice.

'The guy dressed as Severus Snape? Yes.'

'He's THE Nico? As in, the man who's married to Victoria?'

'Yep. Why?'

'That's not even possible.'

I pulled my bunches tighter and shook my head.

'What do you mean?'

'Alice, that man is *so* nice. He's funny and gentlemanly. I spoke to him at the bar ten minutes ago. He was charm personified. A really, really friendly guy.'

I scoured the table for another drink. There wasn't one.

'Well they do say opposites attract,' Alice said.

'What if she finds out I was talking to him? What if she gets even angrier . . . ?'

Alice touched my arm. 'Let it go, Mand. Victoria can't hurt you. She's new here too, remember? She doesn't know anyone either.'

'Well it looks like she's already found her coven,' I said.

'I guarantee she will be as nervous about making a good impression as you are tonight. In fact, it might even be the perfect opportunity for you two to, you know . . . make *amends*.' She shrugged and offered a slightly pathetic smile, which suggested she knew what she'd said was wildly improbable. 'You're both new and could do with making friends.'

'Alice, I reversed over her dog,' I said wearily. 'I don't think I'm going to be the first person invited to her new book club, do you? She's definitely not the forgiving type.'

And then the paranoia hit me. Maybe Victoria had come to Darley Heights for revenge. Maybe she wasn't satisfied with driving me out of St Cecilia's, and wanted to make my life at Darley hell, too. My mouth felt absurdly dry. Did she want to destroy me so much that she would do something like that? Change her children's school so she could get revenge for offing her dog?

I must have been wearing a mask of terror, because Alice read it perfectly, as she often did by virtue of the length of our friendship. 'If you're thinking that Victoria is here to get back at you – which I know is the way your mind will work it – then that's not the case,' Alice said. 'It's as simple as Nico losing his job. Brigitte Denner told me about it – in the strictest of confidence, of course, so you can't tell a soul. Victoria and Nico were forced to choose which of their three girls to remove from private school, and so they took out Darcy and Iris, since they're still at primary school, and kept Clara at Milton Abbey.'

Then she added gently, 'Mand, remember not everything is always about you.'

'I know,' I said sulkily. 'I didn't say it was.'

'Listen, I have your back, and I'm a big deal in this school.' Alice took my hand. 'I promise, no one will mess with you!'

I smiled at her, but I wasn't really listening, because all I could think was that my internal organs were crying out for liquid to anaesthetise them, to quieten the jitters. A glass of something sweet to put a bond on my rising anxiety and soothe my throat, which ached from swallowing back a ball of emotion.

'Can we go back to the table now?' I stood up calmly, while my stomach lurched and pulled like a lump of pizza dough being roughly kneaded on a marble surface. My hands were shaking. 'I really could do with a drink.'

Chapter Five
Alice

Transcript: The voice of Alice Daniels in the office of Dr Martha Davis.

She seemed calm at first. But then I watched her walk back to Ted's side of the table and throw back a glass of champagne like it was some kind of antivenin. She whispered in his ear, relaying the news I guessed, because he looked around him and said, 'What?' and then shook his head and looked at her as if she was mad. I mean, it was a massively bitter pill for Amanda to swallow, to learn that some old bitch who'd made her life hell and to all intents and purposes driven her child out of their school, and away from her friends, was now competing for the Darley Heights award for most popular newcomer.

She looked up at Ted with dog eyes and said, 'I'm serious!' and pouted at him with a girlish petulance. He said something to her which, knowing Ted, was probably something level-headed like, 'Well, you need to go and smooth it over', and she waved her hands at him dismissively, as if to say, 'I can't deal with this right now', which is classic Amanda when she wants to disown something. Denial is her speciality. Drama and denial – usually the former followed immediately by the latter. Shut the door on a topic, swallow it down and put a padlock on it, file it in the 'too hard' basket. If it had been me (not that I would have got myself into a situation like that with another school parent, and I can say that to you since you're my therapist, right?) I would probably have cried and left. But she didn't do that. Cry, I mean. She never cried. The last time I saw her shed a tear was at primary school when her mum came to pick her up, paralytic, and everyone in the playground turned to look. Then Ben Collins, who was the most popular boy in the school and who Amanda had loved for forever, shouted out, 'Oi, Blackland, does that haggard old piss can belong to you?' and everyone fell about laughing. Well, as you can imagine, Amanda was devastated, and that was the last time I saw her cry.

So anyway, after I told her about Victoria, she did the whole classic shut-it-out thing and started knocking back the booze even harder, dancing and basically acting pretty wild, and that's when I had a weird flash of something, call it intuition, that the night would end badly for her. I actually went up to her at that point and said, 'Come on, Mand, slow down,' but I felt quite mean saying it. She seemed happy after all, despite what I'd told her, so when she told me to give her a break, I just nodded, and said, 'Okay then,' and I left it.

Ted agreed. 'Just leave her tonight,' he said, massaging my shoulders as he walked past me on his way to the loo. 'She'll be okay. I'll look after her.'

I'm not passing the buck, I'm honestly not – and this is just a straightforward observation and not finger-pointing – but if Amanda hadn't been as drunk as she was, I don't think any of it would have happened, even if we did all play our own part. But having said that, Amanda wouldn't have been able to instigate anything without the presence of the Hampsons. If Amanda was the flame, then Lara and Luke were the logs in the grate.

You want to hear about Lara and Luke? Well, the two of them arrived late, which had already injected a bit of anticipation, as in, 'Where are the Hampsons?' and, 'Why are they so late?' and, 'Are they even coming?', mainly from Amanda, who evidently fancied Luke because she kept banging on about him, even if it was to slag him off. 'He's so up himself,' she kept saying, which, as I recall, was how she talked about Ted when she first met him. She likes them swaggering, that's for sure.

Anyway, arrive they did, and talk about an entrance. It was like it was choreographed, seriously. Like someone in the sound department was told 'Go!' at the exact moment the doors opened. Miles was standing on my left, wiggling the fat cork out of a champagne bottle, really giving it some welly, but it wouldn't move, and we were all kind of side-watching it with squinty eyes, waiting for the pop, the way you look at a kid chasing a balloon with a pin. Well of course it burst out with the biggest thump, didn't it? It flew off in the direction of the double doors, and, at the exact moment it landed on the floor, they swung open. But it happened to coincide with the opening bars of 'Je T'aime' – you know, that sexy seventies song by Jane Birkin and Serge Gainsbourg where she's basically climaxing – pounding out of the speakers, and that's when Lara stepped in with Luke behind her. And I can't describe it, I honestly can't. It was like the whole room froze. The dads salivated and the mums stared, half out of admiration and the other half out of complete jealousy. She was stunning. She was dressed in a Darley Heights green and white summer tunic that she'd sort of restyled into a strapless mini dress, along with a pair of thigh-high latex boots, which must have been boiling. She just oozed sex appeal. The soft, pretty features she wore at the school gate had been replaced by a vampy look and a steely gaze. Her hair was scraped back in a high ponytail and her lips painted bright red. I recall turning to look at Pete at that point and watching him stare at her as her hips sashayed in time to the music, his eyes glazed like a Christmas ham, and I wanted to tell him to close his mouth, but I didn't, because really, I couldn't blame him. Everyone in the room seemed to be looking at her that way: Ted, Miles, Zoe, Amanda, *me* – all the parents in the entire place – and, when she stepped onto the dance floor with a very smug-looking Luke behind her, the crowd parted to let them through.

When they finally arrived at the table, the chatter resumed. It was literally like a hypnotist had clicked his fingers and announced, 'You're back in the room.' Silence one minute, business the next. She sat down opposite me, and it was like the homecoming queen had just arrived. Her lips glistened under their waxy lacquer and she flicked her head back with a sort of apologetic confidence. She crossed and uncrossed her legs, her left thigh swinging balletic and poised, landing softly on her right. I watched as Pete fussed around her saying, 'Lara, can I get you a glass?' and, 'Can I unscrew that for you?' and, 'Do you want ice?' when he hadn't even offered *me* a drink. Can you believe that? It was almost comedic. And, here's the thing, it didn't bother me. Not a pang, not even the mildest itch of jealousy as he fell over himself to fawn over her like a wave grabbing at the shore. She looked up at me and smiled as he poured her a drink and I felt bad for watching her and wondered if she'd noticed and categorised me as the angry wife. I didn't want her to think of me that way, so I smiled back. You know, all loosey goosey.

'I love your Hermione outfit,' she smiled. 'It looks great!'

'Thanks. You look incredible,' I told her. 'That was quite an entrance.'

'Thanks!' Her smile was warm and generous. She loaned it to me for at least three seconds, before Pete thrust a glass into her hand and clinked it with his, offering a slightly desperate 'cheers' and she passed on the smile, the enthusiasm, to him. I looked at Pete handing over that glass and I thought to myself, *Well fantastic, and they say romance is dead.* And I proceeded to scour the table for a bottle with which to top up my own glass.

Let me say at this juncture that Pete was never much of a romantic, so I wasn't surprised. Neither of us were particularly demonstrative beyond the odd hug and a handhold. We didn't need to be. We'd always been pretty secure in our relationship. We didn't need to be the couple kissing in the corner of the room and trying to ram it down everyone else's throats how loved up we were. I left that kind of behaviour to Amanda and Ted.

Mine and Pete's was a very functional relationship. We worked like the cogs of a wheel. Chores divided up, shared. I cooked the dinner, he took the twins to school; I did the homework, he did bath time; I did the cleaning and the house admin, he paid the bills. We each had our role and we did it seamlessly. It just worked. *We* just worked.

Did he make me laugh, though? What kind of question is that? Of course! I remember we watched a Steve Carell movie the night before the trivia night and we were in hysterics, all of us. So yes, we laughed! All the time!

But, going back to trivia night, when we were all at the table, I felt a charge on the skin of my arm, and looked to my left to see Miles withdrawing his hand from my forearm. 'Shit,' he said. 'Electric shock.'

I laughed and rubbed my arm, pleased to be distracted from the spectacle of Pete worshipping at the altar of Lara.

'I'm so sorry,' he said. 'I didn't mean to make you jump. It's these bloody chairs, they're full of static.' His face lifted in to smile, a genuinely beautiful smile that seemed to transform him into someone else. I hadn't categorised him as handsome before. 'I just wondered if you needed a top-up. This is a really nice champagne, if you want some?'

'Oh,' I said, snapping out of my Lara-imposed trance and smiling back at him. Sincerely, I hoped. 'Sorry, I was miles away.'

'You mean you were miles away or, "Miles, go away"?'

I laughed at that. He was funny.

'The former,' I said. 'And I'd love one, thank you.'

He was drinking beer, and I realised he'd actually gone out of his way to pick up the champagne bottle and top me up – unlike my own husband on the opposite side of the table – and I was flattered. Not to mention reassured that chivalry was alive *somewhere* in the vicinity. The champagne bubbled its way into my glass and I took a sip, and I think it was then that I registered that I was pretty tipsy. Not out of control tipsy – it's very rare I get like that – but a bit sort of *silly* tipsy. 'Thanks,' I said. 'That's really kind of you.'

He said, 'No worries', and turned to his left to attempt to chat to Zoe, his wife, but she was having a deep and meaningful with Ted and all I heard was 'trying for a baby' and I noticed Miles rolled his eyes when he heard that and he leaned in back to me and we chatted about nothing for a few minutes, until Brigitte Denner, who looked just brilliant dressed as Minerva McGonagall from Harry Potter, tottered up the steps of the stage and tapped the mic and told us trivia was about to start and to get our thinking caps on.

Miles had a pen in his hand, and I happened to have hold of the answer paper, so we sort of looked at each other and said something along the lines of, 'Here we go!' or maybe, 'Are you ready?' or something like that. And I looked up at Pete, who was listening to whatever Lara was saying pretty intensely, like a dog sitting for a treat.

Miles clocked my eyes darting to my flirting husband across the table and I think he felt genuinely sorry for me then, so he patted my hand in a sort of reassuring manner, and said with a raised brow, 'I hear from an impeccable source that you're a trivia whizz.'

I smiled, amused at the accolade. 'Well, I'm not sure about that,' I lied, because I knew I was awesome. 'But I've been known to get competitive, that's for sure.'

He laughed. 'Nothing wrong with a dose of healthy competition. Okay, so now we're telling secrets,' he said, even though we weren't, 'I'll let you in on one of my own.' His eyes sparkled. 'I'm a genius at trivia, too, so the victory of this table is in our hands.'

I laughed back. 'Okay.'

I glanced across at Pete again, doing robotic arm movements in a bid to make Lara smile. She looked up and offered an apologetic shrug as if to ask, 'Is it okay that we're chatting?' and so I nodded back at her with a smile, and I thought to myself, *Maybe she's not flirting with Pete. I mean, he is an accountant after all, hardly Lara's type. Maybe tonight will be okay, after all.*

Chapter Six
Zoe

From: Zoe.m8kin79@realworld.com.au
To: pho_e_b_wallis@zapmail.com
Subject: The truth

Well sis, it won't surprise you to know that when we got to the school, Miles and I were still filthy with each other. Absolutely filthy! I couldn't even look at him in the cab, let alone talk. The poor Uber driver must've felt so awkward with us two ignoring each other the whole way. Miles was still pissed off about the lobbed pasta incident, and I was seething because I still hadn't managed to get my ovulation shag and he was all nonplussed about it. He didn't give a rat's arse. It was like his will to fight for us had gone. *I'm fed up of getting the brunt of it*, he snapped. We both just stared out of the windows and sat as far away as you can physically get from one another in the back seat of a Nissan when THE song came on. You know the song I mean, the Annie Lennox one. The one I was listening to that night when I got the phone call. The song that was on when my gut twisted like a wet rag and the bile came up, bitter and sickly.

I heard my breath catch in my throat right there and Miles's hand reached across the back seat because he knew I couldn't deal with that song. *Zo*, he said. *Baby? Are you okay?* But I pulled my hand away. I don't know why, Phoebs, but I just did, and Miles looked hurt and snapped at the driver, *Can you just turn this music off please, mate? My wife doesn't like it.* And that's when the tears started pooling, and even after the radio was off, I could still hear the chords of the song going over and over in my head.

Miles's mood didn't improve when we got to school, and I introduced him to Amanda and Ted (of course I'd already met Ted in the supermarket). He was so unfriendly, which really annoyed me. He only perked up when Alice Daniels came over, and after that he cosied up to her like a leech because she was being all chatty with him and giving him the time of day and I wasn't. She is pretty, but not, like, *sexy* or anything – more sort of athletic in a practical sort of a way, and we all know Miles loves his curves – so anyway, I wasn't that concerned at first, until I realised she was making him laugh. A lot. Those big, teeth-flashing guffaws that make the freckles on his nose fall over themselves, the likes of which I hadn't seen for ages. And here he was, offering them up to Alice Daniels of all people.

I never really told you too much about this Phoebs (you had other stuff on your mind before you left, obviously), but it started to go wrong a few months after we started trying for another baby. It was great at first, a game to play, always fun. Miles would chase me down the hall, pretending he was some monster or something, and I'd giggle and tell him, *Shhh! Freddie will hear us*, and then we'd collapse on the bed and the fun would turn serious, sexy. The lovemaking would be slow and sensuous and afterwards we'd lie together talking about anything, everything, me on my front and him tracing his finger along my spine. Talking about what we'd call our baby, how old he or she would be when Freddie started school, what star sign they would be, what they would look like.

If it's a she, she'll be beautiful like her mummy, Miles would say, and he'd smile his gorgeous smile.

But somewhere along the line, after a few negative tests, it stopped being so much fun. Lovemaking turned to sex. The tenderness, the stroking, the passionate kisses turned robotic, like we were following a pregnancy manual. Step One: Begin Sex. Step Two: Complete Task in Missionary Position. Step Three: Place Legs in the Air for Ten Minutes Until Arse is Numb! About six months in, when I was standing at the foot of the bed in lacy lingerie, he looked up at me and went, *Really? Do we have to? I just want to read my book!* So I pretty much spat at him that he was pathetic, and he said, wait for it, *I would want to do it if you didn't treat me like a walking sperm bank!* He goes, *Look at you, Zoe! You're obsessed with this whole project!* And all I could think, over and over, was, *He called it a project. He called it a PROJECT.*

I threw myself into parenting Freddie when I wasn't thinking about getting pregnant. Tried to nurture the toddler I did have. Obsessively so, Miles said. He said I was wrapping him in cotton wool, worrying too much, stopping him from doing things, that I was being one of those awful helicopter parents.

That's so unfair, I told him.

Zoe, why can't he eat the fruit slice?

Because it might have nuts.

But I've given him peanuts before!

Yes, but I'm pretty sure he hasn't tried walnuts yet. Only last week I read about a girl who went blue after eating a walnut. They couldn't get the EpiPen into her in time.

** cue eye-roll from Miles **

The way I figured it was that I only had one baby, and I might not ever have another (the ship of hope had well and truly fucked off across the ocean by then) and so I had to look after him. Miles seemed to go the opposite way, he was so relaxed he was horizontal and that's how Freddie ended up with the black eye, because Miles was looking at his phone when Fred threw himself off the roundabout and hit the tree! God we had the argument that ended all arguments after that. *For fuck's sake, Miles! What were you thinking?* I'd yelled, and he'd replied, *Zoe, you need therapy! No one is this obsessive about their kid's safety.* And then he felt bad and said, *I mean, you've been through a lot. Therapy couldn't hurt, baby.*

I slammed the door after that and took Freddie for a (nut-free) cupcake.

That's how life went from then on. He said I nagged him. I said he was pathetic. He said I cared more about Freddie than him. I told him to grow up. It became all about tolerating, grabbing a shovel and digging a hole and burying the bitterness, hoping it would stay underground long enough that it wouldn't fight back through the mulch and up to the surface. I know it's wrong, but I resented him – resented that his sperm was okay, but that it was *my* body at fault, my topsy-turvy uterus like an upside-down tea pot. Resented him when he suggested we leave a third round of IVF because of the cost, because he should have wanted to remortgage thirty times over if it meant a sibling for Freddie. And I was still working, Phoebs, selling online homewares like they were coming out of my arse. It wasn't like we were on the poverty line, not *quite*, or like it was him who had to do the hormone injections and the egg harvesting, or to feel those God-awful cramps once a month and wait to send a perfectly good egg to the bottom of the garbage bin aboard a Libra pad with wings.

And here he was, giving away the lesser-spotted Makin laugh to Alice Daniels, who was batting her eyes over a pair of cheap plastic Harry Potter glasses, even though Hermione Granger doesn't even wear them, and getting all into the trivia questions with her. She couldn't stop mentioning that her twin geniuses had read all of the Harry Potter books, even though they were only just seven. I mean, Freddie couldn't even say the word 'Azkaban' let alone read an entire novel, so you can understand why it pissed me right off. I couldn't bear to look at him, so I took out my phone and texted Cassie to check Freddie went to bed okay, since it was so hot in the apartment that night. *Can you check he is cool enough? Did he brush his teeth? What story did he have? What time did he go down?* She replied straight away, *All good, have fun!* Which made me a bit unsettled because she didn't actually answer any of my questions. *Is he asleep tho?* I'd typed back. *Yes, with his duvet folded back* she wrote, followed by a heart emoji. I felt much better from that point onwards, knowing he was safely in bed, so

I popped my phone back and attempted to chat to Amanda. She was already quite drunk because some woman she annoyed at her old school had apparently rocked up to Darley Heights to seek revenge, which seemed pretty unlikely to me, but I was like, whatever. She was behaving really oddly, like she'd just snorted some coke in the bathrooms – on the dance floor one minute, off the next, depending on which tune they were playing between sets of trivia questions. She was jumpy, that's the best word for it, and when she was off dancing, I found myself chatting to Ted, which was pretty bloody pleasant because he was so funny and attentive, unlike Miles who had forgotten I was in the room. It was all a bit fucked up, to be honest.

So anyway, after they'd played 'Wrecking Ball', Mrs Denner (the principal), stepped up to the mic with the next question, which was basically, *Who played Hector in* Troy*?* but she made a show of reading all dramatically, like, *Who was the Oscar-winning actor who played the role of Hector in the 2004 Wolfgang Petersen movie,* Troy*?* And I shit you not, Alice whipped her head round like she'd found the cure for cancer and looked at Miles and said, *I believe it's Eric Bana, Miles!* And Miles cooed, *Yes, you're amazing, Alice!* It made me cringe.

That was when Amanda appeared from nowhere with a glass of red wine in her hand and shouted out, *I know! It's Eric Bana!* and Miles got this crazed look and snapped, *For fuck's sake, table seven* totally *heard that!* and Ted said, *Okay, mate, chill!* and Miles shrugged and said, *Yeah, sorry mate, I was just a bit overexcited!* And Ted replied, *It's okay, no worries, mate!* It was all very civilised, but I was livid at Miles for being such a rude wanker.

Did someone call the fun police? I snapped. *This is supposed to be a game, Miles!* Besides, everyone knows it's Brad Pitt!

Oh, hello, darling! Miles replied, then turned his back on me. Oh, Phoebe, at this point I was seething, but before I had a chance to say anything else, Denner was back telling us we had to hand our quiz papers in, and Alice and Miles were both in a frenzy trying to work out if they should go with Brad Pitt or Eric Bana. Eventually, Alice grabbed the A4 sheet and said, all earnestly, *So, are we going with Brad or Eric?* like she was a movie producer trying to work out which of her celebrity friends she was going pick for an Oscar-winning role, and Miles said, *Well, I'm inclined to go with Zoe's answer. That's the one thing she's good at – film!* THE ONE THING SHE'S GOOD AT! Not work or motherhood, or making babies, but *film*.

Well anyway, Denner started reading the answers, and Miles fist-pumped after every one they got right, and then came question ten. *The answer,* Denner said, *is Eric Bana! For those of you who wrote Brad Pitt, that is incorrect. Brad Pitt played Achilles!*

Just great! Miles piped up.

And all I could really say is, *Oops, sorry!*

Oops, sorry? Miles hissed. *Well maybe you should listen instead of thinking you know everything!*

And maybe you should lighten the hell up, it's a game!

Me lighten up? How many times have you texted the babysitter tonight?

Twice, which is totally normal for any decent parent! I told him.

Alice? Miles turned to Alice, who was pretending to study her phone (but was totally listening). *Have you messaged YOUR babysitter twice tonight?*

Alice looked at me and shrugged and said *Ummmm.*

I poked Miles with my finger. *Anyway, if you're in the slightest bit interested, our son did go to sleep okay, thanks for asking.*

Go to sleep okay? Of course he fucking did. What, did you think he'd gone out clubbing? Did you think he'd climbed out of his Thomas the Tank Engine pyjamas and hit the fucking town?

Oh shut up, Miles!

Alice obviously felt mortified at this point, because she went, *Guys, it really doesn't matter about the Brad Pitt thing! Anyway, it's a great movie. Diane Kruger is my girl crush. She's such a good actress.*

And I couldn't help myself, and I said, *Uh-huh, she's right up there with Meryl Streep, isn't she?* And Miles snapped, *Zoe, don't be such a bitch!*

Thankfully at this point, Lara decided to pour a round of Sambuca shots, so I grabbed mine and downed it, and I was giving the little plastic shot glass a lick out with my tongue, when I noticed Ted watching me out of the corner of his eye. When I put the glass on the table, he looked me dead in the eye and said, sort of absent-mindedly, *That's so hot!* And I felt myself flushing, like, everywhere. Amanda's head whipped up with slitty eyes and she goes to Ted, *What did you say?*

Um, I meant Diane Kruger, not Zoe! he stuttered, and I could tell he was embarrassed because his neck had gone purple.

Five minutes later, Denner, who looked quite dramatic standing in front of the closed stage curtain with the school emblem behind her, announced it was a tie break for the quiz and that there would be one more question to decide the winner. The question was, *Which song by an Australian artist is the only song beginning with an 'X' ever to top the UK singles chart?* She said she was giving a point for the artist *and* for the song and yelled at us to bring our answers up to the front.

Ted turned to me and murmured *Ooh the pressure!* as he swigged his beer, just as Amanda launched herself out of her seat like a rocket and began miming into a plastic spoon like it was a microphone before yelling, *It's 'Xanadu' by Olivia Newton John!*

Alice stuck her arm out, rolled her hand into a fist and pulled it towards her chest like she was pulling a pint in the pub. *Yessss,* she hissed. Then she ran to hand the paper to Denner, while the smarmy surgeon Luke (who's married to Lara – are you keeping up?) looked up from his phone and said with a fake laugh, *Xanadu? Everyone knows Xanadu starts with a 'Z'!* and Ted started to piss himself laughing.

Xanadu starts with an X, mate! Ted told him. *It means a place of great beauty!*

Swallowed a dictionary did you, mate? Luke replied.

Nope, I just know how to spell! Ted shrugged, and it was obvious there was some weird, simmering tension between the two of them, maybe because they were both these attractive alpha males and they looked sort of similar in a preppy, Next directory kind of a way.

Anyway, Ted got out his phone and produced the dictionary definition of xanadu from Google and held it up. And Luke was clearly livid that Ted had made him look like the village idiot, because he pushed his chair back and went to get up, but was stopped in his tracks by Denner, who shouted, *Put your phone down, man dressed as a gym teacher on table six!*, and everyone looked at Ted. *I will have no cheating in this class . . . err, I mean, hall!*

Nice one! Luke said, and shook his head.

Now, I could tell at this point Ted was very close to blowing his top, so I did what came instinctively to the wife of a fiery red-headed male, and that was to put my hand on his knee to stop him getting up. To, you know, tell him to calm down. It was only a second after my hand landed on his muscular thigh that I realised it was highly inappropriate because a) the man wasn't my husband, and b) I fancied the living shit out of him. And I would only tell *you* that!

Ted didn't say anything, but turned towards me with a weird look in his eyes, and it was the first time we looked at each other in a way that was well, *different*, and the breath went completely out of me and bugs danced around in my stomach. And, even at this point, there seemed to be a hint of how things would pan out. I snatched my hand off his knee just as Amanda appeared and stuck her head between us. She looked at Ted and then at me and slurred, *Sorry, am I interrupting something?* and then, *In case you hadn't noticed, Ted, I won us the quiz!*

You're the star of the show, darling! Ted replied, and Amanda grinned like a kid who'd just won a lifetime supply of Cadbury.

Now the moment Amanda appeared, it was like I was no longer in the room. Ted put his arm around her waist and pulled her on to his lap, and said, *Well done, my darling*, and it was almost as if, with that gesture of spousal affection, he was saying to me, *Look, just in case there was a little something between us just then, forget it – I love my wife*! And so I sort of sat there and grinned at them as if to say, *Aren't you two cute!* and then I turned to Miles to try to demonstrate to Ted that I was also deeply in love with my husband, and that the hand-on-knee gesture was purely for the purpose of peacekeeping. I gave Miles an overexaggerated wink and a smile, but he shrugged back at me in a defensive, *What?* way and gave me the stink eye, which was totally awkward.

Anyway, I felt a sudden need to blur over it all with a bit of showiness, so I jumped up.

Let's play our own trivia! I've got a question! I shouted. *Which person at this table has six toes on each foot?*

Luke looked up. *You?* he said, bored.

No. I smiled.

Well it can't be Lara! Pete said, looking at her like a perv. Then he said, all alarmed, *It's not, is it?*

Lara laughed loudly and said no.

Give up? I asked.

Yep, they all agreed.

It's Miles! I squealed for dramatic effect.

Amanda leaned forward on Ted's knee, squinted across the table at Miles and said, *Seriously?*

Yep, serious! Miles replied, momentarily forgetting he hated me. *It's called polydactyly. My old man has it too. A supernumerary digit on each foot!*

Really? Alice asked.

Yep, it's genetic!

Alice pretty much bent herself double to get her head under the table for a look.

Come on then, let's have a gander! Pete said.

Miles kicked off his left Converse trainer with his right foot and pulled off his sock. *Here you go,* he said, giving it a wiggle. *My left side little toe. Isn't she a beauty!*

Alice banged her head on the way out from under the table and rubbed it with her hand. *Wow, that is freaking amazing!* she said, although I get the impression she'd have said the same if I'd told her Miles had genital warts.

Isn't it? I replied. *Miles, tell them what we call her!*

Toe-lene! He turned and smiled at me, offering a temporary ceasefire.

Amanda didn't need any encouragement, and started singing *Toe-lene, Toe-lene, Toe-lene, Toe-leeeene* to the tune of Dolly Parton's 'Jolene', while Ted just smiled and said, *Well, that's a pretty cool party trick!*

Freddie's gutted he didn't inherit it. Isn't it cool? I said, and everyone sort of nodded, unconvinced.

And then it was silent for a moment.

Who's next? Amanda said, looking around the room. When no one replied, she said, *Okay, well I've got one for you!*

And this, darling Phoebs, is when it started to get very weird indeed.

Chapter Seven
Amanda

Technically I should have been reeling from the whole 'Victoria is at Darley' missile Alice had thrown at me, but by this point, I was having such a good time that I'd kind of forgotten the Wicked Witch of the West had landed on my school.

Zoe had regaled us with this gross fact about Miles having an extra toe and I guess I wanted to trump it with my own juicy fact. You know, to liven up the party. I got up off Ted's lap and stood on my chair – which was an effort in the skirt I was wearing, I can tell you – and I told everyone, 'Right, I have a question! Which primary school has some resident swingers? I'll give you a clue: it's *very* close to home.'

Alice glared at me with a 'WTF?' expression, and then glanced nervously at Lara. Lara looked across at Luke. Luke looked at me. It was like a circle of stares. I met Luke's gaze and held it. You know, a bit like, 'I know who I'm talking about and so do you!'

'Where?' asked Miles. 'The Catholic one? Saint Cecil's?'

'Cecilia's,' snapped Zoe.

'Closer than that.' I paused for effect. 'I have it from an impeccable source that there are swingers *here* at Darley Heights Public.'

'Yeah right,' said Miles.

'Swingers?' Pete's head shot up. 'As in jazz performers? Tonight? How fantastic!'

Alice shot him a withering look. 'No, Pete,' she said through her teeth. 'I don't think Amanda is referring to *that* kind of swinger.'

Pete held up his index finger as if he was about to say something insightful. Then his mouth dropped open. 'What, you mean *sex* swingers?' he asked, and I thought, *How the hell you bagged someone as smart and gorgeous as my best friend, I'll never know.*

'They put their keys in a bowl,' said Zoe. 'Then pick a random set out and that's who they end up shagging.'

'You get who you get, and you don't get upset,' said Alice.

'That's what I say to the kids when I'm handing out Paddle Pops,' I shrugged.

Zoe let out a snort, which was really unladylike.

Alice glanced at Lara again and touched her earlobe, which was glowing scarlet.

'Sorry, but I'm calling bullshit.' Pete poured his beer into a plastic tumbler.

'Well good on them,' said showy Zoe. 'Whoever they are. They're consenting adults, after all.' And I know I wasn't imagining this, but she flicked her hair off her shoulder and looked straight at Ted. And bless him, he's not used to being flirted with, and so he sort of spluttered into the top of his beer bottle and reached for my hand.

The conversation was all very light-hearted at this point, and then Alice turned to Lara. 'Well, that was awkward,' she said, distancing herself from the gossip, even though she was the one who'd got it from her 'impeccable' source, and had told me all about it. 'I'm not sure why Amanda asked us all *that*.'

The disco was in full swing (for want of a better word) and Lara, who was sitting on the edge of the table, tapped her leather-booted feet in time to the song 'Maneater' – the irony of which wasn't lost on me. She wound a piece of hair from her ponytail around her finger and said, 'I'm not offended by the question. I mean, we're not shy, are we, Luke?'

Pete laughed and turned to Lara. 'Don't tell me you know these parents Amanda is talking about? These *swingers*?'

'We do, actually.'

The table fell silent.

'Good one, Lara!' Miles eventually said. 'Next you'll be telling us it's you two!'

Lara let out a girlish laugh and looked him dead in the eye. 'Actually, Miles, it is.'

Ted downed his beer as the opening bars of Salt-N-Pepa's 'Let's Talk About Sex' cranked up. 'Shit,' he murmured. 'Not again.'

We'd been propositioned two years before by some parents from Evie's day care. Rachel was a personal trainer with fake boobs and an orange tan, and Paolo a sleazy city-slicker who wore his shirt open due to the ill-informed belief his chest wig was an appetising sight for sleep-deprived mothers. It always amused me to see the two of them walking with their pale Caucasian son Tyler between them. 'That's what her skin looks like under the fake tan,' I pointed out to Ted at the Father's Day tea.

We arrived at the trendy tapas bar on a Saturday night to find Rachel and Paolo in a corner booth sucking face, her boobs hanging over the top of her black bandage dress. She patted the space next to her on the green leather couch, which gave a wheeze as she pressed into the seat. 'Come and sit with me, Ted,' she said. 'I feel like I know *all* about Amanda from TinyKins, but nothing about you.' I didn't think there was anything weird about that, because she was always uber friendly, one of those women who was desperate to know everything about you. But after two bottles of Malbec, the cleavage situation had gone from a teetering-over-the-edge affair to something from *The Magic Porridge Pot*. She squeezed Ted's biceps with her witchy nails and pouted at him with sticky, wet lips. Ted took the flirting in good humour, until halfway through dinner when he kicked me on the shin under the table.

'Ow.' I bent down to rub my leg. 'What did you do that for?'

He nodded his head toward Rachel, who was studying the wine list. 'Help,' he whispered.

'What?'

'Hand. On. My. Balls,' he mouthed, his eyes darting wildly towards her.

'Ar-an-cini . . . balls?' I asked. 'Do you –' I pointed at him dramatically – 'want *me* to order *you* some arancini balls?'

'No,' he hissed. '*Her* hand is on *my balls*!'

'YOU'RE NOT MAKING ANY SENSE!'

He stood up and grabbed my arm roughly, dragging me to the corridor outside the restroom and muttering a lame 'Excuse me, nature calls,' to Rachel and Paolo.

'Ted, what is wrong with you?' I rubbed my arm.

'Rachel is coming on to me!' He spoke slowly, as if he were trying to communicate with someone on the other side of a pane of insulated glass.

'Oh darling, she's just flirting, it's harmless. Besides, what do you think she's going to do exactly, with her husband at the table?'

'He's in on it too.' Ted was panic-stricken. 'He's all over you like the measles.'

'Don't be ridiculous. This is Darley, not the bloody Playboy Mansion.'

He shook his head. 'Get your coat. We're getting the fuck out of here. The last thing I want is to end up in a jizz-filled hot tub with Don Juan DeMarco and fucking Jane Fonda over there. *This* spicy chorizo,' he gestured towards his crotch dramatically, 'is not on the tasting plate. Let's go!' Then he ushered me back to the table and asked for the bill.

In the safety of the cab, it dawned on me that Paolo's hand had, in fact, been on my lower back for much of the evening, making clumsy circular motions like an obstetrician searching for a spot to administer an epidural.

'I suppose he *was* pretty flirty,' I mused.

'See!' Ted was pleased with himself. 'They're swingers!'

'Wow, and I thought all the touching was just a . . . *Spanish* thing.'

Ted sighed, pulling my hand onto his thigh. 'Darling,' he said, giving it a reassuring pat as if he were talking to a dementia patient. 'Paella and Sangria are Spanish things. Flamenco and bullfighting are Spanish things. Espadrilles are a Spanish thing. But trying to cup someone's balls in the middle of a tapas restaurant is not. They would have had us back to their place for a saucy siesta quicker than you can say "Barcelona FC", given the chance.'

'Well, that *is* a first,' I said, and I didn't quite know why – maybe it was all the red wine I'd consumed – but I felt excited by the idea that someone thought I was sexy. I leaned over and kissed Ted on his forehead, which smelled like grilled chorizo.

'You were terrified,' I laughed.

'Of course I was. It's not exactly our cup of tea, is it, darling? The old cock-swap?'

I looked out of the window as I watched Darley speed from view in a kaleidoscope of lights. 'No, no, it isn't,' I agreed.

It was silent at the table, while we all took it in. Alice stared at Lara with her mouth open, a smile fixed on her face. Pete twisted his wedding ring round on his finger repeatedly. Ted drained his beer. Zoe chewed the side of her lip. No one knew *what* to say, and I was praying Ted wouldn't arc up with one of his sarcastic comments. Thankfully, Pete beat him to it.

'Well, cheers to that,' he said, glass in the air. 'Thanks for your honesty Lara. Telling us something like that really does take balls.'

Ted snorted. 'You're right, Pete,' he said. 'It does take *balls*. Lara, please excuse us if we're all a little bit *stiff*, but this has *come* as quite a shock, and I think I speak for everyone when I say I'm *feeling a right tit* I didn't respond appropriately.'

Zoe was trying so hard not to laugh she went purple, like Violet Beauregarde from *Charlie and the Chocolate Factory* right before she popped.

'So,' Pete continued, earnestly. 'How did you, um, get started with the swinging?'

'With a bit of foreplay, I'd imagine,' said Ted.

Zoe laughed so hard the red wine she was about to swallow pebble-dashed Miles and Alice on the opposite side of the table.

'Oops,' said Alice politely, dabbing at her shirt with napkin.

'What I mean is, how does a person *become* a swinger? Is it something you decide to do?'

'Well of course you decide to do it,' Alice snapped.

'It's fine,' Lara said, and touched Alice's hand. Alice jumped about a thousand feet in the air and went bright red. 'Pete has questions and I'm happy to answer them. The fact is, we tried it when we lived in Singapore a few years back, and we've done it occasionally since we've been back in Australia. It's really not that big of a deal.'

I leaned across to Alice and whispered, 'No big deal? Bloody hell. Would you want Pete sleeping with her?'

Alice didn't answer. She was still staring like a fish at Lara.

I clicked my fingers in Alice's face. 'Oi, Alice!'

'Shit, sorry . . .' Alice said. 'I was miles away.'

Miles's head flew up, like he was a wind-up toy that had just been restarted. 'Well,' he slurred, 'there's no way I'll be letting another man puff on *my* doobie while I'm in control of my bodily functions. No way in hell!'

'It doesn't actually work like that . . .' Lara began.

'Ah right, well still . . .' Miles began, before Zoe cut him off.

'Well, Miles,' she said. 'I'm so glad you're more concerned about the emasculating effects of seeing another bloke's penis than you are about seeing me get it on with another guy. That's *incredibly* flattering.'

There was silence, while eyes darted around the table, awkwardly.

I looked up and across the hall. Behind Zoe, three tables along, a familiar blonde head nodded animatedly, and with a click of the fingers I was out of the swinging discussion and into the quicksand of my past misdemeanours. Victoria's head fell back and she let out a laugh that bounced off the walls in the momentary gap between songs. Her peers fell about laughing. *She's already popular, look at her. She's as new as you are! You have to make your mark tonight, show them all how fun you can be! Come on, Amanda! Show them you're a riot! They'll love the 'fun' you!*

Luke's husky voice brought me out of my trance and back into the world of partner swapping. 'We're not talking about a massive orgy here, guys,' he said.

I topped up my glass and took a comforting slug.

'It's about adults deciding to do a consensual swap and have fun. Most blokes would love to do it and fantasise about it when they're at home screwing the wife, but they don't have the guts. In my opinion, life's too short not to enjoy yourself.'

Miles was incredulous. 'There's nothing wrong with my sex life,' he slurred.

'Alice might say differently,' Luke laughed.

'Err, I'm married to Zoe, mate.'

I really wanted to catch Alice's eye at that point, so we could both laugh, but she was chatting to Lara, so I turned my focus to Luke. I watched the muscles of his jaw clench as he swallowed his beer, his Adam's apple popping in and out. His hands were thick and manly, but somehow poised and precise – a surgeon's hands. Long, thick fingers that looked like they knew their way around the female form. He put his bottle down and put one hand on his thigh. A big, muscular thigh that led up to a perfectly packaged . . .

'Sausage?'

'I'm sorry?'

'Sausage!' Ted handed me a snag on a stick, which he'd slathered in tomato sauce.

'Thanks,' I said, flustered. I took the snack on offer, picked up the nearest bottle of fizz and emptied it into my glass to wash away my sinful thoughts.

Chapter Eight
Alice

Transcript: The voice of Alice Daniels in the office of Dr Martha Davis.

After Lara told us they were swingers? Well, that's when it all got seriously loose. Pete was like the boy at the front of the class who not only throws his hand up to ask a question, but holds it up by the armpit with his other arm: 'Pick me! Pick me!' It was incredibly embarrassing, but I decided quite early on to leave him to his own devices. That way I could disassociate myself from some of his more, shall we say, *eager* questions. And they kept on coming: 'What credentials does one need to swing? Do you really put your car keys in a bowl?' You know, stuff that, in fairness, we all wanted to know (but we didn't want Luke and Lara to *know* we wanted to know. Poor Pete was the conduit, bless him!)

Amanda was as fascinated as Pete was. 'Tell us the rules,' she pouted. 'Is it true swingers take pineapples to parties?' And the way Luke grinned at her made me think, *There's no prizes for guessing whose pants he's going to try and swing into later.*

Zoe was all faux worked up because she said she'd taken a pineapple pavlova to someone's house a couple of weeks before, and now she was worried they'd think she was up for a group shag.

'Well, did you get laid?' Ted asked, and she swished her ponytail and let her chin cosy up to her shoulder, all flirty, and was like, 'Haha you're so funny, Ted!' It was a little over the top.

Lara just laughed, keeping a cool visage against the barrage of idiotic questions. 'I've never taken a pineapple anywhere,' she told Zoe. 'Or pampas grass for that matter. They're just old clichés. Or maybe that's what they did in the seventies, when everyone and their dog were at it. I know my parents liked to experiment . . .'

'Just think, if our parents were all at it,' Pete offered, 'we could all be walking around *related*!'

'Calm down, darling,' I whispered, my hand on his knee.

'Sorry,' he mumbled.

Lara clocked me and smiled, so genuine, so sweet. Something in her expression said, 'It's okay, Alice' and I felt myself loosen up a little. After all, who cared if Pete asked some silly questions? Weren't we all pretending to be other people tonight? Younger people? Weren't we the 15-year-old versions of ourselves? I certainly felt a little more frivolous in my polyester Hogwarts miniskirt, all hitched up around the waist, I'd forgotten I *had* legs!

'So, what *are* the rules?' I asked.

Lara sat up straight and pulled her dress down a little on her thighs, which were beautifully tanned, suggesting she was more than used to showing off her legs. 'Well,' she announced like she was reading from a Monopoly instruction pamphlet. 'First up, we don't allow repeats. In other words, if one of us hooks up with someone, we're not allowed to do it again, and we can't text or call that person afterwards.'

'What about email?' Pete asked.

I shot him a look.

'That's a no, too.' Lara smiled.

Beside her, Luke flicked the cap off a beer. 'Yep,' he said and leaned back in his chair. 'That's when it crosses the line and it becomes cheating.'

'So it's not cheating before?' asked Ted.

'No, it's sex,' Luke said. 'If you make contact, it becomes emotional. *That* is infidelity.'

I couldn't quite get my head around it all. Yet as Luke spoke, something inside me fizzed with energy.

'Everyone's different,' Lara said. 'But we have other rules, like no kissing.'

'What?' said Amanda, glancing at Luke. 'That's the best bit.'

Luke's voice dropped an octave like one of those creepy voice-over men in a film trailer and he said something along the lines of, 'Believe me, there are *so many* other things you can do.' He looked at Amanda and she flushed pink.

Lara laid out the rest of the rules: always use contraception; no taking one for the team (which she said meant no sleeping with someone because your partner wants to have sex with *their* partner, which made Pete look confused for a second); only go as far as you've previously agreed with your actual partner (as in the one you live with).

'So, let's see, if I was paired up with Pete, for instance, I wouldn't be able to do anything I hadn't cleared with Luke and Alice,' Lara said. 'So theoretically, I could give Pete a blow—'

'Okay, thanks for clarifying,' I told her. I looked at her petite hands. Long slender fingers, smooth palms, delicate nails. I didn't like the idea of them touching Pete's body.

'Some people might agree on a full swap,' Lara continued. 'That's the whole shebang, so to speak, but other couples might only allow a soft swap, which is, like, oral only.' She said the word 'oral' like she was discussing cake decorating.

'Is that it?' Zoe asked.

'Well, we did have a no singles agreement, but we scratched that and now we do allow unicorns.' She looked at me, as if I was supposed to know what that meant.

Ted let out a laugh. 'Unicorns? This is starting to sound like a fairytale.'

Lara smiled. 'Unicorns are single women. They're called that because they're pretty rare within the community. A few years ago, there would have been no way Luke and I would have let a lone woman in the group because it sort of *unsettles* things, but now we're completely open to it. Single guys are a no-no though. Luke gets a bit possessive of me, don't you?' She looked up at him. 'And that's fine, I totally understand that.'

I remember thinking at this point: How the hell could you look anyone in the eye after this? I mean, how would you hold your head up if someone found out you'd slept with another parent? It would make canteen duty unbearable!

Lara must have read my thoughts. She picked up her drink, took a large sip, licked her lips after. 'There's one more rule,' she said, 'and in some ways it's the most important of all.'

She swept her eyes around the table. 'Discretion. We *never* talk to anyone else outside the group about who we've been with. Never. It stays totally private. What goes on tour stays on tour. That is the number one rule of swinging. And, well . . . .' she flicked her ponytail back over her shoulder. ' . . . I guess that's all, folks.'

How did *I* feel? Well at that point I remember looking at Lara, and I mean *properly* looking at her. Half of me was disgusted, if I'm honest. It was pretty seedy, the idea of swapping your bodily fluids with a school parent and then going about your business as if nothing had happened. I felt a bit sorry for her too, almost as if I'd assumed at that point that Luke pulled all the strings. Like she did it to please him, and not the other way around. Part of me burned with envy. I was jealous of the way she was so unapologetic about who she was, the way she expressed her sexuality so freely, so liberally, without giving a toss what anyone else thought, or expected. Jealous of the way she talked about sex like it was something to be enjoyed, and not scheduled or performed dutifully within the confines of marriage.

And the rest of me? Well, I guess that part felt excited, I suppose. Excited by the prospect of doing something that was, to all intents and purposes, extremely naughty. And we all felt the same, I think, because there seemed to be this gigantic shift amongst the group after that, as if we had suddenly been made aware that there were people in existence who functioned successfully as couples, who were *parents*, but yet had recreational sex with other people without ramifications. Or at least that's how Lara and Luke had sold it. And while we were probably all thinking (or at least I was), that it was highly unusual, but each to their own, and just sat there, observing safely from the smug confines of our own morality, Amanda was the one who let off the handbrake and inched the wheels towards the precipice, as it were.

After Lara's monologue Pete, very politely, offered a 'Cheers!' to Lara and Luke, and we were all a bit jolly, so we leant in and clinked our drinks.

That's when Luke honed in on Amanda.

'You didn't say cheers,' he told her. She was miles away, in her own little drunken world, sitting cross-legged on her chair. I remember she was fiddling with a button on her white shirt that was hanging on by a thread, and she kept glancing over her shoulder at Victoria on the far side of the room. Victoria was holding court with the rest of the Mean Girls, the clique she'd evidently managed to worm her way into within the space of five days, and was throwing her head back and laughing. Poor Amanda was totally spooked by the woman's presence, at least in the moments she wasn't too drunk to forget about it.

'Oi,' Luke repeated. 'You didn't say cheers!' When she didn't register, he banged his fist on the table. It was pretty aggressive and rude, I thought. I don't think Luke was used to being ignored. 'Hello?'

Amanda looked up with a start, and as she did so, her hand jolted and the button flew off and landed on the floor, leaving us all staring at the red lacy Calvin Klein bra she got the last time we were at Darley Mall together. I felt mortified for her and expected her to pull her shirt together and blush, but then I remembered this was not the sober-light-of-day Amanda, but the tanked-up version.

'Ooops,' she said, in a breathless, Marilyn Monroe sort of a voice. Like, sorry, not sorry.

Luke grinned. 'So,' he asked. 'What about you?'

Amanda fixed her eyes on him, Victoria forgotten. 'What *about* me?' she slurred. It was embarrassing, the state she was in, and it was about that moment I gave myself an internal telling off for letting her get that drunk.

'Would *you* ever think about it?'

'About what?'

'About swinging . . . *playing* . . . having sex with another man?'

At this point, I remember thinking holy shit, where is this going? What is she going to do with this?

Amanda looked at me for help, and I opened my mouth to speak but Ted beat me to it.

'Okay Hampson, that's *enough*,' he snapped. He actually called Luke 'Hampson' and I remember that very clearly, because it was uncharacteristically aggressive from Ted. But I understood why he'd done it.

'I was just asking a question.' Luke shrugged, all innocent.

'Fine,' Ted held his hands up. 'Let her answer.'

Bless Ted, I felt for him then. The poor guy had total faith in Amanda and in the notion she would just rebuff sleazy Luke with some cute quip and nothing more would be said. But that wasn't what happened.

'Would you think about it?' Luke repeated, eyeballing Amanda like a seedy predator.

And this was it, the moment I told you about. The moment that changed everything. The moment where what we'd all been talking about went from theoretical to entirely possible. And it was because of what Amanda did next, drunk Amanda who was desperate to show she was the life and soul of the party, that she was the fun new girl who didn't care that her arch nemesis was on the other side of the room. And that was to lean in towards Luke, her boobs squashed against the table like a pair of bum cheeks, her lips in a weird drunken pout.

'As a matter of fact,' she slurred, 'I probably would.'

Ted's eyes were on absolute stalks.

'Shit,' Pete and I said in unison.

Chapter Nine
Zoe

From: Zoe.m8kin79@realworld.com.au
To: pho_e_b_wallis@zapmail.com
Subject: The truth

Ted was understandably rattled by Amanda declaring she would happily shag another man.

Are you okay? I asked.

He glanced at me and smiled, although it was an empty smile, like the ones I doled out to people who asked me when I planned to have another baby, and he said, *I'm good, thanks for asking. She doesn't mean it. Amanda tends to get a little* . . . overexcited *sometimes, but it's harmless!*

I nodded supportively, and placed my hand on top of his, for comfort.

Ted looked at my hand but didn't move. *She'll probably pass out in a minute!* he told me. *I expect I'll have to put her in an Uber within the hour!*

The clock on the wall read ten forty-five and I thought to myself, *I somehow doubt she'll be in an Uber any time soon, she's having way too much fun*. But, of course, I didn't say it, I just carried on making soothing faces, which were probably a little too over-the-top in the hope they might stir up some kind of jealousy in my husband. But they didn't, because Miles was on the dance floor, spinning Amanda around, while Lara and Alice were back-to-back, shimmying to the floor in front of Luke. I felt equally as annoyed by Miles as I was attracted to Ted and his delicious vulnerability. I wanted to pull this poor, neglected man's head into my chest and stroke it. I mean, what was Amanda playing at? She had the most attractive man at the table – what the hell was she doing flirting with Luke Hampson?

Ted followed my gaze to the dance floor, *Yep!* he said again, refilling his glass. *I'll be taking her home soon. There'll be no swinging tonight!* He offered me a weak laugh, and I don't know where it came from, Phoebs, but I said, *That's a shame!* and his eyes shot up to meet mine. He seemed confused at first, but then he smiled, a sort of sexy unconscious smile. I grinned back and looked away, sort of amazed at myself that I'd been so brazen.

At this moment Principal Denner jumped up onto the stage to announce the auction, which turned into a total dick-swinging contest – Luke attempted to outbid Ted a thousand dollars for some crap artwork of the Sydney Harbour Bridge done by a year 4 student, which was evidently about a lot more than fundraising for a worthy cause. Ted was outbid by a guy dressed as Severus Snape, which made Amanda act all weird for a minute and she whispered to Ted, *You can't let* them *get it*, and pouted when he shook his head at her. *It's not worth twelve hundred bucks,* he told her. And all I could think was, twelve hundred bucks . . . that's our monthly mortgage repayment! For a piece of art done by some random kid!

Alice kept shouting, *Come on people, bid! Don't you want air-con in here?* over and over like a lunatic. Meanwhile, Luke was talking Amanda through the ins and outs of doing a nose job, running his finger along her nose slowly and gently while she tilted her head back and giggled. Ted kept glancing over at her, but after a while seemed to decide he'd had enough of her flirting. I heard him say *Fuck it* under his breath and then he turned to me, all seductive.

Since we're on the topic of cheating, he said, *who's on your free pass list? You know, the three celebrities you can sleep with if you meet them?*

Easy, I told him. *Chris Hemsworth, Ryan Reynolds and Matt Damon. How about you?*

Salma Hayek, Mila Kunis and Natalie Portman, I'm not fussy.

Lara leaned in. *Free passes?* She squealed, opening our game up to everyone. *I love this game! Who else has one?*

Amanda's head swung round. *Jason Statham*! she yelled.

Then, get this, Phoebs! Lara leaned in and announced *I have two celebrities on mine, and one person on this table!* One person on this table! Can you believe it? It was shocking!

We all stared at one another, amazed, and Luke started to laugh. *That's my girl*, he said.

Who? Who? Pete asked, because he was desperate for it to be him. Alice looked up to the ceiling and sighed.

I'll tell you mine, purred Lara, with this sort of seductive lilt to her voice, *if you tell me yours! Who would you pick from our table if we were all at gunpoint?*

Shagging at gunpoint? said Ted. *Sounds like a recipe for performance anxiety!*

Come on, Lara giggled. *It's just hypothetical, just a bit of fun. Pete, what about you?*

Well, Pete replied, *I couldn't possibly – I mean my wife is here – but I suppose at gunpoint, I'd have to say, you!* He glanced over at Alice, who, to my surprise, simply shrugged and said, *What a surprise!* She didn't seem remotely upset or like she wanted to rip Lara's ponytail off her head, which said a lot about her character. Or about her marriage.

Amanda, whose shoulder was touching Luke's accidentally-on-purpose, leaned in. *What about you, Teddy?* she purred. *I don't mind you picking someone, it's just fun!* By that, I deduce she was hoping he'd pick someone, anyone, so she didn't have to feel guilty about flirting her arse off with Luke.

Okay then! he said without skipping a beat, watching her as she cosied up to Luke. *I pick Zoe!* He turned to me. *Zoe, I pick you!* As if the first time wasn't confirmation enough. I felt a flush of embarrassment and desire, and it travelled upwards from my toenails to my neck. I tried to stop the smile lifting up my cheeks, but I honestly couldn't. I looked to Miles for his reaction, but he was way across the hall, heading in the direction of the gents. He had that sort of sway he gets when he's starting to get really drunk.

Amanda let out a fake laugh, and said, *Well, I didn't see* that *one coming!* and then she gave me a googly-eyed stare and said, *What about you, Zoe?* She was pouting again. It was evident she hated me for catching her husband's eye as much as she appreciated me for giving her a reason to crack on with Luke.

Well, it's all hypothetical, right? I told her. *So, in the spirit of sportsmanship, I'd say Ted!* Which made Ted grin, and I half expected him to put his arm round my shoulders now that we were going steady, but he didn't. Amanda moved on to her BFF, demanding Alice make a choice, and Alice, who I'm learning is quite diplomatic, said, *It's too hard, I couldn't possibly choose between all these amazing men!*

Pete was on the edge of his seat. *So what about you, Lara?* he said and, get this, she looked right at him and said, *I think that person knows* exactly *who they are!* And for the first time Alice looked rattled, in that her face went puce and she grabbed her earlobe, which was burning red. *That's the beauty of it being a free pass!* Lara shrugged. *You can have anyone on it and there are no repercussions!*

Well that sounds like fun to me! Amanda slurred. *Count me in!*

Ted's mouth twitched – he was SO pissed off. *Yes, it does, darling!* he said. *Well, count me in, too. Nothing like a bit of partner-swapping to liven up a party!* And I realised he was deadly serious. Alice was too. She nodded towards Pete and said something along the lines of, *Well Pete seems keen, so I'm sure he won't mind if I put myself down as a yes, too!* Pete flinched ever so slightly, but evidently wasn't about to give up his pursuit of Lara because of the inconvenience of matrimony. I have to admit, at this point I was relieved Miles had wandered off because he wouldn't be able to even focus on Alice, let alone shag her. I *know* Miles after a couple of beers and the water she poured him wasn't going to help.

After a few seconds, Pete leaned in and said what we were all wondering: *are we still being hypothetical here, or are we all agreeing to some weird trivia night swing?* And Luke turned to him and said, *Why not, mate? It's a bit of fun, no harm done!* Then Lara piped up, like she was asking for the first time, *So, who's in, then? Give me a show of hands! I'm serious!*

Pete's hand went up first, then Amanda's – not even a wobble, but up like a rocket – followed by Luke's and Lara's, then Alice's. My heart raced like I was tachycardic because it dawned on me this might actually happen. Here's the thing, Phoebs – I'd never cheated on Miles, never even entertained the idea, but at that precise moment, I felt like I'd earned the right to make a choice about *something*. A little voice inside of me, somewhere, was telling me, *Fuck it*. You couldn't make a baby miraculously come! You couldn't stop your sister – your *best friend* – from leaving! You couldn't make the man you love understand the depth of your grief for both of these shitty absences! So here's something you can choose! Here's a decision you *can* make. Here's something you can do without someone pulling the plug or stopping you! So I did it: I raised my own hand. Ted's was still in his lap at this point and suddenly I felt exposed, like I'd put myself out there and been publicly rejected, but then I saw him fix his eyes on Amanda, and her defiant, raised palm, and he shrugged and lifted his arm a little. Not a yes, but definitely not a no, either.

Full house, said Luke, before glancing at Miles' empty chair and saying, *Well, sort of.*

I went to the loos after that, so I could breathe. I took out my powder compact and tidied myself up a bit, spritzed on some of the travel deodorant that was in my bag, and started to put my lipstick on, and that's when Amanda appeared behind me in the mirror. She reached her hand to my face and tucked a strand of my hair behind my ear and smiled sort of knowingly at the mirrored version of myself, the one I know. *So pretty*, she said, then she walked away as if we were best friends. I followed her out a minute later and she was there, leaning against the wall of the loo with Luke standing over her, whispering in her ear. I slipped past them to get back to the hall, to Ted.

When I sat down beside him, I was taken back to the time Benny Oden took me to the cinema in year 12. The feeling of desire as bodies don't quite touch, but the agonising pain of wanting them to. My pulse thundered in places I never knew existed! And then he put his hand on my hand under the table. He didn't look at me, just stared straight forward as his fingers weaved through mine.

Miles sat himself down and started chatting to Alice again. He flipped the lid off a beer and skulled it as he leaned in to hear her over the music.

Miles is pretty drunk, I said.

I know, Amanda too!

I bit my tongue, and I thought, *Why not? Why the hell shouldn't I let loose, just this once? I'm a big girl. I can choose!*

So then I did it (and I still can't believe I did!). I said to Ted, *Well, I'm going to the caretaker's room backstage, you know, just to get a breather. Do you want to come with me? I could meet you by the door to the stage and I'll show you where to go?*

He didn't reply for a moment, like he was thinking. He looked pretty anguished, if I'm fair. But just as I was wondering, *what the actual hell did I just do?* he said, *Okay, you go first, I'll come after*, and I thought to myself, *I bet that's his motto every time he has sex.*

Ted arrived in the corridor a couple of minutes after me, glancing behind him as if he was about to get sprung.

He smiled nervously, and took my hand, dragging me up the corridor and further away from the dance floor and the potential to be discovered. We walked, with our feet in time, between the rails of dance costumes that lined the corridor and narrowed it, and I kicked one by mistake and let out a giggle. Ted looked panic-stricken and hissed a *Shhhhh!* that was louder than my laugh or my heels as they clip-clopped on the hollow floorboards. When we got to the room, Ted opened the door and let me go in before him, which I suppose was rather gentlemanly, and then stepped in himself, dodging a bucket on the floor filled with dirty grey water and a mop with twisty dreadlocks. He looked hesitant, so I reached my hand out decisively and yanked him towards me, and weirdly, his body, despite the height and bulk, was somehow light, like one of those air-filled men that whip and wobble outside a car dealership. The room was no bigger than a baby-change cubicle at Darley Mall, with green walls, and dried drips of Dulux where the painter from years ago botched the job. There was a strong aroma of disinfectant and the unmistakable smell of vomit. A metal shelving unit had been rammed against the wall, with bottles of industrial cleaning fluid stacked one in front of the other, and on the wall, in loosely-joined-up scrawl, a kid had written 'Mr. Jones is a dickhead, 1980' in black marker, with a drawing of a penis and testicles sprouting hair. Put it this way, Phoebs, it was more revolting than romantic – but then neither of us was under the illusion that what we were about to do was in the least bit lovey-dovey. I plucked my phone out of my bra and threw it onto a box of blankets in the corner of the room, to free up space in the lace, and Siri popped up on the screen, waiting for me to ask her advice. *What the hell am I playing at, Siri?*

Ted seemed to be thinking the same, but we were at the point of no return, and plus I was craving some attention, some *affection,* so I smiled up at him and said, *It's just a bit of fun! We all agreed. Amanda is doing it too!*

The hit of his wife's name made him come to, and his head shot up, his body straightened. He lifted up his hands and pushed me against the wall and kissed me, his tongue deep in my mouth. It shocked me for a second, because it was so intimate and because it was meant to be against all the swinging rules, but I yielded to it. It was so sensual, and he was so needy. And I wanted to be needed.

He bent down, effortlessly, and reached up my dress and took one of my thighs in each hand and lifted me up and around his waist. *Are you okay?* he asked.

Yes! I told him, my tongue in his ear. *Yes!*

I reached down and unbuckled his belt, yanking at the top button of his grey school pants, then down, down inside his black boxer shorts. *Well hello, Big Ted!* I purred, forgetting I was meant to be sexy, and he kind of half-laughed, half-sighed as I pulled them down. He was breathing heavily, any sense of guilt evidently dissipating with the feeling of my hand on his cock, and reached between my legs, yanking my G-string to the side. My bum and back were pressed up against the wall, and I could see he was beginning to sweat under my weight. *Don't let go,* I whispered as his arm slipped and my body dropped with a jolt.

I'm so sorry about that! he said. *It's a long time since I've done it against a wall.* And he hoisted me up again with one big jig of his arms, and pushed himself inside me. I let out a moan worthy of Serena Williams on Wimbledon Centre Court, and Ted put his hand over my mouth, and we moved back and forth until we were done. There was no time for foreplay, there was a job to do that we both wanted done, and it was over in less than a minute. And when his body relaxed into the pleasure, and he sighed with relief as mine did the same, it was as if a cold wave of shock had blanketed me. In a single minute we had done something that couldn't be undone.

Ted gently dropped me to the floor, stood back, wiped the sweat off his forehead with his hand, and looked me in the eye. Then he said *Thank you, Zoe*, and it was so sincere I felt the tears prickle in my eyes and suddenly I couldn't control them and I started to properly sob.

Are you okay, did I hurt you? Ted asked, concerned, and bent down to look me in the eye.

I looked up, my eyes red and swollen, snot pouring out of my nose and my chest aching, and I shook my head. *No, no, you didn't!* I told him, my voice heaving.

Zoe . . . what's the matter? Please!

But all I could do was shake my head faster. I couldn't explain why it had chosen this exact post-coital moment to come out – the grief, the loss, the sadness. I wanted to tell him how lonely I was without Miles and how much I loved him. I wanted to tell him about you, Phoebe, how much I missed you. But I didn't. I couldn't.

I'm so sorry! I told him instead, as I wiped my nose on the back of my hand. *It's just . . . something I'm dealing with. I'm sorry!*

He pulled me close to him, held me there, but it felt wrong – he wasn't Miles, after all. His skin felt like sandpaper against my cheek. It was too oily. He smelt like musk, not maple syrup and cooking. His chest was too wide, too firm. He wasn't Miles! Ten minutes beforehand, I hadn't given Miles a second thought, but he was all I wanted once I'd done this thing that couldn't be taken back! I felt panicked, like I needed to get out, to get home to the apartment. I needed to check that Freddie was okay, because I had left my beautiful boy with a teenager while I'd been in a dirty broom cupboard with a man who was not my son's father. So I pulled away from Ted abruptly and said *I need to go . . . now.*

Ted nodded. *Of course, as long as you're okay.* He leaned in and kissed me on the cheek, tenderly, but it made me flinch, and I turned and walked out, hot semen dribbling down my leg, leaving him to dwell on the enormity of what we'd done together.

Out in the corridor pissed-up parents sang 'Livin' On A Prayer' and under my feet I could feel the vibration of hundreds of pairs of legs thundering on the wooden floor ahead. I turned to look back at Ted, and saw the face of someone also grappling with regret, his skin still red and sweaty and his hand sweeping anxiously through his beautiful, sandy hair.

When I walked back into the hall, Miles was snoozing with his head on the table, which is his party trick when he's had a few. Alice clocked me and looked behind me at the door I'd just come out of like she knew exactly where I'd been. *Are you okay?* she asked. *Yep, I'm great!* I mustered my biggest I-am-fine smile, but she still eyed me suspiciously.

Are you sure, Zoe? she asked softly, and so I smiled again and told her, *Honestly I'm fine! I just have a few . . . things going on at the moment.* As if I was going to tell her anything when she'd been flirting with my husband all night.

She nodded, like, sure whatever, and then asked, *Where is Ted?* It gave me a bit of a shock that she was asking me that, but I didn't have the energy to deny or lie, so I nodded my head towards the stage door. Behind her, the tall one of the Mean Girls, with the blunt blonde bob and the superior look about her, was on the dance floor taking selfies with her phone. She looked up and gave me a smug, knowing sort of a smile, so I returned it with a 'what are you staring at?' glare and turned my attention to Miles.

I leaned my head in against him to check he was okay, trying not to cry any more when I breathed in the comforting sweet scent of his skin, but he was fast asleep, breathing heavily. I knew, from experience, that I couldn't move him when he was like that. But I was desperate to get the hell out of there, to get home and undress and shower, and to wash Ted and the smell of him off me, out of me. My head ached and my stomach churned with waves of regret that made me want to puke.

Miles! I gave his shoulder a shake. *Miles!*

He grunted but didn't move. I could feel the anxiety pulsing in my chest. I didn't want to face Ted and I could see him striding over already, looking guilty but also just concerned, like Alice had, so I kissed Miles on the top of his head and ran-walked out of the hall, outside into the warm night air where I could finally breathe. I stood there for a second, bent over, my hands on my hips like I'd just completed a ten-kilometre run, and I looked back to see Alice and Ted watching me. I turned, took off my heels, and ran across the playground to the car park, which was empty and dark. Everything was scarily vivid – the stars, the moon, the picture in my mind of Ted's sweaty face as he was coming, and I leaned into the bushes and heaved next to a navy-blue Range Rover with a stupid number plate, but nothing came out. I lifted up the hem of my skirt and bent down to wipe my mouth on it. It was like someone had taken the contents of my brain and put them in a spin dryer. My thoughts were jumbled like cards in a recently shuffled deck. One minute I told myself sternly, *That did not just happen! You imagined it!* And then the next card read something entirely different: *You fucking idiot! Miles will leave you! How will you get out of this? How can you undo it?* I tried to shut off my thoughts as I walked briskly down the hill to Sunshine Parade, which was lit up orange by the streetlamps above my head, and I thought, *I hope to God no one thinks I'm a hooker, because that's how I am dressed, and that's how I have behaved.*

Chapter Ten
Amanda

Luke was waiting for me outside the girls' bathrooms, where I'd found Zoe putting on her lipstick, preening herself for the benefit of my husband.

'There you are,' he said, catching my arm and pulling me towards him, making it look as though I'd accidentally stumbled there. 'Oh, I'm so sorry to trip you,' he said out loud, for the benefit of two women, who, like Alice, were both dressed as Hermione Granger. Then he whispered, 'So, do you want to go somewhere quieter?' and fingered the neck of my shirt. At that moment, Zoe walked out of the bathroom, head down, obviously not able to look me in the eye because she was on her way to seduce Ted. I pretended not to see her.

'So?' Luke said, bending his head down to try and catch my eye.

'Yes, sir,' I said, fingering his tie. 'I've been a naughty girl and I need to be punished by a very sexy teacher.' In hindsight, the whole role play thing was a little inappropriate, but what can I say, I'd had a couple of wines.

Luke gave me a dirty smile. 'In that case,' he said, 'you'd better come to my office.' And he led me to the staffroom door. He wiggled the handle, which was locked. 'Shit,' he said. 'Meet me behind the stage curtain in five.' It sounded incredibly risqué to me, but also pretty exciting, so I waited until he'd taken a few steps before following on behind.

'Ladies,' he said, as he passed a group of women, who I realised were the Mean Girls, and I felt a sudden lurch in my stomach as I remembered Victoria made up one of their party. I studied the women, head by head, but there was no statuesque blonde in the line-up. The only one I recognised was Tansie. She looked me up and down, without a smile, and I felt the confidence leave me then and a feeling of self-reproach wash over me, because I thought Victoria must have told her new friend about the *accident* at St Cecilia's. And for a millisecond I wondered if I should turn and leave, go straight home before I could get myself in to any more trouble, but then Luke turned round and gave me the smallest of winks, and I immediately forgot the sins of my past.

Inside the hall, I watched him bend his tall body around the velvet curtain. I weaved my way through the madding crowds all bending and jumping to the Black Eyed Peas hit 'I've Got a Feelin'', and glanced back at Ted, who was bent in close to Zoe. For a second, the jealousy was so strong that it was as though I was inside a rubber band Ted was holding, trying to walk away from him but being pulled back, but then the Phys-Ed teacher Mr Mattock, who was doing a moonwalk, blocked my view and the band snapped, leaving me free once again to follow Luke behind the musty curtain.

He was sitting on a chair in the middle of the backstage area, his legs spread, and he smiled when he saw me. It almost felt as though I was doing some kind of sobriety test by the side of the road walking towards him, and when I got to him, I stood between his open legs and he patted them, inviting me to straddle him. His aftershave was strong, and I could taste it on my lips as they pulled away from his neck. Sweet, bitter, masterful. Behind my head, voices blurred into one another, offering a sort of humdrum buzz that was broken every so often by a high-pitched squeal of laughter or an impromptu mass chorus to the *Grease* medley.

Luke's left hand was around my waist, the other inching its way towards my bra from the bottom of my blouse. He pushed his hand underneath it so that he was cupping my right breast in his hand. I'm not going to lie – it was a thrill to have a foreign hand there, against my naked flesh, and the desire began to pulse like a drum beat deep in my groin.

He leaned into my neck and began to kiss it. His lips felt warm and soft and his breath smelled like red wine and garlic, but not offensively so. I went to turn my head, to kiss him on the lips, but he pulled back and looked at me instead, in a slightly quizzical way.

'You have the most divine depressor labii inferioris,' he said, stroking my chin, and I was so glad I'd had a go at it with the wax strips beforehand, because, well, perimenopause really isn't kind. 'You have perfect zygomatics.'

'Zygowhaass?'

'Sorry,' he said, all doctor-like. 'It's just surgeon speak. I'm talking about your cheekbones – they're spectacular.'

I grinned, my lips sort of making involuntary movements with the booze, which was a bit odd because I hadn't had *that* much.

'Your upper eyelids are deliciously hooded,' he added. 'You would be a great candidate for blepharoplasty. You should call Louise, my PA.'

And I thought to myself, *Are you trying to shag me or drum up business?* Frankly, the bone structure chatter was a bit tedious, so I grabbed his face in a bid to be sexy and assertive (which Ted usually loved) and told him, 'Just kiss me,' which may or may not have come out as 'Jushkisssme'.

'No,' he said and pushed me away. 'Sorry babe, but I don't kiss on the lips. You heard Lara, right?' I didn't like the fact he was talking about his wife whilst I was astride him and my nipple was between his thumb and index finger. 'Kissing on the lips is cheating. It's against our rules.'

'Like *Pretty Woman*?' I asked glumly.

'Yep,' he said. 'But we can have so much other fun.' He lifted up my arms and ran his hands down my torso like he was feeling me up in a drug bust. Then, out of nowhere, he pushed me off his lap and started to steer me towards the curtain.

'Let's go and find Lara,' he said, involving the other woman again. It was a tad off-putting.

'But . . .'

'Let's get an Uber back to my place.'

'Okay,' I said, acquiescing. After all, I was eager to show that I was the adventurous type.

'Right, I'll go first and you follow me in two minutes.' He edged towards the curtain.

'So, if that was the interview,' I giggled. 'Do I get the job?'

'You sure do,' he said.

He was about to slip himself round the curtain when he suddenly pushed me back against the red brick wall and covered my mouth. 'Shhh, someone's coming.'

The sound of a familiar voice wafted along the corridor, deep and soothing, like a fluffy winter dressing gown, and with it, footsteps, two pairs. One loud and heavy, a familiar flat tread, and the other lighter, a set of pointy heels. The wearers stepped completely in time, each with the other, the sound of two people in perfect harmony. There was a giggle followed by a 'ssshhhhh!' and a woman saying, 'Come on!' Instinct must have kicked in then, because I sort of pushed Luke's hand off my mouth and turned my head to listen to the sound of my husband's feet. From beyond the curtain, the lyrics to 'Should I Stay or Should I Go' floated on the air, and I had a sudden urge to race behind the stage wall and into the corridor and shout, 'Oh, darling, *there* you are! I've been looking for you, I think it's time to go!' and to turn to Zoe and say, 'I'm so sorry, Zoe, but I think you've taken a wrong turn. The hall is *that* way!'

But there was Luke: tall, sexy and . . . masterful, leaning up against the wall with a smile on his face and a bulge in his pants. Luke Hampson, the object of desire for almost every mother at Darley Heights, from what I could tell. Luke Hampson, who was presenting me with a free pass to misbehave, to pretend to be young and hot again, to forget being a wife and mother, both thankless tasks. To revel in an encounter that was making me feel sexy again, and not forty-two with saggy eyelids and wrinkles and washing to be done.

Should I stay or should I go? The lyrics rang in my head, and my brain hurt and I thought, *I could really do with another drink right about now.*

I shut my ears and looked up at Luke. 'Okay, go,' I said. 'I'll follow.'

He smiled at me, a dark and sexy smile, and disappeared out into the hall.

I stood there, behind the musty curtain that smelled like it was straight from the charity shop, and tapped my foot, counting to sixty. It wasn't two minutes but it was enough. I slipped myself out from the curtain, wrestling with it slightly as I tried to push the heavy fabric away from me, and focussed on not falling down the five steps down to the dance floor. When I reached the bottom, I noticed a figure standing dead still amid the whirling revellers on the dance floor, throwing their hands up in letter shapes to 'YMCA'. I couldn't immediately work out who it was because the lights were low and the disco ball entertaining elsewhere, but as it turned and threw its shards of metallic light into the middle of the room, the figure came in to focus. Stick thin, intimidatingly tall, and wearing a pink miniskirt, a matching cardigan and a string of pearls, which she fingered gleefully. Our eyes met for the briefest of seconds, before a tight smile spread across Victoria's lips, and she began to shake her head and click her tongue against her teeth in a silent 'tut, tut'. Then she turned and vanished into the crowd as if she'd never been there.

Chapter Eleven
Alice

Transcript: The voice of Alice Daniels in the office of Dr Martha Davis.

This bit will be very hard for me to explain. I don't want to dwell too much on what happened at the end of the night, or go into any more detail than I absolutely have to. I will tell you what happened, Dr Davis, but please understand that it was all very out of character. You can read into it what you want – that it was a consequence of repressed desires, tra-la-la, but I know myself what it was and what it wasn't. I don't need analysing!

A few of us went back to the Hampsons' house after the school event was over. You know, to continue the party; a nightcap and some banter. Lara and Luke were there, of course, and Amanda and Miles, who had sobered up massively by then.

Pete had been in the men's toilets when we left the school. I think he was feeling a little queasy– Pete has a very delicate stomach at the best of times – so I walked to the house alongside Miles. He was still a little wobbly on his feet, but not too bad. He was telling me a hilarious tale about a customer in his restaurant who'd turned up with his girlfriend when his wife was at a business meeting at the next table – and I remember looking up at him and thinking, *What an unusually attractive man!* and wondering what the issue had been that night with him and Zoe, and whether he knew that Zoe had been behind the stage with Ted. If he did, he didn't seem to care. He was happy as a pig in the proverbial as we walked back to Lara's. Maybe it was because he'd enjoyed an hour-long power nap at the table, or a disco kip, or whatever you call it.

I was feeling untypically frivolous, carefree as I walked along with Miles, and I suppose just buoyed on the success of the night. It had all gone so seamlessly, and I'd had so many people come up to me and congratulate me.

I had enjoyed playing a role, I suppose. It was as if the uniform transformed me for the night. I felt uninhibited, and, dare I say, excited by the general vibe at the table. What's more, I had enjoyed the last half hour of the night talking to Lara and finding out more about her. For all of my early opinions about her extra-curricular activities, I'm happy to admit I was captivated by her ('fan-girling', I think Amanda had called it). She was definitely not the person I'd been expecting!

Anyway, we had only been in the house honestly about ten seconds before Amanda and Luke disappeared upstairs – him pulling her by the arm and her sort of skipping up behind him. I remember almost going to get up, to go after Amanda to tell her we should leave, but I'm ashamed to say I didn't. Partly because I knew what Ted had done with Zoe Makin backstage (and it was pretty obvious because he looked sick with guilt when he returned to the table and proceeded to sit for ages with his head in his hands before leaving to go home and pay the babysitter), and also because I didn't want to. Alice, frivolous party Alice, with her legs on display, didn't want to go home. There was a knot of anticipation in my stomach, the feeling that something illicit, something forbidden, was going to happen. And it did.

I was on my own in the kitchen when I heard the voice call to me from outside, and I followed it, took a tentative step outside into the unknown. The deck was dark, save for the twinkling of fairy lights, hundreds of them, hanging up on high, their strings intertwined like the legs of ravenous lovers. There was the hum of a hot tub to my right; the faux leather spa cover had been unhooked and rolled back to reveal the nakedness of the turquoise water below, water that frothed urgently, lapping and pulling rhythmically, inviting me in.

I stood there for a moment. Watched the figure standing beside the hot tub and I felt the fear again, felt my foot on the door frame, hovering between the inside, where I was safe and I was married, and the murky waters of the unknown. Watched as a hand reached forward, the forefinger beckoning, the lips raised up into a smile, a transformative smile, kind and generous and sexy, that made me look behind me for clarification. Just to make sure. *Who me? Are* you *beckoning* me?

What about Pete, you ask? Well, by that point, any sense of guilt I might have felt about fornicating with someone else had been blinked back. Pete had wanted me to leave, to push my chair back and take my half-drunk bottle of Prosecco and go somewhere, anywhere, with Miles, and to leave him to the spoils he'd been working so hard to procure. To take the prize he'd tried to claim when he said to Lara, 'I couldn't *possibly*, I mean my *wife* is here, but I suppose at gunpoint, I'd have to say you.' And I couldn't let him, I couldn't. I didn't want to make it easy for him! I must have sat there in the hall for the best part of an hour, on Lara's left and Pete on her right, my husband trying to dominate the conversation and failing. I knew that every inch of him, especially the three inches below his belt buckle, was willing me to leave so he could try to secure the contraband on offer. It was laughable really – poor Pete would have been terrified if the opportunity to have sex with a woman like Lara had actually arisen. He isn't the most confident man in the bedroom. I mean he's not shy, but he's more tarmac grey than *Fifty Shades*. Put it this way, there would be more bumbling than acrobatics.

And the whole time, Lara was sweet, polite about the whole thing, kindly put up with the stubbornness of the third wheel who just wouldn't leave. But here's the thing, Dr Davis. It wasn't about jealousy. I didn't refuse to leave Pete with Lara because I was jealous! I had my reasons, of course, but they were not jealousy.

So, back on the deck, I stepped towards the beckoning fingers, the body moving slowly to the rhythm of Marvin Gaye's 'Sexual Healing' pounding out on the speakers inside. I watched as that same hand peeled off its own school uniform, and threw it to the floor, until all I could see was nakedness in front of me. I felt desire and angst pulse equally between my legs. I knew then that I had to step out, I had to let myself go. And I did. I let myself be seduced by someone who wasn't Pete, let another pair of hands unhook my bra, pull down my skirt, my underwear, stand and look at me with that smile. I took the hand offered to me and together we stepped into the water, and it wasn't particularly graceful, but that didn't matter, it really didn't. I let myself be touched, felt another mouth on my breasts, different fingers inside me, and I felt myself reciprocate the touch, the generosity, the pleasure of lips locked, the sensation of taste. Water sloshed from side to side, up the walls of the hot tub and over the sides in torrents, hitting the slippery wood below as our bodies moved together rhythmically, urgently, while the knotted fairy lights twinkled above us, flashing on and off like a helicopter spotlighting the sea.

I heard myself groaning and moaning until I had to pull away to stop it being over too soon.

'Stop, *please*,' I begged in a breathless whisper, as my body arched and pulsed with desire.

But in the end, it wasn't me who climaxed first. It was Lara.

Chapter Twelve
Zoe

From: Zoe.m8kin79@realworld.com.au
To: pho_e_b_wallis@zapmail.com
Subject: The truth

I managed to hold it together enough to pay Cassie when I got home, but she knew something was up because instead of talking to me, she talked to the floor. She was probably wondering why I came home without Miles and assumed we'd had a massive row.

I said an over-the-top-happy goodbye, and then, when I'd watched her mum reverse out of the driveway and given a half-hearted wave to the back of the car, I turned to my reflection in the mirror by the front door. My make-up had smudged in big grey rings around my eyes and I looked like an entirely different person to the well put-together cheerleader of a few hours previously. All I could see in front of me was a cheat – someone who did something utterly stupid because they thought, in a moment of madness, it meant they were seizing control. That it was something they could choose for themself amid the decisions made for them by the fucked up roulette wheel of life.

I kicked off my shoes and crept across the living room and down the corridor to Freddie's room. His night light was on, painting the walls Hulk green. He was on his side and had kicked his duvet off because it was such a hot night. I put my hand on his forehead, which felt a little hot, and my heart jumped. I bent to kiss his head instead, the ultimate temperature gage, and I realised he was fine, just warm from the humidity, so I turned to his cupboard and brought out a single cotton sheet to cover him with, removing the toasty duvet. Even though it was boiling hot and the fan whirred madly at the end of the bed, I didn't like the idea of my little boy being uncovered, for him not to have the comfort of some kind of fabric to soothe him.

I looked at his sleeping face. The freckles on his nose, the long eyelashes, the glimmer of auburn in his thick brown hair. He looked just like Miles. That realisation, even though it happens frequently, stunned me a little, possibly because of what I had just done, and I fell to my knees on the carpet beside Freddie's bed and cried. Tears of shame and guilt – wifely guilt and mother's guilt. I wondered how I could possibly worry so much about this beautiful boy being hurt, day in and day out, by external forces, yet do something that could have an emotional fallout for him for years and years? Maybe for the rest of his life?

I climbed into bed beside Freddie, and watched my thoughts link up like this: Guilt. Cheating. Sex. Babies. And that's when it dawned on me properly – because the thought was only fleeting before – that Ted and I had not used protection and it was my fertile window.

My heartbeat hammered wildly, the familiar sensation of panic whirring around like a tornado. It was a job to control it. I had to say to myself (quietly of course because of Freddie) *Zoe, you are the one with the reproductive issues, so even if his swimmers have motors on them, you won't conceive,* and it made me feel a little better. I reasoned that at least I wouldn't have to worry about that aspect, which is pretty ironic, since I'd spent God knows how many months stressing about why it *wasn't* happening and willing it to.

I thought back to my pregnancy with Freddie, and the first baby days, which were the happiest of my life, hands-down. I don't know if I ever told you this, but we only tried for six months that time, which was no time at all when I look back – not compared to now. But I was still desperate for it to happen. Every month I'd stock up on tests, and sometimes, in the days before my period was due, I'd do, like, three a day: once in the morning, once at lunch and once before bed. One time, I thought I saw a line and actually pulled the test apart in an attempt to see it more clearly. I spent an absolute fortune and I remember Miles saying, *They're expensive, Zo, maybe wait a few days.* But I couldn't wait. I wanted to know! And then of course, at the six-month mark, I got the two little pink lines. Do you remember me sending you a photo of the test? You were in London then, and you were still awake because it was my morning, and we screamed at one another over Skype – I told you before Miles because he was on the bus to work and he'd forgotten his phone! I loved being able to share that with you, sis. I'll never forget your face: the joy on it. *I'm going to be an auntie,* you said. *Auntie Phoebe!*

As you know, I decided to wait all day to tell him after the initial shock had worn off, which was tricky when he rang me from the office and I had to act all normal. It was even harder when he got home – I'm crap at lying and he knows me so well! But I really wanted to make it special, so I made him a roast chicken with proper crispy roast potatoes and an apple pie for dinner and we made all this lovely small talk and he said *You're in a great mood* and eyed me suspiciously. Then when he was done, I said, *I got you a little pressie* and I handed him a little box with the test in. Phoebs, he lost it when he saw it! He stood up, knocking over his glass of sauv blanc (I'd had elderflower cordial in my glass and he hadn't noticed at all) and he grabbed me by the waist and spun me round and said, *Shit are we really having a baby?* and I laughed and said, *Yes yes, honey, we are!* And he said *When? How?* And I said, *Come on, Milo, don't you know about the birds and the bees? Were you skiving off during Sex Ed?*

He looked at me, with tears in his eyes, and he said, *You will be the most amazing mummy. I'm so proud of you!*

He was incredible during the pregnancy. We were in the process of moving out of the rental place and buying the apartment then, and he wouldn't let me do a thing, not so much as lift a pillowcase. He plumped cushions, cooked meals, offered massages, did food shops, everything. And while some of his mates treated their wives like ever-rounding, designated drivers for nine months, Miles was respectful. He kept the drinking to a minimum, and when I got really big, he drove everywhere because I was so worried about having a crash and a seatbelt injury and Freddie being hurt *inside* the womb.

Watching Miles at the antenatal classes was hilarious, trying to wrap a baby doll in a pink chequered hospital blanket and put on a newborn nappy. The whole class erupted in hysteria when he dropped the doll on its head and announced, *Oh shit! That doesn't bode well, does it?* But the weird thing was, when Freddie arrived after that God-awful labour, there wasn't a hint of fumbling or fear in him, only complete ease. Miles switched him from arm to arm like a rugby ball, fed him bottles of expressed milk at midnight so I could get a full night's sleep, sang to him, changed nappies, instigated the removal of peanut-butter-style poo from Freddie's shrivelled little walnut scrotum like a pro. And he'd show Freddie to me, *present* him, like he was a trophy and say, *Look Zo, just look at what we made!* Those days were perfect, they really were. Hard graft with the chafed nipples and the sleeplessness and the hormones whizzing around like flying saucers, but perfect, nonetheless. We were a little impenetrable unit, living our best lives in our own idyllic little bubble.

But back to trivia night. Sometime during the early hours of the morning, Miles arrived home. I don't know what time exactly, but he'd obviously sobered up because he wasn't at the trestle table in the school hall anymore and had made his way home somehow, either on foot or in an Uber. His key fumbled in the lock for what seemed like forever, and I toyed with getting up to help, but my head was pounding with booze-withdrawal, along with pungent waves of regret and grief, and so I screwed my eyes shut tighter and pulled a pillow over my head. Miles clattered around in the kitchen for a while, banging pots and pans on the 1970s orange Formica worktop and I could hear frying. He used to do it all the time – whip up something amazing with basil and chorizo or whatever is left in the fridge, however drunk he was. Eventually he climbed into bed beside me, and I reached out my hand to feel his skin, but he was fully clothed. He could cook gourmet food when he'd had a beer or two, but he couldn't undress himself. Still in his school uniform, still dressed as teenage Miles, and I didn't care because he was home safely, and I was relieved. Eaten up with guilt, but relieved.

Yet again I felt the tears come. Tears of guilt and regret. *I love you*, I told his back, as the warm salty drops pooled in my neck. I wondered if I could fill the whole clavicle, like a bucket. I put my hand over my mouth to stop a sob filtering through and breaking the silence. Not that he would have noticed, he was that sloshed.

Love you too, he slurred, too drunk to remember we were barely on speaking terms, and slung a dead arm over me, before his breath slowed and he began to snore gently. And I felt my breath relax then, too, and I curled myself into him, and all was suddenly normal in the universe, and it was as if the weight of the world was suddenly on someone else's shoulders.

I woke up the next morning with acid in my throat and a sick feeling in my stomach, because I knew what *I'd* done, but I was terrified something had happened between Miles and Alice. I started to wonder if maybe he went back to the Hampsons with her and Pete and Amanda before he stumbled in through our front door, and it made my skin prick with sweat.

I reassured myself that on the practical side, Miles didn't have a great history of success in the bedroom when he was out-of-his-tree drunk, and I seriously doubted that someone who took twenty minutes to get his key into the front door after a few drinks would have been in any state to guide his penis into anything. Plus, he despises infidelity, considers it the ultimate betrayal. At least that's what he'd always said (not that he used those exact words, but you know, if someone cheated on their partner on a TV show or anything, he'd say *scumbag* and shake his head). This thought made me sweat harder – because I was the cheating scumbag in real life – and I could feel the salty dampness pooling on my forehead and between my breasts. I knew what I'd done was not acceptable within the walls of our marriage, and for a moment I began to properly panic. I sat up on the side of the bed and began to rock, feeling my heart race as though I was being chased by someone – and not my own conscience. I did not know what I was going to do. If I told him, surely he'd leave? If I didn't, and he found out, he would hate me. If I veered him away from the topic so that we didn't even go there, would it be lying or just omitting the truth? I took a deep breath to try and slow my heart rate, to reset.

Miles turned over and opened his eyes. He went from sleepy to alarmed when he saw me on the end of the bed, and sat up.

You okay? He put his hand on my back. *Zoe?*

Yes, I said, and told myself to breathe.

He looked into my face. *Oh God, Zoe,* he said. *I'm so sorry.*

I was confused. *What for?*

For arguing last night, for trying to annoy you with Alice, for passing out like a dickhead! He reached out to stroke my hair. *All of the above.*

I sighed, relieved he didn't add the words, *And for shagging Alice.*

It's fine! And when I said it, the guilt almost suffocated me. Here he was apologising to me, when I was the one who had broken our marriage vows in the worst possible way. I was the one who had had a quickie in a cupboard. The tears came again, and this time, unlike inside the broom cupboard, I couldn't keep the sobs quiet, I couldn't swallow them down.

Do you remember the time we went to see *The Notebook* at the outdoor cinema at Centennial Park, Phoebs? Remember that? God, we were both a mess! Well this crying was like that, but on steroids, as in I couldn't breathe and there was proper snot dribbling out of my nose and into my mouth. I could taste my own snot!

Hey hey, Miles grabbed me and wrapped me in his arms, burying me in the soft, downy hair of his chest. I could smell the maple syrup smell, along with the booze. His breath still smelled like it was twelve per cent proof.

Don't cry, Zo, he said, his voice softer than I'd heard it for a while. *Everything's okay, I promise.*

I nodded, but continued to cry harder, the tears clinging to his chest hair like rain on a spiderweb. And I think that's the moment he realised, I really do. Realised that I wasn't crying out of fear he'd cheated, but out of guilt because I had.

I opened my mouth but nothing came out, and when the words did start to form, I knew it was the start of a confession.

Miles, I ventured, my mouth choked with saliva and snot and guilt.

He pulled away from me, held my shoulders and looked down into my eyes. He closed his eyes. Braced himself like his head was on a chopping block and the axe was about to fall.

Oh God, I cried.

He let out a deep sigh and wove his fingers through his hair.

Miles, I did something.

He shook his head.

Miles!

No. NO!

He strode to the wall next to the window with the framed koala print I got from the op-shop that hung wonky. He faced the wall, a large child in his school uniform still, couldn't look at me. The muscles in his back and arms, and even his buttocks, tightened. The veins in his neck pulsed, and his skin coloured red. He clenched and unclenched his fist into a ball because he knew what I was about to tell him. What I had to tell him in order to make our relationship honest again. I owed him more than this dirty secret. I loved him too much for that.

Miles. Turn and look at me. Please.

He didn't turn. Didn't look at me.

Fuck, he spat.

I need to tell you. Please!

NO. He let out a groan, like a groan of anguish, like a childbirth groan. And then he did it. He pulled his fist back.

I closed my eyes, braced myself. Waited for the punch to hit.

And it did. He punched hard. A boxer's jab. The koala print leapt off the wall with the hit of his knuckles on the plasterboard, and smashed into tiny pieces at his feet, shards flying. It took a few seconds before I realised my shin was bleeding.

I gasped and held my hand to the cut.

Fuck, Miles said, the anger melting into concern. *Are you hurt?*

His knuckle was purple already.

Oh fuck, Zoe, he said. *I'm sorry.*

No Miles, I'm sorry. The words sounded meaningless, overrated. But they were gut-achingly genuine. I let my body fall into his open arms.

Zoe, do you love me? he asked. His voice was wrought with pain like an injured dog. I had been with him for twelve years at that point, and I had never heard him sound like that.

I nodded.

He looked me in the eyes. *I'm going to ask you again,* he said and his lip quivered. *Do you love me?*

Yes.

I mean, more than anything? I mean, do you want to stay married, to see it out, whatever the hell this weird patch has been about?

Yes, I told him. *I love you more than anything.* My chin trembled uncontrollably, my cheeks were swollen and hot. I'd forgotten how much until now.

Well if you love me then don't tell me, he said.

My mind whirred. *What?*

I mean it, he said. *I do not want to know.*

I tried to protest but he stopped me.

No, Zoe, he said, the anger simmering again. *Please. I don't ever want to know about it. If you love me, you will keep it to yourself.*

He swallowed back a sob, and I realised that he was protecting himself. Protecting himself from hating me. I realised that his *not* knowing what I'd done was the only way he could forget it and move on.

I nodded, put my face in my hands, and he pulled me into his arms with a knuckle that was bruised and red.

I'm so sorry, I said.

I know, he whispered into my hair. *I know. It's going to be okay, I promise. We need to move on from whatever this shitty stage has been about.*

And it was at that moment I realised I would never find a man like him again and nor did I ever want to. I saw a man who was a good man, *my* man. A man who had been at my side through everything, who mopped up the vomit that spewed from me at the side of the road when that awful phone call came through three years ago, and helped scrape me up and deposit me back into life afterwards. The man who gave up the plan to buy a house for a baby that never came, who let me stray so that I would come back to him. A man who loved me without condition, so much that he didn't ask me *who*. I told him *I do fucking love you, Miles. I do, I do! I can't lose you.*

I put my hand up to his face and kissed him long and deep, and he kissed me back, kissed away my tears, and before long we were making love and it was *making love,* not just sex. It was beautiful and apologetic and forgiving – it was everything it hadn't been while we'd been trying to get pregnant. It was a meeting of hearts as much as bodies, it was understanding, it was kindness, it was acceptance. It was nothing like the sordid encounter of the night before, which I hated myself for, but would try to forgive myself for eventually. Because if Miles could forgive me, surely I could forgive myself? I would show him how much I was sorry, I would take this fuck-up and I would turn it into something, reinvest this energy into us, into our family, into Miles and Freddie. And for the first time in maybe two years, I thought to myself, *You know, perhaps another baby isn't the be-all and end-all. Maybe I'll just settle for what I've got. Perhaps it's enough for me after all. He is enough, and he always will be. Who the hell was I to want more when I have all that I ever wanted in the first place?*

I lay in Miles's arms for a long time after we'd made love, and, even in those post-coital moments when secrets are so often revealed and deepest confidences shared, he didn't ask me anything else. He just stroked my hair gently and held me with a grip that was tight enough to tell me it was all going to be okay. And even though my pregnancy app said I was ovulating, I didn't even remind him of that, because for that moment I wanted to step away from duty, from cycles, from weeks in the month and from legs up, up in the air.

We fell back to sleep for a while, Miles holding me tight as if he was expecting someone to come into the room and take me from him, until we were woken by little feet on the wooden floor and Freddie bursting in. *Hello, mate*, Miles said to him as our blue-eyed boy opened the slatted bedroom blinds and let the sunshine flood in.

Chapter Thirteen
Amanda

I woke on the left side of the bed to see Lara staring at me from a wedding photo on the bedside table. Her face sparkled and her hair threw a golden sash across the white lace bodice of her bridal gown. Haphazard, but somehow fashioned that way. Luke stood beside her, posing in a grey suit, smug. A picture-perfect pair, enthralled by one another and by the vows they had made to be faithful to one another. To let no man (or woman) put them asunder!

Standing amid a sea of hairclips and jewellery, tubes of face cream and lip gloss, and a watch that read 5:52 a.m., were two glasses – one a water glass, filled to the brim but untouched, and another, a red wine glass, drained of its contents, its rim smeared with the greasy white veins of the lipstick I'd worn the night before. I took in my surroundings for a moment, breathed them in. The quiet. The solitude. The comfort of the white linen sheets, the coolness of the air from the window, and the triangular slice of sunlight, whirling dust motes around the room. It was pleasant, *peaceful* even. And then it came, the regret, charging at me like a tsunami towards a tranquil beach, first a rumble, but then a roar. Hot sweat prickled my face, my neck, the skin between my breasts. And I thought, *Amanda, what have you done?*

I glanced around to see if he was there, and he wasn't, so I closed my eyes again, waited for the familiar mini movie to start. The one that played in my head a lot these days, each time I woke up from a heavy night. A cinefilm of moving pictures, images, scenes strung together to create the story that I'd momentarily forgotten, each one a sequel to the one before. This one was *The Night You Cheated on Ted*, starring yours truly in the leading role of adulteress, bad mother. Scene One: pouty stares, the hand up high in the air, leaning into Luke outside the girls' bathrooms. Scene two: behind that musty curtain, astride Luke as he fumbled at my bra strap and whispered into my eardrum. Scene three: the finale! My body lying underneath Luke's, groaning and moaning as he told me how much I was enjoying it. Then going to sleep far away from the body that had, seconds ago, been inside me – as if post-coital affection was as straightforward as switching a light on and off. A body that wasn't Ted's.

Ted. The self-loathing spewed forth with the thought of him, the snapshot of his image in my mind. The softness of his face, his square jaw and his kind eyes. Not quite put together, dirty nails, a hair growing out of his ear. Not sterile, not manicured. My man, my love, my everything. My heart started to race, not just a jog but a sprint, bringing breath-stealing palpitations falling over themselves one after the other after the other. Fear, anxiety, dread, all fighting for space in the boggy mire of my mind. My amygdala was illuminated neon, lit up like Times Square, warning me: Alert! Alert!

I glanced to the floor, saw Luke's underwear lying beside the bed. Blue Armani briefs – *briefs, oh God, he wears briefs?* – and the repulsion flooded me. I knew I needed to leave, get out of the house, because then, in some small way, it would distance me from the situation. Maybe, when I got back home, it would be forgotten, buried as if it had never happened to start with! Maybe whatever Ted had done with Zoe (another lurch, another tsunami, more sweats) would be swept under the rug with all the other shitty dust and debris, hidden for no one to see. Out of sight, out of mind. Maybe.

I needed to find my clothes, to get out of the house before Luke came back, and so I sat up then, despite the protests from my pounding head, drank the water beside me, which tasted stale, and scanned the bed for my underwear. I found them at the end, on Luke's side, and pulled them on hastily, flattening out the crumpled sheet with one hand, as if making it pristine would erase what we'd done on it, or at the very least iron out the disorder in my head. My mother's bed had always been like that, crumpled like a screwed up ball of paper that had been unfurled. That is one of the things I remember about her. Maybe she never made the bed because she was almost always in it, nursing a bottle of vodka and watching *The Paul Hogan Show* playing on her rickety old TV set in the corner of the pink room. The pink room that threw out insipid, mustardy 1980s technicolour and canned laughter. Or lying in the dark calling out to me for painkillers. 'Amanda, darling, would you mind? Amanda?'

'Amanda?' Luke stood at the end of the bed, a crisp white towel wrapped around his waist. His six pack was wet, as if he'd rubbed himself in cooking oil, like Peter Andre. He was drying his hair with a towel, using just one hand, in a showy demonstration of core strength.

'You're awake,' he said, like he was chatting to his wife, not a fellow school parent he'd just slept with and would likely have to swap pleasantries with at the school gates in the not-too-distant future.

'Hi,' I croaked.

'Sleep okay?'

'Yes. You?'

'Like a log.'

Silence.

'Where's Alice?'

'Spare room.'

'Oh.'

Luke put a corner of a white hand towel in his ear and waggled it around, inspected what was on the end.

'Well babe,' he said. 'Last night was fun.'

'Uh huh.'

'Don't be bashful. We're grown-ups, we had fun and we played safe.'

Well, that was one good thing.

'I know.'

He put the towel on the dresser and sat down on the bed, regarding me in the same way you might a child who's making a huge fuss about a superficial splinter. He lifted up my chin in his hands, but there was no tenderness to it. It felt harsh, sanitary.

'Seriously, don't be awkward, babe,' he said. 'We were all in it together.'

'I'm not . . . I mean, I know!' I couldn't quite look at him.

'Right, shall I call you an Uber, then?' He sprung up, back to business. 'I expect you're waiting to get back to the kids.'

The kids. *Oh yes, that's right, I am a mother! I was a mother when I ran over someone's dog, too! I'm a mother now, in another man's bed.*

It didn't occur to me until later that I hadn't even checked in to make sure Ted had gone home after trivia night. I had just assumed it. I had just assumed that he would go home to pay the babysitter and to check the kids were sleeping peacefully. Christ, who was I kidding? I hadn't assumed anything because I hadn't given it a second thought. I was disgusted with myself.

'Uber. Yes, yes please.' I made a feeble attempt to look around for my phone.

'It's on me,' he said, tapping away at his phone.

Oh my God, I'm a prostitute.

'Do you have any painkillers?'

'Sure,' Luke said, opening the bedside drawer and tossing a silver packet of paracetamol at me. It crackled as I popped out two little white pills from their sockets.

Luke gestured to the open drawer, at a packet of Durex inside. 'I just want to reiterate, in case you don't remember, that we used a condom . . .'

'Um, okay, great,' I mumbled.

He shrugged. 'Just letting you know. Oh, look at that! Three minutes,' he said, looking at the Uber map on his phone. 'That's lucky. I thought it would be harder at this time in the morning.'

Thank God we only have three minutes to continue this horrendous small talk.

'Um . . . I can't find my clothes,' I mumbled. I groped at the bed sheets, reluctant to get out of bed semi naked in front of him.

'Here you go, babe.' He bent down and picked up my grey skirt and Sam's white school shirt from the floor, and tossed them towards me. In the cold light of day they just looked slutty. I pulled the sheets up to my neck and backed out of the bed towards the bathroom, my uniform bundled up with the bedclothes.

Luke chuckled. 'Don't worry, I saw it all last night, babe,' he said.

In the privacy of the bathroom, I pulled my clothes on hurriedly, buttoned the shirt up high, pulled the skirt down as low as it would go on my hips. Looked at myself. The messy hair, the dried saliva around my mouth, the chapped lips, the kohl-rimmed eyes. I wasn't even a hot mess.

'Cab's here,' Luke called. 'Martin in a Toyota Camry, FDZ 4RY.'

'Okay, well . . . see you,' I said, grabbing my bag from the table by the door and hoping it had my phone and purse in it, at the very least.

'Ciao, bella,' he said, giving me a nod. A nod. I wouldn't have been surprised if he'd held out his hand for a shake, I really wouldn't.

I had just slipped through the door when he called me back. 'Wait,' he said. 'So, babe, you were quite concerned after we'd, you know, done it.'

I turned to look at him quizzically. 'I was?'

'Yep. You were worried about being seen by that woman. You said she saw you coming out from the curtain and you were stressing about it. You said something about her making your life a living hell. Victoria someone?'

'Thanks,' I said and I felt my legs wobble underneath me. I just about made it down the stairs and out through the front door before I bent over and vomited profusely into a manicured hedge, in full view of Martin in his shiny Camry. He shook his head at me, looked in his rear-view mirror and pulled out into the road, leaving me on Luke and Lara's porch to make my own way home on foot, and I thought to myself, *This is categorically an all-time low. Even squashing that yappy dog was less humiliating than this.*

And the worst part was, it was just the start.

When everyone knows your name for a good reason, it's unsettling enough, but when you have done something reprehensible, unforgiving, you expose yourself to a whole new level of notoriety: infamy. I didn't go to school the day after the dog incident, I couldn't face it. Victoria's high-pitched screams were still ringing in my ear, and the image of her body folded over Mr Perkins' limp corpse still flashing up in my brain like some horrendous subliminal advert. Ted had driven Evie to school for the rest of the week, but by the following Monday, I had no choice but to take her in myself since Ted had needed to be at the airport early for an interstate business meeting. Evie had been contemplative in the car, sucking up the tension as I pulled in outside St Cecilia's and braced myself for the inevitable.

'Mum,' she said, her hand poised to open the door. 'Darcy Day says you killed her dog on purpose. She said you had an argument with her mum on their driveway and squashed Mr Perkins to get back at her.'

I didn't understand why Victoria would have told Darcy that. Why tell a *child* the circumstances, especially when she knew it would get warped thanks to playground Chinese Whispers?

'No,' I said. 'It's true Mummy was responsible for what happened to Mr Perkins. But it was an accident, and not something I did on purpose. You know how when you knocked Sam's school trophy off the shelf and that was a mistake?'

She nodded.

'Well, this was like that.'

Evie climbed into the front seat and hugged me. 'Okay, Mum,' she said. Always forgiving. 'Can you walk me to my classroom?'

'Well darling, I thought you might want to do it yourself today,' I said. 'Like a big girl.'

Her face fell and she offered me a petulant bottom lip. 'No!' she said. 'I want *you* to do it this week!' I stopped short of saying please, and stepped out of the car. I knew I'd have to rip the plaster off eventually.

The walk to the classroom was like proceeding through the quiet zone in a library – no noise, only silent whispers and disapproving eyes, the occasional snigger. Evie was oblivious as she skipped beside me. As I approached her classroom, I saw Victoria, her head in close with a group of women, one with her arm round Victoria's shoulders. Her other arm was in a sling, and my immediate thought was that maybe she had slipped on the wet stairs and hurt herself, and that was my fault, too. I wished the women would go, so that I could brace myself to walk up to her and offer my sincerest apologies once again, but they had circled her like wolves, protecting her, and I was too scared. As I stepped closer, one of them looked up, and then all of them, in sync like some kind of cheerleading team. I sidestepped the group with a wide berth and my eyes cast down – until I made the mistake to look up. Victoria stared at me, at first angrily, until the corners of her lips pulled up into a smile. I felt the blood return to my body, my lungs exhale heavily as my brain registered that I was forgiven, that it was all going to be okay. I smiled warmly in return, until I realised that her mouth had contorted in a scowl. A mean expression that told me, in no uncertain terms, 'You'll get what's coming to you'. Then she turned away again.

Just as I was returning to the car, I saw Nicole – the woman who'd sneered at my job at the Melbourne Cup lunch before handing me a hundred bucks – fumbling with a dog lead around her legs. She saw me and kept her head down, her leg kicking wildly in a bid to unravel the lead so she might avoid an awkward confrontation – these women were not so bold out of their pack.

'Nicole,' I called and took a tentative step forward.

She pretended she hadn't heard, so I walked over and stood right beside her.

'Nicole?'

'Oh Amanda, hello,' she said.

'I . . . I know you must have heard what happened to Mr Perkins. I just want to reassure you, as a good friend of Victoria's, that it was a total accident . . .'

'Amanda,' she said. She was awkward as all hell. 'I'm sorry, but Victoria believes you killed Perky out of anger. Now I'm sure you're not the kind of person who would kill a defenceless little dog *really*, but Victoria is a *very* good friend of mine, so I have to take her word for it.'

It didn't actually sound like she believed her friend's version of events at all, but if I suspected Victoria possessed an ability to manipulate before, I was convinced of it now.

'Look,' Nicole said, her voice softer this time. 'I've known Victoria for a long time, and I know from experience that it's not a great idea to get on her bad side. If I were you, Amanda, I'd keep your head down.'

I didn't know what experience Nicole had had with Victoria, and frankly I didn't want to know. But reading between the lines, Nicole was saying that it didn't matter what she or anyone else believed really happened to Mr Perkins, and whether they felt she was being unreasonable or not – because when Victoria said, 'Jump!' you said, 'How high?' And when she said, 'That bitch offed my dog!', you agreed, 'Let's lynch that murderer!'

So by the looks of things, I had killed my social life along with the dog. And it was bad, yes it was. But it wasn't insurmountable. So what if the most popular girl at school hated me? A bitchy glare was only to be expected – after all, I had earnt that. Facts were facts, and I had reversed over Perky, albeit accidentally, and the only reason I'd been at her house that day was because I was there to atone myself for puking all over her carpet. It was a domino effect that I had caused, so I could hardly expect her to gallop over and envelop me in a hug, could I? If this was the best she had, then I could take it. I could cope with a coven of death stares and a maniacal smile, I could. It couldn't get any worse, I reasoned with myself.

Except the very next day, it did.

'Mrs Blackland?' Verity Watkins, Evie's kindergarten teacher, was waiting for me at the door of the classroom. Her voice was clipped, unkind. 'Mrs Walsh would like to see you in her office as a matter of urgency.' I felt my face crinkle up with confusion. What would the principal want with me? 'Of course,' I said. 'I'll head to the office now.' I kissed Evie goodbye and made my way to the far side of the concourse, feeling the burn of eyes on my back all the while.

I knocked gently on the door.

'Come in.' Margot Walsh's voice gave nothing away.

'Mrs Walsh, hello!' I wondered if she was going to ask me to be on a committee – after all, I'd helped raise eight hundred dollars for the new computer room the previous year when I hosted a wine and clothes swap night at home.

'Mrs Blackland,' she said, her face grey. 'Please sit.' She thrust a hand towards the two seats in front of her desk, positioned for the presence of two parents.

'I'll get straight to it,' she said. 'We've had some very disturbing reports of an incident at Victoria Day's house this time last week.'

I felt my cheeks redden.

'I am aware you were there for the Melbourne Cup and Victoria has alleged you were not only destructive to property, but that you returned the next day and . . .' She clutched her pearls, 'and deliberately ran over her dog.'

I was utterly dumbstruck. Darcy Day believing I'd killed the dog on purpose was one thing, but the principal was quite another. Margot Walsh leaned forward and straightened a photo, dusting it lightly with her fingers. It was a picture of a Labrador Retriever with an older man I assumed to be her husband. She was a dog lady, of course she was.

'No, Mrs Walsh, it wasn't . . . I didn't mean . . .'

'Now I would normally turn a blind eye to this kind of unsanitary behaviour,' she said over me, 'but since Victoria told me the Melbourne Cup event was a school fundraiser, complete with a charity bucket to raise funds for the new netball court, and not a social gathering, I am obliged to address the incident. It would do the school untold damage if this were to get out: St Cecilia's has a clean image, Mrs Blackland, and a school fundraising event cannot be considered a drunken free-for-all!'

'There was no bucket,' I protested. 'It was just a social that happened to have school mums there. Really, I . . .'

'I am reliably informed there *was* a bucket, Mrs Blackland.' The week before, in the playground, she had smiled at me sweetly and called me Amanda. Now we were using titles and surnames again.

'I'm not denying I behaved badly,' I pleaded, 'but to make out Victoria's Melbourne Cup party was a school function is simply not true.'

'Well you must have misconstrued the presence of the bucket in your *condition*,' Mrs Walsh said. Her voice had raised.

'Misconstrued?'

'That is what I said.'

I sighed. 'Mrs Walsh, there was no bucket.'

'Yes there was, Mrs Blackland.'

'*There was no bucket*!'

'There *was* very much a bucket and I . . .'

Now I'm an amiable person, I really am, but I'd had enough by this point. Victoria was lying through her pearly whites and I was being told *I* was the one who was making it up.

'I'm sorry,' I said in my best passive-aggressive voice. 'Were you there last Tuesday and I just didn't see you?'

'Excuse me?'

'I mean, you seem very convinced there was a charity bucket, but I don't recall you actually being at the house!'

'Mrs Blackland . . .'

'What colour was it?'

'I'm sorry?'

'What colour was the bucket?'

'I don't know but . . .'

'What *colour*?'

'Mrs Blackland,' she snapped. 'I was told there was a bucket by multiple sources who were sober on the day.'

'Well then, let's call them all in and ask them individually what colour it was! But they're not allowed to confer first!'

'That's preposterous! And besides if there was, as you say, "no bucket", then why would I have received a very generous donation of four thousand dollars from Mrs Day for the new asphalt?'

I laughed then. *Well played, Victoria*, I thought. *Well played.*

'Well I think it is obvious she wants to make out it was a school event so that I get reprimanded – and handing a wad of cash over is quite persuasive, isn't it?'

'I beg your pardon? Why on earth would Mrs Day do that?'

'Was it in coins?'

'Excuse me?'

'Was the donation in coins?' I said, my voice raised. 'And notes?'

'No, it was a cheque . . .' she said, confused.

'So you're telling me that instead of giving you the *bucket*, which as we've already established didn't exist, she has taken the money to the bank herself, handed it over to the teller and written the school a personal cheque? What rubbish!'

The principal sighed. 'Mrs Blackland, please! I have been told by Mrs Day, who is, I might remind you, a very generous benefactor to the school, that it was a fundraising afternoon, and there was a bucket . . .'

I saw red then. 'When are you going to get it into your head?' I tapped my temple. 'That miserable cow is lying to you to get rid of me. There was no bucket! And if there was, I'd drive my car erratically to her ridiculous colonial mansion right now, and fill it with water and hold her fucking head right under!'

The principal's eyes were like frisbees. 'Well,' she stuttered, looking faintly alarmed and glancing over my head to the door. 'That is certainly not the kind of language we find desirable at St Cecilia's . . .' She trailed off.

'Well,' I said, mimicking her. 'That's fan-fucking-tastic because I am withdrawing my daughter from this shitty, judgemental school right now. Say so long to eighteen grand a year from us, and to our generous Christmas donation to the new asphalt!'

I stood up and brushed myself down. 'Goodbye,' I said. 'I hope the netball team has a shit year!'

Margot Walsh's mouth hung agape as I pushed my chair back with a flourish, stormed out of her office and power-walked to Evie's classroom, my arms marching like I was in the Japanese military.

'Evie!' I screeched, as twenty little heads turned around towards the door. 'Get your stuff, we're having a mummy–daughter day. Ice cream and shopping. Yummy! Now *move*!'

Evie slid her chair back obediently and jumped up. 'Bye,' she called over her shoulder, as Verity Watkins stared at me wide-eyed and open-mouthed, her navy-blue marker pen slipping down the whiteboard in a haphazard manner and leaving a tail on the 'Y' of the word Monday trailing down the board like a snake.

I home-schooled Evie for the last six weeks of term and we had a blast lying side-by-side on lilos in the pool, watching Disney movies and giggling conspiratorially when Sam moaned about having to go to school every day on the bus and asked, 'Why can't you get into a fight with a mum from *my* school?' Aside from reading the odd chapter of a book, I don't think we did a single minute of actual school work during that time, because for both of us, any kind of scholarly endeavour would have broken the little bubble we were in. Evie's bubble was called 'fun' while mine was most certainly called 'denial'. I didn't want to think back to those last few toxic days at St Cecilia's, and focused on the days ahead. As it happened, they tumbled rapidly into weeks and, once Alice had worked her magic and secured us a spot at Darley Heights for after Christmas, the start of term 1, it just seemed better to temporarily forget about school altogether.

It was six thirty in the morning when I eventually walked in through the front door, the sun now fully up, but too early for twitching curtains as I made my way up the drive. I tiptoed down the hall and threw my keys into the china bowl on the stone kitchen bench. They landed with a clink that was altogether too loud for my head.

Ted appeared in the doorway. 'Keys in a bowl. Isn't that ironic?' he said. If he'd been worried about my whereabouts all night, he didn't immediately show it. Instead, he opened his back and shoulders into a wide stretch, nonchalant. But when I looked at his dark-ringed eyes, they told me otherwise. His eyelids were puffy, like they'd been the morning after his father died and he'd cried through the night. He was aching inside, just like I was. He would have been pacing the floor waiting for me to come home.

I smiled at him, a sad smile. A lacklustre drawing up of the sides of the mouth. A smile that told him, 'I need you, Ted. Please put your arms around me, hold me. I need you to look after me.' But he turned away at the sight of it.

I pulled out a wooden stool and leaned forward to rest my upper body on the concrete slab. Watery Concrete, it was called, but up close, its drab grey surface was dry and porous like a pumice stone.

My eyes flicked up the hallway, towards the front room, where Sam and Evie were giggling. I could hear the excitable falsetto tones of *Alvin and the Chipmunks*.

'Are they okay?' I asked. 'The kids?'

He followed my gaze along the hall. 'They just woke up,' he said. 'They don't know you didn't come home, if that's what you're asking.'

I sat down at the bench. 'I'm sorry,' I said.

'What for?' Ted replied, flicking off the kitchen light he always left on for me when I was out late. He was obsessed with the notion I would trip on the stairs. 'For *him*, or for staying out all night?'

He was deflated, dehydrated. Zapped of energy and water and blood. I wanted to offer Ted some emotion then, to show him I understood, and I willed the tears to come, I really did. I tried for them, imagined them pooling in my eyes, spilling overboard from their fleshy sockets, all salty and warm, then rolling down my cheeks and plopping onto the stone benchtop. But they wouldn't come. They never did.

'We need to talk about this Amanda, and I'd suggest sooner rather than later,' he said.

His white T-shirt had risen up to expose his tanned chest. A belly that was not unlike Luke's when all was said and done. They weren't that dissimilar, really. Only Ted was just a little bit rougher around the edges, less kempt. He scratched the exposed flesh overzealously with his blunt, bitten nails, eager to talk, to get it settled, if it could be. It was his way to want to face things head-on, to *analyse*. But I couldn't deal with it – not so soon. I needed to clear my own head before I helped him clear his.

'No, Ted. The kids . . .' I said, gesturing towards the hall with my hand.

'They can't hear us.' He pushed the kitchen door shut as a precaution. 'Amanda, I need to know what happened last night. You need to tell me . . .' He faltered, his voice cracked.

'Don't you want to know about . . .' He took a deep breath. 'About *Zoe*?'

I felt my body stiffen, and my hands fly up to my ears and cover them like warm, fleshy earmuffs. Just like Evie did when she didn't want to hear something. It was childish, I know, but I didn't want to hear that name – *her* name. Not yet, and certainly not in my own home.

'Please, Ted, don't . . .'

'I need to know.' His voice was urgent now.

'Okay,' I shrugged. 'What do you want to know?'

He breathed in thoughtfully through his nose and out through his mouth and fixed his gaze on me.

'Was it . . .' he stopped and looked down at the floor, biting his lip, bracing himself. 'Was it *good*?'

I fixed my gaze on a chipped floor tile beside his big toe, the left one with the blackened toenail. It was a Scandinavian-looking tile, light grey in colour with four white leaves on it. It pissed me off, that chipped tile, ruining the flow of the pattern. It really needed to be fixed. I would need to call for a handyman – maybe one of those Hire A Hubby people. Oh my God, *Hire A Hubby*? Now that *was* ironic! I felt a sudden urge to giggle, but swallowed it down.

Ted sat down at the kitchen bench. He still hadn't made his tea, so I stepped towards the kettle and flicked it on, my back to him. Tea was Ted's answer to everything, a legacy from his British mother. There was no problem that could not be solved, Elizabeth Blackland always said, with a good cup of English Breakfast. *Well not this cock-up, Elizabeth. Oh no! This one won't be sorted by a bit of boiling water and an English Breakfast tea bag! Not enough tea in China to sort out this doozy!*

'Amanda!' Ted demanded, snapping me of my daydream.

I didn't turn to face him, just scooped a teaspoon of sugar into the mug that said 'World's Best Mum'. I couldn't remember if I'd put one or two spoons in already, so I added another, just to be sure. I was elsewhere. For the most fleeting of seconds, I was back inside the white, linen bedroom with the lights on low. Goosebumps rolled up my body, as if a finger was slowly tracing its way up my spine. The hairs on my arms stood on end, teasing me with coldness, until the kettle, at boiling point, let out a shrill whistle of relief, snapping me out of my momentary trance. I leant forward and released it from its clunky base with a click.

'Amanda?' Ted's voice slapped me in the back. Poor, loyal Ted, who had done something stupid and was filled with remorse, was still only concerned for me and whether or not I still loved him. I owed him more than evasion techniques.

'No!' I told him, solemnly. 'No, Ted, it wasn't good.' I shook my head for extra emphasis, like Evie did when we asked her, 'Did you eat the lolly, Evie?' despite having the wrapper in her hand and long blonde hairs clinging to the sticky pink residue left on her lips.

'It was drunken, it was unfamiliar, it wasn't . . .' I searched for a word that would suitably placate him, but I couldn't find it in my vocabulary, inside my jumbled mind. 'It wasn't . . . *right*.'

I looked up into the smoky, mirrored splashback, and saw Ted's reflection exhale. He pulled his hands together, intertwining his fingers and bending them back until he heard the joints responding with a click. He rolled his head one way and then the other, before looking to the skies, giving thanks to whatever, or whoever, was up there.

'There's another thing I need to know.' His hands were together in prayer, fingertips to his chin. 'I need to know if you had thought about it before last night?'

He ran a hand through his floppy golden hair, bracing himself, and took a breath that was so deep his nostrils flared. 'What I mean is, were you attracted to Luke Hampson before last night? When you first met him, I mean. I'm . . . what I'm asking is, have you been looking at him and wanting to fuck him all along?'

I closed my eyes.

'Amanda?' his voice was frail.

'Do you want tea?'

Ted's face flashed with anger.

'For fuck's sake, Amanda! I asked you a question!' he shouted. I didn't recognise that tone. 'Don't you think I deserve some answers?'

I tried again, met his gaze momentarily before it dropped downwards into deceit.

I shook my head firmly. *I did not eat the lolly.*

'No,' I said, and my sinuses hurt. 'I never thought about him like that before. I promise you.'

He stood up, opened his arms and I fell into his chest and let him wrap me up. I could feel the jagged rise and fall of his chest as he tried to hold back the tears, while my own breath remained steady, composed, like it always did: no emotion yielded, nothing revealed.

Yes it *had* been good. Yes I *had* enjoyed it. Yes, I had felt revived in his bedroom, alive. But I had been drunk. Very, very drunk. Did I want to see Luke again? No. I cringed at the way he had reeled me in, despised myself for falling willingly into those arrogant arms. Hated what the whole situation had done to Ted. Ted, who had watched me across that trestle table and had thought to himself, *Right, for once she can deal with her own shit* and who had, because of me, been pushed to do something so alien, so out of his comfort zone, he was now in agony because of it. Ted who had gone against his marriage vows and was eating himself up with remorse, who just wanted to be open and honest and be loved by me and to give love back. I closed my eyes, shut it all out.

'We need to talk about . . . about Zoe,' he said, pulling himself away from me and seating himself at the concrete island.

'No, Ted, I . . . I don't want to know, I can't . . .'

'You can't, so I'll tell you. We did it, Amanda. We did it and it was a huge mistake. A stupid, stupid mistake,' he said.

'No, no . . .' I shook my head.

I felt an unfamiliar sting in my eyes, my dehydrated eyeballs finding warm relief. But I blinked it back, swallowed it down.

'I only did it because it killed me to see you flirting with him like that. It killed me, Amanda. I knew you'd end up screwing him and that's why I did it. I felt like I'd been pushed to it. I felt like I didn't have another option.'

His lips trembled.

'It was over in a second and it meant nothing. It was awkward, horrible. . .'

'Stop, Ted.' I felt the panic rising. I couldn't deal with the images that were flooding through my mind. Did he *kiss* her . . . ? Did Zoe make Ted feel *good*?

'We were in the caretaker's . . .'

'STOP!' I spat, my brain choosing denial as its dominant emotion yet again. 'STOP, STOP!'

The shrill staccato shout was enough for Evie to call out.

'Mummy? Mum, are you okay?'

I took a breath. 'I'm fine darling, Daddy and I are just playing!'

Far from it.

'Stop, now,' I said, softer this time. 'Please. What's done is done. Can we just . . . *forget it*?'

'Yes,' he said. 'I want to forget it too. God, I love you, Amanda. I really do. But there are things we need to sort out. Things need to change.'

He was right, and we both knew it. Somewhere along the line we had become unstuck, I had become unstuck. But I wasn't ready to talk to him about it. I wasn't ready to own it. Not then. But I didn't know where to start, I was too tired. So I stood up and walked back to the kettle, watching Ted carefully in the trusty mirrored splashback, my reflective co-conspirator. It was always on hand to help me when I wanted to study the expressions on my family's faces or catch an illicit exchanged look between the kids, a roll of the eye from Ted. Exhausted and wrangling with himself, I watched as he allowed his head to rest in his hands.

'I know,' I said.

I kept my eyes on him as I reached up to the cupboard to my left and took out a miniature bottle of malt whisky. Then, deftly, I threw a slug inside my tea mug before popping it silently back inside the cupboard, Ted none the wiser.

'Mum!' Evie's feet came padding across the kitchen floor, her arms outstretched for a hug. It was as if she didn't notice Ted at the bench. Everything for Evie was Mummy.

'I missed you. Can I have a cuddle?' she said, squeezing in between me and the bench, wrapping her arms around me. She smelled like biscuits.

'Why are you still dressed as Britney Spears?'

I looked down at my crumbled clothes. 'Oh,' I told her. 'Mummy was so tired last night I didn't even bother to get into my pyjamas!'

Evie laughed. 'That's so silly, Mum! You look beautiful anyway.'

I smiled at her. So sweet and innocent and adoring. My beautiful girl. My daughter. Then the guilt again, like a steam train. *What are you doing?* I thought to myself, as she buried her head in my stomach. *Even by your standards this is early! Really, are you really going to drink this? At seven o'clock in the morning?*

I looked at Evie's head, her hair straggly from sleep, and picked up my mug, brought it to my lips. Smelled the woody aroma coming off the steam of the tea, breathed in its comfort. Felt the familiar tingling in my body, my blood fizzing excitedly, the pulsing in my neck as it called to me. But I couldn't do it, I just couldn't. Instead I turned, Evie still clinging to me, and quietly poured the contraband down the sink, hating myself for even thinking about it.

Chapter Fourteen
Alice

Transcript: The voice of Alice Daniels in the office of Dr Martha Davis.

It was eight o'clock when I woke up, which is so unlike me. I'm usually already in the kitchen making sandwiches and whatnot by six thirty. Pete would tell you I'm an 'up and at them' type of person, definitely not a lie-inner. After all, the early bird catches the worm! But no, the morning after the trivia night, not only did I lie in, but I woke up somewhere else entirely.

I seem to remember needing to move my leg, but it was trapped by a soft limb, a calf without hair, smooth and light like a marshmallow. Nothing like Pete's heavy cumbersome legs. Up higher, a thin arm, Lara's left, reached across my belly, a henna tattoo snaking up her wrist and a single solitaire next to a wedding band on the third finger of her hand. Her fingers were slim, and her knuckles jutted out, almost like she needed more flesh on them. Extraordinarily dainty fingers, not sturdy ones – if that's the best description – like mine. Fingers that might snap easily. I hadn't noticed how slender they were the night before, when they had beckoned me, sweetly, on to the dimly-lit deck.

I felt the urge to stretch, but I didn't want to startle my bedfellow and have to talk, so I didn't move, just lay rigid. Played sleeping lions. I stared up ahead, up at the non-descript white ceiling, and watched the fan whirr around slowly, spreading us in a cotton blanket of air, listened to its hum, like the purr of a cat. I inched my head to the right, taking in the sunlight streaming in from the French windows. The garden beyond was filled with toys, tons of them, that I hadn't noticed the night before: an easel with chalks spilling around the base, a hosepipe attached to a rocket launcher, a pink ball, a red bike resting on its side with a purple helmet swinging from the handlebars. Ridden through the gate and dropped there by Sienna en route to the house. A white-washed Wendy house with its own veranda, and a slide leading down to the lush green grass below, sat in the bottom right-hand corner of the yard. So many toys – way more than Freya and Lottie have (with them it's just books, books, books). I wondered if, had I seen these things the previous night, remembered that Lara was a mother, seen the house as the home of a small child and not a sort of adult play space, something would have clicked in me, woken me up to what I was doing, and I would have gone home. But it wasn't really so much a serious pondering as the moral side of my mind posing the dilemma, inviting me to feel guilty about what we'd done together.

Lara stirred and exhaled deeply, slowly, her chest rising and falling contentedly, as if she were in the midst of a beautiful dream. I shifted my head all gently to the left, looked at her from the side: the glowing skin, the plump lips, the long fine brown lashes, freckles like they'd been dotted on with a kohl pencil, the hint of pigmentation

– either a gift from her pregnancy with Sienna or from the sun, both forces she worshipped equally. The twins would have said she looked like Sleeping Beauty. A wisp of golden hair clung to her lip and I wanted to lift my hand and slowly pry it away but I didn't, because it was too intimate a gesture! Ha, can you believe that? Too intimate, after what we'd done the night before!

I closed my eyes, felt the thudding of the hangover, and let my mind drift back to what had happened in the hot tub and how it had made me feel, how intense it had been – how clamouring, how grasping – how desperate we had been for one another, and I felt myself begin to sweat all over, and I must have gasped then, or made some kind of noise as it all came into focus, because that's when Lara's eyes flashed open, her pupils widened and locked on mine, and she moved in, very slowly, to kiss me. A kiss that broke all of her rules, the rules she had imposed on herself and Luke: a forbidden kiss, a touch which suggested that, for her, this was more than a thing that had happened, casually, the night before. More than a sexual act to be forgotten and never repeated. The intimacy in those few seconds when her lips were on mine was astonishing, and I almost felt my body go limp with it, felt my eyes lock shut as if I was being pulled into a vortex that I couldn't, didn't want, to fight. But then reality kicked in and, like breath refilling empty lungs, the panic hit. I felt as though I was trapped in a tight dress with a broken zip, the fear of something, everything, setting in and regret taking refuge in my brain like a dirty squatter. I pulled away, pretended to cough I think, felt my cheeks colour, heard the confusion buzzing in my brain in tune with the cacophony of cicadas outside the bedroom window.

What the hell are you playing at? I asked myself. You are in bed with a mother at your daughter's school! You are an upstanding member of the school community! You organise cupcake stands and school drought appeals and raffle prizes and cheese and wine evenings! What would Brigitte Denner say if she knew about this? You have two young, impressionable girls at home! Girls who, when they see you, will hug you and you'll breathe in the smell of their strawberry blonde hair and Lottie, because she's the nosy one of the two, will ask, 'How was your party, Mum?' and you'll say, 'Fabulous, darling! It was so much fun, and the best thing is, we raised $24,850 for the new air conditioning system. Isn't it amazing what a fundraiser can do to help? How things can change when the community comes together?' That's the person you are, Alice! I told myself. You're . . . not . . . this woman.

The feelings were gut-wrenchingly familiar, exhumed from a place I had buried them years before. Before Pete. Feelings of shame, of denial, of what will people think? It was too much. Too much! I sat up and looked for my clothes, saw my hand shaking, felt the sweat collecting on my palm. I needed to get out of the room and into the fresh air.

Lara sensed my panic. 'Alice, are you okay?' she asked, reaching up to brush hair from my face – the same gesture I'd resisted doing to her. I turned my cheek away from her.

'I . . . I just don't feel comfortable about all of . . . this, if I'm honest,' I told her.

She laughed. It wasn't unkind. 'We had fun Alice,' she said. 'It was beautiful. We have . . . had a special connection. There is nothing to feel weird about.'

'Well, I do.'

'You shouldn't.'

We didn't speak for a moment and I used the awkward silence to scour for my clothes, but I couldn't seem to focus.

'Have you . . . have you ever done that before?' Lara asked me. 'With a woman?'

I gathered up my various pieces of clothing from beside the bed, still wet from the backsplash of the hot tub. Even after everything last night, I'd remembered to collect my stuff up and bring it inside. Can you believe that? Organised to the letter!

'No I haven't,' I lied.

'Me neither.' She hesitated, and then said, 'But I've wanted to. Luke and I, we're not quite . . . Well, something is missing, I think.'

Part of me felt like I might melt then, like a wax candle, fall in a crumpled mass at her feet. But then the real me kicked in. 'You know,' I said, in a voice that probably sounded quite prim. 'I'm very definitely not *gay*! I'm married.'

Lara smiled in a way that unnerved me.

'I know,' she said. 'I'm married too. But this felt very different. I wouldn't have tried to kiss you again just now if it hadn't. I mean, you know it's against our rules . . . mine and Luke's to kiss on the lips. I just . . . with you it just felt, it *feels* . . .'

She couldn't find the words, and I didn't give her any more time to.

'Yes, well,' I said, as if I was trying to excuse myself from a business meeting. 'Like I said, it's not really . . . me. I really should get back to the twins. And I can hear Luke walking about upstairs too, so . . .'

She held her hands up and smiled, with sad eyes. 'Sure,' she said. 'I understand.'

I wriggled into my Hogwarts skirt, threw on my grey shirt and did it up, realising halfway that I'd buttoned it unevenly. I was rather discombobulated, I was so desperate to get out of there. I picked up my shoes, offered a polite smile at the door. Brisk, business-like, but a smile nonetheless. After all, I hadn't wanted to be rude.

'Okay then,' I said.

Lara stared back at me, and it was like she was looking into my soul. 'Thank you, Alice,' she said, softly, and I felt both confusion and guilt, and somewhere deep inside me, longing.

I let myself out of the house and power-walked towards home, bathed in the cool change in the air. As I passed the playground on the corner of Mentira Drive – that's Amanda's street – I spied Robyn Adams, another year 1 mother. I mean, if there's any time you *don't* want to converse with another school parent, right? I tried to keep my head down, but she saw me – she has a neck like an ostrich, that one.

She called to me from the climbing frame and I realised I wasn't going to dodge the inevitable small talk. 'Hermione Granger! Well, well well! Don't tell me you're doing the walk of shame?' she winked.

'Oh no,' I laughed (probably a little too enthusiastically, in hindsight). 'I stayed at Amanda Blackland's last night. Her daughter is in the twins' class. I crashed out on her sofa bed – much easier than walking home in the dark.'

'I don't blame you,' Robyn said. 'It was a big night wasn't it? That's why I'm clutching this!' She waved her coffee cup at me. 'Well done for organising it all. Thank Christ it's cooler today – last night was steamy!' She fanned her chest with her hand and I remember thinking, *Oh, Robyn, if only you knew* just *how steamy!*

'It really was!' I mumbled and nodded a quick goodbye.

I quickened my pace after that, partly because I didn't want to bump into anyone else (because you can't even fart in Darley without someone knowing about it) but mainly because I wanted to get back to the girls. I had managed to shut them entirely out of my subconscious while I was inside the Hampsons' house, left them on the threshold when I went in, and now I had an overwhelming urge to get back to them. Mother's guilt had well and truly impregnated me, as it were, and I felt utterly wretched that I'd done something so . . . *unmotherly*.

Freya was on the front porch with a book in her hand. 'Mummy!' she called, running down the steps and throwing herself into my arms. I closed my eyes and breathed in her smell. Always the same, the Hello Kitty body spray she'd got for Christmas. Sweet, just like her. Lottie came running out behind her and eyed me suspiciously. 'Daddy said you stayed at Aunty Mandy's. You're supposed to tell us things like that! We didn't know where you were when we woke up!'

'I'm sorry, darling,' I said, wondering why Pete would have told them that. Maybe he just assumed that's where I'd gone. As if on cue, he appeared. 'There you are,' he said, shooting me a disapproving look. 'You should have let me know where you were. I had to message Ted to ask if you were back at their place. I was worried.'

I must have looked confused.

'He told me you and Amanda came home in a right state,' he said.

I felt my cheeks redden. 'Sorry,' I mumbled.

'Girls,' he said, ruffling Lottie's hair, then Freya's, 'pop inside and switch the kettle on for Mum, will you? I think Aunty Amanda forgot to make her a coffee.'

The girls skipped off and Pete nodded to the veranda chairs, indicating he wanted to chat. But I felt I needed to get things straight in my own head first. What was I going to say if he asked me whether I'd followed through with the trivia night swinging pact? I hadn't even been able to think about it on the way home because I'd been rumbled by nosy Robyn, and my head was so jumbled.

'Can I have a shower first?' I asked, gesturing down to my costume.

'In a minute,' he said. 'Please. We need to talk.'

'Of course.'

'Right, well, I assume you went to Amanda's because you were angry with me,' Pete said. 'But you don't need to be. I'm aware I was probably a little too flirtatious with Lara Hampson last night, and I do regret my actions, but I can assure you, absolutely nothing happened between us.'

He was so serious, so earnest, and I felt the sudden urge to laugh. I mean the fact he thought he even stood a chance with Lara in the first place, when, looking back, all of Lara's glances towards 'us' the previous night had been directed at me: the smiles, the 'accidental' brushes of leg under the table, the touch of the finger on parted lips! Poor, deluded Pete! Perhaps he *would* have gone with Lara if he'd had an opportunity, just like I had. It would have been too good an offer to pass up: a free pass, for one night only! But I also knew that, had he taken a step into that world, he would have woken up as equally out of his comfort zone as I had. He is no more able to be out of control than I am, and perhaps even less able to deal with unpredictability. He's a pipe and slippers man, as you know, a creature of habit.

'I mean, Lara went home anyway,' he told me, as if I didn't know. 'Nowhere to be seen. Um, not that I would have done anything with her if she *hadn't* . . .' he trailed off. 'Alice, what I'm trying to say is that I didn't mean what I said when we put our hands up. You know, that I would pick her and whatnot. It was very silly, and drunken and completely hypothetical.'

'I know, Pete,' I said, because in that moment my brain was so scrambled, I couldn't think of what else to say. 'It's okay, really.'

He sighed and nodded.

'Well, that's my confession. Now I'd like for you to be honest with me,' he said and I felt my stomach flip. 'I know you slept at Amanda's last night, but I need you to answer this: did anything happen between you and Miles?'

I looked him right in the eye then. 'No,' I told him. Well, it wasn't a lie, was it?

'Thank God!' Pete exhaled deeply and brought his hands together in prayer.

I looked at him then, so loyal, so apologetic, so grateful, and I felt an awful pang of guilt. I mean really, who was I to lie to him? Who was *I* to proclaim to be this upstanding person, this pillar of the community, this fundraising whizz, and yet come home and lie to my husband's face? But still, I couldn't tell him the truth about Lara. Maybe I would have done if it had been a man I'd slept with. But I wasn't quite ready to confess my antics with Lara to anyone, even myself.

'You're safe,' I said. 'I promise I did not sleep with any of the men at that table.'

And it was true, wasn't it?

'Alrighty,' Pete said with a relieved laugh. He pulled me into his arms so that the side of my head was resting uncomfortably on his chest. 'For a moment there I was worried! It would have been a little troublesome, wouldn't it, if we'd both ended up doing something . . . saucy!'

Troublesome. It was a fucking understatement. It makes me laugh now, to think about it, because it was such a Pete word.

I closed my eyes, stared at the blackness behind my eyelids. Pete kissed my head and I felt a sensation in my throat that tasted like disappointment.

'Well, my dear, I'm glad that's that sorted then.' He turned around and walked towards the garage. 'I'd better get cracking on the lawn.'

'Yes,' I said, looking out in front of me at the garden, at the frangipani tree that held so many of my secrets within the branches and the jasmine that creeped its way up the railings of the fence, pulling tight my deepest desires in the twists of its boughs.

Pete handed me a brush. 'Are you okay to do the porch?' he asked.

And I thought, Yes, I will sweep! Sweep it all under the carpet. Chuck it in the bin. Bury it like it never happened. Make it all nice and neat again so that people think it's perfect. Because nothing can ever come of me and Lara. How can it? I'm a wife and a mother and I'm the events chairperson of the Darley Heights parent-teacher committee!

I turned to my husband, felt my shoulders straighten. 'You'll need to get the strimmer out too,' I told him. 'And give the lilly pillies a good watering, they're looking a little brown. I'll just go and freshen up.'

And as the shower water flowed down the contours of my body, over my breasts, between the goosebumps on my skin, I thought of Lara, and the colour of her eyes, the softness of her skin, the vein in her neck that had pulsed as we stood face to face in the hot tub.

I opened my mouth and let the water in, to wash it out, to cleanse me of my own guilt, of the saliva from another tongue.

'Come on, slowcoach,' Pete had called from outside the bathroom with a sharp knock. 'The garden isn't going to weed itself!'

'Just a moment,' I told him, and I remember watching as the dirty water spiralled down the plughole.

I suppose we had an untraditional start, Pete and I. He was my accountant, of all things. Well, I say *accountant* like I had a lot of money, but what I really mean was he did my tax for me. I was working full time for Creative Occasions during the week, but I also had a lot of freelance clients in the evenings and on weekends, and it was hard working out what cash was coming in from where, and Pete was a friend of my work colleague Don.

'I know a good accountant,' Don said. 'Pete Daniels. He's a good bloke. I'll dig out his digits for you.'

I remember walking into Pete's office, a drab, concrete place, totally devoid of personality and seeing him leaning up against the photocopier in grey suit pants and a white shirt open a little at the top, laughing about something with his PA, and I thought, *that man has a lovely, warm smile*. He wasn't earth-shattering, not a male model by any stretch of the imagination, but not *bad* looking, and with a lovely sort of warmth about him. As it turned out, Pete was friendly, and funny and clever, too. He was a real climber at this company, and when a man is good at his job, it's a very attractive thing, don't you think?

I went to see him mid-week, with a giant envelope full of receipts, organised in alphabetical order according to the supplier. He seemed to find it funny that his new client, who organised rich women's baby showers or sorted out proposal dinners with harbour views for the banking elite, would have such a brazen approach to claiming tax.

'I'm an events planner,' I told him. 'A creative.'

He smiled, fingered a David Jones receipt, and said, 'Well, no offence, but you're certainly creative with your finances. I'm afraid you cannot claim for a pair of three-hundred-dollar Ray-Ban sunglasses!'

And I was a bit uppity at that, as you can imagine. 'Yes I can,' I insisted. 'I work outside all day with my clients. If I don't wear glasses then I'll be claiming for macular degeneration in ten years' time, and that would be an even greater drain on the civic purse, wouldn't it?'

He smiled, intrigued. 'Go on.'

'The fact is, I'm at baby showers and weddings outside in the blazing sun every day of the week and I have to look the part. I can hardly turn up to a celebrity party in a pair of Target sunnies, can I?'

He looked at me as if to say, 'Are you for real?'

'It's true,' I said. 'My friend Belinda is an entertainment journalist and she always claims for sunglasses every year because she interviews people outside, so . . .'

Pete shrugged, flipped a piece of paper over and wrote, 'Designer Sunglasses' in black ink, all the while with this amused look on his face. 'What else are we claiming for?' he said, shuffling the papers. 'Handbags? Couture dresses? Cosmetics?'

Oh, it was supremely sexist, I know. But I was younger then and probably less offended by things like that. The point is, I thought he was funny – which I'd always considered a non-existent quality in accountants (accountants and funeral directors – humourless, the lot of them) – and at that point in life, I really needed funny. My previous relationship had broken me, and he was there. Right place, right time, right sentiment, right level of humour.

'What about my ticket to the Sydney Comedy Festival? Can I claim that? I assume you'll be appearing?' I asked.

He laughed. 'Touché!'

I took my hand out of my lap then, to sign the form, and he clocked the diamond ring on the third finger of my right hand. I remember the look on his face when he saw it. He actually looked gutted, and he'd only met me five minutes before. I think for him, the connection was instantaneous.

'That's a beautiful ring,' he said, his manner turning brisk. 'When's your wedding?'

'Oh,' I said, waving my hand about. 'I'm not getting married. This is my grandmother's engagement ring. She died last week, and this is the only finger it fits on. I like to wear it for sentimental reasons.'

'That's so great,' he grinned, before realising his error. 'Err, I mean it's great you're not engaged, not that your grandma passed away.'

I laughed out loud then, and told him I understood what he meant, and there was no offence taken. He smiled with relief, and I did think to myself, *This guy is sweet, I could really date him.* And so I did. And on our first date, he took me to dinner and to the cinema, as if we were a couple of 15-year-olds, not 27-year-old adults. When he kissed me on the steps of my apartment, he said, 'Is it okay if I kiss you?' which was hardly a moment of intense passion, but it was charming, and I felt respected. And the kiss was lovely and gentle with maybe a little too much tongue, I seem to recall, but we worked on that quite a lot over the next few weeks until we found our groove. And do you know what? Maybe it *hadn't* been New Year's Eve fireworks in that drab office, but that was fine with me, because I didn't want to get burned. I didn't want passion, because passion hurt. Pete was safe. He was everything that, at that point in my life – battered, bruised and lovelorn – I felt I deserved. I thought to myself, *Here is a man who treats you like a duchess, a man who wants to see you happy. A man who loves you for the person you are and for all of your flaws. You deserve that, after everything.*

The sex was fine. God that sounds awful, I mean it was perfectly good, adequate, you know. Enjoyable, even. And the fact was, he wanted me, wanted to nurture me. He wanted to cook me healthy meals and to talk about my day. He bought me flowers and chatted on the phone to my mother. He put up with my closeness to Amanda, and the fact she acted like he wasn't good enough, like she felt we wouldn't go the distance, the fact she didn't invest in him like perhaps she had his predecessor, who knows. He ignored it and pandered to her. He didn't just buy *me* tampons, he even went out for some for her once! And I think that's quite a solid indicator of a good bloke, isn't it?

Right from the start, Pete was content to let me steer the ship, understood I didn't feel the need to 'discuss' our romance, that I wasn't the kind of person to analyse every cross word or happy moment. He didn't whisper sweet nothings, nor expect them back. Well, a few times he tried, but he knew I didn't like it. I'm a doer, and not a talker – in relationships, that is. Maybe that's why I've ended up on your couch, who knows. The point was, I started to *like* myself as Pete's other half, to like the person I was with him – the woman who was functional, who made things happen, who was in control. Not the one I'd had glimpses of all too recently beforehand, the one who cried herself to sleep, the one who was needy, the one with no self-worth.

And more than this, Pete fitted that image I wanted to convey to other people. I liked the way other people loved him. He knew everyone, and I mean *everyone*! He went to Shoal Grammar, which you must know, right? Shoal, on the north shore? And that meant he was part of the most amazing old boy network. I'd tell someone I was dating Pete Daniels, and they'd say 'Danno? Went to Shoal? He's mates with my cousin. I love Danno, he's such a good bloke!' or 'Pete Daniels? You're on to a winner, he earns a packet!' And I'm not going to lie, I loved that everyone had this image of Pete as a top guy and a successful one to boot. Like I said, success is attractive, isn't it? I don't think that's a vain thing to say, or a materialistic one. Facts are facts, and they're the same the world over. I mean look at Donald Trump's dating history! Not that I'm saying I'd go for Donald myself, but you get what I mean, don't you? Success is an aphrodisiac, and so is popularity.

And I thought in those early days, maybe you don't love him yet, not in a Christian Grey way like I said before, but you can *learn* to love him. And I don't know how long it took exactly, but I did learn to love the man, and like in that famous quote from *Captain Corelli's Mandolin* that every woman and her dog picks for weddings these days – including us, I might add – our branches did become intertwined so deeply that it was inconceivable that we should ever part. Just perhaps without the bit about love being a 'temporary madness'.

When we got married, Pete told the story from when we met, about the ring and my grandma, and that became part of our schtick. And the wedding, in case you are wondering, was perfect (and I'm not just saying that because I organised it), me in a white Vera Wang gown, Pete in Armani, two hundred guests watching us, telling us we made the ideal couple. Except Amanda.

On the morning of my wedding, she dragged me into the bathroom at my mother's house and said to me, 'Alice, are you sure?'

I pretended to be shocked, all, 'What on earth do you mean?' But I knew. I knew immediately that she was asking me if I was sure about Pete because of Jenny.

'I just want to make sure,' she said. Her voice was gentle. 'You can't go back on this very easily if you change your mind. Are you sure you love him?'

I snapped at her then. 'Of course I love him! Otherwise I wouldn't be here.'

'I know. I just want to make sure that you're over her . . . that Jenny isn't . . .'

'Why are you talking about Jenny?' I asked pompously. 'This is my wedding day – to Pete!'

Amanda came to then. 'Of course. I'm sorry Al. Forget I said anything. You look beautiful, just stunning. I'm so proud of you!'

I look back at photos now and the fact is, I *did* look terrified when I walked up the aisle. But who isn't terrified when they're trying not to trip in a dress with a train and a veil and sweating like a bastard in the sunshine? And it was a frig of a hot day.

Looking back, maybe Jenny was in my head, but on my wedding day, I didn't want to hear it. To everyone else,

Pete and me *were* the perfect pair – both with uber-successful careers, a white picket fence and eventually, Freya and Lottie, both little prodigies with their early speech and their rapid toilet training. Lottie was out of nappies at eighteen months, can you believe that? Freya was a little slower in that respect, but she was the early reader, you see. And it's not as if that stuff is the be-all and end-all, but you have to understand that when you're seen in a certain light, you get used to it, don't you? I mean, I imagine you like telling people you're a doctor, don't you?

Let me tell you this, Dr Davis. Our marriage may never have been Elizabeth Taylor and Richard Burton, but it has worked. For me, for Pete, for Freya, for Lottie, for *us*. Sure, it might lack passion at times, but that also means we don't have those blazing rows that raise your blood pressure and hurt your heart. Or the tears that are hot and painful and leave a burning in the back of your throat. We're devoid of the exhausting aches and twists and jealousy that eats away at you like a big cat eating a carcass – the kind that ends up giving you cancer or sends you mental from second-guessing yourself. Perhaps desire is overrated! Don't you think? There's a thin line between passion and annihilation, never mind between love and hate.

Do I love him? Isn't that evident? I love him wholeheartedly. It's a deep, respectful love built on the solid foundation of the years we have spent together, the home we have built, the family we have made – and yes, I'll admit it, on the image we have created. The image that serves the vanity of both of our egos to upkeep.

And that was the thing that teased me and tugged at the membranes of my consciousness as I dug in the garden the morning after trivia night. The thing that, along with the sunshine and my thumping hangover, made my brow sweat profusely, and my heart skip a beat when my mind danced between the night before and Monday at the school gates: how would I face my peers, the parent-teacher committee, Brigitte Denner, the school principal, the *neighbours*, if it somehow became public knowledge that I had not only cheated on my husband, but with a woman? I certainly wasn't prepared for that eventuality! But as I wrenched out the prickly Canada thistle roots with my shovel, I thought to myself: *You have it all in hand.* After all, Lara would never tell – that was the number one rule of swinging, according to her – and that meant Luke would never let anyone in on the secret, either. I knew I was safe in that respect. And Amanda might have been pickled in elderflower gin, but she knew how to keep a secret, because God knows I'd trusted her with a few of them over the years, although admittedly, none of this enormity. So, I really believed I had nothing to worry about. It seemed I only had my own conscience to grapple with. Well, at least until later that night, when Amanda forwarded me the text message.

The text message. Gosh, it was a shock. Because that was when I realised that exposure was not only a possibility, but a foregone conclusion, and that it had the potential – no, the *surety* – of sending my perfectly balanced world into an unsalvageable tailspin. And that was when we decided that between us, we would have to do something drastic about Victoria.

Part Two: Revenge

Chapter Fifteen
Zoe

From: Zoe.m8kin79@realworld.com.au
To: pho_e_b_wallis@zapmail.com
Subject: The truth

Sunday ended badly. Like, fucking badly. You know that feeling when everything is postcard-perfect and then, like a windowpane, it shatters into tiny fragments that you can't piece together, even if you get on your hands and knees and collect every single one? Like someone upstairs is saying, *Oooh aren't you having fun?* and, *Isn't everything in your life looking nice and rosy? I'm just going to look at all your perfectly set out things on the table, and yank the cloth out from underneath. Not inch it out, not take away the lovely things neatly stacked on top nice and slowly to ease the blow a little, but let's tug so hard that the whole table collapses, bringing with it the brightly arranged flowers, the water, the food, the life*. Well, that was the evening after the trivia night.

Miles and I got up and we were all sort of loved up after we'd shagged for the first time in forever without it being a mechanical, baby-making bonk, and it was blissful. We were feeling more romantic than we'd been in literally years, because we'd had a taster of what we had to lose and it had made us both really emotional. The sunlight streamed in through the window, the kookaburras laughed up in the trees, Freddie giggled as he pushed himself on the swing, his little legs rising and falling as he propelled himself higher in the air. Even the *toast* was perfect when it popped out of the toaster – not black on the edges, not half soft, half brown, but caramel all over, like Mum used to make it. And it was honestly like something from *The Waltons*. I half expected a bluebird to fly in through the window and land on my hand like I was Mary Poppins. I actually found myself wondering if perhaps what happened with Ted was a bloody big blessing in disguise, because it had made me and Miles realise how precious what we have together actually was. Miles kept pulling me to him for hugs and asking if I was okay (if *I* was okay, after everything I did!) and kissing the top of my head. A couple of times I caught him staring into space, his eyes distant, but then I would touch him and he would turn to me and smile. He'd turn that frown upside down! He knew I was racked with regret, he knew it. But he was willing to try to forget. He could see I was sorry and how much I loved him and he didn't want to ruin it. I watched him sipping his coffee on the deck and told myself, *Today is the start of forever. We can make it. We're okay. We're not perfect, but we used to be and we can get back there, and most importantly, we want to.*

The whole day was good. We went to Bunnings to get some Polyfilla for the bedroom wall that had the fuck-off big hole in it where Miles had punched it, and Freddie and I cried with laughter when Miles dropped a spanner on his foot. When he clocked us holding our bellies, doubled over, he started too, until we were all literally dying, standing there in the hammer aisle, or whatever it's called.

Then the woman came over and asked if everything was okay, and Miles told her, *I think I've just annihilated my sixth toe* and he took off his sock and she actually screamed when she saw it. It was so good to see him laughing like that, for us all to laugh together.

Later, in the afternoon, the three of us squished on the sofa and watched *Jumanji*, the original one from like, 1995, and then, when Freddie was in bed, Miles and I curled up together and watched another film – two in one day, so indulgent. I was lying in the curve of his arm, when I saw a flash on the coffee table in front of me, and heard a ping, like the echo from a cymbal smashing together. I wriggled free from Miles's arm gently and leaned forward to grab my phone. I was feeling pretty sleepy but thought *I'll just read this and then we'll go to bed.* And then came the moment – the shattering of the glass, the clattering of the prettily organised crockery crashing to the floor as the universe flicked its wrist carelessly.

That's how it was when you died, Phoebe. Like someone just walked into a normal day and sliced it in half, twisted it, gutted it. Decided with the flip of a coin to deal me the cruellest blow of all – the loss of my sister and best friend.

I still can't believe it's been three years, can you? I'm still waiting for you to contact me, give me a sign, let me know you're okay. We used to say if one of us died, we would menace one another for eternity, but you've given me nothing, not the fateful cheep of a bird, a meaningful flash of lightning, a rainbow, a white feather on the back doorstep. Why can't you do it for me, Phoebs? For Mum and for Dad? I won't go on about it, cos you know how I feel, and I don't want to offend you in the spirit world, or wherever you are. You always were such a sensitive soul – too gentle, too troubled, for this big wide world.

That medium, the one with the blonde bob and the English accent, said you were travelling, throwing out shards of light all over the place like a glitter ball, and so I always like to imagine you in a different place with every email I send. On a boat on the River Seine, or sweeping through some Mediterranean sky like a paraglider. Maybe balancing atop the statue of Christ the Redeemer in Brazil or the Statue of Liberty, or jamming with Bowie in a maze somewhere, sort of like *Labyrinth*! Miles reckons you're popping some pills and doing some bonkers dancing in Ibiza. How funny is that? He misses you too, you know. You were always the little sister he never had. I see you more with the wind in your long hair and your arms outstretched on a mountain like Julie Andrews in *The Sound of Music* (and didn't we give that movie some mileage when we were kids?). But for some reason I always come back to the damn bridges.

I pushed Miles away after you died. Held him at arm's length. Pushed everyone away, tried to fill my grief with the pursuit of new life. He said to me, a few days after we heard the news, as your body flew home from England to Australia in the freezing hold of a Qantas jet with no one to hold your hand, *Zoe, why don't we have a baby?* and I'd snarled at him that I couldn't replace you. *It's not like replacing a cat,* I cried. He didn't get it. No one did. One of Freddie's friend's mothers told me at day care pick-up, with her hand limp on mine, *I know how you feel!* A gesture that ticked a box, made her feel she'd supported the grieving peer. *I was just devastated when my aunt died! Your aunt? YOUR FUCKING AUNT? Oh sweetheart, that doesn't even touch the surface!* I wanted to shout in her face, *I'm talking about my SISTER! The person who shared parents and hand-me-downs and I've-started-my-periods and* E.T. *on repeat. Who got the same nose with the tiny slope and the same curvy hips and annoying hair kink that will only go with a hardcore squeeze of the GHDs. Your aunt, you said?*

Poor Miles. I punished him for not knowing exactly what I was thinking, not 'getting' my grief, because he'd never lost anyone before. And how meanly, how *keenly* I wanted him to lose someone so that he would know, so that he wouldn't keep saying the wrong things, like, *Why don't you try talking to someone?* or, *Let's put the renovations on hold until you're better,* as if my grief was like the flu. Then the time, about a month after you left us, when he suggested we should plan a night away and not think about you! He may as well have asked me not to breathe! I was revolted, sickened that he couldn't get inside my brain and see my despair. I understood later, when the anger and devastation had abated to tolerable levels, that he was doing everything he could to help me, but at the beginning, he just couldn't do right for doing wrong. I suppose like it was trying for another baby. I blamed him for it because I couldn't control it – he usually had all the answers. Why not now?

You'd have told me to stop being such a bitch and you'd have been right. How *could* he have known? How *could* he?

No one understands what it's like to lose a sibling and to lose them young, when they have so much of their life left to lead. How can anyone imagine the agony of hearing the anguished voice of the person you love the most, bar your child and maybe your husband, and registering they are standing on the precipice of a bridge with a 245-foot drop that's 17,132 kilometres away, and not be able to stop them from climbing over the edge and plummeting way, way down into the murky, freezing waters below? And they *were* freezing, Phoebs, weren't they, because it was January there, and I was complaining of the heat while you complained of the cold! How can another person, even the one who is meant to understand you best, know the feeling of the line going dead and the agony of listening to a loved one's voicemail recording over and over, fifty-odd times, praying they'll pick up, hoping they've just passed out cold beside a tree next to the bridge, the notorious Clifton Suspension Bridge, suicide hotspot, and hadn't actually done what they'd threatened to? The agony of waiting to find out if the phone was dead, or they were, and then finding out from the shrill scream of your mother down the phoneline in Brisbane that one of the two people she gave birth to was, in fact, gone? To know there is nothing you can do to help, that it is all completely out of your control?

I'm sorry Phoebs. I didn't mean to be so intense. Or to make you feel bad. Let's get back to the Sunday evening. To the sofa. To my phone. To the moment I realised I might not get away with my stupid indiscretion quite so easily. The tablecloth moment.

My phone informed me I'd been added to a WhatsApp group consisting of myself, Amanda, Alice and Lara. It had been started by Alice, who must have got my details from the 1S contact form the school office emailed round to parents and carers at the start of term. It was entitled 'Big Problem', and immediately my blood turned cold, my stomach burned, and my heart began to palpitate like I was strapped into a seat on a passenger plane plummeting rapidly towards the sea.

Chapter Sixteen
Amanda

I didn't read the text message for an hour. And in some ways, it was a relief to have been blissfully unaware while we ate dinner.

It had been a pretty normal Sunday afternoon, considering. As normal as a Sunday afternoon can be when you and your partner have both had sex with someone else, and you're trying to act like nothing's wrong for the sake of the kids.

But kids are more clued up than we give them credit for.

Ted was lost in thought as he delved into the KFC bag and handed out the contents. Kids Fattening Centre, as Evie called it. He still had dark circles under his eyes.

'KFC dinner. Best day ever,' Sam sang, grabbing the brown paper bag from Ted and dragging out a chunk of battered chicken. Evie squeezed a large dollop of ketchup into the red and white cardboard box with the Colonel smiling out at her. The smug bastard.

'Dad, why are you looking so sad?' she asked, as she tucked into her chicken burger.

Ted looked up and smiled. 'I'm not, Evie-bear,' he lied.

'Because mum drank too much wine last night,' Sam replied. I had winced at that. I didn't want him to think that his mother was a wino. I was very careful to hide that stuff from both of the kids. But like I said, children are clued up. Sam wasn't my naive 6-year-old boy any more, but a high school student with oily skin and bum fluff on his top lip.

'Do you still love each other?' Evie asked.

Ted and I glanced at one another.

'Yes,' said Ted, and his voice caught on the single syllable.

'Of course, Evie darling,' I sung, a little too enthusiastically. 'We love each other so much, don't we, Daddy?'

Ted bit his lip and nodded.

But even though it was horrible, gut-wrenching, I felt in some way we were heading in the right direction. We both cared. Ted still loved me, and that was something to be relieved about. But there was another nagging thought in my head. I couldn't shake off the image in my mind that kept flashing up, of Victoria on the dance floor. She had seen me, I knew that, because our eyes met as she stood stock-still amid the jumping parents, bending and stretching their arms into letters, as I tottered down the steps at the side of the stage and onto the dance floor. Had I been buttoning up my shirt as I walked down? Would I have been that stupid, that unsubtle? I couldn't quite remember. She looked exactly the same as she had only a few weeks previously – the change in her financial situation hadn't softened her. She still had the same rigid posture, proud ownership of her six-foot frame. The body of the girl who was bullied at school for being too tall, now the bully herself, and dressed the part in her pink tweed skirt and her button-up cardigan. A real life Mean Girl.

If it had been nothing more than a look of recognition, she would perhaps have blinked and turned away, or smiled at me with thin lips before dissolving back into the crowd. But she didn't do that. And that's the bit I do recall – even if the rest of it is a tad blurry – her face. Her open mouth, with a smirk playing on the lips, a knowing half-smile that hadn't reached the eyes, like a kindly one might. A smug smile that seemed to suggest she knew exactly how to destroy me.

I knew my hypothesising wasn't doing much for the alcohol-induced fear, so I tried to talk myself out of my paranoia. I took myself off for a long shower after dinner and washed my hair, pulling at the ends roughly as I combed the conditioner through. I pulled so hard that my scalp hurt – a good pain, a deserving pain. Penance for being a bad girl. I wonder now if I'd known somewhere inside that the text message was going to throw my world into disarray, and that I'd just tried to put off the sucker punch I was about to receive. Because I took my time there, washed my body, shaved my legs, just stood with my head up towards the shower head, let the water pummel down on me until it turned cold. Stood on the bath mat, watched my wet feet make perfect shapes on the soft grey towelling, watched them for a minute more, the water dripping down my legs. The cool air hit as I stepped out of my watery cocoon, and the fear hit with a vengeance. What was I worried about? I didn't exactly know.

I felt miles better after I'd poured a medicinal gin and tonic (in a mug so Sam couldn't accuse me of drinking too much) and settled on the couch. Thoughts of Victoria vanished from my head. Perhaps it was the fact we were sitting together in the living room, and it could have been any other weekend hanging out as a family, and not the day after I put a dagger in my relationship. We put on Bear Grylls and Ted ruffled Sam's hair with his hand, and looked almost carefree if you ignored the heavy eyes. At one point he looked over at me and offered me a weak semi-smile, as if to tell me it would all be okay, and I thought, *If this is the worst it can get, then I will survive. I can swallow it down, and I know he can too, and we can just get on with life. Look at us, watching TV together as a family, without a care in the world!*

When Luke popped into my head again, I sort of shoved him away, closed off the images before they could drive me insane. I told Victoria to fuck off in my head. I sipped my drink, booked an evening yoga class, suddenly felt almost righteous about how well I was dealing with everything.

Then Ted said, 'Your phone beeped while you were in the shower.'

The only way I can explain how I felt in that moment was knowing. I knew it was going to be her. That feeling you get when you fire off a message to the wrong person, or cc someone into an email that's about them. That plummet. That cold sweat. The kind of realisation that makes you sit bolt upright in bed.

I picked up my phone with shaking hands.

Victoria didn't beat around the bush. HELLO, AMANDA, she wrote. DID YOU HAVE FUN LAST NIGHT? ALICE ASKED ME TO TAKE SOME SNAPS FOR THE SCHOOL FACEBOOK PAGE, AND I HAPPENED TO GET SOME RATHER INTIMATE FOOTAGE OF YOU, ZOE AND ALICE. IT'S AMAZING WHAT YOU CAN GET WHEN YOU SNEAK ABOUT! I'LL HAVE TO BE CAREFUL THEY DON'T POP UP ONLINE, WON'T I? XOXO

I felt as if I'd just stepped into an ice bath. I pulled my hand up to my chest and got off the sofa with jelly legs, trying to make my way to the bedroom, to solitude, without collapsing. I sat on the bed and held my breath as I watched the three little grey dots dancing inside the speech bubble as she prepared to strike again. But this time she didn't send words, but photos. The first had been taken from under the bottom of the stage curtain. My back was to the camera, but you could see it was me because I was looking to the side, an expression on my face of euphoria, like a kid taking the first lick of a Bubble O'Bill ice cream. Luke's entire face was visible over my shoulder, and you could clearly see his hand – his left, the one with his wedding band on, no less – gripping my short-skirted arse.

The second photo popped in right behind it. This time of Pete, Alice and Lara, sitting close together, in a semi-circle around the table. At first, I wondered what was so incriminating about it – they just seemed to be chatting, Pete with his hands up in the air, telling a story about something fascinating to do with accountancy, probably – but then, when I realised, it caught my breath. It reminded me of one of those photos where someone's arm is placed awkwardly in the snap, so it makes it look like a woman inadvertently has a giant penis, or something, but you don't get it until you actually *see* it, as it were. And 'it' was Lara's hand, right up Alice's skirt under the table, like Sam's hand in the KFC bag and a Bubble O'Bill look on *her* face this time. I felt my cheeks flush. It was embarrassing, intrusive, unkind. And all the more grotesque because it showed Alice and Lara enjoying themselves while Pete carried on, oblivious. I felt a flash of anger towards Alice. How could she have been so stupid? But then almost immediately realised my outrageous double standard.

I dropped my phone on the side like a hot potato, disgusted with the content, and felt myself rocking as I sat on the edge of my marital bed with its happy, floral duvet cover. A minute later, the phone pinged again, a gap big enough to suggest the sender had hesitated to press the green button, knowing the impact it might cause. I took a breath, picked it up and clicked on the photo. Number three was the pièce de résistance. Three, the magic number. Third time lucky. Three times a charm! It was taken from the door of the broom cupboard and showed them up against the wall. The man struggling to carry the weight of the woman, but undoubtedly enjoying himself wholeheartedly. *Bubble O'Bill.*

I threw the phone down on the bed, felt myself crumple in a heap on the mattress as the photo of Ted and Zoe imprinted itself on my brain. A Polaroid moment. The moment I heard Princess Diana had died. When Sam and Evie were born. When I said 'I do' to Ted. When Ted fucked Zoe in a cupboard. I knew this image would never leave me now, and Victoria knew that too. It was why she had hesitated – not for long, but for a minute at least – perhaps indicating there was something human about her after all. But then, really, there wasn't, because she'd hit green for go. And anyway, how could there be anything even remotely human about a woman who had followed a group of people with a phone in her hand, surreptitious, invisible? Who enjoyed her role as documentary maker, as voyeur? No different, really, to people who go to the park to watch other people have sex.

I lay back on the bed for a while, stared up at the ceiling. Everything I'd told myself about not caring if Victoria exposed me, about it not being the worst thing that could happen, had all been a whopping, bare faced lie to calm myself down. All I could think of was how I *couldn't* be exposed – not at another school. I couldn't go through the ridicule, the embarrassment, the sniggers, the side-eyes, the transformation out of my chrysalis not into a social butterfly but a social leper. And how, if it happened, I wouldn't just have to deal with being seen as a sex-crazed husband-stealer, but also a woman to be pitied, whose husband had banged another mum in the putrid caretaker's cupboard. I didn't know which was worse. I didn't want Ted to face that ridicule, either. Or Evie. Or Sam. Because gossip like this in a community like Darley Heights transcended schools. The thought made my stomach throw spasm after spasm at me as punishment.

I must have lay there for an hour, the familiar hum of Ted's voice outside in the living room. As I stared at the ceiling, I went through the full spectrum of emotions: fear, self-loathing, grief, jealousy, anger – at myself, at Ted, at Zoe, at Victoria . . . until the dice stopped on the one it always settled on: determination. After all, you don't survive being the child of an alcoholic without being steely.

I sat up and felt my shoulders straighten, my head raise, the way it had done as I'd marched from Margot Walsh's office to Evie's classroom the day we had left St Cecilia's. *Who was Victoria Day to treat me like this? To treat my husband and my family this way?*

Evie didn't deserve to be uprooted again, to have a third school uniform in the space of as many months. No, it wasn't going to happen. Not to my family. Not again. And certainly not because of something that had fuck-all to do with Victoria Day.

I picked up my phone again and messaged Alice, realising she would know precisely what to do, since she could talk herself out of a paper bag, and, as I clicked send, I thought to myself, *There's no way you're getting away with this, Victoria. You think you're so tough? You don't know who you're messing with!*

Chapter Seventeen
Alice

Transcript: The voice of Alice Daniels in the office of Dr Martha Davis.

God, it was truly awful. Really it was. I remember that moment, as clear as day. Pete and I were in the middle of our usual Sunday evening routine when I got the message. The twins had just gone to bed, which was a relief as I just wanted to have some down time, and I was serving up the last of the lasagne I'd cooked on Friday, with a bit of salad, foregoing the usual glass of red. Pete was scrolling through Netflix for a good doco, and he'd literally just said the words, 'There's a good one here about a lesbian sex scandal,' – I'm not even *joking* – when my phone beeped at me. That was the message from Amanda.

It said, VICTORIA KNOWS. SENDING PICS NOW.

At that point, I thought, *Yeah! Photos, my arse! If you've got photos, then I'm Gianni Versace*, but then the photo arrived which clearly showed Lara and I at the table at trivia night, and well, how shall I say it? There was a hand up my skirt that clearly wasn't Pete's.

My immediate reaction was acute embarrassment. I wondered who'd taken it, whether it was Victoria or someone else, and how they'd got low enough to snap it from that vantage point, as in, on the ground. I thought, *Good God! If one person was able to see what was happening under the table, how many others saw it, too?* I also remember being outraged about how another woman could be so cruel. I mean, I know the woman was mourning the loss of her dog and everything, but the rest of the shit that had happened to her, with Nico and his job, was hardly Amanda's fault, and it was certainly not mine!

But it's a sad fact that there are women who exist who not only *don't* champion other women, but who actually want to see them go down in a raging fireball. Thankfully, they'd been infrequent extras in my world up until that point, but I knew they existed. You see them in the movies, and they're usually the unstable villain, you know, the psychotic blonde who's gorgeous, but who makes it her life's work to ensure the steady existence of their homely nemesis crumbles like a slice of passion fruit pavlova. They don't allow the protagonist to live their white-picket-fence life and make mistakes, but are hell-bent on exacting revenge for the smallest wrong they feel might have been done to them.

I felt I couldn't breathe. I was petrified! Petrified that everyone would know what I'd done that night. I remember putting my hand to my chest and feeling the thud of my racing heartbeat under my palm. I was so flustered, I told Pete I'd just remembered the pool needed cleaning and could he just pop outside and fish out the two ice-cream wrappers that were floating on the surface before they got sucked in to the filter? And he said, 'Sure thing,' and he did it, and I stood there grinning at him like I was some kind of Stepford wife, until he lolloped out of the back door and started rummaging around in the shed for the pool net. Then I flopped down on the sofa and looked at the photo again, just to check it was still as incriminating as it had been two minutes before, and it still was, and I sat and rocked a bit, thinking, *I actually can't breathe.* In fact, for the first time in my life, I wondered if I was going to have some kind of panic attack. I couldn't collect my thoughts rationally. It was the shock, I think. My amygdala was flashing like a siren, shouting, *What if other people know? What if Tansie Wright knows, because she was a Mean Girl too, and her and Victoria already seemed inseparable? And what the hell will I do if Tansie tells anyone, because God knows she's about as discreet as a drag queen at Mardi Gras.*

I grabbed the brown paper bag the twins' McDonald's meal had come in (please don't judge, we *never* feed them that rubbish, but I was feeling so guilty about being out all night) and started breathing in to it, but it was too small and stank of chicken nuggets, and that just made me feel like I was going to panic-vomit, so I put it back down and tried to remember my yoga breathing. *In through the nose, out through the mouth. In through the nose, out through the mouth!*

Just as I was getting a hold on my shame spiral, the phone went again, twice, and two more photos came through. The first was of Amanda – how do I put it – *dry humping* Luke, which wasn't *that* incriminating when all was said and done because he only had his hand on her bum, over her clothes, but it was still enough to make her look slutty. Too over-friendly to be excused as a cuddle. Enough to destroy the little social headway she had made at Darley.

But worse still was the candid snap that came after, the one that must have killed her to see, and which made me hate Victoria all the more aggressively. The one that showed Ted gasping with pleasure as he hoisted Zoe's curvy body up against the grimy wall of the caretaker's cupboard, her back straight against the graffiti and the cobwebs and the hardened globs of chewing gum.

It took me a few moments to let the fear run its course, but I'm fairly pragmatic, I like to think, so once I'd pulled myself together, I got my thinking cap on.

Just then, Pete walked in, carrying Freya's pink beach bucket.

'Look,' he said, gravely. 'Three raspberry Zooper Dooper wrappers, a pair of goggles and a spoon. Whatever next?'

Whatever next? I thought. Well, I'm about to be exposed for having another school mum's fingers in my knickers, for one. I see your Zooper Dooper and I raise you that!

Obviously, I didn't say it. Instead, I tutted and shook my head in steely support of his rubbish haul and tapped away on my phone to Amanda. She was freaking out, asking, SHE WON'T DO IT, WILL SHE? SERIOUSLY? I replied that I thought Victoria was severely unhinged to send a message like that in the sober light of day and that people like that were unpredictable. I told her we would need to let Zoe and Lara know, so I messaged them and it was as simple as, VICTORIA HAS PICTURES OF ALL OF US LAST NIGHT. THEY'RE BAD. Lara was the first to respond, which for some reason made my stomach flip again, and she said something like, OOPS. NOT IDEAL AT ALL. Which was of course the biggest understatement in the history of all time, but typically Lara – so chilled out. It occurred to me that for her, people knowing what she'd been up to probably wasn't the worst thing in the world. It was all part of her allure – that bohemian, free love kind of persona. She seemed to gloss over, or perhaps simply not notice, what people thought of her.

Zoe's reaction couldn't have been more panicked. SHIT she wrote. I CAN'T BREATHE! WE NEED TO STOP HER! MILES CAN'T SEE THESE PHOTOS. AMANDA, CAN YOU CALL HER? WHY IS SHE DOING THIS? WHAT DOES SHE WANT FROM US?

And Amanda replied simply, REVENGE.

Chapter Eighteen
Zoe

From: Zoe.m8kin79@realworld.com.au
To: pho_e_b_wallis@zapmail.com
Subject: The truth

What do you make of all this, Phoebs? It's so fucked up, right? And it gets way, way worse.

Well as you'll expect, it filled me with absolute horror that some woman I'd never met had photographic evidence of me cheating on Miles, and that she felt compelled to stand in the doorway of that mangey little room and click her camera at us. I know, I know, I was doing way worse in there, but anyway.

I knew things with Miles would be irreversibly screwed up if he saw the photo – because telling me he didn't want to know about it and then being confronted by basically a graphic porno pic was the difference between it all being imaginary and real. I wasn't sure he'd be able to get past actual pictorial evidence, as much as I wasn't sure I'd be able to get past him seeing it.

Alice, who, like I said before, is the biggest control freak on the planet, demanded we all down tools (and by that she meant TV remotes) and meet on the corner of Darley Road where it hits Mentira Drive, by the postbox. Say you're going to post a letter or something, she wrote. It'll only take five minutes. It was the last thing I felt like doing, and I was sure I wasn't alone, but we needed to sort it out, so I replied saying I'd be there and threw my coat on. I grabbed a letter that had already been delivered to me and told Miles I was just popping to the postbox. He didn't even look up from *Deadliest Catch* or whatever it was he'd switched on.

Alice was already there, wearing a hoodie, like she was about to rob a bank, even though it was like a fucking sauna outside. She kept looking to her left and right, and when she was satisfied that she wasn't being watched, she pulled her hood down. That's when Lara floated up in some kaftan thing, stinking of patchouli. Alice just nodded like an embarrassed teenager and muttered *Um, hi Lara*. Lara flicked her hair back and chewed on her lip and said, *Hi Alice*. You could have cut the sexual tension with a knife, Phoebs, like seriously!

Amanda rocked up next, in activewear and clutching a mug. She looked awful, like properly rough, and I couldn't work out if it was because she was hungover or just because she wasn't caked in make-up. She made a point of not looking at me, even though she said hello to Lara and Alice. *This is messed up*, she said. *She is fucking insane, that woman. We have to stop her*. She waved around the mug in her hand, which said World's Best Mum or something ironic like that, and I could hear the ice cubes crashing against the sides. It definitely wasn't Earl Grey in there, put it that way.

What's that you're drinking? Alice asked, and Amanda shot her a massive death stare.

Mineral water? Amanda said it like it was a question, like, *duh?* But it looked like it was G&T to me because it had a lemon dancing round in the top and Amanda was guzzling it the same way she'd been enjoying her Prosecco the night before.

Lara was nodding whenever Alice spoke, tucking her hair behind her ear and saying *I agree, Alice,* which made Alice really flustered. She kept touching her earlobe, which went bright red each time Lara spoke (it would have made a great drinking game – a shot for every ear touch!).

We need to trap her somehow, Alice said, when she'd stopped acting like a lovestruck skateboarder. *To get her in a metaphorical corner, so that she feels threatened by us, and agrees not to do anything as fucked up as posting our sex pics on the school Facebook page.*

And she was right, it was messed up to threaten that, wasn't it? I mean who in their right mind behaved like that?

Amanda was so worked up she thumped the postbox with her fist and then said, *Ow, fuck.*

Alice told her to chill and said, *We're not going to do anything harsh, we simply need to engineer a meeting and try and reason with her, try and convince her that she doesn't have to do anything stupid.* It's like she was hoping Victoria and Amanda would hug it out, or perhaps both have a little mutual cry, then say, *I'm sorry, no I'm sorry, no really, I'm sorry.*

Agreed, I told them (while Amanda pouted and gulped down her 'water' and purposefully didn't look at me), *but in my opinion, Amanda should apologise for whatever it is she's done. After all she's the one Victoria has beef with and not the rest of us.* I proposed that once she'd apologised, we could gently suggest to Victoria that it would be in everyone's best interests to kindly delete those grubby pics. *If we point out we're all mothers, it might help,* I said. *As a parent herself, surely she'll understand how damaging this could be for our kids?*

Lara nodded. *We should remind her that blackmail isn't cool. It isn't a good look.*

Good idea, Alice said, pulling at her ear again.

Amanda shook her head. *It's unforgivable, the woman is sick. You expect me to apologise to her? If she wants a fight, she's got one.*

Amanda was all for marching over to the woman's home and stealing her phone, or, if needs be, grabbing it from her hands and deleting the offending photos, but Alice wasn't having it.

Stealing Victoria's phone wouldn't work, she said, because a) she would have a six-digit passcode, unless she happened to be using a Nokia from like, 1995, and b) even if we did manage to get all three photos off her camera roll, we'd also have to remove them off her WhatsApp messages, and then potentially her email too, and God knows where else she may have sent them.

Lara agreed (of course), and Alice touched her earlobe, which was still burning crimson.

Maybe her passcode is her birthdate like everyone else's? suggested Amanda, who was obviously clutching at straws now.

Alice shook her head. *We are not stealing it,* she said. *It will put us at risk of exposure and arrest for theft. We could contact the police and explain there's an unsavoury blackmail situation going on.*

NO! we all said in unison.

I, for one, didn't fancy sitting in the interrogation room at Darley Police Station explaining that we were being bribed by a fellow school mum for shagging one another's spouses.

Alice obviously realised how mortifying that would be – especially as one of the mums from year 4 works on reception at the police station – and said, *Okay, fine! Well, Zoe's suggestion seems like the best course of action. Are we all agreed?*

Lara nodded.

Amanda? Lara turned to Amanda who was pouting into her mug.

Whatever. Amanda shrugged.

Lara, who was more laid back than bloody Tutankhamun, said, *I have a good feeling about this. I'm sure we can talk Victoria round, she's not a monster! Maybe she just wants to be heard?*

And it made me think maybe she had a point and that it might actually be as easy as popping over to Vicky's massive mansion with a nice big bunch of flowers and saying, *Right Victoria, what's your problem and what can we do to make it better?* And even though I was loath to spend a single cent on the devious old cow, I do think in these situations you can kill people with kindness. She'd have to be highly irrational to want to expose all of us, after that, wouldn't she?

And also, I thought, if it comes to it, I could say to her: *Just hold on, lady-I've-never-met-but-who's-seen-me-shagging-someone's-husband! Isn't it Amanda you want to destroy, at the end of the day? Not myself, or Lara or Alice?*

Okay, said Alice, *well that's our plan then. We'll go there, all of us, and Amanda can apologise.*

Amanda chewed her cheek and looked up. *She's not exactly the forgiving type,* she said. *I've been there before.*

Well, we don't have much choice, said Alice. *Plus, if we're all there, maybe she'll be a bit more reasonable because she'll be outnumbered.*

Amanda didn't look convinced, but to be honest I was trying not to look at her too much, so I couldn't really tell. *Well, if we're going to do it, Monday works, I suppose,* she said. *Victoria always has lunch on her deck on Monday before she goes to Pilates.*

Alice offered to buy the flowers and said we could settle-up later. She'd obviously realised that Amanda wasn't quite ready to go bouquet shopping yet.

Right then. See you tomorrow! Alice pulled her hoodie up again, like the illuminati, and told us we should meet at Victoria's the next day at twelve. *I'll do the talking if that helps* (she knew Amanda would fuck it up, presumably) *so you don't need to worry, Mand.*

Fine. Amanda shrugged.

Twelve it is, said Lara. Then she said, *Well, on the bright side, at least we won't need to have that awkward, post-coital meet up at school.* (And she said it like it was an everyday occurrence.) *We've got that over with, right here on the street!*

Alice smiled, grabbed her earlobe and turned, while Amanda sighed loudly and strutted off without saying goodbye to anyone.

Miles was still in the same spot on the sofa when I got back.

You okay? he asked and kissed my forehead.

Yep, I told him, because, now we had a plan, I honestly felt okay.

But once we were in bed and the lights were out, my heart started to race. The images came thick and fast: Freddie in the playground holding a photograph with kids circling him, pointing fingers; Miles opening his messages in the kitchen at work and gasping in shock as his team of chefs leaned in over his shoulders to look; giant posters of me and Ted doing what we did on every lamp post in Darley, like the ones you see for lost dogs.

Each scenario entered my mind with such ferocity I had to switch on the bedside lamp to banish them, and only snuggling up close to Miles's warm back, breathing in time to the rise and fall of his sleeping chest, could calm me down.

Chapter Nineteen
Amanda

I couldn't believe I was going to have to go back to Victoria's house again. I'd last been back there two days after Mr Perkins died. I was aching with guilt for what I'd done and I needed to make amends, to show Victoria I was truly sorry. I had barely slept thinking about her girls and how devastated they would be without their beloved dog. When Evie's fish had died halfway through kindergarten, she'd been inconsolable – and even now, when she is sad, she'll say things like, 'I wish Dory was here, I miss him.' But a dog? A yapping, licking, adorable little dog with the body of a sausage? I was disgusted with myself.

When I'd arrived home after the incident in the car, hysterical and breathless, I'd hoped for some kind of redemption from Ted, something along the lines of, 'It's okay darling, it's really not that bad', but he didn't offer any such platitudes, because it *was* that bad. He just held me tight while I moped, and said, 'Shit – those poor kids' on repeat until I asked him to stop.

Nestling atop my regret was terror. Pure and unadulterated fear about what would happen at school on Monday – to me and to Evie. I was painfully aware I needed to get the whole mess sorted so that the act of walking through the gates of St Cecilia's did not become akin to entering the pit of hell. Oh, how deluded was I?

In preparation for my apology, I ordered a bunch of stunning Australian natives from the artisan florist in Darley Exchange, right next to Luke's surgery as it happens, and collected them in the morning. I didn't intend to knock on the door this time, especially since it was a Friday and there was a chance one of the girls would answer, which would have been pretty upsetting for them. Instead, I left a handwritten note, with five crisp green hundred-dollar bills. In the card, I wrote in black ink, *Dear Victoria, Nico, Darcy, Iris and Clara. Words cannot express how sorry I am for the tragic accident on Wednesday. Mr Perkins was a beautiful dog and I can't begin to understand what you must all be going through. I hope I can, at some stage, make amends to you all. Please accept my sincerest apologies as well as this contribution to the carpet cleaning. I will obviously pay any extra if this is not enough – please do not hesitate to reach out. With kindness, Amanda xoxo*

Her driveway was empty, suggesting no one was home, but I parked on the street because I couldn't bear the idea that I would have to reverse the car back down her drive again, just in case another beloved family pet decided to lodge itself behind my rear tyre. Although if I *had* eased my car onto the concrete, it might have hidden the shouty red blotch that screamed 'dog killer' at me as I crept up the driveway. A vivid snap of Mr Perkins flashed into my mind. To my left, an oblong mound of earth stood up above ground level, and two paddle pop sticks fashioned into a headstone stood proudly in the top. A child's handwriting on the vertical stick read, 'Perky RIP' and at the base, a handful of white and yellow frangipanis were fashioned in to a 'P'. Halfway down the drive, a fat kookaburra burst into spontaneous laughter from the electric wire above my head. *You're screwed, you're screwed, you're screwed*, he screeched, each cackle distorting and dying out at the end. Then his mate arrived and joined in the hysteria. Maybe they'd been there on Melbourne Cup day, and seen it all from their vantage point, up high on the wire, watched as I slipped my heels off at the door and crossed the threshold of the show home, towards my fate of social fire and brimstone.

'Fuck off,' I hissed, as I tiptoed up the steps of the front porch, eager not to be seen, and they laughed even louder. I lay the flowers down on the mat and retreated backwards, my body hunched, and as I neared the road again, I looked up to see a shutter on the living room window snap angrily shut.

I didn't hear anything that day, or the next. But when I drove past Victoria's house on the way to take Evie to school on Monday, I saw that the flowers were sitting on the top of the green recycle bin, still in their cellophane, the unopened brown envelope still stapled to the front. The bin didn't look full, and so I knew she had left them there in full view of the road for my benefit. She knew I would drive past and see them – her message as loud as, if not louder than, a verbal 'fuck you'.

Ted was aghast when I told him Victoria hadn't read the note. 'Get that envelope back,' he insisted. 'There's five-hundred bucks inside.'

'No! What if she softens and decides to open the card?'

But I should have realised there wasn't a snowflake's chance in hell of that happening, and the confirmation of the rebuttal of my white flag came when Evie climbed into the car at pick-up.

'Darcy Day said her mum said you're going to get what's coming to you,' she sang, as brightly as if she were discussing a trip to the zoo. 'Does that mean you're going to get a *present*?'

The 'present' of course had been the grand finale in Margot Walsh's office the following day arguing about charity buckets, and Ted was so livid about the whole thing that he marched over to Victoria's and snatched the flowers and the envelope from the green recycle bin, which was now sitting on the road awaiting the Wednesday biodegradable waste collection.

'Enjoy not having our money, dickheads,' he said when he got home, thumbing the shiny green banknotes.

This was now my fourth journey to Victoria's house, and instead of feeling repentance, I felt determination. I had a wine with lunch, which added to my sense of self-righteousness. The fear of the consequences of photographic exposure had given way overnight to outright anger, as if I was going through some weird incarnation of the seven stages of grief. My current emotion was indignation that someone would be so fixated on revenge that they would drag four innocent women into the fray. And yes, I counted myself as one of those four, because as far as I was concerned, I'd paid my dues. I'd tried to make amends. I'd written a note, I'd grovelled, sent flowers, offered recompense . . . My child had been booted out of her school for it, because *she* had made up the story about the Melbourne Cup afternoon being a school fundraiser and donated a large sum of cash to prove it. It wasn't my fault that her implausibly nice husband (I was still utterly bemused as to how she managed to snag such a solid bloke) had lost his job and she'd been forced to follow me and the other mortals up the public pathway alongside the kiss-and-drop at Darley Heights. As far as I was concerned, I'd done my penance and it was literally time for Victoria to let sleeping dogs lie.

Alice was already outside the house, loitering in the shrubbery. She hugged me, then stepped back with an angry face.

'Have you been drinking?' she asked in that prim way she adopts when she's criticising someone, but attempting to hide it as a question.

'Why do you always ask me that?'

'Well have you?'

'No! I mean, I had a wine with lunch . . .'

'Just *great.*'

'Chill out! I had a white wine with my salad, okay?'

'Whatever,' she sighed, and then she softened. 'How are you feeling, anyway?'

'Angry, actually,' I said.

Alice's concerned expression amplified about twenty-fold.

'Oh, don't worry, I'm not going to kick off,' I said.

Just then, Lara's SUV with its naff plates, HAM 50N, pulled in opposite. She stepped out in some ground-skimming floral number that looked like it was from a Balinese street market, and a pair of Ray-Bans perched on her nose. 'Hi,' she called breezily, as if we were all meeting for a playdate at the park. 'How are we all?'

Her non-plussed response may have been irritating as all hell, but the fact was, she was the one who had least to lose.

'Fine,' Alice mumbled into her hair as she kissed her awkwardly on the cheek. Lara pulled her in for a hug, and Alice, burning puce, stood with her hands by her side like a tree trunk. I half wanted to cover my eyes and watch it through my fingers.

Lara let out a sigh. 'Right, I'm going to say this right now. We are not going to be awkward like we were last night on the street. Sex is sex, okay? It is natural! All animals do it. It is nothing to be embarrassed or ashamed about. We had a special connection . . .' She looked at Alice. 'And we acted on it. So let's not be awkward, okay?'

'Sure,' mumbled Alice.

'Are you going to suggest a group hug?' I snapped. I knew I was being a misery guts, but I couldn't help it. I was so worked up about Victoria.

Lara ignored me. 'Right, well let's try and sort this thing so you guys can relax,' she said. 'Where's Zoe? Ahh, over there.' She nodded to the brow of the hill as Zoe emerged over it, dressed in purple activewear, her hair flapping about her shoulders like she was in some weird hybrid shampoo/tampon commercial. It was almost as though she'd parked just out of sight on the other side of the hill just so she could run over it like that, just to show us all, 'Look at me with my curvy hips and my glossy hair!' It felt as though someone had plunged a steak knife into my guts and was twisting it, gleefully, before taking it out and thrusting it back into a new spot, slicing through pristine new skin. Yet again I was being forced to look at the beautiful woman who had had sex with my husband, who had felt the strength of Ted's arms, smelled his skin, tasted his sweat on her tongue. I felt my shoulders stiffen, the anger heat up my blood, and I pulled off my top layer to cool myself. Alice caught my eye and touched my arm gently in a show of support.

'Hi.' Zoe bent over, her hands on her hips, a runner's pose. She gulped down air, which made me think of the noises she would have made when she was with Ted. I felt nauseous.

'Hey Zoe,' Lara said, leaning in to hug her. Zoe was obviously taken aback by the intimacy of the gesture, but hugged her back regardless.

'Hi,' she said again, this time to Alice. Then she moved around to face me. 'Amanda,' she said. 'How *are* you?' The concern she was peddling seemed genuine, but I wasn't buying.

'Never better,' I said to her left shoulder. 'Shall we do this then?'

We walked up the driveway in a row (not unlike the line-up in front of a firing squad, come to think of it), and Alice leaned forward and rang the bell. There was no noise from inside except Tina Turner's smoky voice crooning, 'You're Simply The Best.'

'I'd expect more from Maleficent than Smooth FM,' Alice muttered.

Zoe stepped up and glanced through the window, her hair falling into her face. 'Ugh,' she whispered, flicking it back over her shoulder.

'Maybe tie it back?' I hissed.

'Anyone got a spare hair elastic?' she asked, eyeing the one on my wrist.

Oh for fuck's sake, I thought. *Let's share everything.* 'Sure,' I said, yanking it off and thrusting it at her.

Alice offered me an encouraging smile.

'There's no one in there,' Zoe said. 'I don't think she's home.'

But I knew she would be. I cast my eyes up towards the plantation shutters in the upstairs bedroom. But there was nothing, not as much as a quiver. *Please be in*, I thought, *I can't go through this again*. Plus, there was obviously quite a big sense of urgency. The longer she had to contemplate, the more likely she would be to click on the button and doom us all to a lifetime of social media hell.

Emboldened by my lunchtime tipple, I stepped in front of Alice and rapped on the door briskly, before stepping backwards to look up at the window. Nothing.

'Let's check around the back,' I said, marching towards the side of the house.

'You can't do that, it's trespassing,' Lara said, and I thought, *Really? This from someone who aided and abetted the flouting of marriage bans.*

'Amanda's right, we should try,' said Alice. 'It's only the garden.'

Lara shrugged. She bent down to admire the little shrine in the front garden, which she obviously didn't know was the final resting place of Mr Perkins.

I lifted my hand up over the fence and clicked the gate latch under my fingers like a burglary pro (or a real estate agent, come to think of it), and we all filed in along the manicured pathway towards the back deck. A half-eaten salad sandwich sat on the whitewashed garden table along with a glass of iced water, ice cubes still bobbing about whole and a Diptyque candle, still burning. *Aha!* I thought, feeling a little like Miss Marple. *She is here! And I'm going to find her.* The least she could do was to answer. I wagged the handle of the bifold doors, but they were locked shut. Which meant that, when she'd seen us coming, she'd locked up and retreated indoors. The laundry door was locked, too. I jiggled the handle up, a little too enthusiastically, apparently.

'Amanda, chill,' Alice snapped.

'Yes, we are here to make things better,' Zoe added. I glared at her and continued waggling the door handle as I did so. It was a trick I had deftly learned from my 7-year-old.

'What are you going to do if it opens?' Alice's voice was firm. 'You can't go in. That really *is* trespassing and I, for one, don't fancy getting arrested today!'

'She's in there,' I hissed, loud enough for someone inside the house, and probably across the street, to hear. 'She owes it to us to talk.'

'Calm down,' said Alice, as if she were disciplining an unruly child.

'She's in there!' I shouted, so that whoever was inside would hear. 'And she really should do us the courtesy of coming out now!'

I looked up, saw a shutter flicker just like I had when I'd left the flowers. Only this time I wasn't going to leave without an audience. I couldn't. She had photos that I couldn't let slip (or be evilly thrust) into the wrong hands. Not at Darley. I couldn't go through it all again. I couldn't drag Evie through this again.

'See!' I said, looking around at the others. 'See! She's up there. I saw the shutter move!'

I raced back to the bifold doors and began banging on the glass. 'Victoria! Victoria! We know you are in there. Please! You can't ignore us!'

'We . . . we just want to talk,' called Alice gently.

'Please, be reasonable,' Zoe shouted upwards. 'We just want to chat.'

'Victoria!' I screeched. I'd pretty much contorted my mouth to fit inside the inch-wide crack in the laundry window. 'Come downstairs! You're a *mother* for God's sake! This isn't the way to behave! You need to come here now, you need to . . .'

Alice, who evidently didn't miss the irony in what I was saying, yanked my hand, and me, away from the window.

'Amanda,' she snapped, her hands on my shoulders. 'If you want those photos online then you're going the right way about it. Just calm the hell down!'

I nodded sulkily and turned to see a shadow at the frosted window of the laundry door. There was the click of a key in the lock inside and the door opened a crack. Victoria's left eye peeked out of the crack.

'Get out of my garden,' she spat.

'Victoria, we just . . .' began Alice.

A bony finger squeezed through the gap. 'I said, get the *fuck* out of my garden you bunch of . . . of *perverts*!'

Alice's mouth dropped open. I watched as her body rose up out of its hunched, apologetic pose, her muscles stiffening with anger. 'Excuse me?' she demanded.

'Get. Out. Of. My. Garden. Or. I. Will. Call. The. Police.' She said each word slowly, her fingertips now gripping the side of the door in its place, just in case one of us should try and push it open.

Lara wafted in from the front garden with a frangipani flower in her hand and another tucked behind her ear. Her brows had knitted and her lips twitched with purse. 'Hey, Victoria, that's really not cool,' she said.

'Well if the cap fits . . .' Victoria hissed. 'What does the "S" in class 1S stand for anyway? Is it *SWINGERS*?'

Lara gasped and Alice touched her shoulder. When she realised what she'd done, she did a speedy exit of her hand and cleared her throat, awkwardly.

'You absolute–' Zoe stopped, changed tack. She took a long breath. 'Please, Victoria,' she said through gritted teeth. 'You owe us an explanation.'

'I owe you NOTHING,' Victoria snapped, finally raising her voice. She sounded deranged, the voice of a lunatic.

'But you *do*,' Zoe said. 'You might have issues with Amanda, but what have I . . . I mean the rest of us . . . ever done to you?'

'She's right, Victoria.' Alice's face was pink with anger.

There was a dramatic pause. Victoria's pupils shrank to pin dots. 'Yes? Well you can have an explanation . . .' she said, removing her fingers from the door frame, '. . . over my dead body!' Then she slammed the door.

The anger was already simmering inside my chest, but now it had started bubbling over.

'Well,' I wailed, my nose now pressed up against the wooden door. 'I'm sure that can be arranged.'

I turned to Alice. 'God, I could kill her right now,' I raged, my hand up to my throat. 'I could really fucking kill her!'

Alice bit her lip. 'You know what, Amanda? So could I.'

'Yep,' said Zoe, her hand on her hip and her eyes still focused on the upstairs window. 'Me three.'

And the way we all said it was in some ways just like it had been at trivia night when we'd all made the pact to swing – which of course was what ultimately led me to that perfectly manicured lawn with its stupid white play house and festoon lights.

'What are we going to do?' Zoe's lip quivered.

'We're going to stop her, that's what,' I snarled, loud enough for Victoria to hear. Then I aggressively ripped the head off a nice-looking lilac hydrangea and tossed it at the laundry door. I don't know why I did it, but I just did. And that's when I noticed Victoria's elderly neighbour peering over the white picket fence, a look of horror on her shrivelled face.

'Can I help you?' I asked, with what must have been a rather manic smile, because the old woman's head immediately retreated back behind the fence like a turtle.

Chapter Twenty
Alice

Transcript: The voice of Alice Daniels in the office of Dr Martha Davis.

I was seething for the rest of the night, but obviously I couldn't tell Pete. I wanted to throttle the woman! Do *I* have anger issues? Oh, come on, I think you know enough about me by now, don't you? No, I don't at all, but I'm a human being, and if I get pushed enough – if someone is on at me going poke, poke, poke – I will snap. This chat is private by the way, isn't it? I mean, I know it is, with doctor-patient confidentiality and everything, but occasionally I feel like I need to check. It's not easy to expose so much about yourself and your actions, your emotions, to a stranger, and even harder to imagine that there is a possibility your confidence may in some way be betrayed.

Thank you, yes, I believe you, of course I do . . . I just needed to check. Now, where were we? Ah yes, anger. Like I said, I am no angrier than the next person, but there was something about that interaction with Victoria that made my blood boil like a whistling kettle. I don't know if it was her tone, or the fact she called us perverts – I mean, can you believe that? – but something snapped in me, like a hair tie that's been doubled over a ponytail one too many times. Isn't it the same for absolutely everyone, if they're pushed too far? Like I said, Dr Davis, I'm only human, just like you.

It was even worse at the school gates the next day, which was the Tuesday. I was walking towards the canteen when I spied her in her little witchy coven of five, heads bent in. She was the tallest, of course. You can't miss her in the playground, not with that military bob and long neck. Tansie was next to her, of course. I kept my eyes down because even though I was livid, I didn't want to make a scene. I queued up to order the twins their lunches and I heard the name 'Daniels', in her snippy voice. My head whipped up, of course, and I looked over and she and Tansie were staring in my direction, as if Victoria was divulging something about me. Tansie didn't look shocked or amused or anything like that, just had her usual bitchy face glued on, but when Victoria turned to me, despite her huge designer sunglasses, the message delivered by her pursed lips was clear. She was telling me she was biding her time, that she was going to wait for the perfect moment and then do a massive number on all of us. You know, let everyone know what we'd done.

The coven broke apart then and Victoria headed in the direction of the car park. I felt my shoulders straighten and my skin prickle with goosebumps, and I was all set to march on over to her, when Brigitte Denner swept in.

'Alice,' she called across the quad, her jacket flapping as she walked. 'I haven't had the chance to tell you what a marvellous job you did with the trivia night! Mr Vincent is still totting up the dollars we made, because we had a few late payments for raffle tickets, but suffice it to say we'll all be nice and chilly in that hall next summer! I'm just off to do playground duty, but I'll speak to you properly later in the week. Mwah!'

She gave me a wave and headed off.

'Wonderful,' I called back, and turned to hurriedly order two tuna sushi boxes and two freshly squeezed orange juices (I cannot abide those boxed ones, way too drenched in sugar and preservatives).

Tansie swept past me, her eyes boring into my skull. 'Great party, Alice,' she said without any kind of facial movement. 'Victoria tells me there's a bunch of titillating gossip she's yet to fill me in on.'

'Oh, um . . . really?'

Tansie leaned in. 'Apparently,' she said, 'some year one parents were caught doing something very naughty indeed. She's going to fill me in on all the gossip when I see her later in the week. You don't know anything about it, do you?'

I wondered if it was a test and Tansie already knew which parents, and exactly how naughty they'd been. But it seemed she didn't.

'Search me,' I mumbled.

'Maybe someone was doing coke off the toilet seats,' Tansie squealed. A delighted smile danced on her lips. 'Christ, that would be an effort, wouldn't it? Imagine the squatting you'd need to do to get your head close to one of the tiny kindergarten seats! But I suppose you could do it on the cistern,' she mused. 'Anyway, better go.'

And she wafted off, leaving me shell-shocked. I distinctly remember lifting up my hand and watching as it trembled in front of me.

I left the school and just as I was turning into the car park, I caught sight of Victoria a few yards ahead of me, unlocking her shiny black Tesla.

'Victoria,' I called. '*Victoria!* I need to talk to you!'

She flinched, but she didn't turn back, only clambered hurriedly into the driver's seat.

Inside my own car, I put my head on the wheel and took a moment to calm myself down. I remembered my yoga breathing again and once I began to feel my breath steady, my heart rate return to normal, I had a strange, overwhelming urge to call Lara. Just for the soothing effect she seemed to have, the caramelly sound of her voice. I wondered if some of her composure, her general sense of self-possession, her *collectedness*, might rub off on me, as it were. Perhaps there was some comfort to be had in the sound of her laugh. I scrolled down through the alphabet list of names in my contacts list and stared at her number. I must have looked at it for two whole minutes. But my finger just wouldn't do it, I couldn't make the call. I was still too shaky.

Instead, I waited for Victoria's car to leave the car park, and, after a few seconds, I followed her – I can't tell you why, but I did. I followed her past the chemist, along Darley Parade, until she pulled in at her home. I sat outside her place for a minute or two before I drove away.

I stewed on it all for the rest of the day and the night, mulling it over in my head and wondering how one woman could cause such a ruckus, and why she was such an evil cow. I wished someone would take a dagger to her or run her over in their car, so we wouldn't have to worry about her again. They're not the kind of thoughts I usually have, you understand, but Victoria had just been so horrendous to us.

And I suppose I got my wish in a roundabout way, because the very next day, Victoria was declared missing.

Chapter Twenty-one
Zoe

From: Zoe.m8kin79@realworld.com.au
To: pho_e_b_wallis@zapmail.com
Subject: The truth

She'd been gone for three days, and even though she was new to Darley, people were acting like they'd known her forever, like she was suddenly the patron saint of parenting. That awful woman Tansie Wright set up a Facebook Page called Find Victoria, with a picture of Victoria pouting and holding a glass of something sparkling. She'd posted a link to Darley Area Command's own post with the same photo and the words: HAVE YOU SEEN THIS WOMAN? VICTORIA MERCY (oh, the irony) DAY, and some blurb about who she was and where she was from and how many children she had, and a list of stats – her height (six foot), eye colour (brown) and hair colour (highlighted to shit). Tansie totally did it to look good rather than out of genuine concern (I mean, she'd only known the woman five minutes), and pretty much everyone, whether they knew Victoria or not, was leaving messages and tagging her, saying stuff like, *Come home safe Victoria Day, we are praying for you xoxoxo!*

There was a rota on the page for leaving food parcels on her doorstep for Nico, her husband, and everyone was going nuts for it, falling over themselves, like, *Ooh, I'll take round a lasagne*, or, *I'll bake some cookies* or, *I'll drop round some meringue*. As if the man wants a meringue when his wife's gone AWOL. I mean seriously! And I thought to myself, *This bloke's going to be a right fat bastard by the time she shows up, and then no one will want to leave him a food parcel.* It's like he was suddenly on *The Bachelor* or something, even though they hadn't found a body – but let's face it, that's what everyone was expecting to happen, because you don't just disappear for three days and leave all your shit at home. She took her Chanel crossbody everywhere, and apparently it was sitting on the kitchen counter with her purse (she hadn't touched her bank account) and her phone. The fact she had no phone made all the Facebook wishes people had written to her slightly pointless, since she couldn't read them, but it also meant that, unless she happened to be swanning about an Internet cafe somewhere, she wasn't about to post those photos of us all any time soon either. It filled me with so much relief that I went to bed on the Thursday night sort of hoping they'd find her in a shallow grave, or beside the freeway, because that's where bodies are always found. I know it was wrong to think like that, but I couldn't help it. I wondered whether, if someone or a *group of people* had, say, stabbed her and partially buried her or something, whether her body would get disturbed by all of the rain we'd been warned about. And I began to feel a bit nervous, like there was going to be some kind of announcement.

Miles was as obsessed with it all as I was. He said, *Why would anyone want to off a Darley mum? She looks like a sweet lady in her photo!* And I was busting to tell him what a cow she was, but I couldn't because then I'd have to have told him why I thought that, and that would've meant admitting there was a soft porn photo of me with my thighs wrapped around Ted Blackland doing the rounds.

Her two youngest girls weren't at school that week, and that *did* make me feel pretty guilty – you know, just thinking about what the poor kids were going through with their mother missing. A couple of days after she'd last been seen, I bumped into her husband at the supermarket and felt I should say something to him instead of just staring at him with the sneaky side-eye like everyone else in the store seemed to be doing. So I went up to him and was like, *Hi, you must be Nico, I'm Zoe, one of the year one mums. I'm so sorry to hear about Victoria. You must be frantic. I don't suppose there is any news? Is there anything I can do to help you and the girls?* And he looked up at me with sad but kind eyes, and said, *I just hope she comes home safely, Zoe. We all love her so much.* He looked devastated, the poor man.

Even the sky was mournful that week, which wasn't a great omen. Large, brooding clouds settled over Darley, and the swell was rough when I walked along the promenade. On the Friday, a queasiness hovered over me from the moment I woke up, which had all the hallmarks of anxiety, and I realised that whenever I thought about Victoria and what happened when we went to the house, it amplified by about three thousand per cent. After all, that old biddy next door had seen us threatening her and Amanda had thrown a hydrangea at her house, for fuck's sake! We would be numbers one to four on the list of murder suspects if Victoria ended up being found wrapped in carpet at the bottom of Darley headland. Knots formed in my guts and I was completely off my food, which I suppose was no bad thing. I felt like I was observing my life as opposed to participating in it, so I busied myself at home: cleaned the house and cooked a chicken curry with a big hit of spice, the way Miles liked it, even if I couldn't stomach it myself. Miles licked his plate after dinner and said, *Why don't you drop the rest at Victoria's house tomorrow, for her husband, whatever he's called*, and that made me feel even more sick because the last time I was at that house, I was agreeing with everyone that I'd quite like to stab his wife in the neck. Did I say in the neck? I can't remember if I was that specific.

Thank God no one else is ever going to read this, unless *I* get bumped off and the police read my emails. In which case, they'd also go through my Google history, which would have shit on it like, 'Can you be implicated in a murder for arguing with someone and threatening to kill them?' and, 'Can you get pregnant having sex upright?' (I mean obviously I know the answer to the last one, I'm not *stupid*, but I was looking for some comfort, maybe a stat or two saying it's less probable.)

That night, the three of us played Scrabble and watched the rain pour down outside and pummel on the pavement. I thought of you and the way we would pull on our boots and our rain jackets at home the moment it began to rain and jump excitedly in the puddles that would collect in the dip where the drive met the road. Memories I'd love Freddie to have with a sibling one day, but which seem ever more unlikely. If it had been earlier, lighter outside,

I'd have let him out. *Daddy, it's pouring*, he said, his little eyes wide with wonder. *I know*, Miles said, *I love the rain and so does Mum. Don't you, Mum?* I just replied with a nod because it made me think of you and then of bodies being dredged up from water.

I clicked on Victoria's Instagram page, which was set to public, as a distraction. The photo from the missing notice was there: the one where she was holding the glass of Prosecco and smiling into the camera, her head lopsided. A dead head? Then my phone started to buzz. I watched it dance in my palm, wondering whether or not it would be a good idea to pick up. After all, Miles was beside me and I very much doubted this particular caller was ringing to ask me to get their washing in. So I left it, let it ring out. I couldn't deal with it tonight.

Not going to answer? Miles asked, and I shook my head and returned my attention to the Scrabble board. Ironically, the letters I pulled from the bag spelled the word CHEATS and I couldn't bear to use it, even though it was a decent score.

I'll call back tomorrow, I told him.

But the phone flashed and buzzed again and a message arrived in my inbox. I'll be outside your place in the car in two minutes. You need to come out, it read.

I felt a whoosh of adrenaline and stood up before turning back to kiss Miles and Freddie. I told them I was off to evening yoga and flew to the bedroom to put on my Lorna Jane tights and a yoga top. I didn't even put on a bra. Miles walked to the window and looked out after me, and I wondered for a moment if he thought I was meeting *him.* Desperate to show him I wasn't, I blew an over-the-top kiss over to the window. I huddled under the porch of my apartment block and waited for only a minute before I saw the yellow headlights of a car navigating their way haphazardly through the downpour and towards me. The headlamps darted upwards to the heavens dramatically as the vehicle flew over the sleeping policeman in the middle of the road, and back again, when the wheels hit the level ground. The rain dumped in buckets on the windscreen and the wipers whipped back and forth urgently like the tail of a dog.

When I looked back at the window, I noticed Miles had gone, and I felt pangs of guilt and relief that he hadn't waited to check I was telling the truth. He had trusted me.

Chapter Twenty-two
Amanda

We were on our way back from the cinema when we noticed it.

'Is that the Bevan house?' Ted asked, nodding his head to the large white colonial-style home on the brow of the hill, as we drove down Lyre Street. There was a sold sign outside with the bright yellow logo of Fair & Brewer on the top.

'Yep,' I said. I knew the house. I'd taken the photos inside prior to it going on sale, a couple of weeks before the trivia night.

'What's it like inside?' His tone was polite, and I knew I didn't have him back yet. I wondered if I ever would. In the six days since the trivia night, we'd performed life robotically, despite the apologies and the declarations of love dished out the morning after. Because, as much as we wanted everything to be the way it had been just a week earlier, no amount of apology could change what both of us had done. It didn't matter that it hadn't meant anything to either one of us. To give us our dues, we were trying to make it okay, to play our parts for the sake of the kids – and that meant our usual Friday night cinema trip.

'Amanda?' Not honey, not darling, just Amanda. 'What's the house like inside?' Ted said again, bringing me back to the inside of the car, with the wipers swishing dully back and forth, and the soundtrack to the movie *Frozen* whining unpleasantly in the background, much to Sam's annoyance. He wouldn't want to come to Friday cinema nights for much longer. He was growing up, and fast. I watched him push his headphones deeper into his ears to drown out Evie's favourite song, 'Let It Go.'

'Sorry,' I said, shaking my head. 'I was a world away.'

Ted flicked the wipers up a notch and squinted at the road ahead through the sideways rain.

'It is beautiful,' I said. 'Well, at least it was when it was styled for the sale. It's empty now, nothing in there at all. They were spray-painting it again last week. The new owners move in next month, apparently.'

'What did it go for again?'

'Two point six million.'

We drove past the house silently. The sky above was an ominous charcoal, making everything around us a foreboding shade of grey. I should have taken it as an omen, really.

'The rain's picking up,' Ted said, turning off the music so he could concentrate. Sam took his earphones out, his silent protest over. 'Look at that sky, there's going to be a massive storm. Should think so after the crazy heat.'

'Everyone in the underground bunker,' shouted Sam in a southern American accent. 'There's a storm a' comin'!'

You're not bloody wrong, Sammy, I thought. *Victoria's going to rock up dead and we were arguing with her the afternoon before she disappeared.*

I felt my body give an involuntary shudder. I wrapped my arms around my stomach to comfort myself. I hadn't done it for a while, because I'd had a husband and kids to fill that role, but it had been a daily habit when I was a child left alone to clean up my mother's mess, literally and figuratively.

'I hate thunder.' Evie put her hands over her ears.

'It hasn't started yet, dummy!' Sam poked her meanly.

'Mate, don't be rough with your sister,' Ted said. 'You shouldn't hurt the people you love.' He glanced across at me. I wanted to put my hand on his knee, but for some reason I was scared to. My husband of fourteen years and I was scared to touch him.

'Maybe we'll get flooded in and we won't have to go to school tomorrow,' Sam said, punching the air.

'Since when has that ever happened?' Ted laughed, immediately snapped from his melancholy. 'Besides, it's Saturday tomorrow, doofus.'

'Oh yeah.'

'Look,' Evie said, her body twisting round to look out of the back windscreen. 'There's someone at the window of the house you showed us.'

'Which house?'

'The one Mum pointed to with the sold sign.'

'Can't be, Evie-bear. The house is empty,' I said, studying the worn tips of my bright, Shellac nails. It dawned on me that the upper side of my hands looked middle aged, the blue veins of my mother winding their way from the base of my fingers to my wrist. I wondered if they'd been like that last week, even.

'No, Mummy,' Evie continued. 'I saw someone. A lady I think, looking out through the curtain.'

'That's weird.' My brain searched for an explanation. 'I don't think there would be anyone inside the house on a Friday night. It's officially the weekend.'

'If you're worried, call someone from the office.' Ted clicked on the indicators. 'I don't want to stop in this weather. We'll all get soaked if we get out. It's not like anyone can steal anything if it's empty.'

'Let's get out,' said Sam. 'This rain is epic.'

'No way,' I said, 'but let's just slow down a second so I can look.' I twisted my body round, heard the bones in my back click. There was no light on inside the house, it looked empty, but Evie had noticed what Evie had noticed, and she wasn't a kid who made things up.

'I can't see anything,' I said, taking another long glance at the stately abode. I don't know what I was expecting, Mrs Danvers up at the window, maybe. Ted put his foot on the gas and I turned to face the front again.

It all felt wrong. It was possible that someone from the office was in there, making final tweaks to the building before the new owners moved in. But surely they wouldn't be there after hours? Or could it be that someone was hiding out there? Someone who had a key of their very own, and could let themselves in? Someone who could get by undetected, knowing that the house was vacant and no one would go there, and who could hide away at night, maybe with the aid of a dimly lit lamp or a torch, curtains closed. Someone who wanted to get away from everything, who wanted to make out she was missing for whatever reason.

Hadn't Victoria told me on Melbourne Cup day that her parents used to live on Lyre? It had been Lyre, hadn't it? I grabbed my phone and logged on to the Fair & Brewer internal server and typed in the address, 29 Lyre Street. The blurb read: *Previous owners: Victoria Mercy and Nico Day (bequeathed by Mark and Paula Bevan, April 2013). Sold January 29 2022 to Eleanor and Marc Atkins of 28 Dierdre Street, Newcastle. Sale price: $2.6 million.*

Bingo! Maybe Evie had imagined seeing a woman at the window, but it wasn't beyond the realms of possibility that Victoria was hiding out there, even though she technically didn't own the place any more. It was vacant, a shell of a home just waiting to be claimed. She could go undetected there, if there was something she wanted to get away from.

Back at Mentira Drive, Ted pulled into our own driveway and told the kids to get out.

'Eww, I don't want to,' said Evie, wincing.

'Come on,' he said, pulling her arm gently and hurrying her towards the door, Sam following behind slowly as he attempted some rap moves in the rain. He was still my little boy in a lot of ways.

I didn't move from the car. Ted looked at me from the front door.

'You okay?' he mouthed.

I wound down the window.

'Do you . . . do you mind if I whizz round to Alice's?'

'Now?'

'Yep, I just need to get her denim jacket back to her. I promised I'd drop it back tonight.'

'Well . . .' Ted gave me an odd look. 'You'd better come in and get it. Last time I saw it, it was in the hall, not the car.'

'Oh, yes!'

I moved to get out of the car, but he'd already reached in through the front door and grabbed the jacket, which he used to shield his head as he ran back to me.

'Drive safely,' he told me, and turned away.

'I will.'

'Ted,' I called after him through a crack in the window. 'I love you.'

He looked back at me. 'You too,' he mouthed through the rain, and I felt at that moment that maybe, we might be okay. We still loved each other, and that was a start.

Alice answered the door in her pyjamas. 'Listen, I think I know where she is,' I said.

She didn't reply, just grabbed her trainers and pulled them on, shouting something to Pete about popping to the shops. 'Okay,' came a voice from upstairs. 'Can you get milk?'

'Uh-huuh!'

'Where?' Alice whispered.

'I think she's at the empty house.'

'Which empty house?'

'Hers,' I said, impatience creeping in, as we clambered into my car. 'The Bevan house. I accessed the Fair & Brewer internal server and checked. It's her house. Well, it was her parents' house. She put it up for sale early January when Nico lost his job. I can't be sure, but we drove past it fifteen minutes ago and Evie said she saw someone at the window.'

'Well, that's creepy,' Alice said, strapping herself in.

'Why do you think I'm getting you to come with me?'

'It's bizarre. Why would she be hiding there and letting people think she's missing?'

'Who knows? She's not exactly rational, is she?'

'True. But say she *is* there and that was her up at the window, she's hardly going to answer the door and ask us in for a cuppa, is she? It'll be like her garden all over again.'

'Ah, but it won't,' I said, with a flourish. 'Because I still have a key.'

Alice smiled. 'How?'

'From when I was taking the photos. The office made a copy for me, because the photos clashed with some maintenance work they were doing in the upstairs bathroom and I never gave it back. I mean, I meant to, but I just didn't quite get around to it. I remember thinking to myself that I would put it there –' I nodded at the dash in front of her – 'for safekeeping, out of the way of sticky hands. Then I just forgot about it. So, unless Evie's been rummaging around in the glove compartment, which she knows she's not allowed to do, it should still be there.'

Alice twisted the knob in front of her and felt around with her hand. She pulled out a coffee cup lid, a Barbie doll head, a tampon and a single key on a piece of hessian string, with a canary yellow post office tag that said '29 LYRE' in black marker pen.

'Talk about lucky.'

'I know!'

'You're right,' she said. 'Let's check it out. We need to get Zoe and Lara.'

'Should we check Victoria's in there, first?' I didn't particularly want Zoe in my car – or my general vicinity.

'No, let's get them and go. Easier that way. If we're all there, she's going to feel more intimidated. Plus, Lara is just so chilled out, she'll be able to keep things calm. I think we should definitely get her.' Pink crept up Alice's neck.

'You're blushing,' I said.

'No, I'm not,' she snapped.

'Okay, chill!' Evidently she wasn't ready to discuss her table grope with Lara.

I started up the car and threw Alice my phone. She scrolled down the list, and the green of the screen illuminated her face in the dark. There was no answer from Zoe, so she sent a text. Zoe was outside the house in a blue rain jacket when we pulled up a minute later.

'Ahh, my lift to yoga,' she said loudly as she pulled open the car door, which I remember thinking was completely futile, since Miles would never have heard her from outside the house, especially not in the pouring rain.

'Hi,' she said, climbing in the back seat.

'Hey Zoe,' Alice shouted. 'Ready for yoga?'

'Hi,' I mumbled.

'So?' Zoe said, leaning forward in her seat. My instinct was to tell her to put her seat belt on, but frankly I wasn't that bothered if she went through the windscreen. 'What's happened?'

Alice relayed the information about the mystery woman in the house.

'Shit,' Zoe said. 'I hope it's her. Imagine how it would look for us, if she ended up dead after we were overheard threatening her! And obviously, that would be pretty crap for her husband and kids too . . .' She trailed off.

I wound through the backstreets, completely off course. 'Isn't the house you're talking about on Lyre Street?' Zoe asked, looking slightly alarmed on account of the weird route.

'Don't worry, we're not about to dispose of you, too,' I said, cheerily.

'We're going to Lara's,' Alice said, a little less menacingly. 'She's waiting for us.'

Five minutes later, the three of us, plus Lara, had pulled up on Lyre, a little way down from the house. The street was lit orange, thanks to the street lamps that had switched on for their night shift, and the grass verges were squelchy underfoot.

'We should knock first,' said Lara. 'Otherwise it's trespassing.'

'What is it with you and trespassing?' I asked. 'Anyway, she doesn't own the house anymore – the new owners are in Newcastle.'

'Still . . .'

'Lara,' I said, wearily. 'I work for the real estate agent and I have a key, okay? I'll just say I'm checking out a report of vandalism if we get caught.'

She shrugged, leaving me once again astounded at the indignant moral standpoint of the woman with the open marriage. She was like an oxymoron in tie-dye.

'Amanda's right,' said Alice. 'If we knock, the chances are she'll do a runner, and then we might never get the chance to talk to her about the photos.'

'If it even *is* her inside,' Zoe shrugged, pulling the hood up on her raincoat.

'Look, I highly doubt she'll publish the photos now, anyway. I mean she hasn't done it yet.' Lara sounded hopeful.

'Yes, but we still need to get them off her. I don't particularly want her holding on to them,' said Alice.

'Good point,' said Zoe.

'Well come on, then,' I said, waving the little silver key in front of my face as if it were the holy grail. 'Let's do this, shall we?'

We filed along the watery grass verge towards the house, and I tried to get the words to Sam's favourite toddler book *We're Going on a Bear Hunt* out of my head.

I don't know how I was feeling at that moment, really. I guess you could say emboldened. I hadn't been able to enjoy so much as a sniff of booze that night because of the cinema. The multi-screen duplex did have a bar, but Ted had seen me eyeing it up on approach and had yanked my hand by very pointed means of distraction, pulling me unceremoniously away from it and into the darkness of screen one, where I had sat through a breath-zapping tear-jerker about a missing dog, wishing I had a bottle of chilled rosé with a straw instead of a plastic gym bottle filled with lukewarm tap water.

I was stone-cold sober and about to do something that terrified me, not just because of the illegality of it, but because the ramifications of it going wrong were not worth thinking about, even *with* the soothing knowledge that Victoria didn't have her phone. But oddly, I felt good. I found I had a reserve of energy, of confidence even, that I didn't realise I possessed without a glass in my hand, and it actually felt empowering. My thoughts were clear and uncluttered, the colours around me vivid, not sepia. I'd forgotten how it felt to embrace the challenge of fear without a crutch, but I was surprised to learn I liked the feeling, even if it unsettled me a little. I was nervous, yes, but not angry this time. I just wanted to have it out with the woman rationally, to reason with her, and get some reassurance she'd stop with the whole photo thing, assure us she would delete them when she got back home.

We crept up the gravel drive like robbers, shhhhing one another if a foot was placed down too heavily. Gravel isn't the most burglar-friendly material and every crunch seemed like a glass windowpane shattering. There were no apparent signs of life – no torch light darting about inside, no curtains twitching.

'She's not here. This is completely pointless,' said Zoe when we reached the porch.

'Well, we're going to go in anyway,' I said. I liked the decisive edge to my voice. 'Evie knows what she saw.'

'Okay.' Zoe shrugged.

I lifted the key to the lock and tried to slide it in gracefully, quietly, but my hands were shaking and I ended up fumbling about like I was drunk and trying to let myself in the house late at night.

'Quick, before someone sees!' Lara rolled her eyes upwards. 'God, I am far too boring for this kind of caper!'

Three pairs of incredulous eyes turned to glare at her. 'Lara, you're a *swinger*,' Zoe said.

Alice and Lara looked at one another and smiled.

'Yeah, but not a cat-burglar,' Lara said.

'But we're not breaking in,' I told them. 'I have a key! Besides cat-burglars let themselves in the *back* door . . .'

'And we all know that's against Lara's rules . . .' Zoe giggled.

'Shhhh!' I could feel the sweat on my brow. I wiggled the key again, and in one silky motion the door slid open. 'Voila!'

Zoe gave a little clap.

'Where do we go?' Alice whispered.

'Kitchen's this way.' I nodded to the left. I took my phone out of my pocket, flicked on the torch and led the way to the home's airy, open-plan kitchen. On the stone benchtop sat a half-eaten bar of Lindt chocolate, some packet noodles and a bag of Doritos. The bright packaging was the only touch of colour in the whole white-washed room.

'Well, it's not her,' whispered Alice. 'There's no way she'd eat any of that shit. Have you seen the size of her?'

'That's ridiculous,' said Zoe. 'Everyone loves Doritos.'

'They might belong to the tradies who came in after I took the photos. Let's keep looking. I only have one per cent battery.'

Alice sighed. 'Why didn't you charge it?'

'I was in the cinema watching a bloody remake of *Lassie*. How was I to know we were going to be breaking and entering?'

'It's not breaking in, apparently,' Lara said, sarcastically.

'Well, I didn't bring my phone,' said Zoe.

'Mine's in the car,' said Alice.

'Awesome,' I sighed.

We walked from room to room on the ground floor – into the living area with its lonely wooden floorboards and faux fireplace, the downstairs bathroom with the sliding door and the faint smell of disinfectant. Everything was sterile and lonely looking, like a shell vacated by a hermit crab. The smell of people, of life, was still there, yet there was nothing living or breathing inside.

That's when my phone ran out.

I led the way upstairs in the darkness, treading softly on the carpet runner. I nodded my head to the right. 'Master bedroom first.'

We filed in. 'Nice room,' Zoe whispered, her face lit by the street lamp outside. She turned her body round so that it was facing the mirrored wardrobe, and jumped back dramatically at the sight of herself.

'Holy shit!' she screamed, her hand to her chest. 'Who the fuck . . . ? Oh, it's only me!'

There was a moment of silence before Alice let out a snort of laughter, followed by Lara, then Zoe and then, to my surprise, me.

'I thought to myself, "Shit, she's hot",' Zoe said.

We all began to giggle again, and it was just like the squeaky fart someone does in assembly when you're a kid, a fart that isn't all that hilarious in itself, but is when you consider the gravity of the situation you're in. And I'm not joking, we all laughed like idiots, out of control with the craziness of the situation, momentarily breaking the seal of whatever dislike we had for one another, or whatever sense of awkwardness there was. I remember my eyes meeting Zoe's as we laughed, and God, it felt so . . . liberating.

When we'd wiped our eyes, and were all done with the customary, 'God, how funny was that?' chatter, Alice said, at normal volume, 'Well she's not here, is she, so we may as well put on the light because I can't for the life of me work out where the door is.' Which of course made us all start up again.

I reached up for the switch and threw the room suddenly into wakefulness.

'Shall we go?' Alice motioned towards the door.

Zoe moved towards the mirror and began inspecting her eyebrows, looking at herself from one side, and then from the other. 'It's a good mirror,' she said.

The rest of us began to file out of the door, and were following each other languidly to the top of the stairs when I heard Zoe let out a scream.

'Zoe?' I turned and ran back into the room, to see her crouched down in the doorway of the en suite bathroom with her back to me. She was bent over someone, and all I could see was a blonde head resting on her shoulders, face down.

'Victoria?' I whispered.

The peroxide head lifted up, and its eyes fixed on mine. Eyes that were purple and black, with a ring of yellow underneath. Eyes that were puffy and grotesque. She pulled away from Zoe to face me as I stood in the doorway, with Alice to my left and Lara to my right, squeezed into the wooden doorframe. And it was then I saw the enormity of the injuries. Her face was yellow, apart from the eyes, her arms black and blue. Her eyes, make-up free and tired beyond measure, were dry, as if they were resigned to their fate. Eyes that had no more fight left in them, which were utterly and irrefutably defeated.

'Oh, Victoria!' I stepped forward instinctively, towards my nemesis. The only proper enemy I'd really had in my entire life. I reached out, took her bruised hand in mine in a gesture that – and I can't really explain why – came completely naturally. A gesture that Alice told me later was one of the kindest, most genuinely forgiving things she had seen in her entire life.

'Victoria,' I said, as though I was talking to a wounded child. Which I suppose I was. 'Victoria, sweetie. What on earth . . . what on earth happened to you?'

Chapter Twenty-three
Alice

Transcript: The voice of Alice Daniels in the office of Dr Martha Davis.

She appeared out of nowhere! God, it gave us all the fright of our lives! Not just because she was hiding inside the en suite, but because of the way she looked. Her face was yellow, like morning urine, all jaundiced, almost *treacly*, and she had these large purple – no, *black* – rings around her eyes. Her lips were fat, abnormally fat. Swollen. Honestly, it was like she was one of those women you read about in the newspaper who says, 'I only went to the clinic to get a millilitre of fillers, and I came out like this!' It was grotesque, cartoon-like. And to top it off, there was an angry scarlet wound on her top lip, which had crusted over with a yellow scab and was weeping some kind of clear sap.

She was just sitting there, on the white tiled bathroom floor, her hands wrapped around her legs, hugging herself, and every so often she would emit a sudden tremble, like the tremors you get with the flu. It was pretty shocking, I have to say. But the most shocking thing of all was the look in her eyes. She looked dead. Like she didn't give a shit about anyone or anything. Like she'd given up on life. I'll never forget it, as long as I live.

Amanda, bless her, stepped over to her instinctively. She crouched on the floor and coaxed her to look up with a gentle touch of the hand. I felt really quite proud of her, for that. For putting her feelings out of the way to comfort this bitch of a woman, who'd brought her nothing but grief. And she wasn't doing it for any other reason than compassion. She'd forgotten about the photos at that point, I'm sure – she genuinely wanted to help Victoria. 'Sweetie,' she kept calling her. 'Are you okay, sweetie? Talk to me, sweetie.' But Victoria didn't want to talk at first – that was until Lara said, 'I'm calling an ambulance', and Victoria's head shot up, which must have really hurt, and she said, 'NO!' and Lara lifted her hands up in surrender, and said, 'Okay, it's okay.'

We sat in a sort of circle on the bathroom floor, which, I recall, was really cold, and which in other circumstances would have been nice, because of the overbearing humidity outside. Amanda and Zoe were on either side of Victoria, and Lara and I sat opposite, facing the full-length mirror. At one point, I realised my leg was touching Lara's, and I looked up into the mirror and our eyes locked there for a second, and it was strange, because Lara looked almost a bit . . . *lovestruck*, if I'm honest, and I thought, *Oh dear, I can't be doing with this*, so I blinked and turned my head pointedly towards Victoria, moving my leg away from hers.

Did the issue of the photos cross my mind? Well, of course it did. After all, we'd gone to the house for a reason, hadn't we? But strangely, for those few minutes on the floor, it was simply about the circle we were in. The circle of support, as Amanda called it later. We sat like that for five minutes, maybe ten, no one uttering a single word, all of us just kind of contemplating, listening to the rain beating down outside and the wind whipping up a frenzy, while Amanda held Victoria's hand, gently.

After a while, Amanda asked her, 'Have you been here the whole time?'

Victoria opened her mouth to speak, which obviously hurt, because she winced and just nodded.

'You know, everyone's been so worried about you.'

Victoria looked at her and blinked, eyes still dead.

But Amanda pressed on. 'What happened to you, sweetie? Who did this?'

Victoria sighed. Her eyes filled up with tears, which was a surprise, since you don't expect that kind of emotional response from someone as brutal as her.

'My husband,' she said, with a crack in her voice. 'He hit me.'

'Nico?' Amanda asked.

Victoria nodded.

'Oh my God,' Lara gasped. 'But why?'

Victoria fixed her gaze on Amanda, as if she didn't want to converse with the rest of us, only her.

'Because he's a monster,' she said. A tear raced down her cheek, over the bruise, and stopped in the cut on her lip. 'A fucking monster.'

'Has he done it before?'

'More times than I can remember.'

'Why this time?'

'Because he's in deep shit, and I'm the fall guy.'

'What do you mean?'

Victoria did a fake laugh. 'He didn't just get fired, Amanda,' she said. 'He was arrested for insider trading and he's being investigated by the Australian Federal Police. We had to sell this house, the house I grew up in, to pay his bail. We're finished,' she said. 'Finished.'

Zoe and I exchanged wide-eyed glances.

'And that's why he hit you?'

'Yes, because it's my fault. I'm the one who throws the lavish parties and who wants the excessive life, apparently. I'm the one who's always buying clothes, and shops at Only Organic and will only go to the Jean-Michel Cousteau resort!'

'Where?' Zoe asked.

'It's a five-star resort in Fiji,' Victoria clarified. 'You wouldn't have heard of it. It's very luxurious.'

Zoe looked like she was about to protest but thought better of it and closed her mouth.

'That's why he was under so much pressure to make money,' Victoria continued. 'Except it has nothing to do with that, because he hit . . . *hits* me all the time, regardless.'

'How often?'

'I missed the St Cecilia's fete last year because he'd beaten me up so badly, I had a cut next to my eye. He usually goes for the face, you see.'

'So it happens regularly?' I asked her.

'Maybe once a month, if I'm lucky. When you came over for Melbourne Cup day, Amanda, I had a swollen eye.'

'Yes,' Amanda looked pensive. 'You told us all you'd walked into a door.'

'Did I? A door, a post, the stairs . . . I've honestly lost track of what I tell people. I can't even *remember* what that beating was for. When he found out about Mr Perkins, he lost it, because he said it was my fault I'd let him out of the front door when you turned up. He smashed me up against the outside wall for letting the damn dog get out, hurt my wrist.'

'That's why you were in a sling when I saw you up at school afterwards,' said Amanda. 'Victoria, I am genuinely sorry.' She leaned forward and took Victoria's hand again. It was like she'd forgotten that the woman had us all over a barrel. But that's Amanda for you – compassionate to the letter.

Victoria half-smiled. 'Yeah? Well I don't care anymore. I can't go back there. Maybe it was worth the pain to finally make me realise that I'm done.'

I thought of the twins, about whether I'd leave them with an abusive husband. It made my stomach churn. 'What about the girls? Are they . . . *safe*?' I asked. I mean, it stood to reason this volatile man might do something stupid to his children.

'They're fine. They've been with my sister all week in the city,' she said. 'Things at home have been so bad since he lost his job, I just thought it would be best to get them away for a few days. Believe it or not, he's never touched the girls, and he never would,' she told me. 'He shouts and they are scared of him, but he's never raised a hand to them. That's one thing he wouldn't do. I am positive about that. They all know I am safe, by the way. The girls. I wouldn't have gone without telling them I was okay.

I told them I'm on a top-secret mission for their father's birthday and they can't tell anyone, especially him. Clara knows what he's really like, of course. She's old enough to understand.'

Zoe turned to me. 'That's fucked,' she mouthed.

'You do know you've been listed as *missing*, Victoria?' said Amanda. 'It is serious.'

Victoria didn't seem remotely fazed by that nugget of information. 'Oh, he reported me missing did he? Must be shitting himself I won't go back. Or that I've done something stupid. As if! I'm going to get my face cleared up and then I'm going to take the girls and get away from him for good. But wherever we go, we won't have to stay there long because, by the looks of things, he's going to be put away for a long, long time.'

'He's going to go to jail?' asked Lara.

'He's been caught using the proceeds of an illegal deal to . . . to fund his gambling and the kids' school fees among other things,' she said. 'Even his lawyer says there is no way he can escape it. She thinks he'll get at least two years, maybe one on a good behaviour bond.'

'But surely beating up his wife could make things so much worse?'

'You'd think,' she said. 'But he knows I'll never make an official complaint.'

'But surely this time you will?' I offered.

'Never,' she said. 'I will not let my younger children know their father is a monster. I won't do it.' She looked at us all, one by one, her eyes glazed with panic. 'You cannot tell a soul.'

Now, it may have been highly inappropriate, but I thought to myself, *If you don't mention it now, you never will*, and I said, 'Of course we won't, but you need to delete those photos you have of us. It is only fair, Victoria.'

Amanda's eyes snapped up to meet mine, alarm written all over her face. 'Alice, not now,' she snapped.

Victoria smiled, then winced and put her finger to her lip. 'Those? Oh please, I had forgotten about them completely. I was just angry – angry about Mr Perkins and my husband's reaction, and the fact we were about to lose everything. I was still reeling from the fact we'd had to leave a school like St Cecilia's to go to a *public* school. *No offence* . . .'

'None taken,' mumbled Zoe.

'It was a silly error of judgement.'

'What were you going to do with the photos exactly?' I asked.

'I hadn't quite decided. At the trivia night, I talked myself into emailing them to Mrs Denner.'

Amanda's hand flew to her mouth. 'But you didn't . . . ?'

'No! Amanda, I was so riled by seeing your face at school at the year one assembly, even though you didn't see me, and everything came flooding back,' she continued. 'The carpet, my darling dog, the faces of my beautiful girls when I told them about Perky. Then to see you and Ted so happy when *he* was being such a bully at home. It made me angry. I felt as though you'd fucked everything up for me, yet here you were, lapping up your new persona at Darley Heights.'

'Life isn't perfect for me, Victoria,' Amanda told her.

I jumped in before Amanda could make it a pity party. 'Why did you threaten to put them on the Facebook page?'

'Humiliation, Alice!' She shrugged. 'Why else? Or maybe I might have just held on to them just to make you sweat, I just don't know. I wasn't thinking clearly. And then as it happened, I got a royal beating from my husband, and so I didn't do anything with them.'

'Why did you involve the rest of us, though?' Zoe asked. 'What did we ever do to you?'

'You were friends with Amanda,' Victoria sighed. 'Like I said, I was irrational, angry. If I was going to drop a bomb, I wanted to make it a big one, I suppose.'

Zoe shook her head angrily, but to her credit, she didn't speak.

'So where are they now?' I asked, very gently. I didn't want to go in all guns blazing, you see, just in case it annoyed her.

Victoria was silent long enough for us all to sweat a little. 'The photos? Oh, I've deleted them from my phone, please don't worry. In fact, I'd done it even before you all came and yelled at me in my own garden.'

'Really?' Amanda asked, hopefully.

Victoria nodded. 'The girls play games on my phone all the time. I was hardly going to keep those pornographic photos on it, was I? And besides, I wouldn't want my children associated with this whole mucky scenario at school.'

I must have still looked anxious, because she said, 'Oh, don't worry Alice, I deleted them from the cloud, too.'

I felt my shoulders drop.

'But tell me,' she asked us, 'what were you all *doing*? At trivia night of all places?'

It was a fair enough question, I suppose.

'Don't ask,' Amanda and I said in unison.

'Swinging,' said Lara brightly.

Victoria smiled, and it was the most genuine smile I'd seen from her yet. 'And I thought I was messed up,' she said.

It was about this point that it seemed to dawn on the rest of us that we had partners at home. I imagined Pete standing in the kitchen waiting for the milk to make his nightly mug of cocoa, fretting about why I wasn't home. He would assume I'd gone to Amanda's, and no doubt Ted would think Amanda was at my place, chatting, handing over a jacket and staying for a wine. And, of course, Zoe was at '*yoga*'. That was one good thing, we all had an alibi. Although Christ knows what Lara's was – I still don't know. I don't think I ever asked, actually.

'Yes, please, go. I'll be fine,' Victoria sniffed. She sounded like Oliver Twist asking for more.

'Where have you been sleeping?' Amanda asked. 'There's no bed in here.'

'On the hammock on the porch,' she said. 'It's been so hot outside. I don't care. I used to sleep there all the time when I was a teenager.'

Amanda was incredulous. 'Well you can't do that,' she said, and she gently hauled Victoria up by the hand. 'It's pouring with rain. You're coming home with me. You can sleep in the spare bed. Ted won't care. He won't ask you any questions, he is very discreet, I promise.'

Victoria looked up at her, with tears in her eyes, as if she were asking why Amanda would be that kind to her, after everything. Even if she did think Amanda was only making the offer for penance, she didn't seem to care. The gratitude was pasted on her face like cheap foundation. She stood up. I'd only met her a couple of times, but I'd been blown away by her stature, she was so tall and sort of stately. Terrifying, really. But she seemed to have shrunk in the last few days, her upright frame now oddly shrivelled with humility, and also, I presumed, fear.

'What day is it?' she said in a small voice. 'It's Friday, right?'

'Yep,' said Zoe, shrugging her raincoat back on.

'My husband has squash and then beers from seven o'clock until about ten on Friday nights. He won't change his routine because of me being gone. Maybe I could just go home and get some clothes if you girls would come with me? I mean, I'm pretty sure he won't be there, but just in case? I can't see him right now.'

Amanda nodded. 'We'll go there now, all of us, and I can ring the doorbell first to check he's out.' And we filed out of the house obediently and into the car, Lara wedged in the confines of Evie's car seat, which she was petite enough to fit into, and drove to the house with the blood-spattered driveway and that pitiful, frangipani-laden dog shrine.

Nico wasn't home, as Victoria had predicted, but he'd definitely been there recently, because all of the lights were on, and later, when I went inside after Amanda and Victoria,

I noticed there was a Tupperware pot with a blue lid covered in condensation on the kitchen counter and a Post-it note on top that read, in a loosely joined-up scrawl, *Nico, if there's anything I can do to help, holler. Love, Tansie XOXO.* I remember that because she'd underlined the word anything, which made it sound pretty suggestive, like she was offering a pot of chilli and a blow job.

Amanda had waved to the car from the doorstep to show the coast was clear, and Victoria slid out. I watched her scurry up the driveway, evidently fearful she would be caught by the neighbourhood watch. Together, the two of them entered the house.

Everything from this point onwards is a little blurry, I'm afraid, because of what happened next. I vaguely remember tapping my hands on the steering wheel impatiently, because I wanted to get home and relax now that we'd realised we were no longer about to be exposed by our blackmailer. I had so much to do at home, plus I'd promised Freya I would watch a YouTube tutorial on how to do a fishtail plait so she could show it off to Evie because 'Auntie Amanda's plaits are really bad'. Lara and Zoe were deep in discussion about the fact neither of them had eaten dinner and they were both starving. Maybe we even said a few things along the line of, 'Thank God for that' – you know, because of the photos and the fact they couldn't come back and bite us on the arse. I just don't really remember, to be honest, save for the fact we were all bloody relieved the whole icky ordeal was well and truly over. I presumed they'd grab a few things to chuck in a bag, Amanda and Victoria, and then get straight out before Nico got home. I guessed they'd be five minutes, tops.

But they'd been gone less than a minute when we heard the scream. A sort of animalistic wail that echoed in my eardrums even though there were two sets of windows closed between me and it. A cry that was so voluminous and high pitched and terrible that it could have pierced the night sky and shattered it into a billion pieces. And it came from Amanda.

Chapter Twenty-four
Zoe

From: Zoe.m8kin79@realworld.com.au
To: pho_e_b_wallis@zapmail.com
Subject: The truth

The scream was blood-curdling. You know that episode of *One Born Every Minute* I made you watch before I had Freddie? Well think about one of those God-awful labour howls, and multiply it by 5,000. Seriously, it was enough to give you tinnitus a kilometre away. Alice was like, *What the actual . . . ?* And the three of us literally propelled ourselves out of our seats, up the drive and up the stairs where the noise came from. It was unmistakably Amanda's wail and I seriously wondered if we were about to find her dying in a pool of her own blood at the top of the stairs, and Victoria standing over her with a carving knife and a psychotic smile on her face. Alice was evidently wondering the same and was completely shitting herself, you could tell by the way she flew up the stairs ahead of us all crying, *Mand? Mand?*

Alice got to the door of the master bedroom first and took a single step in. She realised immediately what had happened, and kind of pushed Lara and me back with a shake of the head, as if to say, *Don't come in here, it's not something you want to see.* But I *did* want to see, because I already knew what was in there beyond that door, and

I felt like I needed to go and look for myself. Like it was going to be cathartic or something.

Through the doorway, all I could see was Victoria standing opposite Alice. Her face was blank and she started to walk towards us, her hands hanging limply by her sides like a zombie. She was staring at the floor, and as she got to the doorway, to us, she raised her eyes up to meet Alice's, then Lara's, then mine. And I noticed the way she did it, like a woman who was so tired of everything, of sleeplessness and of life. It was as if her eyelids, which were the colour of blueberries, forgot to move up at the same time as her eyeballs, which also contained a whole lot of nothingness. Black pupils that didn't care. I turned to watch her as she descended the stairs below, her hands hanging and her head slumped. Lara turned to follow her, grabbing onto her arm and leading her safely to the bottom step. I could hear her talking to Victoria, asking her questions, but she didn't get a response. Victoria was like Goldie Hawn in the movie *Overboard*, when she's so exhausted that all she can do is sink into the giant water bucket and go bub-bub-bub-bub-bub.

I followed Alice into the bedroom and turned the corner and that's when I saw the bed. Amanda was slumped down beside it, in shock, and Alice broke the silence by shouting, *Can someone make some sweet tea?* and Lara yelled back *I'll do it after I've called triple 0.*

He was lying there on his back, Nico, the cover thrown off him, in white Bonds boxer shorts. His skin was a kind of a yellow colour and waxy, and the hairs on his chest protruded like bits of curly wire. Maybe they had been soft once, but now they were kind of gross, like thick, wiry pubes. His toenails were purple. His eyes were closed, but his mouth open, like he was in a deep sleep and I half expected him to sit up and say, *Who the fuck are you lot? Get out of my bedroom!* He looked pretty relaxed, pretty chilled, and if it weren't for all the foil pill packets lying around him, labels showing loads of 'O's and 'X's and 'Y's in their names, along with the empty bottle of whisky on the bedside table, I'd have assumed he just went gently, in his sleep.

Alice was standing behind Amanda, her feet sort of nailed to the spot, and as she reached to stroke Amanda's head, I noticed her hands were trembling. But I don't have it, the fear of death, which most people seem to have. I just felt sad for Nico that he was alone, and that no one was with him when he passed. Even wife-beaters don't deserve to die alone, do they? Or do they, Phoebs? I just don't know.

It's okay, I found myself saying to him, touching his face. *You're not alone.* And as Alice walked Amanda to the doorway and down the stairs, I heard myself talking to Nico, the insider trader, the wife-beater, the man who had seemed so nice at the supermarket when I'd expressed my concern about his missing wife. *You don't have to worry about any of this shit any more.* And then, because it felt like the most natural thing in the world, I kissed his forehead, and even though it was warm outside, his body felt like ice. And I couldn't even tell you why I did it Phoebs. Before you, I was terrified of death, of the shock of it, the finality, the way someone else's morbidity reminds you that your own is to come. I would never have been able to look at a dead body before, let alone touch one.

But after you died, I realised that there is something achingly peaceful in death. I never got to see you or hold your hand, but I could do it for him, and whatever kind of a man he'd been in life, I truly believe he deserved the warm touch of a living hand before he was handed over to the morgue. Everybody deserves that, don't they? I only hope someone held your hand like that, or touched your beautiful, thick hair, as you lay on the bank of the River Avon on that frosty night, after those poor kids had pulled you out. I'll never know, because the people who found you didn't want to make contact with us – and that was their choice – but I'll never stop hoping, or believing they comforted you in the minutes after. Nico went, like you, through his own choosing, and having some understanding of the tempest that must have been raging in his brain right before he took the last of the pills and washed them down with the single malt, was enough to warrant a touch of the hand and a kiss of the brow, in my humble view.

I called Miles from Victoria's en-suite toilet, which is bigger than our bedroom. I told him we'd found Victoria and explained what happened to Nico. He didn't ask me anything else or say anything about the fact I was meant to be at yoga, he just listened and said, *Do you want me to come and get you?* I told him to stay with Freddie and that I'd be home when I was home and that the police were on the way. Then I told him, *Miles, I love you so much. If I never told you how amazing you were when I lost Phoebe, then I want you to know it now.*

I do know, baby, Miles replied. *I do know.*

The police had arrived by the time I got back downstairs. There were two of them, and they looked like they were both about twenty-one and had been shoved on the weekend shift because they were rookies. They called for their superiors, and then for an ambulance to triple check Nico was dead (even though it was obvious because he was stiffer than a paddleboard) and then advised that none of us could go back in the bedroom until officers from Crime Scene had been to take photos and assess the area 'just because it's not your run-of-the-mill in-your-sleep death'. Victoria looked a bit weirded-out at the suggestion that someone might have *done* something to Nico and spent the whole time the crime scene cops were upstairs snapping away with their cameras in their blue overalls, twisting her enormous diamond ring around on her wedding finger and biting her lip.

Soon after this, two detectives – a man and a woman – arrived with their notepads and trench coats, like they do in the movies. They took a good look upstairs and then came back down to chat to us. They were keen to know about Victoria's bruises, and she told them the whole story, about the insider trading and the court appearance, and about how he would beat her up whenever he was under any stress. She told them she thought he took his own life because he couldn't live with himself for fucking everything up financially. He'd been seeing a psychologist, she said, because of his anger issues, and added that he had mentioned a couple of times that he was suicidal. She said, with a sob, *I never actually thought he'd go and do it!* and gave them a number for Nico's psychologist just in case they needed any professional notes to corroborate his troubled state of mind.

While she was talking to the police, Victoria was animated, almost more alive than she had been all night. It's like she'd slugged a triple espresso or something. The adrenaline had kicked in, obviously, but what I could see from my vantage point was relief. Her pallor had changed, she was pinker, and her eyeballs seemed moist again. Her abuser was gone. Her body was straighter as she spoke about him, the man who was dead and quietly decomposing on top of the 300-count Egyptian cotton sheets in the room above our heads.

For the next couple of hours, the detectives chatted to us individually. We each told them how shocked we were about Nico, and how we all knew he couldn't live with himself for what he had been doing to Victoria, and that she had told us all about it. I told them he was a Jekyll and Hyde man – lovely to your face, but a monster on the inside – and that he probably just couldn't live with himself. When they'd spoken to all of us, and checked in with Nico again upstairs, they had a little chat amongst themselves outside the front door, and I heard one of them say, *I'm pretty sure we can rule out foul play, here, Fiona! Crime Scene said it's pretty obvious he downed the pills!* Fiona replied, *I couldn't agree more, Tim. It looks pretty self-explanatory to me.* Fiona came back and told Victoria that there would be no need for an autopsy, because the coroner's findings were likely to show Nico offed himself (although she didn't use those words, obviously), which was all the more conclusive since he was having counselling for mental health issues. She told Victoria to presume the matter was finished because it would be very unlikely to end up in the coroner's court, and said there were plenty of counselling options available to her and her girls and that she should utilise them. Then she smiled and nodded at the photo of Victoria with her daughters on the fridge in their school uniforms and said *What beautiful girls* and then, *Thank you for the Scotch Fingers and the tea*, and then, *Come on Tim, let's call it a night.*

Just as the sun was beginning to rise, a private ambulance arrived. The two men who emerged had grief-stricken looks pasted on their faces. *It's okay, I'm the friend*, I told them, and they seemed to brighten up. *Okey dokey, let's go up and get him*, said the taller of the two, and I pointed up the staircase, following behind as they dragged the stretcher up the stairs with a grey plastic zip-up bag slung over the top.

The ambos thanked us and left shortly after and we knew we should all get some rest after that, but none of us were tired, none of us wanted to sleep. We were still in the kitchen, Victoria and Lara at the bench, Alice stirring sugar into a cup of tea and Amanda, who had finally got her shit together, was studying the photos on Victoria's fridge.

What will you do now? Lara asked her.

I don't know, she said. *Focus on my girls.*

Alice asked her then if she would be okay, like, without Nico.

Yes, she replied and she didn't hesitate. *He was my abuser.* Then she told us, *I know why he did it. He did it to do one last good thing for us.*

We looked at her, like, *How do you mean?*

And this I remember as clear as day. She stirred her tea and locked her eyes on each of us, one by one, and spoke very slowly and clearly. *He knew we were going to lose everything when he went to jail*, she said, *so that's why he did it. His life insurance policy was over two million dollars. He did it for the girls.*

I swear, Alice spat out her tea so violently, it hit the wall.

Shit, we said, pretty much in unison. *That's insane.*

Victoria nodded, and took a sip of her own tea, leaving us all a bit speechless.

It wasn't until the early hours of the morning, when I was standing in my own kitchen with a mug in my hand, that I realised in the whole time we'd all been talking, Victoria never actually called Nico by his name. That's how much she must have hated him.

Chapter Twenty-five
Amanda

The police said we could strip the bed after they'd moved him, so I did it with Zoe. Victoria wanted to throw away the sheets, not wash them, which I understood completely. Who would want to sleep on sheets their husband had gone out on? They didn't smell or anything, but when I unhooked the fitted sheet from one corner of the bed, I saw a big, black pube, which looked like it was a man's if you know what I mean, and I actually felt the vomit come into my mouth. My head thumped angrily, and if ever I needed alcohol, it was then.

'You okay?' Zoe asked.

'I just feel a bit queasy.'

'I'll get you some water.' She walked into the bathroom and ran the tap. When she came back out, she said, 'You know, my sister died.'

'I didn't,' I said. 'That's awful. Can I ask how?'

'She killed herself, like Nico.'

'Oh, Zoe,' was all I could say. I looked at her and saw her eyes fill with tears. I felt a new urge to total myself on whisky, but even my giant cravings couldn't extend to drinking the dregs from the bottle of single malt on a dead man's dressing table. Even I drew the line at that, although admittedly, I did have to think about it twice.

'She jumped off a bridge. In England. Two years ago. She struggled with depression and she hit a bad patch.'

'I'm so sorry,' I said, seeing Zoe for the first time as someone other than the woman who slept with my husband.

Zoe shrugged. 'I was on the phone to her when it happened, so it was pretty tough.'

'Oh my God.' I touched her hand. 'How awful.'

'I haven't told anyone else at Darley. I don't know why I'm telling you.' She shrugged.

'Maybe because it's Suicide Friday,' I offered.

She smiled and shrugged. 'Maybe.'

'I am so very sorry, Zoe,' I said. 'I had no idea.'

'I'm sorry too,' she replied. 'I really am.' And I knew she was no longer talking about her sister.

Later, Victoria gave me her clothes to wash, or rather I asked for them, since she'd been wearing the same stuff for four days and she actually smelled bad, like really bad. The kind you get a whiff of when you pass some old guy in the gym who thinks it's manly to stink. Put it this way, she didn't have the waft of Dior Poison she always had back in the days when she was glamorous.

She didn't want to sleep in the house that night, even though they'd taken Nico away in a body bag, and I got why. So instead we all got back inside my car – five of us by then, not four – her in the front seat by virtue of trauma suffered, and the others in the back seat, Lara in the booster again, and we dropped them off, one by one, driving from house to house until it was just the two of us.

We drove along in silence, Victoria looking out of the window, her hands in her lap.

'I really am so sorry,' I told her as I pulled up in the driveway and turned off the engine. The lights were out, everyone asleep.

'People always say that when someone dies, don't they?' she said. 'As if it's their fault. I've always thought that was a little strange.'

'I didn't actually mean that,' I said. 'I mean, I *am* sorry about Nico, but I actually meant about everything else. About your dog, the staircase, the carpet . . .'

'Amanda,' she said, her tone weary. 'That stuff is small fry. I honestly couldn't give a shit about any of it now, even Mr Perkins. Yes, it was traumatic at the time, but it was nothing in the grand scheme of things.'

We sat in silence for a moment.

'I have to know, though,' I said. 'How did you work out what we were all doing on trivia night? I mean, was it that obvious?'

'I guessed.' She shrugged. 'One of my frien— *acquaintances* had heard Lara and Luke were on the swinging scene. Then I saw you all flirting wildly with one another and I worked it out. You were all over Luke like a rash and Zoe was all over Ted – sorry, I know you probably don't like to hear that – and I just kept watching and it was just, well, obvious what was going on and how it might play out. It probably wouldn't have been obvious to anyone else, but I suppose I was looking for something.'

'But photos, though?'

Victoria looked out of the window in silence, like she was choosing her words.

'I've already told you,' she said. 'I was angry. I suppose I wanted you to suffer as much as I had.' She put a hand up to her swollen face. 'But I took it too far. I shouldn't have done it.'

'But what about Zoe and Lara and Alice? They didn't run over your dog.'

'What can I say? I was dealing with domestic violence and a husband who was about to be jailed for insider trading. I watched you, from the start of the evening, knocking back the booze and dancing and having fun, all of you at that table. Everyone was merry, everyone was enjoying themselves, and I was miserable. I'd just been booted out of St Cecilia's and I was on eggshells at home, thinking he would blow at any time. I guess I just wanted every one of you at the table to suffer, like me and my girls were suffering.

'You have to understand, Amanda, that every action I've ever taken has been to protect my girls. Why do you think I pushed for you to leave St Cecilia's? Because my beautiful girls, particularly Darcy, couldn't bear seeing Evie every day and remembering what happened to their sweet dog. I wanted you gone so they wouldn't have to deal with it at school as well as at home.'

She stared ahead. 'And I suppose emailing the photos to Mrs Denner would have seen you pushed out of Darley Heights too – I liked the idea of having that option if it became too much for the girls to deal with having you and Evie there. As it happens, they're okay. Darcy is obviously a lot more forgiving than me because she's ecstatic to see Evie again.'

She laughed, then winced as the cut on her lip stretched and reddened with fresh blood. 'What can I say Amanda? A mother will go to extraordinary lengths to protect her children. Surely you appreciate that?'

I felt bad then for bringing up something that seemed so trivial given what she'd been through. For somehow twisting the situation and making it about me.

'I'm sorry for asking,' I said. 'It wasn't the appropriate time to mention it. I . . . I just wish I'd known what was going on at home, Victoria, and then I could have helped you. Or I could have tried to help you, at least. I would have tried to make it better.'

She turned to me.

'I wouldn't have let you,' she said, not unkindly. The pride, the anger, the one-upmanship all seemed to have evaporated, and it brought a softness to her face I hadn't seen before. I'd always thought her harsh, angular, perhaps ugly even, but right then, even with the angry bruises and the fat lip, she was incredibly beautiful. And in that moment, it seemed amazing to me how kindness, or lack of it, could determine someone's aesthetics.

She flicked open the headboard and looked in the mirror, slamming it shut almost immediately with a grimace.

'I'm like you, Amanda,' she said, fingering the cut on her lip. 'In fact, we're far more alike than you think.'

'How do you mean?'

'Pride.'

I must have looked confused, because she smiled and took my hand, enveloping it in her bony fingers. She was still wearing her platinum wedding band, along with her engagement ring with the giant, emerald-cut diamond. It was about four times the size of mine.

'I need you to do something for me,' she said, and for a moment I panicked, thinking she was going to say something sinister and that maybe she hadn't got rid of those pictures after all, and she was going to make me do something awful or she would hit 'post'. When all was said and done, I still hardly knew the woman and she was far from my BFF, even if we had just shared a moment. She still had the capacity, I knew, to be incredibly mean.

'What do you want me to do?' I asked, and felt the panic swelling. 'Sort the Facebook page? I can do that . . . do you want me to put up a post explaining about Nico? I think the followers of the Find Victoria page need to know you're okay.'

I knew I was grasping at straws, playing the sycophant so she wouldn't go for the jugular.

'Amanda?'

'Yes?'

'I would love you to post on the page, thank you. But what I would really like would be for you to get some help,' she said, staring into my eyes. She didn't blink.

'You mean, like, domestic help?'

She laughed, which made her wince, and she touched her lip again.

'No. I mean with the booze. I'm going to be very honest with you now, because we have crossed a threshold tonight and learned some very intimate things about one another. You need to get professional help for the sake of your family. It's not . . . it's not normal to behave like you did on

Cup day, to get that trashed every time you go anywhere. I can see it, Amanda, and I've heard whispers about it – and I barely know you.'

I looked at my knees and bit my bottom lip. If it had been Alice or Ted who had thrown that little bomb at me, I would have completely kicked off, shouting and ranting and then sinking a wine. But I was scared of Victoria still, and didn't have the balls to defend myself. And plus, after all she'd been through that night, I didn't feel I had a right of reply. I heard a little voice inside my head protest, 'I didn't drink tonight so I can't be an alcoholic', but I didn't say it out loud, because even the part of my brain that controlled denial realised that this woman, who I had hated so passionately just twenty-four hours ago, had hit the nail bang on the head.

I knew it on Cup day, maybe even earlier. I knew it at trivia night. I knew it when I almost drank the whisky in my mug the morning after I returned home from Luke and Lara's place. I knew it when I yelled up at Victoria's window. I knew it way before any of these events had happened. Events that had snowballed to put me here, in this car, beside Victoria. I knew it on the first day I had the booze van deliver vodka to me at midday, a couple of weeks after the Melbourne Cup. I knew it when I panicked on the school run one time because I'd been out of it the night before and occasionally, just occasionally, the police would be on the corner of Sunshine Parade doing random breath tests.

Even though the dependency had crept up on me slowly, I had known for a few months that I needed help. I hadn't been able to vocalise it, though. I had let the thoughts swim around in my brain like tadpoles, nudging the membranes, prompting my conscious to act, but I'd blinked them back, shaken them off. Not now. Not now. *Not now.*

But sometimes, it only takes a word from a stranger to open your eyes.

I felt the tears pooling, hot and urgent, but they didn't quite fall even though I wanted them to, even though now felt like as good a time as ever to let them go, to cleanse myself.

'I know,' I said and I looked into the face of my tormentor. 'You are absolutely right.'

Part Three:
Present Day

Chapter Twenty-six
Alice

Transcript: The voice of Alice Daniels in the office of Dr Martha Davis.

I'm so sorry I'm late today, Dr Davis. I've been racing around like a blue-arsed fly, what with school and the new house and PSSA sport. Lottie is playing winter soccer now because I felt that maybe I needed to pull back a little on the academia. You know, give the twins a physical outlet. She's actually very good for a child who's only just turned eight! She's a striker and she tears strips off the boys! The other day a 9-year-old boy told his teammates to 'watch that girl – she's good'. Oh, you should have seen Lottie's face, she was so pleased with herself. She isn't remotely fazed about versing the boys. Freya still only wants to read, of course, but I got a trampoline for the new house last week, and sometimes she actually bounces with a book in her hand. She's currently devouring *Anne of Green Gables*. Ahh, what a book! I remember that one from my own childhood. Lottie bounces and shouts out her times tables. I'll be in the kitchen and I'll hear, 'Nine-times-nine-is-eighty-one!' It's a way to make learning more fun, I suppose.

I've been meaning to set up a session for the last three weeks, but honestly, with all of that, and with my rather significant domestic change, I've been so frantic I just haven't had time. But in all honesty, I haven't really felt I've *needed* to come and see you, which I guess is a good thing, isn't it? I seem to have worked out a good deal of stuff in my own head.

How have I been, *generally*? I suppose you want more detail than Lottie's soccer, don't you, otherwise this will be a very short session! Well, I got asked to be chair of the parent-teacher committee, for starters. As in, the main chairperson and not just the head of the entertainment committee – Victoria Day is doing that role now. Do you remember she helped with the preparations for trivia night? Well, she put her hand in the ring for entertainment chair and she landed the role. We voted her in. There were five votes a piece between her and that awful Tansie Wright woman, and I had the casting vote and so of course I chose Victoria. I mean, she's an organisational genius – a little haphazard with the grammar, but a genius nonetheless. She's just the kind of woman you want helping you sort things out. The kind you want on side! Would you believe she is already thinking ahead to next year's trivia night, seven months out? She's so impressive, an absolute marvel.

I assumed my new role around four months ago, right after Nico's death. In fact, Brigitte Denner phoned me right after his funeral, just as I was leaving the crematorium. She informed me Madeleine Spotfink was leaving the school and asked if I would step up to be the chair. Let's just say she didn't need to ask me twice. I was utterly thrilled and I had to bite down on my smile until I was out on the street.

It's taken every spare moment of my time, but God, it has been fulfilling. And I'd only say this to you, but it's fabulous being in such a position of authority. Not in a power-trippy kind of way, but just, you know, being able to represent our wonderful school and get things done.

How is Pete? Ah yes, Pete – I was about to get on to that! Well obviously there has been a lot of change at home. A new home, in fact. The girls and I have recently moved to a delightful little weatherboard cottage on the outskirts of Darley – a pleasant distance from the stifling school community, I'm pleased to say. No, no, not with Pete! Pete is staying put in his parents' home. A week after Nico's funeral, I told him I wanted to separate. Not a divorce – not yet anyway – but a separation with a view to making it official at a later date.

You don't seem remotely surprised, Dr Davis! I suppose it was inevitable, it just took me a while to realise it. Was it because of Lara? No, no, not at all! Well, perhaps indirectly, but not *because* of her. Just . . . just let me explain.

Nico's death was such a shock for all of us, you know. The idea that a man can go to sleep one night and wake up dead the next (or, not wake up, more to the point) shocked me to the core. I didn't sleep for a week afterwards. I couldn't stop thinking that my life was going to end without me finding any more personal fulfilment. The idea of waking up a whole year down the line, with Pete still snoring beside me, filled me with absolute horror. My mind kept flitting to Lara and what we'd done, and I realised I just didn't have the same sense of . . . *excitement* with Pete. I realised I felt trapped, *stifled* and, at the heart of it, wholly unfulfilled. Moreover, the sense of sadness I had been carrying around with me since the trivia night, along with the feelings Nico's death had stirred up in me, seemed to be affecting my girls. Freya hadn't picked up a book in days! I hadn't realised how morose I had become until one day, a few weeks after the trivia night, Lottie said to me, 'I wish you'd smile more', and I thought, *She's right, I don't smile, and that's because I am fundamentally unhappy.* I realised it wasn't my work, or my children that were making me feel unfulfilled, but my marriage.

I didn't do it lightly, Dr Davis. I thought long and hard about the implications of what I was about to do, about the impact it would have on my girls. About what people would say. But I kept coming back to the same thing: fear. Fear of being in the same marriage in ten years' time. Of growing older, and menopausal, and ultimately grey-haired, alongside a man I cared deeply for, but no longer truly loved. I knew I had to act, before I shrivelled up like a decaying apple core.

Pete was very gracious when I told him. Stoic, in fact. I've always found the fact he is somewhat emotionally vacant to be a drawcard really – we have never done 'drippy' with one another – and I was glad of it then. I sat down beside him on the sofa on a Thursday night and I came right out with it.

'Pete,' I said, as my heart thundered and my throat ached. 'This isn't working any more.'

'What?' he asked. 'The remote control?'

'No,' I told him. 'Us. Our marriage.'

He looked up and fixed his eyes on me, flicking off the David Attenborough documentary on the Fijian crested iguana. 'Go on,' he said.

So I told him I felt like life was passing us both by, that as much as we loved one another, it felt as though we were living like siblings, not lovers. That our marriage had, regrettably, become less than I needed it to be.

And then he surprised me.

'You're right, Alice,' was what he said. 'We have certainly aged one another.'

And while I thought I was delivering the cruellest blow, that I was shattering poor Pete's heart beyond repair, I hadn't considered that my husband might agree. Had I been really looking, I would have seen it at the trivia night, the way he had transformed around Lara, how his whole body had livened up with the possibility of some kind of fresh affection, some passion. How he lumbered around as if a cloud were above him the rest of the time, in a marriage where he was afforded little affection or intimacy.

'I think we both need more,' I said.

'You're certainly looking for something, Alice.'

'What do you mean?'

'I don't know. I just know I don't make you happy any more. You're more content to be with your friends. I mean, the way you light up whenever you talk about Lara . . .'

He looked at me and smiled. 'I just want you to be happy.'

'I'm sorry,' I told him and leaned in, my head on his shoulder.

'Me too,' he said, and we sat and held one another for a long time.

The next day we set about finding me a rental place, and Amanda and Ted moved me in two weeks later. I was melancholic at first, but the feeling was fleeting. Less regret than nostalgia – we had had many happy times in that home. We had taken our babies to that house from the hospital and crossed the threshold with them in their matching Maxi-Cosi capsules. We had celebrated numerous birthdays and Christmases in that home. But it was incredible to be in my own space, to have somewhere of my own, somewhere that will take me on a new path in life.

The girls love it. Two homes is proving such an adventure for them, and I've told them Daddy is welcome to visit any time. And he really is. We still do love one another, Pete and I, and we are not hurtful people. We truly want the best for one another, and for the girls, even if it meant dropping the veil of perfection and admitting, publicly, that our marriage had failed. Yes, it was hard when the stream of condolences came flying at me at school – because God knows I do not like to fail at anything, as you may have gathered – but the sense of freedom I have now outweighs all of that. The view from the chair on my own little veranda negates all the gossip. I can breathe again. I can plan. I can get excited about what the future holds. Amanda is thrilled for me. She came over for dinner the other night and she was all over me with questions. 'So, are you going to start dating? Have you thought about Lara? Have you looked up Jenny?' It was all too much, if I'm honest, but I understand she wants to see me happy.

Jenny? Ah yes. I know you'd like to know about her, wouldn't you Dr Davis? Right, well I might as well tell you, since this is our last session.

Jenny Dobson was beautiful. Quite strikingly so. Aqua eyes and a smile that went off like a flare, magnetising everyone around her. We met when I organised her father's birthday party. It was a bigish affair for about a hundred people and she wanted the whole room at Coral Plateau RSL decorated with blue balloons and Chelsea Football Club paraphernalia. Bill was a fanatic supporter, you see. He was British but had lived in Sydney for forty-odd years and hadn't been to a match in donkey's years, so Jenny wanted a whole football theme to remind him of his roots. We worked together closely to organise it over a month or so, and we became close friends, often sending text messages to one another late at night or just meeting for the odd glass of wine to discuss the party plans. I'd never do that now, of course, but back then, life was generally less professional even if you *were* a professional. The party went off without a hitch and Bill was ecstatic since we'd managed to get him a shirt signed by Ashley Cole and Frank Lampard, two of the team's players that year (it was 2006). Jenny wore a silver dress that was like a 1980s prom dress. Strapless, on the knee, very retro. She looked stunning with her blonde hair pulled up high and her blue eyes lined with kohl, and towards the end of the night, I found myself holed up in a corner chatting to her, oblivious to the rest of the world, unable to take my eyes off her delicate fingers as she twisted her straw and bit on the end of it as she talked. Watching her mouth as she spoke, her teeth, her tongue. At the end of the night, when everyone had left, she pulled me in close and kissed me, and it was like fireworks that I *hadn't* organised were lighting up the night sky.

We spent every moment together after that, night and day, couldn't stay away. She wanted to meet Amanda, so, after much soul-searching (because I didn't even want my best friend to know I had fallen for a woman) I introduced them. But as it happened, Amanda didn't seem that shocked. She didn't care. She encouraged the relationship, asked questions, listened to anecdotes, told me she was so happy that I was so happy. And the months went by and it was blissful. We were so very content together.

Then Jenny said, 'I want to tell everyone.' And that's when it all went wrong.

I couldn't introduce her as my girlfriend to anyone but Amanda, even though she was my girlfriend by that point. I just couldn't do it. The thought of telling my parents I was in a same-sex relationship was enough to bring me out in hives.

'Give me time,' I kept telling her, and she always accepted it without pressing me.

But then six months went past and I was still telling people Jenny was my best mate. When she tried to take my hand in the street, I would unfurl my fingers and take out my phone.

'Do you love me?' she asked.

'More than anything,' I would tell her.

'But not enough to let people know you're mine?'

It was a good point. And a question I didn't have an answer for.

Jenny left me on 5 March, 2007. She walked out of my apartment and told me to look her up when I was ready to be honest with myself. She sobbed as she said it, but I stood mute.

'I'll always love you, Alice,' she said, and she shut the door behind her. I never saw her again.

It was only in the days after that I let myself unravel. Sobbed on Amanda's shoulder, let myself grieve for the woman I loved. I let the heartbreak diet starve me, forced down the soup made by Amanda from scratch for me because she would sit over me until I'd had it. You know what I was saying about my friendship with Amanda being cyclical? Well, this was one of the times she looked after me. She was only just back from her honeymoon, and she invited me into the marital home, and Ted did too. She was there day after day, week after week, month after month, until I pulled myself out of the fug I was in and decided to live again. I will always be grateful to her for that.

Did I ever look for Jenny? God no. I owed her more than that, than to restart something that I couldn't own. Amanda bumped into her in the city about a year after I married Pete and told her about the wedding, and apparently she smiled weakly, nodded and said, 'That figures', and asked Amanda to pass on her 'warm regards'. The last I heard she was living with a school teacher, a woman, up the coast somewhere. Noosa, I think. Do I still think about her? Well, I do still wonder what she is up to sometimes, but it's rare these days. I suppose what happened with Lara dredged it all up again, and I did think about the whole situation a little after the trivia night, about what might have been. But I suppose life worked out the way it was meant to, because I wouldn't have the twins if I hadn't made that particular life choice, would I?

As for Lara, well she is living in Byron Bay now – did you know that? She and Luke moved there. He got offered a position at a swanky cosmetics clinic on some mega salary, she told me, and so he closed his Darley practice, even though he'd only just opened it a few months before, and they upped sticks and left. It's just reopened as a Thai massage place, can you believe that? It got a quickie kit-out and is called Spa Lotus, all pink flowers in the window, and wafts of frangipani as you walk past and beaded curtains in the doorway. Can you imagine? Lara would have loved that, being the consummate hippy. The Darley mums are mortified, because not only do they have to go to Darley Mall for their injectables these days, but they are jabbed by women in white coats with orange faces, balloon lips and fake lashes – and not by the tender hand of Dr Luke Hampson. It caused quite a furore when he announced he was hanging up his white coat and putting down his syringe – apparently his business phone was engaged for about an hour after he put up the notice on his Instagram page, as half of Darley fought for a bit of time on the couch with him before he left. What a shit fight! You should have seen the wrinkle-free faces at the school gates the week after – honestly, I don't think there was a single eyebrow that moved in the whole school.

I'll admit part of me felt sad that Lara was leaving, but like I said to you just now, I think it was probably because the whole thing had brought back memories for me. I saw her before she left and the whole encounter was horrifically awkward. We met for a coffee at Della's Cafe the day before she and Luke flew to Byron and we were having a very pleasant chit-chat about the school and our kids, and about how lovely it was that Sienna and the girls had bonded so well, and then after a while she looked at me with this kind of anguished expression and started talking about trivia night and what had happened between us, which took me completely by surprise in a cafe at eleven o'clock in the morning. I just looked at her, sort of dumbstruck, and didn't really respond. She was quite emotional, saying things like, 'I've never really loved Luke in the right way,' and, 'Something is missing, Alice,' and, 'You can't deny there is something between us,' and, 'I don't *have* to go, you know.' I'll admit, seeing her cry was gut-wrenching, and I had to swallow a few times to get rid of the lump in my throat. But I was completely out of my comfort zone with a show of emotion of this kind. It made my heart race and my chest ache, and so I gripped her hand, those slender fingers, for a millisecond and said, 'You guys will have the most amazing time,' and offered the obligatory, 'Do stay in touch,' and then I asked for the bill.

We had an awkward hug outside Della's. I could smell the scent of sandalwood on her skin and feel her hair brushing across my cheek. We held on to one another for a few moments before I pulled away to indicate I was ready to leave. It was too much for me at that moment in time. I watched as she wafted off down the street in the lovely green dress she has with the blue flowers, which she wears with a tan belt and sandals and her hair up in a messy bun that kind of falls out all of the time. I watched her go and swallowed back the lump in my throat, and I couldn't work out what the feeling was, but it was a flicker of the same feeling I'd had when Jenny closed the door of my apartment for the last time.

But here's the thing. I couldn't get that last meeting with Lara out of my head for the life of me. Even three weeks on, it seemed to pop into my head when I least expected it. I'd be pouring myself a tea and I'd think of it, or I'd be making the bed and I would think of it, of her. I kept smelling her perfume everywhere and seeing women who reminded me of her. Not to mention the dream I had – no, not one of *those* dreams – but just a dream that we were walking somewhere and laughing. When I woke up, I wondered if I had been a little cold towards her when we said goodbye and whether I should have been a little bit kinder, you know, and not pulled away and scarpered so quickly. After all, she'd been so upset.

I felt I had to rectify it, to make it good. So one night last week, when the girls had finally gone to sleep, I logged on to Hotmail on the laptop and dropped Lara a line. And I can pretty much remember what it said, because I wrote it a couple of times, just, you know, to get the tone right.

Dear Lara, I wrote. How are you? Are you settling in well up there? I really hope you don't mind the email, but I wanted to ask your advice. I'll be staying at a health retreat in Byron next month and I wondered if you had any tips for things to do or places to eat? I'm coming on my own for a long weekend from 13–17 of next month and I don't know where to start. Frankly, I'm a little lost.

Warm regards, Alice

I don't quite know what possessed me, it was rather spur of the moment! The weekend of the fourteenth was

Pete's weekend with the girls (we alternate, you see), and so I had this little gap in my diary with nothing to do, just waiting to be filled. The fact is, I've always wanted to go to Byron – it has always been on the bucket list, and, as Pete always used to say, 'There's no time like the present!' I mean, Ballina is only an hour's flight away from Sydney and I still haven't got around to visiting. Isn't that appalling?

And I figured, it couldn't hurt having a friend up there, could it? You know, a local to look up if I'm bored or I've had enough yoga and meditating for a day? Who better than a brand new resident of the area who I knew would have been busy scoping out all the exciting new places to eat and drink?

Anyway, ten minutes after I sent the email, Lara jumped into my inbox. Hey you, she wrote. I'll be here then and I'd absolutely love to show you around Byron if you want a tour guide. I know some amazing places. You will just love it here, Alice, I know you will. You won't want to leave! I can't wait to see you! Lara Xoxo

Twenty minutes later, I booked my flight. The online transaction was lightning fast, but the smile stayed with me for a while.

Chapter Twenty-seven
Zoe

From: Zoe.m8kin79@realworld.com.au
To: pho_e_b_wallis@zapmail.com
Subject: The truth

Halfway now, Phoebs! When I peed on the stick and got that faint pink line the day after Nico died, I was so friggin' happy. I was sitting on the edge of the bath, and I kind of slipped down and sat on the bathmat and sobbed. I must've cried for like, twenty minutes. I remember it so clearly because Miles was out playing golf with Pete Daniels because they've struck up this weird 'dad' friendship, and I'd woken up feeling a little bit peaky. I hadn't wanted to eat my breakfast, which, as you know, is so unlike me.

I thought, *I'll just see if I have a spare test in the bathroom cabinet*, and I did, right at the back with all of the stuff you don't use, the weird conditioners and the bottles of body lotion. Can you believe that? Just the one test left over out of like, twenty. It was so bizarre, it felt like the Wonka bar with the last golden ticket. My stomach was fluttering like a butterfly in a jar and I felt saliva pooling in my mouth, like you get before you're going to yak. And then just as the line was starting to show up really, really faintly, that bloody song you used to love, 'Peanut Butter Jelly', came on the radio. And that was it – I knew you were there. You were there, weren't you, Phoebs?

Later on, when I told Miles about how the jelly song – that's what Freddie calls it, the jelly song – came on after I did the test, he said, *Well, there's the sign you've been waiting for*, and it made me sob all the more because he was right. It was perfect, Phoebe. You certainly made me wait for it, three years to be precise, but when it happened, it was so right.

That week I was so happy, and it made me happier still to see Miles. He was just ecstatic about the pregnancy (you couldn't wipe the grin off his face if you tried), and, of course, I believed deep down that the baby was his. I really did. At that stage, it didn't enter my mind that the single sperm which had beat all of the others to the finish line, and burst through the ovum like a runner tearing through the ribbon, was anyone else's but his. I'd tried to blot the ill-judged moment with Ted out of my mind because I'd been given permission to by Miles. That sordid broom cupboard encounter hadn't been worthy of the beauty of creation. It hadn't meant anything for a start – and there was also the fact it was over faster than a rat up a drainpipe. I wasn't even lying on my back, and without getting too icky, standing up isn't the best way to send baby batter up the vag canal, now, is it? That's what I convinced myself, anyway – that the only true and legitimate father of my baby was Miles. Plus (and this might sound a bit weird) in some way I felt that you'd delivered the baby to me, Phoebs, like a sort of stork of the spirit world, and I knew you wouldn't do that if the baby was Ted's.

When I had the Harmony test at ten weeks and found out I was having a girl, I felt that sort of divine conception thing even more. That you'd been there in your disco ball, waving your fairy dust over us and putting a living being inside me that would help our family move on from our loss. A girl for a girl. Oh, if anyone else suggested that, I'd deck them for insinuating I was replacing you. It isn't replacement, Phoebe, it is life moving on.

I didn't tell anyone until twelve weeks, but as the days rolled between the first scan and the twelve-week one, I started to feel uneasy again, those old thoughts starting to flare up once more. My inner voice chatted non-stop, asking me if there was a faint chance that one single, speedy sperm had made its way from the top of my thigh (where I'm pretty sure Ted dumped it, if you really want the gory details) into my teapot shaped uterus.

On the morning of my twelve-week scan, I properly vomited and I know it's because I was terrified, and not because my hormones were making me nauseous. I kept thinking, what if the baby looks like Ted? What if it has Ted's Roman nose? What if it is like a mini Ted staring at me? What if Freddie pipes up and says, *Mummy, she doesn't look like dad, but she looks like Evie Blackland!*

Miles held my hand and Freddie stared at the screen as a woman called Anita squeezed KY jelly on to the plastic camera thing and started wiping it all over my lower belly. *Ahhh,* she said, *I'll turn up the volume,* and there it was, a whoosh-whoosh-whoosh-whoosh-whoosh, the baby's heartbeat at a million miles an hour (151 BPM, to be precise). *Ah,* she cooed, *a healthy heart,* and I felt a tear drip from the side of my eye and down my cheek, and Anita thrust a tissue at me, not unkindly, and Miles laughed and said, *Don't, you'll get me started.* Freddie freaked out, asking *Are you okay, Mummy? What's that noise?*

It's your little sister's heart, I told him. *It's tiny right now but listen to the sound it's making!*

Freddie climbed up on Anita's chair to get a better look and the wheels skidded and he wobbled and I felt myself start to sit up, my heart quicken, but Miles touched my arm and said, *Honey, he's fine. I'll catch him if he falls.* And I felt myself relax into the bed again.

Okay let's take a look at her! Anita said, and started pressing down on my full bladder, and I thought I was going to wet myself. She did all the head measurements with a click, click, took a screen-grab, and said the fluid at the back of the neck was in normal proportions, and then, *Okey dokey Mum and Dad, let's move on to the hands and feet!*

Look! She exclaimed after a minute. *Ten little fingers! There's the thumb on the left hand,* click, and then, *look, there's the thumb on the right!* Click. She wiggled the probe around a bit, pressing down on my bladder again really hard and I was like *aaaaarrrgggh!*

Damn it! This little lady is a wriggler! I can't get a toe! She told me to cough, which I did a few times, which made Freddie laugh, and then she said, *Here we go!* She looked at the baby's feet, and suddenly her smile disappeared. *Oh!* she said, as if she'd just realised the baby was conjoined to another one, or something. *You seem to have, um, a polydactyly baby!*

She has six toes? Miles asked.

Yes! she replied, obviously surprised he knew what that meant.

Freddie whooped with happiness and yelled, *She got the toes! She got the toes!*

Anita looked at him strangely.

I have it too, Miles told her.

Really?

Yes. A supernumerary digit on each foot.

Well, it is genetic!

I know! Miles replied. *My dad has it!*

Oh! Then you'll probably know there are options, um, after birth, for correcting the condition, Anita began. *I can put you in touch with Westholm Children's Hospital, and they can talk you through it.*

And I told her, *No way*, and I started to cry my eyes out because I loved those twelve tiny toes because they were made by me and Miles – and there was absolutely no doubt about it.

A few days later, I ran into Alice at school. She was with Victoria, because they're in each other's pockets for all the parent-teacher committee business these days. They want everyone to know they're super important, and that's obvious because they both prance around together with iPads and serious expressions like they're solving the world's problems, one by one. They're like the Elton John and Bernie Taupin of Darley Heights Public.

Anyway, I was keen to tell them both about the baby and reassure them (and that means by default, Amanda too, because Amanda and Alice, and now Victoria too, seem to share information about the consistency of their shit these days: tight as anything) that the baby I was expecting was very definitely Miles's. I didn't want Amanda thinking for one minute that I was carrying her husband's child or her children's half-sibling for that matter, and so I even got out the scan photos, where you can sort of make out the extra toes, for proof.

Congrats darling, Victoria said in a sort of sweet, but superior, way, which wasn't remotely offensive to me, because we've all been at rock bottom together and I've smelled her BO. I know her now, and we have shared something so deep, so intimate, that we are bonded for life. Even Amanda has to admit that there's no room for awkwardness between us – not after we've changed a dead man's bedsheets together. You can't get much more real than that.

It's because we have all shared so much that I felt I could say it, so I did. *Alice, the timing of my pregnancy isn't ideal considering what went on at trivia night,* I said, *but I wanted you to know, the baby I am carrying is very definitely Miles's baby. We know for certain, we found out at the scan.*

Alice laughed, held her arms out and pulled me in for a hug and said, *God, I wouldn't have thought anything to the contrary! Amanda sent Ted for the snip, like, six years ago, right after Evie was born. He won't be fathering any more kids any time soon, unless he goes back and has the tubes in his balls reattached.* And I started to laugh so hard I actually weed myself a little bit, and Victoria said, *Who knew Ted's nuts were so funny?* And I had to clutch my stomach and tell her, *Stop!* It was only later I thought, *Shit, why didn't someone tell me this, like, three months ago? It would have saved a whole lot of anxiety!*

As I write this message to you, Phoebs, I can feel her moving inside me. They say you feel the second baby quicker, and I swear I got those gorgeous little kicks at the end of the first trimester, and I'm almost twenty weeks now. I knew what it was, my body remembers. They start out like tiny popping bubbles, like gas, or popping candy, maybe. It's just the most amazing sensation! Did I ever tell you that after Freddie was born, I still felt the kicks for a few hours after he came out? I guess it's a bit like getting off a boat and still having jelly legs – your body gets used to what it gets used to! But anyway, I love it! I can't even begin to tell you how many nights I dreamed about being where I am now, and how much I wished for it and begged the powers that be for a baby inside of me.

Miles can't get enough of touching my belly. He comes up behind me when I'm making brekkie and kisses my neck and sort of rubs my tummy with both of his hands, and I always do this sort of lean back into him where I let him nuzzle into me. Freddie's just intrigued, asking us every single question he can think of about eggs and sperms and how they get up there! You'd laugh at our explanations. Miles gets all embarrassed and says things like, *Well, son, you see, there's a mummy rabbit and a daddy rabbit and they love each other very much!* I'm a bit more matter-of-fact, and use the proper anatomical words. I mean, I can't stand these people that call the sex organs the cookie or the lady garden or the winkle. That's just gross. Plus Freddo is a smart kid, so I'm not hiding it.

He's so excited to meet his baby sister – he's made up a dance routine for her to keep her amused when she's out of the womb, how funny is that? I'm not sure how he'll react when he realises she can barely turn her head for the first few weeks and that she'll be way too sleepy to play with. I've asked him to help me decorate the nursery, so he's been drawing endless pictures in art class and bringing them home for the wall. Now *you* know I think he's a prodigy, right, but I'm serious when I say that Freddie's artwork has something totally Ken Done about it. I'm hoping he'll keep me and Miles in dentures in our old age. Stranger things have happened, right?

In case you can't tell, I'm walking on air right now, even if my hips are wider than the Harbour Tunnel. We all are, all of us, the Makin family. And I know it's a very odd way to look at things, but in some ways I feel like what happened at the trivia night did me a massive favour. I regret cheating on Miles, of course I do, and I will always feel guilty, but I honestly think, right now, he does not care. We have never been as solid as we are today, and I mean it when I say I never realised before that night quite how much I love him. How I cease to function without him. It's almost as if I'd only had the entrée before the trivia night, but now I've had the dessert and the pudding, and I don't want to eat with anybody else, anywhere else, ever again. Talking of food, you'll never guess what I'm addicted to right now? Melon! Catalan or cantaloupe, is that what it's called? I'm not even kidding. I used to hate it as a kid and now I am like to Miles at every meal, *Can you put some orange melon on the side?* Miles keeps joking we should call the baby Melanie!

Sissy, I'm going to sign off now, and if it's okay with you, I'm going to have a rest from writing to you for a bit. I love to be close to you, you know that, but sometimes it sort of unsettles me, too. It takes me back a couple of steps when I've just taken one forward. I suppose a part of me wants to have some distance and I think I am finally ready for that now. I mean, I *know* I am.

I'm sure I'll want to check in with you after our daughter is born, when the hormones are raging like crazy and I'm all sleep deprived and emotional, all that delightful post-partum stuff that's somehow manageable because of the sweet reward you have from it. I also know that when she gets here, I'll have a moment, realising I can't physically share her with you. But I know you are always here for me. Feel free to throw me the jelly song whenever you want, I'll listen out for it, every single day, we all will: Miles, Freddie, me and our little girl.

Only she'll have a name by then. We're going to call her Phoebe.

Chapter Twenty-eight
Amanda

I've been sober for forty days now. Forty days without booze numbing my senses. The way I like to describe it is as if someone's taken a filter off. Life is more vivid, colours more primary. I can smell things I couldn't smell before, like the flowers in the garden in the morning. I was too hungover to notice them before, blocked nose, blocked senses, blocked brain! Yesterday I sat on the deck with a cup of tea and just breathed in and out, catching the smell of the grass and the faint waft of the coffee beans roasting down the road at Della's.

Sobriety does wonders for your sense of smell. But the best thing about it is what it does for your marriage. That's a generalisation, of course, because I can only speak for my own, but for Ted and me? Well, it has made us. Ted feels like, for once, I have chosen him over anything else, and when I say that, I mean over the bottle. I lean on him now, not on the grog. More than anyone, I credit him for helping me when I felt like I was slipping down a well and trying to grip the walls with Vaseline on my fingers. And of course, Evie and Sam, who tiptoed sweetly around me, especially in those early days when I fought an icy temper and slept a lot. They never once pushed when Ted told them I needed space. They returned my anger with hugs, with kind words, with motivational notes on the fridge – wordy and loving from Evie ('You are the most beautiful and kind mum in the world. I love you!') and just a basic, 'You got this, Mum!' from Sam. Simple, but effective. Enough to remind me why I am getting sober – and I will always be 'getting' sober, in the present tense, because it will be a battle I'm in for the rest of my life. But one I definitely plan to win.

We chose to be open with the kids right from the start, told them Mummy has a few problems, that I have a tendency to drink wine a little too much and a little too often, just like my mother did before me, and that it is an illness that needs to be controlled. And that I'm taking responsibility for those problems, because I love them both, and their daddy, so very much. It's okay to be fallible. It's okay not to have all the answers, I told them. Mums and dads are human, too. We don't always get it right, we just do our best.

I had my last drink a week after Nico's death and Victoria's very frank finger-pointing in the car. I didn't give up immediately. I didn't *literally* go home and empty the drinks cabinet as a result of what she'd said to me and I didn't tell Ted straight away, either. I knew she was right, and I knew I had to act – I'd known that since trivia night – but I wasn't quite ready to rip off the band aid, especially since there was a funeral I needed to attend, and one I knew would involve three children mourning their father. I couldn't get through that without a crutch, and frankly, I didn't think I should have to.

The funeral, at Darley Crematorium, was held a week after we found him in the bed, and it was as awful as I had expected. There was an open casket for a start, and even though I'd been one of the first people to see his body, it was still pretty confronting watching his three girls sobbing at the foot of the coffin in their neat black dresses and velvet headbands. The funeral home had put make up on Nico, to make him look less, well, *dead*, I guess, and that was just freaky, because I was convinced he was going to open his eyes and yell, 'Surprise!'

I couldn't stop staring at him from the third-row pew. It didn't help that Alice said, 'Why does it feel like he's looking at us?' even though he had his eyes shut. After the service, where Victoria very nobly played the dignified widow despite being terrified of the man, I raced outside to have a swig from my little silver hip flask behind one of the trees that lined the church. It seems unbelievable now, but that's what I did.

Ted caught me and said, 'Really? At a funeral?' and I said, 'Well it doesn't sit well with me that we are saying a fond farewell to a wife-beater.'

He said, 'Amanda, it's eleven o'clock in the morning.'

That night, when we got home, and with a glass of whisky in my hand that I didn't have the appetite to drink, I asked him to help me. I looked into my glass and realised it was time. I'd just been to a funeral where children had said goodbye to a parent. Life was too short, too precious. I was tired, so tired. Tired of the hangovers, the upsets, the dependency, the memory loss, the arguments with Ted, the glances when I'd twist the top off a bottle of rosé on a Monday night, just for the hell of it. The arguments with Alice, the dead dogs, the swinging, the yelling up at windows. I owed it to myself to straighten out. But more than anything, I owed it to my children. There were times I could have hurt them. Not willingly, but as a consequence of my escalating habit. My mother had been a functioning alcoholic once – she had started to drink after my father died – until it had taken hold of her and she didn't function any more, just existed. I didn't want Sam or Evie to have the same memories I had growing up – a tanked-up mother slurring at the school gates, the forgotten packed-lunch boxes and excursion notes (God knows how many trips I missed because my mother forgot to sign the slips), the dirty uniforms, the burnt dinners, the forgotten birthdays.

As a child, it hadn't been unusual to hear the scratchy turn of a bottle cap as early as seven in the morning and I'd pull a pillow over my head to drown out the sound while my mother drowned her sorrows in the other room. Sometimes, she would call to me, a shrill slur that would echo through the pink plywood walls, and I would trudge along the hall and into the pink boudoir with its always-present aroma of chip fat and diluted perfume. There was never a time she didn't have a glass in her hand, and, as I got older, it became normal practice for me to pour the pungent liquid for her on demand from the turquoise bottle, knowing that her favourite glass tumbler must be filled right up to the 'J' of the embossed words Jenolan Caves, otherwise she would fret.

'I asked you to do one thing,' she would snap with an audible slur. 'Up. To. The. J, for Christ's sake!' Then, a couple of moments later, she'd be filled with remorse. 'Oh, come here baby girl, it doesn't matter. Mum's just being grouchy! Just ignore me and my silly grumpiness. I do love you so! Oh darling, please don't cry!'

I knew I wasn't as bad as that, but that's what my mother must have thought, once, long before the cancer took her. I wasn't as bad *yet*, but I was headed there. There was the time Sam fell off the trampoline and sprained his wrist because I'd been grabbing a refill and I hadn't been watching him; the time I rode my bike home from the RSL with Evie and crashed into her from behind because I'd had one too many wines; the time I left Evie in the car to go to the off licence and came back to find a crowd of people outside the window trying to get to her because she had a tummy bug and had vomited up the windows. The numerous times I'd let the kids stay up too late on a school night, because I wanted them to dance around the kitchen with me, even though they were desperately tired and just needed to go to bed. I would justify it by saying, 'God, everyone's so uptight, they just need to relax!' and paste myself up as some paragon of chilled-out parenting. Oh, I'd been the fun mum, that's for sure, but my children needed more than fun – they needed a mother. They needed boundaries. Sam was on the verge of turning into a man, he wasn't clueless as to what I was up to. And just because I was functioning – just because I got up in the morning and got my kids dressed and breakfasted and deposited at the school gates before the bell rang, just because I didn't lie around in my dressing gown all day with a vodka glass in my hand like the woman who gave birth to me, it didn't mean it was acceptable. It didn't mean I didn't have a problem.

It had crept up on me, stealthily, the dependency. What had started as a couple of glasses a night around the time Sam was midway through primary school, became a bottle. The bottle became the desperate need for a 'crutch' to take the edge of social situations. To the point I was behaving like a performer in the story of my own life, with Melbourne Cup, and then the trivia night, the great crescendo. And while it had taken Victoria's comment to wake me up, she was just the messenger. I had known for a while, the greasy slide I was on. Alice had gently tried to suggest I was 'getting pickled' a little too often, but I'd shot her down each time, ignored her for a while afterwards. She didn't know the half of it, anyway – only what I let her see. She didn't see the private drinking. Ted saw some of it, of course, but I was in denial. When he asked me if I'd been boozing because the red wine bottle was half empty, I'd tell him I'd poured it in the bolognese. Or that a friend had popped by for a quick wine. He never pushed it because, I think, he was scared to drive me away. Sometimes I filled up the white wine bottle with water to make the meniscus level go up, and I knew Ted would never catch on because he didn't like white wine.

I'd got tired of the lying. I knew it was time to stop. I had experienced trauma in my life for sure, but then I looked at Zoe. If she could move on from her sister Phoebe's suicide, from the pain of quite literally failing to talk someone she loved beyond measure off the ledge, without becoming dependent on alcohol or drugs, how long could I blame my mother or my social anxiety, my longing to be liked by strangers, for pushing me slowly, but forcefully, towards the bottle?

'Teddy, we need to talk,' I told my husband as we sat side by side on the veranda.

Ted put down his book and gave me his full attention. Even that small gesture showed me the man he was. Always attentive, always patient, always selfless. I had pushed him down so many times, but, like a jack-in-the-box, he always popped back up.

'What's up?' he said.

'I think I should have some time off drinking,' I said. It was the understatement of the decade. 'What I mean is, I'd like to stop. For good.'

Ted pulled himself up in his seat. 'Okay,' he said. No sarcasm, just a single word that sounded like relief. He knew the first step to me getting help was admitting, out loud, that I had a problem. He had been waiting for me to say it for a long time.

'I think . . .' My voice quivered. 'I mean, I *know*, I have a problem, Ted.'

He stood up and pulled me into his arms and held me, stroking my head as I began to cry. Tears I hadn't shed in years. Tears that were big and fat and heavy. Tears for my teenage self, devoid of maternal affection or interest. Tears for those three beautiful little girls following their father's coffin, and how God forbid, I didn't want my kids to end up in the same situation. Tears for putting Ted through shit for as long as I could remember, the way my own mother had done to me – again and again and again – and for my children, who I didn't want to carry the same burden, because I loved them so much. Tears for my best friend Alice, who had been the primary giver in the friendship for the last year, while I sucked energy from her like the dominant twin in the womb. Tears because I'd broken promises a hundred times, but the most reprehensible was shattering the promise to be faithful to my husband, because if our marriage was fucked, then so was our family.

It wasn't that swinging was evil or bad or sordid by any means, it just wasn't acceptable for us, because we had vowed we would never cheat, right from the moment we had the chat about whether we were boyfriend and girlfriend, almost two decades before. We had always said that cheating would be a game-changer. The trivia night smashed our unbroken record of fidelity to smithereens, and it had been down to me. It had shaken us, twisted us and made us strangers for a time, and I can say with absolute certainty that if I hadn't been annihilated that night, I would have laughed at the suggestion when Luke flung it my way.

Ted held me as the tears continued to fall, and my body became somehow lighter as it shed its terrible burden, all the while recognising there was a long way to go. He cried too. With relief, I think. He'd spent so long being terrified about the capacity I had to harm myself, to do something even more stupid the next time round, to walk in front of a car or take an ill-judged dip in the sea and get caught in a rip. What if I'd fallen down Victoria's staircase and broken my neck on Cup day? What if I'd choked on my own vomit? What if I'd walked in front of a car any number of times I'd stumbled back from Darley across the busy high street?

When we were both done with the tears, we googled residential alcohol programmes and found the one I was looking for, the one Victoria had mentioned to me. The Stour House Clinic was located in bushland a little further up the peninsula and so we booked an appointment with my GP for a referral. I went to meet the therapists there and told them I was an alcoholic and I needed help, and I was immediately accepted for the clinic's fourteen-day programme, to be followed up by weekly group sessions.

During those two weeks, when I was separated from my family, I confronted some home truths. I dredged up some memories of times I'd hurt people with my drinking. It was deeply unpleasant. The times I'd fucked up had once been funny to me. I'd giggle and think, *Oops! I fell over and flashed my arse*, or *Oops! I stole some shot glasses from the pub* or, *Oops! I had a massive row with Alice and called her a meddling cow!* Aren't I funny? But it was only when I'd been alcohol-free for a few days, when the opaque blinds of my mind were finally opened and the sun had streamed in, that I realised some of it wasn't so hilarious. Like the time I was so drunk that I puked in front of Evie on the bathroom tiles, and she just watched me, from the bath, on my hands and knees as my body heaved and hurled. How terrifying must that have been for a small child? That time I threw Ted's beloved guitar from the bedroom window because I wanted to see if I could make something land in the pool from upstairs, but instead I reduced it to firewood. That time I let some random woman try on my engagement ring and I had to go back to the bar and literally stalk them for credit card receipts to get her name and get it back, all the while wearing a ten-dollar fake from the mall so Ted would never know. That time I got so trashed at Melbourne Cup, I had to go round and grovel and apologise, which led to the death of a dog, three children's grief, and a woman being smashed into the wall by her husband. That time I allowed my husband to have sex with another woman at the school trivia night because I made it clear I wanted to do the same, and for one night only, he had enough and he flipped and did something that still eats him up with regret. That time, that time, that time, they spewed forth from me like lava.

When I got back home from Stour House, Ted had emptied the booze cabinet. Gone were aged whiskies, his prized collection of aged Merlots and about thirteen varietals of gin – elderflower, grapefruit, cherry, strawberry, rhubarb . . . you name the fruit, I had the gin. The crystal decanters had gone to the charity shop, along with the other booze glasses – white wine glasses, red wine beakers, champagne flutes, whisky tumblers, shot glasses, plastic wine glasses for camping that slotted one into another. My little silver hipflask, hidden away in a drawer but hunted out by Ted like a pig sniffing out a truffle, and chucked in a charity bin somewhere. My mother's Jenolan Caves shot glass, which I'd used in the bedroom to stash random earrings and stacking rings – gone. A beautiful ornamental gin bottle with dried silver eucalyptus that spilled from the top – recycled. Cards from my last birthday, with various references to me being 'Gin-Vincible' or wishing me a 'Happy Beer-day!', taken down and likely lobbed into the recycle bin. The fridge magnet with the 1950s housewife in a gingham apron, that read, 'Me? I don't cook dinner . . .

I drink it!' The tea towel that shouted, 'When life gives you lemons, add gin!' All gone. It was paraphernalia that had been important to the old me, in my old life. That had been part of my identity. Paraphernalia as dangerous as a syringe or a spoon and aluminium foil to a heroin addict. Tools that had enabled me, that had made my addiction a light-hearted and frivolous pastime. All of it, gone.

Ted didn't want any of it either. 'We're doing this together,' he said.

'But I can't make you give up too,' I said.

'Amanda, I don't care about it. I've never been a massive drinker anyway, have I? I can take it or leave it. For me it's not a sacrifice. I'll still have a beer every so often when I'm out with the boys if I feel like it, but never when I'm with you. I promise you, darling. More than anything, I just want you to get better. For us to get better.'

Alice has been incredibly supportive, too. Of course, I made my apologies to her for my bad behaviour. She just pulled me in for a hug and said, 'Come here, you old softie. You hit a temporary bad patch, that's all. I still love you.'

Then she said, 'Now I'm separated, I'm going to be hanging round your place like a bad smell, you do realise that, don't you?'

'Yep,' I laughed. 'Just don't expect a glass of wine.'

Alice smiled. 'It's swings and roundabouts with us, isn't it? It's either one of us having a drama or the other.' Then she said, 'Talking of drama, I never thanked you for being there when Jenny left. Having me move in with you two days after you got back from honeymoon must have been hard. Seeing me wander about crying . . .'

'Like you said, it's swings and roundabouts. That crisis was yours. This one is mine.'

'Let's just hope neither of us has an existential crisis at the same time,' she laughed.

'I think we are at the moment,' I smiled, and lay my head on her shoulder.

Victoria (and I bet you never thought I'd say this) has also been amazing. She helped a lot in the early days, popping round with meals for Ted and the kids, much like we'd all done for Nico when she was missing. Lasagne, chilli, bolognese – all the mince dishes! I still never tire of telling her over an almond latte at Della's how lucky I feel that we became such good friends, especially after the way we started out. We go to classes together at the gym (Body Pump is my new obsession – they say you replace one addiction with another, right? But this one is way better for my stomach) and we take one another's kids for playdates. She's still a complete snob, of course, possibly more so now she has Nico's insurance money through and the cash for the Lyre Street house, but these days I just wind her up about it. Alice calls her 'Mrs Moneypenny'.

When I was in rehab, I started making friendship bracelets with beads, and I made one for her. I could tell she loved it – she was so touched when I gave it to her. Well, she must have been, because she came over a few days ago wearing it, and carrying the maroon YSL bag of hers I just adore and said, 'Here you go, you're thirty days sober. This is a little congrats.'

'What?' I told her. 'I can't take this!'

'Darling,' she said. 'You've been dragging around that bloody dated Kate Spade sack forever. I'm sure it was nice before you overused it, but . . . just no. Anyway, I don't want this one anymore. It's yours.'

'Is it real?'

'Oh, purlease. That's incredibly insulting. Do I look like the kind of woman who needs to buy a fake anything?'

She smiled and I hugged her, which I know she found so uncomfortable. She's not a hugger, Victoria. 'I love that you're such a snob,' I said. 'Thank you.'

This weekend she's even asked me to dog-sit for her cavoodle puppy, Billy. Although she's made me pinky swear I will not let him anywhere near my car. That's a real sign of friendship, don't you think? Trusting me to take care of him after what happened last time? Evie and Sam are so excited to have a new house guest, although I'm well aware the next question will be, 'Mum, can we get a dog?' To be honest, I'm not against the idea. I know I'll be the one who ends up walking it, but I don't mind that – I've found a new appreciation for the outdoors. Like I said, I notice things more: the colour of the grass, the clouds, the sky.

As for Zoe, well I'd love to tell you that she and I are best friends, but I can't. We never will be after what happened. But that doesn't mean we can't be acquaintances who sometimes stop for a chat in the street. When I was clearing out the attic the other day, I found a bag of baby girls' clothes – sleepsuits, dresses and stuff – that I'm going to drop round to her for her baby girl. She might not want them, but, well, it's a gesture. They'll be going to the charity shop otherwise. At the end of the day, Zoe only did the same thing as I did that night – she made a bad decision. I can't hate her for that.

As for Ted and me? Well, he said to me the other night in bed, 'You laugh so much more these days,' and he is right. We're like we were when we were first married – teasing, joking, playing. He is lighter, happier, and that means the kids are, too. We still have Movie Night Fridays, but now we have Board Game Mondays too, and Yahtzee is always a hit. It's my favourite time of the week, all of us playing, chatting and arguing. But one of the things I've loved the most is standing on the soccer side lines on Saturday mornings watching the Darley Bulls (Sam) and the Heights Hawks (Evie) playing their matches with a clear head, just breathing in the air and chatting to other parents like it's the most natural thing in the world. No raging headache, no breath mints, just maybe a strong coffee in my Lululemon activewear (my two new vices, but hey, it could be worse).

Workwise, I'm about to start up a little photography business of my own, called Renew Photography, because I'd rather take photos of families than the sterile insides of homes. I never had the balls, or the enthusiasm, to do it before. I've taken photos of Victoria and her girls, and Alice and her twins for my portfolio. Sam is learning web design at high school and he has made it his term-three project to make me my own site. Unfortunately I'm a complete Luddite still, and so he has to help me on a daily basis, but that's okay, I think he enjoys it as much as I do. It's also our time to catch up about school and what's going on with his friends and all of that stuff. Sam invites his mates to the house a lot these days, and I love having the house full of noisy teens. With Evie, it's those precious moments before bed when we talk about whatever's on her mind, and the new me takes my time with it instead of trying to rush the bedtime routine so I can go and pour myself a wine.

What can I tell you? Life is good. It is not without its struggles, and I've had a couple of moments I've thought about drinking, craved a glass in my hand and the taste on my tongue. But the highs of my new, sober life taste way better than anything from a bottle. The buzz of being the Amanda I am now is a bigger pull than any drink could be.

When you look at it like that, maybe what happened at trivia night wasn't so bad. I came out of it with a new lease of life, a second chance. It pushed me to realise the fragility of life and the importance of relationships – romantic or otherwise. It exposed me to a straight-talking woman who told it to me like it was the night her husband died. A woman at rock bottom wearing dirty clothes. And I listened.

So there you have it. My story. I hope in some way this helps you, especially those of you who are at the very start of your journey to sobriety. And well done for that, because it really isn't easy to give up that crutch and to shrug off the warm booze blanket when the world outside is cold and dark. It has certainly helped me to write all of this down, even if it has been uncomfortable reading sometimes. But that's the thing about alcoholism, isn't it? It is not comfortable, it does sting and it is not pretty. But you can come out of the other side shining. I still have a long journey ahead of me, but I am living, breathing proof that you *can* do it. I wish you all the luck in the world. You really have got this!

Epilogue

Dear Nico,

My psychologist told me I should write to you, so here I am, at the desk downstairs by the window, looking out on to the garden, which is basking in the autumn sun, with a black biro in my hand and a stack of A4 paper. After I finish writing this, and no doubt sign it off with kisses I don't mean, I'll burn it in the kitchen in a little bowl I've prepared. The lighter is all ready to go, and I've got that Moët you bought for our anniversary chilling in the fridge to drink afterwards.

Well I guess the first thing I should tell you is that everything worked out perfectly, but I'll start with the present before I dwell on the past. Nico, do you remember how much I hated the idea of the girls going to Darley Heights? How much I worried about losing my social status when we left St Cecilia's? Well guess what? I'm back! You would laugh to see me now, in my element as the events manager of the parent-teacher committee. I have so much sway at that school it is insane, and what's more, I've acquired a genuine group of friends that I'm honoured to be able to call my inner circle. Who knew one of them would be Amanda Blackland? Who'd have thought that the woman who killed darling Perky would end up being one of my new allies? I have to give the woman her dues – she stepped up to the plate when you died: took me home, washed my clothes, cleaned me up and then held my hand as I walked to the front of the church to look at your yellow, decaying body in that cheap coffin that looked like it was expensive.

So really, in a weird way, I should thank you for that, for bringing us together: Amanda, Alice, Zoe and I (the group of women who you would have laughingly called my 'entourage'!) Well, you *and* the events of the trivia night, that is, because that's where it all started. Oh, what I did with the photos was naughty, I know, following them round and snapping them during their sex fiesta with my trusty iPhone. But I just wanted to teach Amanda a lesson, you know, for Perky, and for thinking she could be top dog at Darley. I wanted to show her who she was messing with – to shoot myself right up there to the top of the pecking order at my new school, knock her off any perch she thought she could get on because she was friends with Alice. And at Darley, Alice was top dog. Not any more, though – there's a new boss in town! And God, don't they just adore little old me! Amanda especially – she even gave me a gaudy little friendship bracelet that she'd made in rehab, as a 'token of our new friendship'. Bless! It's like they feel this perfect blend of pity and fear – pity that I was the beaten wife, and fear that I'll turn around and bite them! They've seen what I'm capable of.

But the photos . . . Oh, my head was everywhere back then! Sometimes, when things go drastically wrong, you don't think properly, and I was at sixes and sevens about you, and about what we were going to do without money. How I'd cope if you went to jail. The point is, what I did actually brought me together with my crew, and your death solidified it in a fateful kind of way.

I think I did that right, didn't I? I'd had it planned since your arrest. The moment I arranged to have the girls away for the week, I knew what I had to do. And actually, it wasn't as hard as I thought it would be. Killing you, I mean. I'd only been missing forty-eight hours and I knew you'd be fretting, downing the whisky in the front room, sitting on the edge of your chair, waiting for the police to call. You never did like being alone, did you? I knew you'd have popped a couple of pills to calm yourself, and that all you needed were a few more. It was hot that evening – the rain came the next night – and I waited until nightfall to walk from the empty house to ours. I couldn't risk being seen, so I did it about a minute before the street lamps went on. I'd been watching them for two weeks – did you ever see me at the window and wonder what the hell I was doing, looking out into the darkness with my glass of pinot noir? They always went on at 8:02 p.m. precisely, so it was eight o'clock on the nose, as dark as it was going to get before the lights went on, when I hurried down the side of the house, and in through the laundry door. Oh, your face when you saw me! 'Oh my God, where have you been?' you said. 'Oh God, I am so sorry I hurt you, you have to believe me. I'll never do it again!' Blah blah blah.

'It's okay,' I told you, even though all I could see in front of me was a failure of a man. 'I'm sorry I left. I just needed some time.' You nodded and offered to make me a drink. 'I'll do it, darling,' I said, and I went into the kitchen and pulled down a crystal tumbler and emptied in the bag of white powder containing the sedatives I'd ground with a mortar and pestle. I was so paranoid about drinking from the wrong glass, but after about fifteen minutes when you started to feel woozy and disoriented, I relaxed, knowing I'd given you the right one. I think you were already that numb that you didn't notice the chalky taste, and so, when we sat up in bed and I poured you another, you were oblivious, only muttering that you felt a little strange. 'Poor Nico. Have these pills with water, they'll help your headache tomorrow,' I said, handing you three more, which you very trustingly consumed. Then I gave you some more sedative-laced milk, to settle your stomach, and you drank that down so trustingly that it was almost sweet to see – you downing it, like a child taking medicine, despite its revolting bitter and chalky taste, because you trusted that I was taking care of you, in sickness and in health. By the time I was done with you, you'd had enough drugs to take down an African elephant! All of them ordered on eBay from your own account, NicoLives76, and delivered to our address in *your* name. I'm just thankful you were never there to receive the post (although I did make sure you were home when I hopped online and ordered them – one has to cover one's tracks!). Why do you think I encouraged you to spend every waking moment of your bail time playing golf?

When you were unconscious, I scattered the pills around you, and lay beside you watching the slow rise and fall of your chest until you slowly left me. It took quite a while, actually. I played Minecraft on Clara's iPad while I waited, watched half an hour of Netflix. Then I sat with you a while longer to make sure you didn't make some miraculous recovery. I told you a few home truths then, you won't remember them of course. I told you how important it is to keep your enemies close: just like I did with you, just like I'm doing with my new 'friends'.

And then, at about one in the morning, I scurried back along the dry grass verges and across three roads and back to the empty shell of Lyre Street and celebrated with a glass of single malt, your favourite.

The fact you beat me up was convenient, actually. First up, it allowed me to ensure you had a mental health record, so that your suicide would be more believable, so that there was no need for a coroner's report and no need for an investigation in court. I mean, those anger issues had to be sorted, didn't they? How fortunate that you agreed, in one of your tender moments, to go see the esteemed Dr Patrick Leyland! How lucky you happened to tell him in one of your more vulnerable sessions, that when you thought about all the things you'd done to me, it made you want to kill yourself. You might not remember imparting that information to me after a whisky or two, my darling, but you did. And I'm so very glad you did, too! Like the beads on that awful friendship bracelet Amanda gave me – each one needs to be exactly in place to make the finished pattern, and I couldn't have pulled it all off without you giving Dr Leyland that juicy little snippet! So thank you, Nico. Thanks for helping me out.

I had to be out of the house, missing, when you killed yourself, just in case I was ever implicated, and I suppose I should also thank you for giving me a reason to hide away – a whole face full of reasons, actually! I was planning to return to the house and 'discover' your body a couple of days later (why do you think I left the air-con on? It's so hot that such a gruesome mission would have been all the more horrendous!). I had no idea Amanda and Co would show up, although in hindsight, I should have considered it an option seeing as she works for the real estate agent. But as it happened, it only helped to strengthen my story, to have those women there when I found you, corroborating to the nice detectives that you were a bastard wife-beater, and that's why you took the easy way out.

Oh Nico. I know you were sorry for hitting me. You were every single time, weren't you? But if you think that was the only reason I killed you, then you're flattering yourself. As if I'd risk jail time, and leaving my girls (and I call them 'mine' because you never deserved them) for a bruise or two. Oh my dear husband, I'm tougher than that! If it was the beatings alone, I'd have offed you years ago, and probably in a much less gentle manner. Perhaps a knife to the throat or a dagger in the back. Yes, the violence made me hate you and therefore made my actions easier – but darling, it was what you were going to do to *us* – to me and the girls – that was the catalyst. You stole our future. How would we have survived if we had lost the house? I couldn't have my beautiful girls out on the street, or, God-forbid, living in some tawdry rental apartment! I couldn't have Carla pulled out of Milton Abbey Ladies' College, could I? It was bad enough that Darcy and Iris had to leave St Cecilia's, but I can live with it, since Darcy is only seven and her serious education hasn't started yet. And poor Iris, so sweet and sensitive, but with such expensive taste in sport! How could I deprive her of the horse riding lessons and our annual ski trip to Whistler? I just couldn't!

How would the girls have faced their peers knowing their father was in jail for insider trading? You did a very stupid thing getting caught, Nico, and now you've paid the ultimate price. You can blame yourself for dangling the carrot of the two-million-dollar life insurance policy in front of my face, because once I knew about that, I had a fallback plan, for when the shit hit the fan. And not only did the shit spray everywhere, but you beat me up because of it. Surely, you must have known it was the perfect storm? But then I suppose you never thought I would do anything like that, did you? Not the loving little wife, who basked in her husband's wealth and cowered from his 'manliness'.

I like to think if I hadn't given you a helping hand, you'd have come to the same conclusion yourself. That death was the only way out. I mean, you did tell Dr Leyland you were a man on the edge, didn't you? It's because of this I don't consider what I did as the M word (dare I say it? *Murder*) because I know you would have taken the brave route eventually, Nico, wouldn't you? If you like, we can forget the way you treated me: the bruises, the split lips, the winded ribs, the broken arm, the wonky nose. Instead, we'll consider you akin to a noble Japanese Kamikaze pilot – making the ultimate sacrifice for the collective good. And I suppose all I did was help you fuel the plane.

Anyway, I've said all I need to say. Rest assured, Nico, that your timely death, and the sale of Lyre Street, of course, have secured the happiness of our beautiful girls (oh, they're almost over your death already – it's amazing what a new winter wardrobe can do for the spirits!) and for that, I am beyond thankful. It has also given me something for which I am eternally grateful – a new life at Darley and a group of girlfriends who I believe will be at my side through thick and thin. They'll never know I helped you pop off this mortal coil, of course – they are all far too trusting and naive for that. But if any of them do happen to find out, I will simply go to my laptop, click on the file marked 'Private', and pull out the three, deliciously incriminating photos I promised them I'd destroyed. Then I really will have something to bargain with. It is not evil, my darling, it's just survival.

I remember you once told me I was like a blue-ringed octopus – beautiful, resourceful and deadly. You never said a truer word in your life.

Rest easy, Nico.

Your loving widow, Victoria

Acknowledgements

It's agonising deciding who to thank first, so, like movie credits, I'll start with the cast in order of appearance. There would be no Darley Heights Public School without my agent, Marina de Pass. Marina, it remains the biggest thrill of my life to be offered representation by you. My heartfelt thanks go to you Araminta Whitley, Helen Mumby and all at The Soho Agency for championing this little book and loving it unconditionally from the get-go. The bottom line is, I wouldn't be writing these acknowledgements without you. Have I earned the right to call you Nina yet?

I haven't worked with a book editor before, but I could not have asked for a better one. Thank you Kimberley Atkins for taking a punt on this novel during the madness of the first Covid 19 lockdown. I am in absolute awe of your talent as an editor - your incredible instinct took the bones of a story and shaped it in to something so much more. Thank you for sharing my love of Australia, cats and Moscato (in no particular order). My heartfelt gratitude goes to you, Amy Batley and the teams at both Hodder & Stoughton, and Hachette Australia, for nurturing and fan-faring this rookie author.

The Trivia Night was written on the Faber Academy Writing A Novel course in Sydney, and it was a comment from newspaper editor Tim McIntyre (quite literally, 'Have you thought about writing a novel?'), and the kind advice from novelist Jaclyn Moriarty that gave me the push I needed to apply. I am indebted to you both. Tim, you joked I should name a character after you – well check out Chapter 24. Detectives aren't unlike journalists after all, are they?

Michael Robotham, I am in awe of you as an author, and that phone call at the very start of my journey meant a great deal to me. Thank you for giving me your time and for putting up with my random 'remember me?' text messages.

Kathryn Heyman, I owe you so much. The advice and encouragement you gave me on the Faber course and during our coffee-fuelled mentoring sessions afterwards was invaluable. I hope you think the end result 'hums'.

Jill Walters, thanks for the crime advice and for not rolling your eyes at questions like, 'what colour is police tape, again?'

To my Faber pals: Andrea Sophocleous, Jen Marshall, Kim Arlington, Judy Pettingell, Shona Parker, Carla Simmons, Helen Signy, Liz Dzelmanis, Kate Horan Williams and Lucy Elliot. You guys are so talented and I'm lucky to be part of your writing gang.

Vanessa McCausland, our Rosebery Street chats are the best – I am so grateful for them and for your friendship. Emma Levett, here's to more random jaunts stalking authors and taking selfies.

It takes a village to write a book. I owe so much to the friends who stepped in to help with childcare so I could binge-write. Fiona Pogson, Jayne Murphy, Leonie Lincoln, Debbie Wise – you girls are my village and I would be lost without you. Cath Adelbert, Pip Prentice, Alice Ierace, Janaya Laws, Sheridan Millward, Ann Byrne, Etta Watts Russell, Georgina Blaskey, Chrissie Reeves and Nina Dorn, you cheered me on even before this book had a deal. I love you girls! To Mitch Pogson, Bryan Murphy, Richard Wise and Simon Lincoln – thanks for never failing to quip, 'Watch out, Ali might get her car keys out!' on nights out, and for taking on the chin the inevitable assumption within our community that you're all swingers. You're welcome!

Lastly, but most importantly: Mum and Dad. Thank you for encouraging my writing career, for being unashamedly proud and promising to buy numerous copies of this book, even if it is 'a bit rude'. I love you both 'all the world' and am so grateful for all you've given me.

Annie Wick, Craig Miller, Vicki Fox, Susie Lowe: your love and support means so much.

Jo Miller, no one else shares my obsession with bookshops, expensive stationery and micro-bladed eyebrows. It's in our DNA. Remember 'there's nothing like a sister to understand the *real* you'.

To Raff, Sav and Bug: thanks for understanding when Mummy had to write, and for the computer Post-it notes and hugs. Who needs motivational quotes when I have you? I love you all so much and will never stop trying to make you kiss me goodbye outside school.

Rob, my person and my trusted first reader. You championed this novel from the start, and never thought for one second I couldn't do it. You're the best man I know. I love you. This book is for you.

Finally, to Chris. I miss you, bro. You should have been here longer. I hope you're tripping the light fantastic listening to *Peanut Butter Jelly*, just like Phoebe. And more than anything, I hope your little sis has done you proud.

Read on for an extract from

THE RUNNING CLUB

The gripping and twisty new novel from Ali Lowe

Prologue

I turn left onto the pavement, always left. Glance down the hill towards Esperance Reserve, stop at the lights to tighten the laces of my brand-new running shoes. The rules of the running club are the same as they have always been: keep your breath steady, keep your mind sharp, record your laps! Only now there's a new one: don't get killed.

I slow down as I reach the seafront, turn to admire my slender silhouette in the French window of Esperance's most extravagant beachside home. A polished red sports car in the driveway just adds to the grandeur, sitting pretty on the verge of the expansive front lawn with a gaudy designer water feature as its centrepiece. Next, a large, white-fronted home with bottle-green Italian-style shutters and out-of-control jasmine creeping up the façade, wily in its efforts. Worth six million dollars, I heard. Every house comes with a hefty price tag in Esperance. You pay for paradise – for neat front lawns and infinity pools; for snaking, flower-lined pathways and white picket fences; for polished bus-stop windows and fancy lattes: soya milk, rice milk, oat milk, goat milk!

You pay a premium.

Perhaps even with your life.

The air is pure today, with a faint waft of sea spray. It is only if you close your eyes you might sense it: the cloying scent of death. It hung heavy in the air after they found the body in the tree-lined clearing that runs parallel to the running track. Eyes open and face set in a smirk. A fingernail neatly lacquered with her favourite shade, Cajun Sunset, standing erect, like a tiny tombstone in the mulch, long hair spread about her like Medusa. And she *was* like Medusa! She could turn you to stone with just one gaze.

That scream when her body was found was shrill enough to pierce the pendulous, grey clouds and force out the last torrents of warm spring rain. The residents of Esperance heard it as keenly as they heard the secrets that came spurting out like champagne through the neck of a shaken-up bottle in the days that followed.

So many secrets.

So many lies.

So much vengeance.

But could anyone honestly say she didn't have it coming?

Now, six weeks on, the sun has cleared the charcoal clouds that bathed our beachside town in grey in the days after her death. Esperance has a new aroma: summer. A season where things prosper and grow, where nothing dies.

In this tiny, pristine patch of the world, everyone knows you need to be perfect to survive.

I bend down, touch my toes, my legs ready to pound the pavement alongside the mulch that cushioned the decaying body of a woman who was once just like me. Who was one of us.

I really must stop thinking about it now. Lay it to rest. You can't dwell on the past, you must move on, just as I have done. I am the butterfly emerged from a cocoon, a chick fleeing the confines of the nest, a phoenix from the ashes!

I've been given a second chance at life.
I am alive. She is not.
So traumatic.
So unfair.
So wasteful.
So pleased I got away with it.

Part One: Jealousy

Six Weeks Earlier

Chapter One
Carole

The house is a hive of activity.

I find it easier to dedicate a particular day of the week to tradesmen, since it lessens the general household upheaval. Today the cleaners are here, and the gardener, too. I am very particular about Summerfield's lawn. I must have the stripes, in alternating shades of green, and Ryan is the only tradesman who knows this. Lottie would flinch at the word 'tradesman' – apparently they are 'trades*people*' these days – but I don't have time for any of that.

Ryan has been doing our lawn for a long time. He travels all the way down the peninsula from Shivers Beach (there are no trades*people* living in Esperance, they're rarer than hens' teeth here), but the money is worth it. We pay him a lot, because good staff are always worth the extra dollars.

'I'd like it to look like Wimbledon,' I told him when he first started gardening for us, five years ago. That's the way the lawn has always been, even before my parents handed this house over to Max and me. Alternating stripes in olive and fern.

'Wimble-*who*?' Ryan had asked.

'Don,' Max told him with a smile. 'My wife likes her lawn nice and tidy.' He winked at Ryan as if he was making some kind of lewd innuendo. 'With stripes.'

Ryan hadn't even tried to hide a look of consternation, but nodded and set about with the mower. The result?

Flawless! Alternating hues of green along the length of the front yard, only broken up by the large marble water fountain in the middle of the grass. It's very tasteful, the fountain, no kissing dolphins or anything like that, just a simple cherub with a spout, but Freya still likes to have a dig when she can.

'Oh Carole,' she lamented just last week. 'The *least* you could have done was get a chiselled Michelangelo with his cock out.'

So uncouth. But that's Freya for you. You can take the girl out of Shivers Beach, but can you really take Shivers Beach out of the girl? Although Shivers Beach is only thirty-five kilometres north of Esperance, it may as well be in another state. Esperance sits pretty at the very southern tip of a peninsula that rolls languidly along the coastline, a few kilometres north of the bright lights of Sydney. Shivers Beach sits poverty clad and unkempt at the northern point with its bulbous, ragged headland, separated from its affluent bedpartner by a buffer of coastal enclaves that get progressively rougher as the coastline unfolds: Esperance, Mooney Waters, Nash Lake, Boorie Point and then finally, Shivers Beach. It's where Freya and Lottie grew up, and my husband, too, although you wouldn't know it.

My phone pings with a text message. Speak of the devil. **What do you mean, it is "mandatory to run in our fluoro vests"?** Freya has written. **Is this a new government measure I'm unaware of?** I didn't say she wasn't smart. Sarcastic may be a better description. The kind of person who has an answer to everything. You would have thought a request to 'stay safe, stay seen' would be self-explanatory for any responsible member of a running club. But I don't have the time to get into this with Freya right now – not with tradesmen to organise. She will have to wait.

Today Ryan is topless, pushing the mower down the slight slope of our vast front lawn that leads to the fence that's almost touching the sand of the north end of Esperance beach. From the front garden, I can see the dunes on the other side of the beach. They mostly block the view of the running track, save for the far corner where the water fountain sits on a square of mosaic pavers, a haven for thirsty runners and dogs. From upstairs, you can see the twinkling lights of the city after dark, and even enjoy the New Year's Eve fireworks over Sydney Harbour. It's a much more sophisticated spot to observe the festivities than on the ground with the masses. This is prime real estate, and as such, the house needs to be well-kept. I like it to be the most attractive property on the seafront, to ensure it keeps the highest price tag in the row, should we ever decide to sell. Not that I can see that happening, because I grew up in this house and it is as much a part of me as my right arm.

I watch Ryan out of the window, his torso glistening in the stifling heat that's unexpected in September, the very start of spring. A single drop of sweat trickles between his glorious thirty-something pecs and down towards the elastic waistband of his pants. I chew on my cheek; I'm a sucker for a bit of rough. I *married* a bit of rough!

Max walks into the kitchen. I turn from the window and throw my arms round his neck. He's only been in the next room, but I like to be as affectionate as possible as often as possible. I truly believe that if you don't give your man what he needs, emotionally *and* sexually, he will stray. And I'm not giving Max up to anyone.

He puts his hands lightly on my waist, kisses me on the forehead and gently extracts me from his torso. I resist the urge to try and snuggle back in, because there has to be a sort of 'treat them mean' element to wifely behaviour, wouldn't you agree?

Max fills a glass of water from the fridge. The chiller churns and gurgles as it spits out cubes of ice. He gulps down half of the glass and exhales loudly.

'This heat's unbearable. It's meant to break on Friday.' He gestures at the laptop screen on the benchtop, where a document emblazoned with the title *Your Running Club Needs You!* strobes out of the screen. 'What's this?'

'A flyer,' I tell him. 'I'm trying to recruit a few more members to the running club. I mean it's lovely having so many husbands and wives' – all of them except Shelby – 'but it would be nice if it gathered some momentum. If we got a few more members, we could raise a little more money for charity.'

'Are people paying to join now?' asks Max.

'No, but the mark-up from the merchandise goes to Meals on Wheels.'

Max smiles. 'Well done, darling,' he says. 'Very worthy.'

I nod. It *is* worthy! I mean, we all have to do our bit, don't we?

The running club consists of myself, Lottie and her husband Piers, Freya and Bernard, although I hardly classify what he does as 'running' – it's more of a senior power-walk. Then there's Shelby and Tino. The three husbands are a late addition to the club. It started as women-only: myself, Freya, Lottie, and, by default Shelby, because she's Lottie's sister, but somewhere along the line Tino joined in and then Piers and Bernard jumped on board (I use the term 'jumped' somewhat loosely as Bernard is far too old to mount anything). By all accounts, all three of them love it, and as well they should – it's the perfect antidote to the stress of their demanding jobs. Tino creates apps for Android, and he's very kindly made one for the group which enables us to keep track of our kilometres and measures our speed against one another. I don't care where I come in, as long as it's before Shelby. A little competition is the best thing for upping anyone's fitness, in my opinion. Competing pushes you to be better, to test your limits.

The running club officially runs five nights a week at seven o'clock, although annoyingly some members seem to regard the start time as a free-for-all. Of course I run every day, rain or shine, but not everyone is quite as dedicated. Lottie runs three nights – Monday, Wednesday and Thursday – because those are the nights Piers, who is an obstetrician or gynaecologist or whatever you want to call it, is generally home on time and Lottie likes to be there when he arrives with dinner on the table. Fifteen laps of the purpose-built 400-metre running track, Olympic size, that backs onto the same scrubland that nestles the sand dunes at the southern end of Esperance beach. We meet at the water fountain and then we begin, in formation. I am the fastest of the females with a lap record of 119 seconds, so I'm always ahead of the pack. I have to be if I want to feel the burn. The only person who doesn't seem to have any routine is Shelby. She shows up when, and if she wants to, there's no rhyme or reason to it. She marches to the beat of her own drum in that arrogant way she has, like the world owes her a giant favour. She will stride out in front, or wait until we're all half a lap ahead before she starts, so she doesn't have to talk to anyone. It's incredibly rude.

'So is all this talk of recruiting runners a roundabout way of you asking me to join the running club again?' Max slices through a green apple and offers me an indulgent smile.

'Well, all the other husbands are involved, as you know,' I say, coyly. I don't want to *pressure* him. 'But it might be a little low-energy compared to what you normally do.'

'I might stick to surfing,' he says and pats my behind. 'It's more my scene.'

What's more Max's scene is keeping to himself. He finds the husband and wife cliques of Esperance a little too much to bear. 'We see them for drinks, I don't want to work out with them too,' he says.

I'd be lying if I said it doesn't hurt a little that I'm the only wife who can't persuade her husband to accompany her on the running track. Still, no matter. If I'm honest, I don't particularly want Max to see me all beetroot and flushed with sweat patches left, right and centre. It's not exactly sexy, is it?

'What have you got on today?' Max asks as he drops his apple core in the bin, and it feels a little like a change of subject.

'School drop-off, a bit of admin.' I look up at him and smile. I need to book more piano lessons for Otto – now he's in year 3 we feel he may benefit from an extra session a week, and pay Olivia's extortionate school fees. 'Keeping an eye on the tradesmen . . .'

Max glances out of the window. 'He's a good bloke, Ryan. You really don't have to worry about him.'

'Oh, I wasn't . . .' I lie.

Max is very touchy about me making generalisations about people from the town he grew up in. 'We're not all rough,' he says.

'Oh darling,' I pout. 'I know *that.*'

I do, however, have my doubts about the cleaners who also hail from the other end of the peninsula. I still can't find the diamond bracelet Max bought me for my birthday and I know for a *fact* that it was on the dresser when Leah was at the house last. Otto said, 'It's your fault Mum, you shouldn't have left it *Leah*-ing around.' That's a private school education for you.

'Are you still out tomorrow night?' Max asks.

'Yes, I'll be at Lottie's. Is that okay?'

'Of course. It's just I thought I might pop out to look at the car. Perhaps Hannah could stay on for an hour or so?'

My husband throws back the remains of his icy water. His skin is lightly tanned and his stubble fashionably short, with distinguished flecks of white. He is as handsome as he was the day I met him. More so. He still turns heads. I mean, he is so much more than a pretty face – he's a wonderful father, for starters. *Present*, I believe that's the word. Always there for the children.

'Of course,' I tell him. 'I'll speak to her. Can't have you missing out on seeing the car!'

Max is almost the proud owner of a Maserati MC20. It's a nifty little thing. It's my fifteenth wedding anniversary present to him – a few months early, but when your name rolls around on the waiting list, you have to jump on it. The car was meant to be a surprise, but the morons at the garage ruined it when they called him directly about the window tint (as in, did he want one or not?). I was livid about it at the time, but now I don't mind a jot because Max is so happy about his impending gift. It's like watching a child wait for Christmas Day to come around when they know they've got exactly what they want.

'I take it you like your present?' I say with a girlish pout.

'Are you kidding?' my husband asks, but not in the over-excited way he did the first couple of times I asked the same question. 'It's incredible. Now I have to think what the hell I can get you for our anniversary. What do you get the woman who has everything?'